The Boy
in Abruzzo

Louis A. Rosati

For information about this title or to order other books by the author and / or electronic media, contact the publisher: Louis A. Rosati at *lrosati@cox.net*

Website: *larosatiauthor.com*

ISBNs:

   Print: 978-0-9849621-3-6

   eBook: 978-0-9849621-4-3

Printed in the United States of America

Cover and interior design by Joseph DiPastena, 705 Market.com

To my parents who gave me and my brother an
appreciation of our Abruzzo roots while instilling
in us the love and promises of our American life.

To my wife, Rosalie, for the love and support
she provided through the writing of this novel
and so many other projects, and for the nourishment
that sustained the effort, some of which found
its way onto the pages.

To my children and grandchildren who I hope will
always cherish our family tree and its origins.

Oh how beautiful is youth

And quickly does it flee!

Be happy if you want

For tomorrow may not come

Lorenzo de' Medici

Song of Bacchus

Francesco's Journey

Part I
A Time of War

Chapter 1

Roccamorice, Italy. September, 1943

Francesco was seated at the kitchen table in the farmhouse chatting with his aunt when he heard the vehicle rumble down the lane. Looking out the window, he craned his neck to see an olive-green lorry slowly sway side to side, its brakes grinding and suspension straining as it inched down a narrow track. The tires finally crunched to a stop on the gravel in front of the house. His breath caught at the sight of the iron cross on the door panel. He clenched his fist. *Merda*, he whispered. An officer stepped out and adjusted his cap, pulling the visor low over his eyes. A blunt-featured enlisted man wearing a flange helmet emerged from the driver-side door with a rifle. The two doors slammed in rapid succession.

"*Donato, fuori, subito!*" the officer shouted, as he walked toward the house. Francesco understood the officer wanted his uncle to come outside quickly.

He rose and whispered this to his aunt as he ducked out of view of the window.

"*Chiama Zio Donato—I Tedeschi sono qui.*"

Aunt Carmela struggled to rise and limped to the door of the root cellar. She looked back and forth worriedly at Francesco as she called down to her husband: "*Veini su! I Tedeschi...*"

A white-bearded man stepped into the kitchen in his soiled work clothes to face his wife. Taut and tight-lipped, he motioned to Francesco to stay back; then the couple shuffled to the door and emerged onto the small landing above the yard.

Francesco stood at the window looking at the assembled group, the couple close together facing the Germans. He stepped back a bit from the window and pressed his back into the shadow of the wall. He had walked down to the farm from his home in the village of Roccamorice to collect a package of beef from a cow his uncle had butchered. He hadn't anticipated any problems, but the unexpected arrival now had pinned him to the wall, his face swiveled to the window. He thought, this isn't worth dying for.

The stern-faced officer peered out below his visor at the couple. "Bring us the beef," he uttered matter-of-factly. His square-cut jaw hardly moved as he spoke.

"What beef?" Donato replied. "I sold my cow in San Valentino weeks ago."

"Don't lie to me. I have it on good authority," the officer responded more sternly. "More than one person has informed us that you butchered the cow and sold some of it. We also know you still have most of it, so where is it?"

"Believe me I don't have anything left. It's all sold."

The officer pulled the luger from his side holster and quickly got off two rounds that hit the framing of the house above their heads sending shards of wood into the air. "Listen to me, Donato, if you don't fetch the meat in the next two minutes, the next time I shoot it will be at your wife—understand?"

Donato and Carmella ducked their heads together as Francesco recoiled and slid to the floor. Donato, wide-eyed, held up a trembling hand and said, almost in a whisper, *"Va bene, aspetta,* I'll get it." Leaving his wife standing there, he went back inside. A few tense minutes passed. Francesco remained still, taking shallow breaths. No one moved, then Donato emerged, his arms cradling a large cloth-wrapped bundle. Francesco sneaked out behind him.

Staring intently at the officer, he shouted, *"La gente ha fame.* Don't take their food!"

Donato turned to Francesco, mouth ajar, his face contracted in shock. Carmela had raised her hand covering her mouth, her wide eyes exhibited unspoken horror. The officer abruptly threw back his shoulders and scowled. He returned his pistol to his holster and asked, "How old are you, boy, and who are you to make demands?"

"I'm fifteen. I'm their nephew, here for a visit. Please don't take the meat. It's all they've got." Francesco had not spoken to any German military man during the occupation, let alone an officer. He had heard stories about the attitudes the soldiers manifested toward village residents, but had not had a direct experience. His stomach felt unsettled and he could feel his heart beating faster as he struggled to maintain control. He hoped a plea might work. "It is all the family has left to share."

The officer stepped forward, brushing past Donato who had turned to face Francesco. Walking up to the outside landing, the officer motioned Francesco to step down. Standing a few feet apart, the officer hooked his thumbs in his black leather holster belt and stared down at Francesco. His voice had a hard edge. "Never speak to an officer of the *Wehrmacht* unless in answer to a question. Is that understood?"

"Si."

"Yes what?" He raised his voice and said, "Yes, sir is the response I expect, always and without exception."

"Si signore," Francesco responded sheepishly, looking down at the ground.

"Look at me, boy. Now let me ask you, do you know why we are here, why the German army has occupied your village?"

Francesco knew the recent events of the war but decided to shake his head no. "Well," the officer said, sneering, "I'm not surprised. For a boy your age who should know, you display appalling ignorance. You Italians have betrayed us. If your government had not broken the pact between our two countries and your soldiers had not abandoned their posts like cowards, we would not have had to come here."

"But why take our food?" Francesco asked.

The officer's face hardened. "Don't be stupid, boy. We need all the food we can get. Your needs, the needs of your family, your village are your concern, not mine, I could care less about *la fame.*" With that he abruptly turned and motioned to his stone-faced companion who shouldered his rifle and stepped forward to retrieve the bundle from Donato. The soldier placed the bundle in the already full cargo compartment. Then the officer stepped toward Donato and ordered him to get into the vehicle.

Anger welled up inside Francesco. He clenched his fists and opened his mouth to scream an insult, but hesitated. The officer's back was to him and events were moving too quickly.

Donato had regained some degree of composure, but now his face was unmasked in fear. *"Per favore, hai pieta—la fame,"* he pleaded for pity with the officer.

"You lied to me, Donato. There is no mercy for that. Now get in the vehicle!"

"No, you can't take him, per favore, no!" Francesco screamed as he rushed forward and reached for his uncle's arm.

His aunt rushed to Francesco's side and pulled him away. *"Fermarti, Francesco! Non peggiorare le cose*—don't make things worse. God will take care of him."

"Unless you want to join your uncle, I suggest you listen to your aunt, and move away from the lorry. I won't ask a second time." He turned and gave Donato a shove toward the vehicle. Donato slumped his shoulders in resignation and lifted himself into the vehicle.

As the officer was about to step into the vehicle, Francesco pushed him aside and reached in for his uncle, shouting for him to get out of the vehicle.

The officer stumbled, nearly falling, but he regained his footing and pushed Francesco away from the open door, poking his leather crop hard into Francesco's belly.

Visibly stunned, Francesco buckled over and let out a whoosh of air.

"Such audacity," the officer of the *Whermacht* said coldly. "I warned you once. If there were room in this vehicle for one more item you would be coming with me. As it is, consider yourself lucky to have only been double-warned. I tell you this in no uncertain terms." His voice slowing but growing colder, he stepped forward and pressed the crop to Francesco's chest. "If you come to my attention again you'll find yourself in a work camp or worse. Do you understand? I only need to hear one more complaint about you. Now get out of the way!"

Francesco, who had straightened up and recovered his breath, backed off in silence.

The officer got into the vehicle next to Donato who sat uneasily with bunched- up shoulders between the officer and his driver.

Turning the ignition, the driver cranked the engine to a low rumble. He swung the vehicle around, and as Donato craned his head back at the house, the lorry lurched up the lane to the road back to the village.

Francesco's body went slack as he watched the men drive off. Then he turned and embraced his aunt.

****

The scent of autumn was in the air on this late September day. Yellowing hardwood trees flanking the road ascending from the Pescara River valley partially shielded the cluster of stone buildings of his village, but he wasn't thinking about the change of seasons. He was angry, but one thought kept repeating in his mind as he walked—it just wasn't worth dying for. The blue-gray slope of the Maiella range that rose above the tiled roofs and bell tower of the church had always had a spiritual significance, but pangs of hunger in the midst of his reflections on the confrontation distracted him from any such thoughts this day.

Francesco walked into the main piazza just beyond the village entrance. To his left he frowned at the group of German soldiers, rifles slung over shoulders, standing next to their military lorry in front of the municipal building. A Nazi flag, featuring a black swastika on a circle of white against a field of red, hung over the entrance. Smoking and chatting with one another, the soldiers paid him no attention as he spit on the cobblestones in their direction. At the fountain, a woman in a wool shawl and cotton skirt flared by layers of petticoats raised a copper amphora to her head, balanced it with one hand, grabbed her young daughter's hand in the other, and walked off. Francesco's mouth was dry; he licked his lips. On the far side, the village baker, a stout man in a black jacket over his white apron, was sweeping the pavement in front of his shop. Francesco thought the villagers should have come and gone by now for the bread ration. He winced at the remembrance of his mother coming home in tears when the bread for the day had run out before she got to the head of the line. His grumbling stomach hoped that hadn't happened today. He continued around to the right where he passed three village men seated on chairs at a café table holding cups of espresso in one hand while engaged in an animated conversation. Coffee, as with so many other items, was in short supply, but every occupied village had at least one café supported by the German military.

Francesco knew these men, always arguing over nothing, even the jowly town mayor who looked ridiculous in the black fedora with red-feathered hat band tilted jauntily on his head. Francesco frowned at the Fascist lapel medal on the mayor's jacket, a fascicle of birch rods tied with a red cord to an axe. He had been told Mussolini chose it as the symbol of his Fascist Party because it represented the power of the magistrates of the Roman Empire. He, like most Italian boys, was a member of a Fascist youth organization, but he was becoming disillusioned. He had begun to question *credere, obbidiere, combattere*—believe, obey, fight, the credo the Fascist government tried to instill in him and his friends. On the one hand he felt an allegiance to the country, and he knew that most of the people in the village supported the government; on the other hand he was aware of rising anti-Fascist sentiment. Mussolini was in trouble now that the war had come ashore in Italy. But it was a matter for the adults; not something that he and his friends thought about very deeply. Besides, one could get in trouble with Mussolini's secret police, the OVRA, and there were spies everywhere.

"*Ciao*, Francesco. Where have you been this morning?" the mayor asked. He answered he'd been to see his uncle.

"Where is that smile?" he chided. "Didn't he give you anything to eat?"

"*Niente*," he mumbled. His stomach growled as he spoke; he wasn't in the mood to discuss the incident.

The site of the coffee cups annoyed him. Beneath his voice , he groused. "There are things more important than coffee." He walked off with rounded shoulders thinking back to the farm: if not for the hunger, none of it would have happened.

Turning a corner, he entered a winding cobblestone walkway lined on both sides by two-story attached buildings constructed of locally-quarried, light gray Maiella stone. Many of the homes had windows bordered by shutters with scattered spots of color from red geraniums in terra cotta pots on iron-framed balconies. Neighbors often chatted with one another across the alleyway. The slightly recessed doorways, a step up from street level, also saw people standing in the stoop engaging neighbors or passersby. Francesco always enjoyed stopping to chat with friends, but the street was empty, matching his gloom, and no one looked down from the balconies. Two German privates approached from the far end of the alleyway. Francesco narrowed his eyes at them and stepped up on a door stoop to let them pass. "*Asini*," he mumbled.

The soldiers were chatting to each other when suddenly one of them stopped, unshouldered his rifle, and glared at Francesco. His partner took a few more paces before he stopped and looked back in anger. Francesco suddenly felt heat flush his temples as he recognized that the soldiers understood the Italian words. The second soldier now unshouldered his rifle. He started walking toward Francesco frowning, but his partner held him back. Francesco stepped down from the stoop and stood defiant. "So, you're going to shoot me?" he shouted in Italian, not knowing if they would fully understand what he said. A tense moment passed. Glaring at Francesco, the soldier pointed the fingers of his free hand at his own eyes and then at Francesco, sending him a clear message. Francesco responded with a time-honored, Italian up-thrusted arm gesture meant to communicate contempt—"up your ass!"

The two men turned to one another and mumbled something Francesco could not understand. Then, looking back at Francesco with the disdain of someone not worth bothering with, the soldiers both shouldered their rifles. As they walked off, Francesco felt his heartbeat slow as he breathed more evenly. He turned away and walked on.

Francesco's home was at the head of the street, separated a few paces from the others. His father, Luigi, had built it in 1925 with money he had earned the first time he went to work in America. It wasn't his first departure to find wages that were adequate to support his family. He and his brothers had first tried their luck in South America, first Brazil, and then Argentina, around the turn of the century as migratory workers—*galandrinos*, swallows they were called. They were part of the great Italian migration that had begun in the 1860s when Italy bled out its citizens to foreign shores. The United States became the ultimate magnet to draw Francesco's father and uncles.

The house was a simple construction of Maiella stone. It was situated at the edge of the village on a sloping plateau with a deep encircling ravine, and had a panoramic view of the countryside at the back. A mulberry tree framed the east end where morning sunlight slanted through the leaves and dappled the patio doors of a balcony enclosed by a waist-high wrought iron railing. A fig tree framed the west end.

Francesco's father had since returned to work in the United States and was hoping to send for his wife, Francesco, and his older brother once he had accumulated enough money. But war had broken out and the future proved uncertain. For Francesco, who missed his father, the house lacked not only his presence, but his spirit.

Francesco approached the weather-beaten front door at street level and paused to consider what he would tell his mother, fretting like any teenager who was about to give a parent disappointing news.

Finally, he opened the door and entered the main room, a kitchen and sitting area with a table and a few mismatched chairs. The residual stale, smoky scent of a cooking fire permeated the air. His mother rose and turned away from the hearth where she had placed a bundle of wood. Francesco saw she was surprised to see him empty-handed.

"Where is the meat?"

"The Germans have it."

"What happened?"

"They found out about the butchered cow." "But how did they find out?" she scowled.

"Who knows?" His fists were clenched as he continued. "You know how hard it is to keep a secret in this town. When someone knows something, soon everyone knows."

"I can't believe it. Now what?" Her face continued to register displeasure.

Francesco began to pace about the room gesturing angrily, clenching and unclenching his fist, and repeated the events that had transpired, leaving out his personal involvement with the officer at the farm and the soldiers on his way home.

His mother waited for him to finish. Casting an accusatory look and tone she asked about her sister-in-law, "What happened to *Zia* Carmela"?

"They left her behind. On my way back here I stopped at Margarita's and told her what happened. She went over to check on her. I think Zia will be okay for now."

"*Dio Mio!*" his mother exclaimed, slapping her hands together as she looked upward. Light filtered through a cloudy window in a door that led out to the rear balcony. She walked out nervously twisting her apron and peered down over the iron railing looking for Francesco's older brother, Antonio. He was working in the small terraced garden below. The ground was nearly devoid of produce. Her eyes were drawn to the garden's grape arbor backdrop where Antonio was tending vines with clusters of purplish fruit ripening in the late morning sun. Antonio was a good-looking, slender young man, slightly taller than Francesco with a full head of dark wavy hair. "Antonio!" she shouted. "Something terrible has happened."

Moments later Francesco's brother hurried into the room removing a soiled gray beret and tossed it on a chair. He walked over to the tarnished copper sink to wash his hands. "*Che successo*, what happened, what's the problem? The Germans, right?" The annoyance in his voice was clear.

Antonio listened as Francesco repeated his story, again selectively excluding his involvement with the officer. Pouring water from a copper amphora into a bowl, Antonio rinsed and dried his hands. He turned to face his brother who looked weary; plainly clad in a cotton shirt that hung loosely on him. His faded corduroy trousers bore tattered cuffs that draped on his dust-covered shoes. The sturdy adolescent with dark, ruffled hair, mature beyond his years, had lost weight. They both had. But as they had always been good friends as well as brothers, they had always discussed their situations rationally. Antonio's annoyance with him now, however, was clear in the tone of his voice. "Francesco, we've talked about this. Some of the Fascists here have difficulty accepting what happened to the government, and they sympathize with the Nazis," he growled. You have to be careful what you say and to whom you speak; nothing anyone says can be kept in confidence." He turned to pour the used water down the drain and leaned back against the counter.

Francesco thought about the mayor's comment. "Look, I didn't say anything to anyone about the beef. Don't blame me for this," he snapped.

His mother exhaled a sigh. Her face had relaxed the scowl. "No one is blaming you, Francesco. We all need to be careful."

Shrugging and throwing up his hands, Francesco signaled he had enough discussion. "I have things to do," he said, angrily; then turning, he quickly descended to the lower level before anyone could say another word.

At the foot of the narrow stairway he opened the door to his bedroom which resembled a cell, and tugged the string that turned on a light bulb dangling from the ceiling. He had been frustrated by his inability to satisfy his hunger, and the presence of German troops everywhere added more misery. Still upset about the latest incident, he thought it would be best if he just left home. It was not the first time he had that thought.

A cloth drape covered a narrow gap in the wall he used as a closet. He pulled the drape aside and looked at his shirts, trousers, and a sweater hanging on a wooden bar. The approach of winter required warmer clothing, but what else would he need? There was not much to ponder. The room held only a metal-framed cot on one side; a small chest of drawers on the other. A small crucifix hung on the wall above his bed and a team poster of the 1938 World Cup Champions, *Gli Azzuri,* was pinned to the side wall. He looked at the players. A wry smile broke on his face. He was very proud of the Italian National Team. They had won Italy's second World Cup and were the undisputed kings of football. The onset of the war had postponed a possible repeat.

He shook his head disappointedly and went through the chest of drawers searching for anything that might be of use. He wouldn't need his old football jersey or the sack of marbles that he used to shoot with his pals in the schoolyard. The hunger had made his friends listless and bleary-eyed. No one wanted to do anything anymore; no football, no nothing.

He picked up an old football magazine with a smooth, glossy cover featuring Sergio Bertoni, one of the team stars. The musty scent of old newsprint wafted up as he flipped through the pages, remembering the times he shared stories with his father who knew all the old players. The magazine had covered a book a teacher had lent him in the spring—*Fontamara* by Ignazio Silone. He replaced the magazine and picked up the book, quickly flipping through the pages surreptitiously. His teacher warned him to tell no one about it, to keep it hidden, and to read it secretly because it was critical of Fascism. He was about to read it when the fighting in Italy began; in the turmoil he had forgotten about it.

Muffled footsteps on the floor above him caused him to quickly replace the book beneath the magazine. His brother, Antonio, called down to him.

"Francesco, don't be foolish. Come up here. Let's talk about it."

"When I'm finished," he responded, closing the drawer and opening another. The drawer contained his writing journal and several articles and essays he had written. He had developed a special bond with his teacher who recognized his intellectual aptitude and encouraged his writing. He leafed through the journal pages, pausing to reread a poem. He smiled as his eyes glanced over the first stanzas, but the smile faded quickly. There would be no time for that sort of thing and Silone's novel would also have to wait. In another drawer that held his socks and underwear he picked up a small wooden box tucked away in the corner. It contained a wooden whistle his grandfather had carved for him. It seemed childish now. His hand reached for the Jew's harp his father sent him in a family package. He had honed it from steel and tin scraps at the steel mill in America where he worked. He thought about him now as he placed the harp against his teeth sensing its ferrous metallic taste, and plinked the flexible tongue piece while rapidly inhaling and exhaling. The instrument sounded discordant twangs and the vibrations rattled his teeth. He put the device back deciding one try was enough. He slipped on the steel ring his father had also sent him, but it was still too big. Frowning, he replaced it and grabbed a pocket knife.

Francesco clenched his fists and with a firmly set jaw was about to ascend the stairs determined to state his case for leaving when he was startled by a loud pounding on the door to the house. Footsteps across the floor above him were followed by sounds of the door opening and a voice demanding in heavily accented Italian: "Where is your brother? We passed him a short time ago heading here."

"He is not here now," his brother said with a voice loud enough to alert his brother. "He left a few minutes ago to join friends on the football pitch."

Francesco's heart began to race as he listened wide-eyed to the exchange between German soldiers, his mother, and brother. Although the sound through the ceiling was muffled, he got the gist of the conversation as he imagined the shocked looks on his mother's and brother's faces. The soldiers, who Francesco imagined were the two he encountered on his walk home, were there to bring Francesco to headquarters for questioning. Their commanding officer had overheard their discussing the run-in with Francesco on their return from patrol. The officer, eliciting further details, had concluded that the boy was the one he had warned at the farm, and he ordered the boy's arrest. When Francesco heard they were going to search the house, he turned away from the door in a panic and slid to the floor by his bed.

His father had added a trap door when he built the house. It was barely noticeable, covered with a chest in which Francesco kept his boyhood games and toys. The door opened to the lowest outdoor level of the house, enclosed on three sides but open to the ravine. It was where they stored farm implements and sheltered the few goats they kept. Living with livestock was not uncommon for the *contadini*, the farmers and shepherds of Abruzzo. He pushed the chest aside sending a soccer ball bouncing around the room. Then he slid the latch and lifted the door enough to bend himself in. He dropped to the earthen floor below. The lingering scent of corn from an empty crib barely registered as he darted out. His heart raced as he scampered along a path on the side of the ravine to an overhang a few yards away. From that vantage point he was able to keep his eye on the comings and goings to the house. He squatted, taking shallow breaths as he waited.

It didn't take long to make the search. Francesco watched the soldiers leave the same way they came. His anxiety eased and he resumed normal breathing. Judging it was safe, he rose, climbed to street level and reentered the house.

His mother was standing by the kitchen sink twisting her hands in her apron; his brother was pacing. *"Madonna Mia,"* his mother exclaimed when she saw him. "What did you do to make the Germans so angry with you?"

Francesco shrugged as he retold the incidents making light of the encounters and insults. "They overreacted."

Antonio stopped pacing and turned to him. "I don't think so. What's the matter with you? What's going on in there?" he asked, pressing his finger on Francesco's forehead. "You know how they are. They expect complete cooperation, no questions asked, and certainly no insults."

"What are we going to do?" his mother asked. "They will be back when they don't find him with his friends. Where can we hide him?"

"I need to leave," Francesco said. "There is no place to hide here." "Where will you go? Who is going to take care of you, feed you?"

Antonio said, " I think what Francesco did was relatively minor. But at the same time, until it blows over, we need to send him somewhere safe. What about the Sanelli's place in Caramanico?"

"What made you think of them?" his mother asked looking surprised. "It just came to mind. You remember when we were last there with Papa before he left for the United States?"

"Yes, but I don't remember your father talking about your brother going there."

"Papa and Pierluigi talked about it on a *passaggiata* after dinner. I was with them. He offered to let Francesco help out with the sheep and chores since Pierluigi sons were away in the army. That business of his in Sulmona keeps him away from home quite a bit. He just has his daughter at home."

"That's a great idea," Francesco chimed in. The mention of the Sanelli daughter rekindled a flirtatious memory; but putting it aside for the moment he said, "Antonio is right, it's safe there and they could use the help. Germans don't occupy that town, they just patrol from time to time. And best of all they can feed me. I would be happy to work for food and a bed."

"Wait a minute," his mother said with a scowl. "That was a long time ago and your father never talked to me about it. We don't know what it's like there now. The occupation changed everything. I just can't let you leave, to impose on friends we haven't seen in a while. There needs to be an explanation."

But Francesco's mind was made up. "Listen," he said in a raised voice, "we don't have time to waste talking about this. You said those soldiers would soon be back. I need to pack some things and leave now!" With that he left and descended the steps to his room, leaving his mother and brother looking at each other.

Francesco gathered the shirts, pants, sweater, socks, and underwear he had looked over earlier. Lifting a canvas sack from the closet floor, he sat on the edge of the bed and stuffed the clothing into the sack. He looked around one last time. He thought about how it had come to this—how all the bad days, especially today had begun.

****

He had seen the headlines bannered across the Pescara newspapers months earlier. He picked up the discarded papers in the piazza; that's how he learned the Allies had landed in Sicily in early July and driven out the Italian and German armies. In the aftermath the Italian government had collapsed and *Il Duce*, Mussolini, had been forced to resign at the end of the month. The king replaced him with the old former military chief of staff, Badoglio. Francesco listened to the men scornfully discuss what a bad choice he was. Too old and incompetent they said, all the while mocking the stupidity of government decision-makers.

But what no one knew until later was that Badoglio was extending peace feelers to the Allies all through August. In September, the Italian army withdrew from the field of battle after the government agreed to an armistice on the eighth of the month. The armistice was a big front-page story in the newspaper that arrived in the village a few days later, just ahead of the Anglo-American invasion of the Italian mainland. Until then, the newspapers contained only positive war stories and no hint that things were unraveling, just as the radio had played only patriotic songs and newsreaders spouted propaganda. Details of the capitulation were sketchy because there was little information from Rome. Who was in charge, they couldn't tell. The Germans, anticipating the Italian surrender, rushed in several divisions of troops through the Brenner Pass to secure a line of defense across Italy, occupying many towns and villages.

The townspeople of Roccamorice learned the details for the first time when the Germans sent a garrison of soldiers into town. That was a bad day, Francesco remembered. When the army arrived in lorry after lorry, with columns of foot soldiers following up behind, a meeting was called in the main piazza in the late afternoon. The man in charge, dressed in a black uniform with red Nazi banner on his right arm, introduced himself as an officer of the *Staatspolizei*, the Gestapo. All adults were required to attend and listen to the rules and regulations regarding curfews, control of the food supply, and the requirement to turn in all guns and contraband, including radios, under penalty of death. The soldiers took down the

Italian flag hanging over the entrance of the municipal building and replaced it with the Nazi banner. Francesco remembered the grim look on his brother's and mother's faces when they came home that day. Later, a house-to-house search was made and all livestock and produce was inventoried. Then the German soldiers took nearly everything of value. Anything considered a weapon or contraband was confiscated. They commandeered many of the larger homes and turned the convent into a military barracks. In homes not entirely taken over, families were forced to take in one or more officers. Francesco's home was one of the lucky ones that avoided a billet, the modest living space apparently not good enough for the officer corps. But Francesco didn't care—living in the same house with a Nazi would not be fun. In the beginning villagers did little to resist the occupation. They knew it would be hopeless. No one wanted to be a martyr; they shrugged and went on, just wanting to survive.

Francesco, his friends, and families were well aware that food products were in short supply all over Italy even before the Allied invasion. But the social, political, and economic disintegration that followed the surrender, made food more scarce along with all sorts of common items like razor blades and light bulbs.

The one item that still seemed to be available was coffee, the luxury the Germans could not do without. For many, however, the awful tasting ersatz coffee made from grain and acorns became the daily beverage.

The local garrison of soldiers was grudgingly tolerated at first. Sometimes they gave their leftover evening meal rations and the dregs in the soup cauldron to the village children. Francesco and his friends were often grateful for those random acts of kindness even though most of the officers seemed to be casually indifferent, leaving half-eaten food on plates. But it was a point of pride for the adults to decline a dish of food. The Germans expected orders to be followed and exacted harsh penalties on those who resisted. Occasionally, a soldier would display some empathy, helping a child cross a street bustling with military traffic; but most often they walked around aloof, seemingly oblivious to the anguish they were causing. Francesco's family made do. He took pride in their resourcefulness. His mother ranged far and wide to put food on the table. Going from farm to farm she was often politely refused, but sometimes returned with an unexpected gift. She knew every wild plant that was edible and scraped together many a meal, seemingly out of nothing. Villagers that had the land planted every available square foot with *gran turco*, maize they ground into cornmeal for polenta. But the worst was yet to come. The German occupation brought heavy rationing. Francesco's family, like the others, was limited to 100 grams of flour or pasta per person per day; most of the livestock, sheep, goats, and the few cows in town were seized by the occupiers. Cupboards were largely bereft of food, holding at most some bottles of tomato sauce and other vegetables from the canning season. Mothers carefully doled out canned fruit by the spoonful to their children. In the summer when fruit trees were resplendent with figs and apricots, and the hedgerows heavily laden with the sweet blackberries, *morre*, or gooseberries, *uva spina*, Francesco's job was to gather the fruit for the family; and what was left, he peddled the rest to neighbors.

His father had shown him where all the best fig trees were in the village and countryside. It was a lip-smacking thought to recall his breakfasts of figs, of going from tree to tree, climbing them and gathering as many ripe figs as he could before settling in a nook and eating his fill; some he brought home. The figs might be his only meal of the day, but they gave him the energy to forage. The growing season, except for the berries, was long over and as winter approached, he scavenged anything edible; not a single dandelion or other edible wild greens could be found in the village meadows after he had combed over them. He considered the insects, even the mice, but he hadn't yet reached that point of desperation, although others had. Birds and frogs and every sort of wild creature became targets. He and his brother scoured the forest floor for edible snails and mushrooms, and stripped hazelnut trees bare.

A limited number of bread loaves were available from the village bakery, but often the loaves had run out by the time his brother or mother reached the front of the line. The same was true of the large pot of soup that was boiled in the main piazza on weekdays. The butcher and grocer had little to offer; their shops were usually closed. Francesco recalled walking the village streets in hopeful desperation, picking up cigarette butts which he repaired and sold in the in the piazza.

The town barbers gave the Germans haircuts, but asked for food in exchange instead of money. It was the same for other services. Food was most coveted. Ration cards provided the opportunity, but not the assurance that there would be any food available. Money was in short supply and more to the point, it was essentially worthless.

All able-bodied men between 15 and 45 were required to join labor gangs. Francesco, just shy of his 15th birthday, looked older than his age, but he had escaped conscription when he was challenged thanks to the baptismal records. The Gestapo officer had announced at the village meeting they had chosen Roccamorice for occupation as a base to build an artillery position, the Block Haus, as he referred to it, on one of the four peaks comprising the Maiella range. The position had a commanding view of the slopes for miles in all directions. Located a few kilometers above the village, it was one of a number of fortification points along a defensive perimeter known as the Gustav line. The villagers learned later that Hitler had ordered this heavily defended position built across Italy from the Adriatic to the Tyrrhenian Sea. He had placed Field Marshal Albert Kesselring in charge of preventing the Allies to breach it. In the Abruzzo region the line extended along the Sangro River Valley and was anchored at its strongest point in the west near the mountain village of Casino. Francesco's curiosity about these places was piqued because he had never traveled far from his village.

Francesco's brother, Antonio, was among the men impressed into the labor gangs; he spending days lugging supplies up to the Block Haus. Those who refused or failed along the route suffered dire consequences. The Germans were quick to display deadly vengeance for any excuse after what they believed was Italy's betrayal in capitulating to the Allies. Impressment was one of the greatest fears during the occupation, especially for the older men. One of Francesco's neighbors, a small, slightly built man, tired from constant service on various work details with little nourishment, plunged his hand into boiling pasta water, sustaining a significant burn, so as to avoid assignment to a crew a day after he had returned from a work detail completely exhausted. Although it had worked for this man, the Germans quickly caught on to malingering.

However, the SS squads in their ominous black uniforms patrolling through the village on a regular basis brought the most fear. The thought of their insolent actions made Francesco shudder, such as the time he saw an officer slap a neighbor's wife across the face because he didn't care for the answer she gave to a question he asked. Her husband could only stand and watch, powerless and humiliated. Incidents like that rankled Francesco.

Emerging from his reverie, he shook his head sadly. Then he grabbed his *mantello* from the hook behind the door, took one last look and left the room, closing the door behind him.

*****

"It's time to leave," Francesco said to his mother as he emerged on the first floor. He saw the anguish on his mother's face. She looked as if she had just brushed away tears, but he steeled himself not to show any emotion.

"Okay," she frowned. "Your brother has tried to convince me that sheltering you with the Sanelli family is the safest option for you and us. I don't know. I just know that I'm angry. It's too much, too fast. I want to talk to Pierluigi and Angiolina, but your brother reminded me the telephones are not working. So, my son, you are going to have to speak for me."

"Yes Mama I will, I promise. But there is no time to waste. I need to leave now; I can't wait for permission. I know they will understand when I explain it all."

"Tell them about what happened at Zio Donato's. Tell them we think it will soon be forgotten; until then I thought it would be safer for you to stay with them for a little while, and please apologize for me."

"I will explain it. Don't worry. I have to go."

"Let me give you something to eat first."

"What is there to eat? The cupboard is bare. There isn't even a crust of dry bread in the house."

"I have cornmeal for polenta."

Francesco was hungry. That day he had eaten only a hunk of bread with a cup of water earlier in the morning, and only water since he had returned home, but he resisted the temptation. "No Mama, but thank you. I suppose it's a good thing that the Germans think the cornmeal is only good for animals. 'Food for swine' they call it. Little do they know it kept the Roman legions going!" he said scornfully.

"But it will hold you until you reach Caramanico."

"Save it, I'll be fine. I better get going. If I take the ravine, I can reach Caramanico before dark. I'm sure *la Sinora* will feed me."

Antonio stepped back into the room; overhearing Francesco's last remark, he said, "The days have grown short this time of year. By the time you get through the ravine it will be dark."

"That's why I have to hurry. I think I can get through while there is still enough light. Please don't worry about me. I'll be fine, I promise."

"Listen to me," his mother said finally, her eyes filled with sorrow. "I want you to be careful. If you run into Germans, don't argue again, just do what they say! No risks! Promise?"

"Yes, I promise."

"And promise me you will do what Pierluigi asks, no complaining."

He assured her again not to worry. "Remember your prayers!"

Antonio gave Francesco a serious look. "Come home when it's safe. I will try and get you word one way or another, or come for you myself. Call us if the telephone is working, but try to stay in touch. I don't want to worry; I've got enough to worry about here."

Sadly, his mother embraced him, and with tears in her eyes, traced the sign of the cross on his forehead with her thumb. "God bless you, my son; may he keep you safe," she said, wiping away the tears with a handkerchief.

****

Under the midday sun against an azure sky layered with brush-stroked clouds, Francesco walked up the street named for the medieval stone watchtower dating to the 14th century, now in ruin at half its original height. He knew the town was old: it was once a fief of the Valignani family, but now he wondered what grief they may have witnessed. He turned to look back toward his home. His mother was standing in the doorway still holding the handkerchief to her cheek. Antonio stood grim-faced behind her. He waved to them and then turned up the road out of town that rose toward the Maiella peaks.

The road was bordered by a rock wall covered with brambles that were once leaf-covered vines that hung heavy with juicy blackberries. He wished he could savor them again. Continuing on he passed through rocky meadows dotted with tholos, the stone shepherd huts that were a characteristic feature of the Abruzzi countryside. The scent of autumn leaves wafted softly on the breeze as he walked along. Arriving at a trail that veered off to the right, he followed it as it declined toward a long and deep ravine. At the ravine's edge he paused and looked back toward the village and the roofs of a few houses that he could still see in the distance above the trees. As he took in the panorama of the Maiella, the mountain whose resources had often saved them, he thought about past autumns when he and his brother scavenged mushrooms and snails, and cut and sold wood from the forested slopes. Why was he leaving home? Apart from his present dilemma, where else would he rather be? In America with his father. But that would require a lot more wherewithal to find his way to him. One thing was for certain—there was no going back.

He turned and descended the narrow, steep, and tortuous trail along ridges and through crevices dropping into the lower ravine. At the bottom, a dried river bed, he paused to get a handful of water that trickled from a spring. He surveyed the scene above him and saw the recess in the sheer rock-faced cliff where L' Eremo San Bartolomeo, the Hermitage of St. Bartholomew, was barely visible in the afternoon shade. The holy mountain had been the home of hermits and saints, but he knew it was also a place of refuge for outlaws, kidnappers, and now, by foreign soldiers. He thought that ironic because Roman legions had difficulty penetrating and establishing themselves in the rugged mountains. Somewhere in the distance a wolf howled, and Francesco reflexively patted the knife in his pocket.

He shouldered his pack and resumed the trail, boulder-hopping along the wash. He then climbed gradually through a series of switchbacks on the opposite side of the ravine. The sky toward Caramanico had begun to cloud up threatening rain and the muffled sound of distant thunder reached him in his climb. As he gained altitude, he reentered forested terrain and emerged in meadowland. The dark gray overcast sky stretched nearly to the western horizon where an orange setting sun cast a glow on the stone buildings of Caramanico, nestled on the slope of the mountain. He had made it before dark and breathed a deep sigh of relief.

Chapter 2

Caramanico, Italy. September, 1943

A brief shower had left the cobblestone streets glistening in the amber light cast by street lamps as Francesco entered the village. There was a chill in the air and he gathered his *mantello* close about him. The trek had taken effort and left him drained. His stomach was knotted with a hunger that ached at his core.

He encountered no one as he approached the Sanelli home on one of the secondary piazzas. It was one of the more substantial residences in town reflecting the family's relative affluence. The façade with its muted coral masonry fronted the piazza, and a tall Mulberry tree rose above the tiled roof from the courtyard at the rear. A narrow alley on one side separated the home from neighbors to the left; on the right the house was connected to a series of older stone houses that had been added to one another over time.

He knew the village well. The roots of his family, he was told, began there with a great-great-grandfather, Vincenzo, who was born in Caramanico at the beginning of the 18th century. No one knew what brought his ancestors to the Maiella in the first place. Some believed their ancestry may have dated to the Greeks who had migrated to the coastal areas of Southern Italy and Sicily in the pre-Christian period: what the poet, Ovid, referred to as Magna Graecia. But while Italians had acknowledged the significant imprint Greece had on their culture, the idea of Greek ancestry in the mountainous Abruzzo was speculative.

Eventually Vincenzo moved to Roccamorice where he married and raised a family. The circumstance of the move from Caramanico to Roccamorice was also lost in history. Francesco had visited Caramanico often with his family, especially during feast days, and he had become acquainted with some of the boys his age through football competitions. The Sanellis were almost extended family. His father and Pierluigi Sanelli had been friends from childhood; and they had remained close over the years growing up, and as they married and raised families their friendship continued. After Francesco's father had left the country looking for work in America, Pierluigi tried to maintain contact to see that his friend's family's welfare was not unduly threatened by the exigencies of the war, but the war had placed increased demands on his time.

Mr. Sanelli maintained a large flock of sheep and goats; however, his principal source of income was his shop in Sulmona, a food distribution business, primarily dealing in regional produce. He had working relationships with local farmers, and he brought in foodstuffs from all over Italy that varied with the season. In the winter, he had citrus shipped in from Sicily, North Africa, and countries in the Levant; but the war had completely altered and largely curbed his import business. His local business arrangements had also suffered recently with the shortages of food in the region, and now from the added demands of the Germans intent on supplying their own troops. His relationship with the German officers, particularly the quartermaster, however, had allowed him to secure enough food for his own family to make them comfortable. He had only a small staff of workers to begin with, one of whom was a supervisor, but the demands of the shop required his close attention, especially with the occupation. Without his sons to help he struggled to maintain both his rural flock and his urban business. A local man had helped him care for the sheep but the arrangement was temporary, and when a better opportunity presented itself the man left.

A man and woman walking along huddled together eyed Francesco suspiciously. He waited for them to pass and then stepped up to the door of the Sanelli home. He waited a few minutes to gather energy and then summoning his courage, he knocked, and hoped the Sanellis would not be upset by his unannounced visit. He was uneasy when moments later the door was opened by Pierluigi Sanelli.

"Francesco!" Pierluigi was wide-eyed, the look of surprise and puzzlement wrapped in a smile. "Please come in."

"*Ciao, Gigi,*" Francesco said, using the familiar term of endearment.

"I am so happy to see you, Francesco; I didn't know you were coming,"

"We would have called, but the telephone at the *municipio* is not working," he said as he stepped inside.

"Lots of things are not working anymore. We've had that trouble in Sulmona—people cutting phone lines to frustrate the Germans. What brings you here?"

"I was hoping you could use my help now, you know, what my father and you talked about when we were last here. Is that offer still good?"

Pierluigi glanced down as he pressed his forefinger to his chin and knitted his eyebrows. Then his face registered the remembrance. "Yes, yes, of course," he responded. "I could use some help, but why come all this way now? That's a good walk."

"I could have waited for a ride with someone, but I didn't know when that would be. There have been some problems with the Germans, too, so I decided to take a chance and take the direct route through the back country." Francesco knew that he would have to provide more details, but how much to divulge then and there was the problem. He described the incident at his uncle's farm, but downplayed his involvement, and he left out the fact that the German soldiers had come looking for him. "My mother and brother felt I would be safer here for a while. My mother wanted to talk to you and your wife first, but with the telephone problem, she didn't know when that would be. She hoped I could explain for her. Will that be okay?"

"Yes, of course," Pierluigi said. His faced turned serious. "I can understand. I see situations like that almost every day in Sulmona. The Germans have made themselves a terrible nuisance there. Fortunately, they have not had much of a presence here."

Francesco felt a little guilty for not telling the whole story. "There is more to tell, but I will save it for later."

"Fine," Pierluigi said, his face more relaxed. "So tell me, how are your mother and brother? I assume you have not heard much from your father, the mail being what it is now."

"As well as can be expected considering," he said, "but you're right— nothing from America in a long time."

"I'm sorry I have not been in touch. Lots on my mind lately; not that it should be an excuse. Well, come with me. We are about to have dinner. Leave your bag here, we will retrieve it later."

Pierluigi was a tall, good-looking man with a patrician's bearing, a persona he had acquired over the years in business. Francesco was fond of him because he always treated him like one of his children. Now in his mid-fifties, he had a full head of dark hair, combed back symmetrically. He was just beginning to gray at the temples. His strong face was animated by lively eyes; a thin, well-trimmed mustache traced his upper lip. He was comfortably dressed in dark slacks and a pale yellow shirt. A tie hung loosely below an unbuttoned collar. Francesco assumed he had recently returned home after a day at his Sulmona shop.

Sanelli turned and Francesco followed him through the foyer and living room and down a hallway to the dining room, suddenly aware of the aroma of food drifting in the air. Francesco was always impressed by the well-appointed home.

The sofas, chairs, tables, and chests were solid and handsomely designed, lending a comfortable and cozy look to what Francesco thought was appropriate to the Sanelli lifestyle.

Francesco's face lit up as he entered the dining room and saw four people seated at the table. He smiled at Mr. Sanelli's wife, Angiolina, while his heart leapt at the sight of their teenage daughter, Annamaria. The two men, strangers, were a surprise. One was slightly built with blue eyes and ash blond hair framing a gaunt face that otherwise seemed distinguished. The other man, a bit younger, had a more rugged demeanor with a square-jawed athletic build, dark eyes, and dark tousled hair. Both men were cleanly shaven, and wore clean cotton clothing that hung loosely on their bodies. However, they didn't appear to be villagers or Italians for that matter.

Mrs. Sanelli and her daughter rose to greet and embrace Francesco. *"Ciao, Francesco,"* Angiolina said with a big bright smile, clearly surprised. "What brings you here; where is your mother, your brother, is everything okay?" she asked in rapid-fire fashion.

Francesco answered that they were at home and well.

Angiolina frowned and wondered why Francesco was alone. She gave her husband a puzzled look, but turning back to Francesco, she smiled, and quickly offered him a seat and a bowl of thick minestrone soup. Annamaria, wearing a blue sweater and dark skirt, smiled modestly. She was an attractive, auburn-haired young woman with full lips, high cheekbones, and dark sparkling eyes. Francesco returned the smile before turning his eyes to the partially filled bowls of soup before each of the diners. A large pot of minestrone sat in the middle of the table next to a loaf of bread, a bowl of olives, a carafe of wine, and a jug of water. He savored the wonderfully fragrant herbal aroma that filled the air. Pasta, beans and rice, or polenta were the major components of most meals for those who were lucky enough find those commodities. This meal, modest for the Sanellis who could afford meat, was a special treat for Francesco. He took a seat at the table, an expression of boyish happiness on his face.

"Si, grazie, thank you. It's sort of a long story," Francesco finally answered.

He was very hungry, but he did not want the pangs in his stomach, elicited by the sight and aroma of the food, to give voice to just how hungry he was. Angiolina ladled a generous portion of the soup into his bowl. Annamaria smiled again and filled his glass with water.

Mrs. Sanelli was slightly shorter than her husband. She had nicely arranged brown hair laced with gray, and her skin was smooth and clear. Her shoulders and upper arms appeared a bit fleshy, and her heavy breasts outlined by the conservative floral dress she wore combined with her other features to give her a matronly look.

Annamaria slid a basket of sliced bread toward Francesco's bowl before sitting down. Francesco looked at her and smiled. Her eyes briefly met his before she demurely glanced away. Annamaria was about two years older Francesco remembered. He was sorry about their age difference because he had grown fond of her. In fact, he had developed a real crush; it was the first romantic experience of his young life. They had flirted a bit the last time he had visited back in the spring. After dinner one night they had walked along Via Belvedere, the village's lover's lane laughing and talking. As they sat, on a bench, Francesco tentatively reached for her hand and when she allowed him to hold it, he slipped his other arm around her waist. She turned her face to him, and as they stared into each other's eyes they stopped talking. He thought about kissing her, but he hesitated. Another couple suddenly appeared arm in arm and sat at a bench across from them. His heart was racing, but he didn't know what to do. He hadn't seen that gesture coming or the emotion it evoked. Feeling self-conscious he leaned away from Annamaria and that moment vanished as if it never happened.

On the way back to the house he had feelings he had never felt before. But he wasn't sure how she felt. He thought she might have acquiesced to his intimate gesture. That was the last opportunity they had to be together. His family left to return to Roccamorice the following morning.

Now, he glanced at the swell of her breasts and the outline of her shapely hips beneath the apron that was fastened about her. He found it hard to avert his eyes. She seemed to have become more alluring since he had last seen her. When she noticed him looking, he quickly looked away, a blush rising on his face.

After inquiring if anyone at the table needed anything more, the women left the room. Francesco picked up his spoon and began to eat. The minestrone's strong aroma and rich herbal flavor almost overpowered his senses; he stifled his urge to gobble it down.

"Francesco, let me tell you about our guests," Sanelli said. "I tell you this in confidence, understand?"

Francesco nodded, as he lifted his spoon.

"These two men have escaped from the POW camp outside Sulmona. They made their way here to Caramanico with the help of a partigiano. I did not expect them, but I have offered them temporary refuge."

Francesco's eyes widened as he looked from Pierluigi to the men. "I knew about the camp near Chieti," he said, as he looked back to Pierluigi. "But didn't know there was one near Sulmona."

"One of the largest in the country, Francesco. It's officially known as *Campo Prigionieri di Guerra, 78.* It holds, or it did hold, thousands of British soldiers, mostly those captured in Africa and Sicilia."

Famished, Francesco sat back again and rapidly lifted spoonful's of soup from the bowl. With his mouth full he managed to ask, "So these men are British?"

"*Piano, piano,* Francesco, No need to eat so fast," Pierluigi said.

Francesco swallowed and nodded, holding his soup spoon above the bowl. "Well, one of them is," Pierluigi continued. "Major Denis Jones," pointing to the slender, blond-haired man, "was an officer in the Royal engineers. He was working in in North Africa, assigned to what became the British Eighth Army."

The two men sat and listened to Sanelli's account of their circumstances, but it wasn't apparent that either man fully understood much of what he was saying.

"Is that where he was captured?" Francesco asked.

"Yes, about a year ago in the African desert."

"Parlo un poco," Denis said smiling. "I'm not terribly fluent in Italian, mate," he said to Francesco, not knowing if he understood the English version.

Francesco appeared surprised. "He speaks a little Italian," he said, dipping his spoon into the bowl again.

"Yes, he knows quite enough. He understands pretty much everything he hears including much of what we're saying. He's just being modest. His grandmother was an Italian woman. He learned to speak Italian by conversing with her."

"And the other?" he asked, nodding toward the dark-haired man while continuing to eat. He glanced up and smiled at Annamaria who had returned to retrieve a sweater she had left on her chair.

"Lieutenant Roger Ellis is his name. He was in a Canadian division of the British Eighth army. After North Africa, he was with them when they and the Americans invaded Sicilia. That's where he was captured a couple of months ago." The Canadian appeared more rugged and physical than the Englishman who seemed more restrained, but his face offered no clue to his thoughts or understanding of what was going on.

"Does he speak Italian?"

"Very little. He grew up on a farm in Canada that employed Italian immigrants as day laborers. He learned to communicate with them, but only in the most basic way. But, he also studied French in school, and that helps."

"What did they tell you about the war?"

"Not too much. Denis gave me some information he learned from the newest prisoners who arrived in the camp just before they left. The rest I fill in with news from London's BBC on my shortwave radio."

"You still have a radio?"

"I have it in my apartment in Sulmona. My relationship with the German quartermaster gives me certain privileges."

Denis nudged Roger and whispered, "Hey, mate lets go out for a smoke and let them talk." Turning to Pierluigi he said, *"Andiamo fuori a fumare."*

"Si, va bene. Take your time. It's cold out there so take something to keep you warm. And remember, the walls are high, but one never knows who might pass and hear English."

After the men left the room Francesco said, "Wow, Pierluigi, such a risk you're taking. Aren't you worried about the Gestapo?"

"Yes, I know the risk and I'm concerned about the authorities finding out, but this family is committed to the resistance now, and this is just part of it. So much has changed since you were here last."

"We hear stories but we get so little information about the war in Roccamorice.

Most newspapers that reach us are already many days old, and they only give the good news; now there is none at all. The radios in town we used to listen to the news and *Il Duce's* speeches on were confiscated when the Germans came. Anyone caught with one risked being shot."

"The Allies bombed the Rome railroad yards back in May. Were you not aware of that?" Pierluigi asked. "How about the bombing of Sulmona and Pescara at the end of August? That must have brought the war home to you as it did for us here."

Francesco had laid down his spoon by the soup bowl. The women returned and moved about clearing the table and tidying up. Francesco kept his bowl stealing glances at Annamaria, excited at her closeness. He said, "We did hear about Rome and Pescara, but nothing about Sulmona."

Pausing to sip some wine, Pierluigi continued. "I was in my shop that day. Nearly a 100 people died when bombs hit the piazza by the train station. The Allies were trying to destroy the railroad yards. But some bombs struck the buildings. Much of the rubble remains to be cleared. Collateral damage they call it."

"You were lucky then?"

"Yes, he was very lucky," Angiolina said, as she put away her pots.

"After that, we were afraid every day papa had to go to Sulmona," Annamaria said.

"It's true," Pierluigi said. "It was worrisome after that. And the shortages became another burden to deal with."

"Getting supplies in Roccamorice certainly got worse after the bombing began, that's for sure," Francesco said. "That's one of the reasons I'm here now. To answer your earlier question, Angiolina, there just isn't enough food in the village to feed everyone. So, I thought I would come and see if I could work for food and stay awhile. There is more your husband will tell you."

Pierluigi looked at his wife shaking his head in a way that signaled it wasn't an urgent matter.

"*Va bene, Francesco. Non tin preoccupare,*" Angiolina told Francesco not to worry as she continued to put things away. "We'll try to help you out as much as we can."

"*Grazie.* So where do things stand now?" Francesco asked turning to Pierluigi. "What do you plan to do with these two men?"

"Well, at the moment their army is somewhere in the south moving slowly along the Adriatic coast."

"And the American army? What about them?" "Dealing with the Americans is out of the question."

"Call us if you need us, Gigi," Angiolina said. "Annamaria and I have to finish the packages we were working on this afternoon."

"*Nessun problema,*" he said, turning to the women who were leaving the room.

Facing back to Francesco, he continued. "I heard on the BBC that the Americans had a very difficult landing at Salerno, they had thousands of casualties, but they eventually managed to establish a beachhead. The problem is they are penned in and bogged down in a tough fight with the Germans."

"How long have these two been here?" Francesco asked as he reached for the bread basket and broke off a piece of bread. He took a bite between spoonful's of soup.

"They broke out earlier in the month, toward the end of the first week of September. It was after Badoglio announced the capitulation. Suddenly one day the guards at the camp disappeared."

"I remember when word of the surrender reached us. No one knew what to think at first," Francesco said.

"Yes, I know. Other than the announcement, nothing useful came out of Rome so there was chaos and confusion all over Italy. There still is."

"What happened at the camp?"

"Denis can give you the details, but when the prisoners found they were unguarded, they simply walked out. They decided to scatter in different directions to avoid recapture by the Germans. The guards discovered that the German army intended to occupy the country because Italy was preparing to reenter the war on the side of the Allies."

"Is that true? That Italy has switched to the Allied side?"

"Maybe in spirit, and maybe even on paper in disorganized brigades, but not as an effective army—it's completely disintegrated."

"So what about your sons then? Where are they?"

"God knows. We hope they are trying to get home from wherever they are. We wait for news every day."

"If these two strangers found their way here— all the way up the Maiella from Sulmona, your sons should make it back," Francesco said, trying to sound hopeful.

"We are hoping and praying for that, Francesco. I just haven't been able to learn anything. I've lost the sources I had in the government after the collapse, and my German connections have not been able to give me any information yet."

"So how did these men get to your house of all places?"

"Well, Francesco that's a long story. Actually, it's a sort of complicated two-part story, mine and theirs. Denis, as I said is being quite humble when he says he knows only a little Italian. Actually he knows a fair amount from conversing with his grandparents as a child, and with the Italian guards at the camp for over a year. He also picked up quite a bit from Fascist newspapers and pamphlets in the camp."

"He could read those?"

"An Italian-English dictionary he received in a Red Cross package helped."
"How about the other one?"

"Roger was a prisoner only a short time. He knows much less of our language, but he surprises me from time to time with the Italian words and phrases he comes up with."

"That you can understand?"

"Fairly well. He is trying to learn as much as he can, as fast as he can. He spends a lot of time with the English-Italian dictionary that Denis gave him, and as I said, his background in French helps too. Annamaria has been helping him. She found a useful book to teach Italian to foreigners. I am impressed with the progress. Roger is getting better day by day. If you speak slowly he can understand much of what you tell him."

"I wish my English was better," Francesco said. "The course we took in school was very basic."

Pierluigi got up while Francesco was speaking and walked over to a cabinet where he pulled out the book Annamaria was using: *Corso di Lingua Italiana per Stranieri*. He handed the book to Francesco. "It's a book designed for foreigners, but maybe you might study it. Maybe some of the English will come back to you." Francesco nodded. "Speaking of studies, what about the liceo in Sulmona?" he asked.

"It's closed now. The headmaster told me he didn't expect to reopen this year." Francesco looked disappointed, but he expected it. "We thought that might have happened. Last spring I don't think any of us would have imagined this situation."

"Things have changed since that visit Francesco. I never conceived of harboring enemy soldiers either. But recently, a close friend of mine, a lawyer from Chieti, became very unhappy with the war and policies of Mussolini. Very quietly he organized a group of men who shared his views and asked me to join."

"I know something is happening. I overheard my brother speaking to friends who were upset with the Germans. They talked about leaving the village to join others hiding out in the mountains. I don't know what their plan was. I think Antonio was considering it—he couldn't stand the German's arrogance either. But now that I'm here, I doubt he will leave my mother alone."

"Well, what you overheard is probably true. There was always an anti-Fascist movement, even from the beginning. Mussolini had fooled most of us, me included, but not everyone. I knew about the early *resistenza*, but I was never seriously interested—too risky for my business so I tried not to get involved. I never wanted to be the target of Mussolini's secret police. My first loyalty was to my family and what was left over to the people who worked for me."

Francesco stopped eating, held his spoon with one hand and casually leafed through the Italian course book glancing back and forth from the pages to Pierluigi.

"But I remember you and my father discussing politics around the kitchen table. Neither one of you had anything bad to say about *Il Duce* then."

"When I was young, I must confess that I did support Mussolini and, obviously, my business depended on support from the government. As you know by now, *raccamandazione*—special references are how businesses like mine flourish. In this country, influence is important. Even beyond education, it creates a comfortable lifestyle. Hard work alone is no assurance for success."

"My father used to say that, but now I am beginning to understand," Francesco said, resuming his meal. "Everybody with a business today looks for all the favors they can get."

"I admired Mussolini for trying to unify the country and bring about order from chaos after the last war when we were in danger of falling into communism. But the danger of Fascism was not recognized until it was too late. Twenty years ago he rebuilt the military and stabilized the lira. He also created many public projects all over the country including here in Caramanico and Sulmona. He drained the marshes and increased farm production, and that helped me in my business."

"Someday I hope to visit the Foro Mussolini in Rome he built for the 1932 Olympics," Francesco added. "I have only seen pictures of it."

"Well, not everything was a work of art, like that sports complex in Rome. But in those days, I believed in him. I was young and inexperienced. He was impressive when you saw him give those speeches and heard him on the radio. There is still a fascination with him. I overlooked the tyranny and idolatry behind *'Mussolini ha sempre ragione*—Mussolini is always right,'" he said, gesturing quotation marks.

"When did your attitude change?"

"When he declared war on France and Britain. It was a big mistake. It's become all too obvious that what he called the "Axis," or the "Pact of Steel" he signed with Hitler was a disaster for this country," he said, again gesturing quotation marks.

"You were okay with North Africa?"

"Yes, although I'm ashamed now. We had reestablished ourselves in the eyes of our European neighbors so I thought, like others, if it's okay for them, why not us?" Pierluigi spoke regrettably about how the invasion, colonization, and domination of the dark-skinned races seemed appropriate at the time. "But it turned out to be an atrocity, and twenty years of Fascism—its belief in the glory of war, has left us with nothing but ruination. Still, those die-hard Fascists shout the same old stupid slogans."

"When did the *resistenza* begin?"

Pierluigi rose and went to the back door to check on Denis and Roger. He opened the door but could not see them in the darkened yard. He closed the door and returned to the table to answer Francesco's question. "I can't say for sure. About five years ago a group of intellectuals who had stopped believing in Mussolini and his Fascist ideas left the country and gathered in Paris. This was before the pact with the Nazis. They sensed another war was coming and knew we were not prepared for it. They began printing and smuggling journals and newspapers with their anti-fascist views back into Italy. I was aware of some of the publications as they passed from hand to hand in Sulmona."

"I was given a book by my teacher that was critical of the Fascists. I came across it when I was packing to come here. I had forgotten to read it. Now I wish I had."

"What was it called?"

"*Fontamara.*"

"Ah yes, it's a very good account. But your teacher should not have given it to you." Pierluigi scowled. "If it's discovered the authorities can make it difficult for you and the teacher."

"I left it covered up in my bedroom. Now I wish I brought it."

"Be careful when you read it. Silone wrote it here, but it was published in Switzerland. It's a *romanza*— a work of fiction, but it shows the bitter reality about life in the Abruzzo under the Fascists better than a nonfiction story." Pensively, one hand propped on his forehead, Pierluigi continued. "I read provocative anti-Fascist articles that questioned Mussolini's policies. My attitude began to change, but personally I never responded to their call to action. As I said, my focus was my family and my business. However, that movement led to the formation of *partigiani* around Italy including here in the Abruzzo."

"In town I heard the Germans call them bandits."

"Here as well. In any case, we Abruzzese have always been drawn as much to bandits as to holy men."

"How big is this *resistenza?*" Francesco asked, as he put the book aside.

"It's still quite small around here and not well organized. It seems to consist of units with just a few men in each."

"You say you didn't want to get involved, but you did, so how did that happen?"

"Well, sometime after I started attending the meetings, just to listen more than anything, I was approached by a young *partigiano*, Fumato, who came into the shop one day. That was his *soprannome*, nickname or code name. None of them want you to know their true identity. My position as a collector of food for the army and now the Germans would be important to the resistance, he told me. Would I be willing to help them? He said he was just one of five men in his resistance group hiding in a grotto above the town, but his group along with other partisans intended to interrupt the food supply to the Germans. The Nazis want the same thing as the Fascists: food and manpower; "We plan to deny them."

"I told him that I was neither Fascist nor anti-Fascist, but what he was asking me was a big risk and sacrifice. Did he appreciate I would have to walk a fine line between assisting the *partigiani* and cooperating with the Germans? He didn't seem to care much—everyone sacrifices was his attitude. I realized that if I said no I could expect trouble from the *partigiani*, but if I said yes and made a mistake the Germans would make it even worse for me. I needed to think about how to work it out, so I said I would think about it. He nodded he understood and told me he would contact me again soon.

"The next day I was approached in my shop by an undercover British agent in disguise. Badoglio's people had made arrangements with both the American and British secret services to become involved in espionage here in this country. The British agent told me that he had had contact with Fumato. He asked if I would also be willing to provide a safe house for British prisoners of war who escaped. I told him about my commitment to aid the resistance, but what he was asking for was entirely different. I told him I couldn't answer him until I discussed it with my wife.

"That evening Angiolina and I talked late into the night about the risks and opportunities. The risks were obvious, but we saw an opportunity to discover the whereabouts of our sons, and get them back here safely. Locating them has now become the focus of our lives."

Pierluigi sipped his glass of wine while Francesco broke off another piece of bread. His hunger had quieted, but he felt the need to put something in his mouth. Putting his glass down, Pierluigi continued, "We had not heard from them in many months, and now that the army was disbanded, we did not know where they were. Were they in Italy or some other battlefield? Could they have been shipped to Germany? We just didn't know. We thought that there were many vulnerable sons and husbands out there, as well as escaped prisoners who needed help, and we believed there would be other villagers like us who would be eager to assist. So when the agent returned I agreed."

"You must have known the danger," Francesco said. "The Germans have posted notices everywhere— death to anyone found guilty of helping prisoners. I've seen the posters with the black borders here in Caramanico. They're posted all over Roccamorice. They must be in all of the villages."

"Yes, I knew. Badoglio made a speech to the people urging them to help the British and American POWs, but it wasn't necessary because the Mussolini government had lost popularity, and from the first many of us sympathized with the plight of the allied prisoners. Stories have already circulated about families in nearby villages who risked their lives hiding men, working hard to feed them until they could move them on."

"So how did they get here?"

"After they escaped, they were first sheltered and fed by a man in a village near the prison camp. When they reached Caramanico they found a *partigiano* who knew to bring them here."

"How long has it been?"

Pierluigi studied the wine in his glass. "Just a few days," he said. "I am getting worried, and so are they. They have seen the notices and heard the stories. Just before you arrived they told me they were very grateful to me, but they decided it would be best for everyone if they left."

"Yes, let them go, why take the risk?"

"I would feel guilty. I know how tough it would be on their own," Pierluigi continued. "You know how difficult the Maiella can be for those who don't know their way. Someone has to guide them."

"But who? There are patrols everywhere, and it is difficult to keep something like this a secret. There are many OVRA spies and Nazi sympathizers around. Word is bound to leak out, it happened in our town." The incident at his uncle's farm still troubled him; he recalled his thought—it was not worth dying for. Holding his hand to the side of his mouth to mimic a villager informing on Pierluigi, he whispered, *"Pierluigi nasconde i fugitivi."* Dropping his hand he picked up his spoon and continued, "A casual remark to the wrong person, a collaborator, who knows who you can trust."

"I know the risk, Francesco. It's not just my life, but my wife and daughter and even my sons wherever they are. I've heard the rumors that some people in town think I give my best produce to the Germans. I give what I have to, but I have tried to be a good citizen and a good friend to the people in this town. I have helped those who have asked for whatever food I could spare."

"You have to hope and pray they will repay you with silence."

"In any case you're right, Francesco. They cannot stay here much longer. So, I have come up with a plan for their departure."

"Whatever it is it has to be less risky than hiding them, at least they will be gone." He noticed the concern on Pierluigi's face and a twinge of guilt crept into his thoughts. "Maybe I can help you get them away from here." Where did those words come from? Francesco wondered. He hadn't expected to say anything so bold as to volunteer for a risky mission in a country crawling with German soldiers.

"I don't know," Pierluigi said, looking critically at Francesco. "I want to involve as few people as possible. My first thought is absolutely not. If your father were here, I would naturally discuss it with him, and knowing him, he would probably say no; but since he's not here, I would have to ask your mother."

Francesco's tone suddenly became desperate. Waving his hands expressively he said, "No, please don't! Let me tell you why. Hunger drove me here hoping I could take care of that by working for you. But I had run-ins with German soldiers in Roccamorice today. Afterward, two of them came looking for me. I was lucky and got out before they knew I was there."

"Do they suspect you came here? What did you do?"

"I don't think so, not yet. But they might figure it out in time. So it may be good for all of us if I'm not here." Francesco laid out the details of the encounters he had with the German officer and soldiers so Pierluigi could judge for himself.

Pierluigi sighed. "I'm not that worried, Francesco. I don't think insolence is high on their reprisal list, at least not enough to initiate a search beyond Roccamorice. But I think it is better for you to stay here for now. Meanwhile, you've given me something to think about."

"I am fed up with the German occupation of our town, and after what happened today with my uncle, I want to fight back," Francesco said angrily, realizing that he harbored a deeper-seated resentment than he had previously acknowledged to himself. "I think I should forget what my family and I thought was best, and help you in a bigger way. You might think I am too young, but I don't think so. I want to fight like other young men here in Abruzzo. I know I can do it, so let me help you, whatever your plan is."

Chapter 3

Francesco knew he had more convincing to do, not only with Pierluigi, but probably with Angiolina as well. At the same time, he was worried with what his mother and brother would think. He was supposed to stay safe and lie low in Caramanico, doing simple chores around a friend's house. Aiding escaped enemy soldiers was not part of the understanding, but he was upset not knowing his uncle's fate.

The door opened and Roger followed Denis back in. Denis cupped his hands and blew into them. "Chilly night," he said; Roger closed the door behind him.

Pierluigi gestured for them to take a seat and refilled their wine glasses. He propped his arm on the table pensively, his hand on his chin, and poured himself another glass of wine. "I was just telling our friend here about a plan I had for you, so let me elaborate."

Francesco sat up straight, pulled his chair closer to the table and leaned in. He was anxious to learn the details of what he thought would be an adventure. His hunger satisfied, he was feeling pretty good.

"It's time to move the sheep to lower pastures," Pierluigi began. "Actually, it's getting late, but the war has upset usual time tables. Ordinarily, moving them further down the valley is not a problem. However, I am thinking of a far longer route this year— to my brother's farm near Casoli." Looking directly at them he said, "Denis and Roger I want to send both of you with the sheep."

Francesco looked puzzled. Casoli is a long way from here, he thought. He had never been anywhere near there; in fact, he had hardly strayed very far from home. He tried to picture himself with the men and a flock of sheep.

Denis piped up, his face registering skepticism, "How's that going to get us back to our army?"

"The farm is close to the German's defensive line along the Sangro River," Pierluigi answered.

"Is that where Montgomery's headed?"

"British Eighth is now in Pulia. I want to get you as close as possible." Francesco knew that The Bloc Haus above Roccamorice at Passo Lanciano the Germans were building for their artillery was a part of that defense. He wondered how they could possibly get past the Germans unnoticed.

Pierluigi said, "The Germans are using Abruzzo's elevated positions for artillery and the rivers for defense." Looking at Denis and Roger he continued, "I want to get you two across the Sangro before the British army engages the Germans. So far, I'm told the British are moving north slowly, so with reasonable haste, it might be possible to get the sheep to the farm, and both of you across the river before the two armies confront one another."

Denis turned to Roger and quickly updated him in English on Pierluigi's plan. Roger nodded he understood.

"How are you planning to get these men with the sheep to Casoli?" Francesco asked.

"As shepherds—disguising them as shepherds."

Francesco frowned as he tore off a piece of bread. He was skeptical, but he was also worried about his fate if he were caught with these men, even though Pierluigi had not yet made him part of the plan. "If the Germans see these men they won't be fooled," he said. "They just don't look like shepherds, or even Italians." He glanced at the men. "For sure if the Germans stop to question them they will know in an instant they are fake."

"We'll have to make them look Italian," Pierluigi said. "That is critical, the whole idea depends on it.

"Blimey! I don't know Pierluigi. Sounds a bit wild. Can't you sneak us onto a train with your supplies?" Denis asked.

"The trouble with the trains," Pierluigi said, "is that the Italian railroad schedules are chaotic and the workers have not left their jobs. I just can't box you up like a carton of vegetables. Conductors check all manifests and packages; and they see the passengers up close. If someone looks like a foreigner they would likely examine the travel documents with more care than usual. They might spot forgeries. More important the Germans are also monitoring the trains, including the loading of materials, you can be sure of that. And then there is the added problem that the Allies have begun to bomb railways."

Francesco was deep in thought. He understood the danger, but boys shepherding with men together might not draw suspicion. His father crossed an ocean to help his family. Could he be as brave and do something that would make a difference—be a man and help these men foil the Germans? "I have moved sheep before," he said.

"True," Pierluigi said, "but this drive will require much guile and shepherding experience taking sheep across the Maiella. There will be days of difficult travel and a lot of unknowns. Crossing the mountains on foot with few roads or trails is not so easy. You and the men could do it, but the sheep are not goats and the passage will be difficult in spots. It's a route no one has done before."

"I think I can do it, or try anyway," Francesco said. "The Germans would not suspect a young boy like me."

"Well, Francesco, consider the consequences. If the Germans catch you, you will be sent to a labor camp or they might just kill you—you've seen the posters with the penalties for those who aid the enemy. And what am I to tell your parents?"

Francesco frowned and nodded. He understood the risk, but he was willing to take it he decided. "If your plan works, you won't have to tell my parents anything."

"Francesco, I admire your courage, but there is no way I can let you have the responsibility for the lives of these men as well as your own. But you might be very helpful to the man I have asked to do this."

"A fourth shepherd? Quite a crowd don't you think?" Denis asked. He turned to Roger with a skeptical face and indicated he would fill him in.

"I have a good man, Ennio, a shepherd who lives just outside the village. He has the experience and knows where to go."

A real shepherd, Francesco thought. A wave of relief washed over him, realizing he wouldn't have to shoulder the full responsibility. He relaxed in his chair, sensing the men were just as he was with that news.

"Why would your friend be willing to do this?" Denis asked.

"The Germans confiscated his flock. It was the only thing of value he inherited when his father died. The house and property went to his older brother, so you can imagine what a loss it was to him. I promised to help him."

Francesco sat back with the men and listened to Pierluigi describe the life of Abruzzo's *contadini*. Francesco didn't know Ennio, but he was familiar with his plight and thought the information would be useful for Denis and Roger.

Pierluigi described how the families eked out a living with meager plots and sheep. He told them most of the people did not own the land they farmed. The big landowners divided their holdings into many small plots as part of the *mezzadria* system, whereby the people gave up half of what they produced to the *padrone*-landowner. "In the end they can't produce enough to buy land of their own. It's the reason Francesco's father and men like him left to find work in America."

"The system is not fair," Francesco said. "My father told me he wanted to break the chain from his father and his grandfather before him. He talked to me and my brother about how he refused to be at the mercy of the *padrone*. He went overseas to earn enough to be independent of them. I know he did it for all of us—the family, and I'm glad for that, even though I miss him."

"When this war is over, I know many will leave like Francesco's did to earn a better living for their families," Pierluigi said.

Denis explained the unfairness behind the basic concept of the *mezzadria* to

Roger, as they sipped their glasses of wine and listened to Pierluigi and Francesco.

"Some of us will stay, of course," Pierluigi said, "if only to hang onto what we know and to what we have become accustomed. Not everyone has the temperament to pack up and leave the country, even to go elsewhere in Europe."

"Or cross an ocean, but that's what I want to do," Francesco said. He missed his father, not that they were close pals or anything like that. His father was a man of few words—his eyes did the talking, but he was the father he needed.

"Ennio knows he is in a difficult position," Pierluigi continued, "but he is willing to bide his time. In the meantime, he sees the chance to move my flock as an opportunity to acquire some of my animals in return for his service and start over again.

"Does he know how to get the sheep to your brother's farm?" Francesco asked.

"Yes, he has been to my brother's farm. I took him with me to look over some stock my brother wanted to sell. He has traced a route from here across the Maiella to Passo Lanciano, marking it with rock cairns and strips of cloth. He feels the route will be reasonably safe for the sheep. From there the route will be more straightforward.

"Too bad we can't count on the Germans to cooperate," Denis said.

"There are bound to be circumstances that can't be predicted and where he will need to rely on all of you as a team. In any case, I trust Ennio's judgment. He's always had a good head on his shoulders."

"How do Ennio and I get back here?" Francesco asked.

"I will send one of my trucks. It seems natural enough even though my brother has no produce at this time of the year to ship back. But he will find something to send."

"Lots of logistical issues, Pierluigi. German checkpoints, petrol, who knows what else," Denis said.

"You're right. I know I have not thought of every possibility. There is still more planning to do, but we still have time to put our heads together, and there are people out there, *partigiani* with safe houses who I hope will help."

Denis and Roger got up and said that they were going out for a *passaggiato* and would be back soon.

At the door, Denis turned back to Pierluigi. "May I have a word?" he asked.

"Certainly, Denis. I will be right back," he said to Francesco. He got up and followed Denis who lingered at the door, while Roger went on ahead. "Do you think this boy is up to the task?" Denis asked quietly.

"He is reliable and more mature than you think." Pierluigi whispered. "I've known him since he was born. Don't worry, I would never allow him to do this alone, but Ennio has the knowledge, and I think Francesco could be of great help to him and both of you. And a boy with you men should lessen suspicion."

"Just thought I would ask. There is a lot at stake here."

"I can understand your reservations. He is, after all, very young, but he is more mature than the usual 15 year old. I have not made a decision. I need to speak to Ennio again and my wife. Go on the walk with Roger. I will talk to you later."

Pierluigi stepped back into the room and sat down by Francesco. "I must speak to Ennio tonight. We must move quickly. There is still much to do and little time to do it. Annamaria will have to finish making *carte d'identita.*"

"Identification cards?" Francesco said, looking surprised. "How did she learn to do that?"

"With a machine the British agent passed on to me through Fumato. Cameras have been confiscated but our druggist, a man I can trust, has taken the photos and will make the prints. The cards for Denis and Roger need to be done quickly." Pausing in thought, he wrapped his arms around his shoulders, "The weather is turning colder. There will be mouths to feed, warm clothing to assemble, and *mantelos* to shield the autumn rain. I just hope it doesn't turn to snow. But I have enough to worry about for now."

Angiolina and Annamaria returned to the room to clean up the few remaining items on the table.

Francesco's heart fluttered when he saw Annamaria. He smiled at her; more demurely, she returned one of her own. He wanted to talk to her alone and hoped they would have the opportunity that evening. Now that he was part of Pierluigi's plan, he suddenly realized he was conflicted between choices of spending time with Annamaria in Caramanico versus going on the road.

Angiolina finished her work and asked if they wanted anything more before going to bed.

Pierluigi said they were fine, but that he would be up shortly to discuss something. "I need your opinion on something."

"I will wait up for you," she said and left, with her daughter.

"Francesco, pick up your pack and let me show you to your room," Pierluigi said.

Francesco followed Sanelli down the hall from the dining room and up the stairs to the second floor. He was shown a well-furnished room with a large comfortable- looking bed covered with a thick comforter. It was one of Pierluigi's son's bedrooms. Francesco remembered the great view it had of one of the Maiella peaks from the tall, now shuttered, window. More importantly he thought, it was close to Annamaria's room.

"Put your things in there and get a good night's rest." Pierluigi said.

"Yes, thank you, I will," he said putting his sack down on the floor by the bed. "I'm not feeling very tired right now. I'm too excited. I think I'll talk to the men some more. I'd like to get to know them better. I would like to know how much of what you told them they really understand, and if they are willing to take the chance crossing the Maiella. Do you have a map of Abruzzo?"

Francesco followed Pierluigi to the lower level where he retrieved a map and handed it to Francesco, quickly tracing the general route. " Show it to them when they get back."

Francesco was about to leave the house when he encountered Annamaria in the hall. *"Ciao,"* he said, feeling his heart beating faster. "I need to talk with the men about your father's plan. Do you want to go for a walk later?"

"It will be too late for that, but I will wait up for you. Did my father actually describe the plan?"

"Yes, the basic idea, not the details. It sounds very clever. I asked him if I could go along to help."

She winced. "What did he say to that?"

"That he would think about it."

"I'm surprised he said that. It's pretty risky. There are still many things to work out. I know that our friend Ennio has agreed, but he needs the work for the sheep my father will give him, so he is willing to risk it. But he is an experienced shepherd, and he has studied and marked out the complicated route."

"I would be his helper, that's all. I really want to do this. I don't think I understood until I talked to your father how much I hate those Nazis who have taken over our country. "

"I can understand how you feel, but don't know if taking part in the plan is wise, Francesco. Too risky. We should talk about this some more."

"Yes, let's do that. I need to tell you more about why I'm here and why I need to do this. I'll try to have a quick talk with them," he said.

They left the kitchen together and walked down the hall. Annamaria turned back to Francesco as she climbed the stairs to her room. *"Ci vedremo piu tardi,"* she said, as Francesco continued toward the front door thinking, yes, but not too much later I hope, still feeling the warmth from being near her, wanting to take up where they left off a year ago.

Francesco opened the door as he heard the men approach the house. He waited as they put out their cigarettes and walked in. He had gotten the impression from watching Denis and Pierluigi converse that they had little faith in his ability to help them out of their predicament. He wanted to correct that, show them he was mature enough.

"Ciao," what's up, Francesco"? Denis asked as he entered.

"I want you to know I am happy to help you and Roger get away safely, so it might be good if we knew each other better. First, should I call you Major?"

"Please call me Denis, mate. And I'm sure Roger here won't mind if you use his first name. We don't need to be so formal now."

Roger nodded understanding, and stepped forward to shake hands with Francesco. *"Piacere!"*

Francesco smiled. Roger knew a basic response to being introduced. He shook his hand firmly. Then he turned to Denis and asked. "So first, tell me how did you get here?"

"It's a long story."

"I've got time. Let's sit in the living room and talk."

The room had a cozy ambience with its mix of comfortable sofas and chairs, wall paintings, and classic Italian ceramic pottery. Francesco turned up the lamp's brightness and sat down in a chair. Roger took a seat on the sofa. Denis walked over to the window and pulled the edge of the curtain back to look out. Seeing no one, he settled into a seat on the sofa next to Roger. Francesco leaned in and Denis began his tale.

46

Chapter 4

Sulmona, Italy. July, 1943

Sendere subito," the guard yelled to step down. *"La guerra e finita per voi."*

Denis knew enough of the Italian language to understand the guard shouting that the war was over for them. He was hopeful when he arrived at the camp in Sulmona. In his mind, his predicament didn't seem real. Magical thinking, perhaps, always believing he would be rescued from his unfortunate situation, even at the last moment. But when he looked out from the panel truck and saw his comrades shuffling around behind barbed-wire in their disheveled khaki uniforms and downtrodden looks, reality hit. He sighed as his heart sank, and his face quickly came to resemble theirs.

He clamored off the truck following the men in front of him through the main gate and into the yard escorted by a phalanx of Italian guards on either side who jeered, pushed, and shoved the grunting and groaning men in various directions toward washing and delousing stations. Afterward they were assigned randomly to various barracks. The camp was built with a twelve-foot-high barbed-wire fence that enclosed several U-shaped cement buildings each housing three hundred men in double-tired bunks of rough-hewn planks on tiled floors. Denis and a handful of others were ushered to the door of one of them and told to find a bed. The room was dimly lit and gloomy; the air was stale. Denis caught whiffs of the sour scent of unwashed men as he walked the aisles. He tossed a bag he had been given containing a sweater and eating utensils on an empty bunk across from a fellow prisoner. The man was seated on the edge of his cot looking at a yellowed pamphlet, smoking a cigarette. He was slightly built with sallow skin. His face seemed sunken beneath his cheekbones much like the other men.

"Denis is the name," he said, reaching out his hand.

"Harry," the man responded evenly, putting his cigarette in the corner of his mouth and extending his hand. "Where did they haul you blokes in from?"

"Naples. Before that, Libya."

"Where did you get captured?"

"Near Knightsbridge."

Harry took a drag on his cigarette, exhaled a stream of smoke and asked, "What happened?"

"When Rommel's forces broke through I was caught completely unaware with my sappers trying to undo pipeline we had laid earlier."

"Ah, you're one of Wavell's engineers. I was in armor. We got caught up like you. I was part of the screening force near Sidi Baranni in '40. We had some small skirmishes, but then the Italians, attacked in force and we were not ready for it."

"We weren't either. So you were one of the unlucky chaps that got captured."

Harry shook his head sadly. "I couldn't believe it." He sighed and took another drag on his cigarette.

"I know the feeling," Denis said frowning. "So you've been here awhile. What's it like?

"Not so bad now." Harry's face brightened a bit. "But it wasn't always like this." He went on to explain how his treatment, when he first got captured by the Germans, was tolerable. But when they turned him and his comrades over to the Italians things got worse. "They practically starved us while they shipped us to Lecce and then to Bari on the train. Bread and water only, and very little of that." He explained when they got there the stockade was overcrowded. The yard was an open cess-pit— the smell of the open latrines was gagging—there was shit and flies everywhere. Everyone had dysentery. "When you crowd that many men together without proper facilities you live in a sewer."

"The sanitation was a little better for us," Denis said, "but they treated us like crap. They would toss biscuits over the fence and jeer at us."

Harry grimaced as he continued. "The rest of the trip here was just as miserable. On a lorry at first and then on foot with very little nourishment—a death march really. It's a wonder any of us made it."

Denis leaned forward and asked, "So how is this place better?"

"At first we were on starvation rations, although they tried to make it bearable with variety—macaroni, thin soups and stews, and tins of Italian bully."

"Yeah mate. I've tasted that gruel," Denis said, screwing up his face.

"And then there were some guards whose jobs they said was to rough us up."

"And now?"

"What happened is that they let the Catholics out for Mass in town on Sunday, and they complained to the priest." Harry explained that the priest got word to the Vatican and the Papal Nuncio came to inspect. "Everything improved after that. We got more food and clothing; Red Cross packages we hadn't seen in weeks started to arrive."

Denis relaxed a bit and leaned back on his cot to let a man pass. Looking around other men were lying back sleeping or chatting quietly with bunk mates. "What's the routine here?" he asked, seemingly less concerned than he had been. "The main thing you have to get used to is the boredom. There are work details, but since they started feeding us better, they're tolerable. How you adjust to the before and after gets a lot of guys down. Old newspapers and magazines, mostly Italian, keep some of us occupied. The Red Cross stuff is heavily censored; not much news there, but some things to read and games to play."

"What's that you're reading?" Denis asked, referring to the old pamphlet Harry had set down on his bunk.

"Oh this," Harry said, picking up the pamphlet titled *L' Eremo di S. Spirito alla Maiella* with the subtitle *S. Pietro, Celestino V*. It's a story about a local bloke who became the pope back in the 1200s. It's written in Italian which none of us could translate. Joe, they call him Pepino, one of the more friendly guards who speaks pretty good English, translated it for us."

"That sounds friendly."

"It took a bit of pestering and he did it grudgingly at first; but he's a bit of a history nut so I could tell he enjoyed it. I'll point him out to you; maybe he will read"iIt mtoigyhotub, teo."o, if you're interested."

"Well the gist of it is there was this holy fellow named Peter who became a hermit and built a hermitage, what the Italians call an *eremo*, near here. Actually, he first built one quite close to the camp and later left it for a higher elevation. Somehow he was chosen to be the pope, but he quit shortly after they chose him."

"I never heard of that. Is it true?"

"Well, according to this pamphlet and Pepino it is. It was published around here," he said, flipping the front page open, "Pescara in 1937. Here take it," Harry handed it to Denis and lay back on his bunk, snuffing out his cigarette on the tiled floor. He turned over in his bunk and then turned back to Denis. "By the way, mate, we were happy to learn Wavell's guys beat the Italians back and ended it a few months later. Sorry the Krauts got you." Turning over again he said, "Get some rest. You'll be on one of the work details tomorrow morning."

Denis sighed, fell back on his bunk, and leafed through the well-worn pamphlet. He stared at a couple of images it contained, but he did not understand much, recognizing only scattered words. His eyes grew tired and after a while he drifted off to sleep.

Harry had been right—tedium became an issue. Everyday sameness. The camp was roused each morning at 6:00 AM and the men given bread and coffee. Then they were marched off on work details. Denis was assigned to a group sent to repair the rail yard and terminal in town that had sustained Allied bomb damage. Work as a gandy dancer brought on an appetite that the evening meal could never satisfy. The repair work went on week after week and month after month.

After the yard repairs were completed, they were put to work extending a rail line south through the woods. Denis chopped trees with a double-edged, wide-faced ax, blistering his hands, or alternated with a partner using a six-foot cross-cut saw to cut down the larger diameter trunks. Then the snows came and Denis and his crew was diverted to road clearing. After Christmas the weather turned much colder, but they still had to work. They were allowed breaks to warm up around a fire in a steel barrel. Red Cross packages were sporadic. Denis's clothes—the sweater and light jacket he was provided, gloves and boots were starting to wear out, and the volume of macaroni and bean dinners did not match his caloric needs, so he lost weight.

Spring brought with it changes at the camp and a shifting of mood among the guards and the camp commandant. Denis had adjusted to the labor and his barbed-wire existence; he was one of the British officers who played a key role in the morale of the camp, providing discipline and communication while pressing the commandant for improvements. "It's warming up, old chap. How about letting the men play some games in the yard?"

Surprisingly, supplies, including clothes and packages, arrived more regularly and the rules became more relaxed. The men were given more latitude to entertain themselves. They formed clubs and teams, played games, and advertised their skills in barbering, tailoring and other handicraft. They organized musicals, and stand-up comedy shows. Neither Denis nor Harry were particularly gifted in sports or the arts, but both were enthusiastic members of the audience that included the Italian guards, most of whom had a limited understanding of the shenanigans going on at the shows—*"Dimenti. Tutti dimenti,"* one said of the performers. *"Pazzi,"* said another.

By June, 1943, the commandant and guards became increasingly preoccupied with their own fate. The war was not going well. The Allies had not yet established a foothold on Italian soil, but the military had sensed a shift in the confidence of the government leadership, and the changing mood had trickled down to the prison system.

"Have you noticed how friendly the guards have become?" Denis asked. "Pepino has spent more time with me translating that pamphlet on Celestine. He was eager to answer questions, even volunteered stuff I hadn't asked." He and Harry were lounging about in the yard with the other POWs, enjoying a smoke after returning from their daily work detail on the railroad line. At first they collapsed on their bunks when they had returned from their daily grind, but over time they adjusted and less was demanded of them. It was a pleasant afternoon; no one was anxious to enter the dreary barracks.

"Yeah," Harry responded, exhaling a breath of smoke. "Today out on the job there was more grumbling about ruination by government leaders."

On July 9th the Allies pulled off Operation Husky—the invasion of Sicily—with British and Canadian forces making an amphibious landing on the beaches between Cassibile and Syracuse, and the Americans landing to the west at Gela and Licata. News of the landings reached the camp in Sulmona raising the spirits of the POWs even as new captives were brought in. Now the guards became openly critical of the Germans, *"Terribili Tedeschi!"* They claimed they didn't want to fight the Allies, but were forced to by the German military.

"Now they want to be our friends," Denis said, chuckling with a group of fellow prisoners lounging about the barracks after dinner. Skepticism aside, the mood of the group was hopeful. In that manner the summer weeks passed with fewer prisoner arrivals and increasing rumors that the camp was going to be evacuated.

As August rolled into September the guards seemed increasingly agitated. Something big was happening in Rome, but what? The Fascist newspapers the guards were reading indicated the possibility of an armistice, but no one thought it would happen anytime soon.

It was unusually quiet one evening when they turned in for the night, but when the stillness continued into the following morning, Denis who had woken early, was curious. He rose and walked to the one small window that offered a view of the yard. Not a single guard was in sight. He was puzzled. Usually by six in the morning, the guards were rousing the men for breakfast before assigning them to work details. Walking back to his bunk, he patted Harry's shoulder, "Hey, no one is out there," he said excitedly. "Something's up. Let's take a look."

Turning over in the low light, Harry saw the excitement etched on Denis's face. He quickly got up and grabbed his clothes and the two of them began to rouse the others. By then many of them were rising and making their way to the entrance. The door, surprisingly was unlocked. Cautiously, they walked out onto the grounds. They saw no guards anywhere.

The sun had come up but it was a brisk September morning. The leaves on the trees surrounding the camp manifested the hues of autumn augmented by the sunlight, and its scent was in the air. Men from the other barracks had emerged and were milling about talking. Someone yelled that the guards' quarters were empty; moments later another came running from the perimeter shouting that the main gate was unlocked and open. Suddenly, there were whoops and hollers as men began to run about sensing freedom. Some moved aimlessly while others ran to the guards' storeroom and gabbed clothes, sacks and tins of food, and other supplies. Denis and Harry ran to join them but when they got there, the cupboards were bare. Denis frowned disappointedly and said, "Hey, mate, lets grab our things and go!" Harry nodded and they retreated to their bunks to gather their personal items. Denis stuffed his haversack with the heavy woolen sweater and cap, water bottle, and the Monopoly game from a Red Cross package that had arrived months earlier. Pausing to light up a cigarette, he shouldered his pack and scampered back outside with Harry.

Their senior camp commander, Major Louis Fitz-Hugh, was standing on the guard platform speaking to the large assembly of men that had gathered around him. Denis and Harry joined the group at the rear. "The Italian army has disbanded," Fitz-Hugh said. "That's the reason the guards are gone. They walked out in the middle of the night." He explained that a farmer from the nearby hamlet of Fonte d' Amore had given the news to one of our men outside the main gate. "I expect the Germans will get here soon," Fitz-Hugh continued. "Word is that several divisions have entered the country through the Brenner Pass. My advice is that we all leave right away, no time to waste."

The men grew highly agitated, milling about talking to their mates, undecided as to what to do. One shouted out to Fitz-Hugh: "Where do we go?"

"I suggest you scatter in all directions if you can," he responded. "And in small groups, no more than two or three. Makes it harder for the Germans to round you up. Use those maps in the Monopoly games, that's what I am going to do."

Harry and Denis each pulled the small silk maps from the Monopoly game pack and unfolded them. A couple of Harry's friends from the barracks had gathered around him asking what he thought. "Pacentro looks good to me," Harry said, as he pointed to the town marked with a blue dot. Let's try for that. What do you think?" He asked as he turned to Denis.

Denis didn't think it was a good choice, but he didn't want to get into an argy- bargy. "Probably one of the first places the Germans will search when they get here," he said frowning. "We should split up, like Fitz-Hugh said."

"Are you sure that's what you want to do, Denis— go it alone?" Harry looked doubtful.

"Yes, I'll be fine," he said with the narrowed eyes of serious intent. "I have options. You and your mates be careful. My advice is when you get to Pacentro keep going— it's too damn close to the camp. Don't count on being hidden and protected—they won't have time to prepare before the Germans get there. "

Harry and his friends chatted a moment, seeming to agree on their course of action. Then they bid Denis good luck. As they walked off, Harry looked back to Denis, gave him a thumbs-up and shouted, "See you in London."

Denis folded his map and shouldered his pack again. He had decided to head for the hills. On his way to the fountain to fill his water bottle, he recognized one of the men who had recently been assigned to his work detail. "Roger, have you decided?"

"Not yet. The question is where to. I don't have one of those maps. Where did you get those anyway?" He asked looking puzzled. "The major said in the Monopoly game. I guess that was before I got here."

"The game was one of the past-time items along with decks of cards that qualified for packages distributed by the International Red Cross. Some clever guy in our M-5 came up with the idea of printing maps on silk sheets that could be quietly folded and unfolded."

"So, you think the map is reliable, good enough to guide us out of here?"

"Not much choice, my friend. I'm comfortable knowing maps like this were placed in American Monopoly games that were made in London. There are more details that I can explain later, but for now, let's make a decision," Denis said as he unfolded the map. "We need to pick a destination. Notice that the towns and villages with safe houses have a blue dot; the others have black dots."

Roger studied the map and pointed to the village of Baddia Marronese. "What about this place? It doesn't have a colored dot."

"I'm not keen on that one. It's a small village with an interesting history though. It revolves around a 13th-century hermit who became a pope.

"Sounds like that might be a safe place. You would think people there with that history would offer sanctuary."

"Maybe. I also learned that people in those tiny rural villages are wary of strangers. But in any case, it is much too close, and has no safe house, so we need to go farther." Denis pointed to the mountain that rose to the east of the camp. "That's Morrone, one of the Maiella peaks. There are a number of hill towns and villages on the slopes toward the peak."

"Yeah, but which one?"

"Well, some of them are just small collections of houses and farms difficult to reach; others are more substantial with roads." He pointed to one of them on the map. "How about this blue-dotted town of Caramanico?"

Roger nodded. "Looks as good as any," he said. They filled their water bottles and started out moving east. Not knowing their exact route, they chose to follow a meadow between two strips of forest thinking it an easier climb than the woods. But picking their way over the uneven terrain proved challenging. The lack of a visible horizon and Denis's lack of conditioning after a year in captivity made for slow going. Even though he had worked, he hadn't hiked much; his legs felt weak, he had lost weight, and his endurance was poor.

"Hey, Roger, hold up a minute," he said, grunting and bending over with his hands on knees. Between deep breaths, he said, "I need to get a bearing." He straightened up and pulled out a small compass the size of a coin.

"Where did you get that?" Roger asked. He had turned and was also breathing deeply.

"It was one of the play pieces in the Monopoly game," he said breathlessly. "It was in there along with a two-part metal file I can assemble if I need to." He pulled the pieces from his pocket and showed Roger. He also pulled out a small stack of currency. "Italian lire! It was buried in with the play money. Also, this 'Get out of Jail' card."

Roger stepped closer for a better look.

"Notice Mr. Moneybags with the pipe and red beret," Denis said. "We need to find the guy who looks like him in the town with the safe house."

"Clever. They designed the game pieces like the map for use in different countries. How did you learn about this?

Denis had regained his breath and looked less stressed. "Word of mouth from the prisoners. Most Royal Air Force pilots and Army officers were given the details during their training in England."

"I guess I never got the word."

"Well, let's keep going. I have no idea how long this trek is going to take." Looking up and taking a deep breath, he shook his head and said, "The terrain on this slope is deceptive. I thought it would be steady uphill."

As they climbed they had to go around one buttress after another and from ridge to ridge using their hands as much as their feet. Stumbling and falling from time to time, the sweat was pouring off their heads when they reached an exposed outcropping in the late morning. Sitting down to rest, they looked back at the camp where they saw a German column moving up the Rome-Sulmona road toward the village of Baddia adjacent to the camp. The convoy consisted of a dozen lorries and assorted military vehicles, some of which had mounted machine guns.

"I'm amazed the Germans got here as fast as they did," Roger said. "They must have known the Italians were capitulating."

"Fitz-Hugh was right, mate. He warned us. Too bad not everyone took his advice—look at those guys still hanging around."

Hundreds of men scurried into the gullies and trees around the camp as the vehicles came to a stop outside the gate. German soldiers jumped out of the trucks in active pursuit as men began to clamber up the slope. Gunfire— the crackling of rifles and stutter of Tommy guns carried up to where Denis and Roger were standing on the rock outcropping. Some of the men were hit running and fell awkwardly; others had reached cover in the copse of trees in the meadow below them, but the Germans kept after them shooting and shouting, their voices carrying upwards—"come out English." The words struck fear in Denis who did not want to relive his capture. He gave Roger a wild-eyed look and yelled, "Let's get going!" They scampered off climbing through the trees and brush. The undergrowth was thick and the brambles scratched their arms and snagged their clothes. They encountered more rocks and outcroppings; there always seemed to be more ridges and ledges above them with drops of thirty or more feet. They never looked back to see the fate of their fellow prisoners but pressed steadily ahead. Time passed— minutes, hours, they lost track of time, even direction. Denis stopped periodically to check his compass to make sure they were moving southeastward. The shadows from the afternoon sun grew longer as they entered a ravine filled with a deep bed of autumn leaves. They laid down to rest and drink. Their water was running low, finding more was a priority, but first they lit up cigarettes.

"I think we're safe. I doubt the Germans are on our trail," Roger said, exhaling a breath of smoke. "We were too far away for them to spot us."

"I hope you're right, Roger. My legs ache like hell. I need to rest. It's late anyway. We should probably spend the night here and start out at first light tomorrow."

"We need to find some food and water. My stomach's churning, but you're right, no sense pressing our luck on this ground in the dark," he said, pulling his wool sweater from his haversack preparing for a cold night.

Denis did the same, put it on and laid back in the leaves. In the setting sun they half-buried themselves in the leaves for insulation, and used their haversacks as pillows. The organic scent of decaying leaves filled their nostrils as they drifted off to sleep.

The next morning they were startled awake by a covey of birds flapping up from the trees. Pangs of hunger gnawed at them as they climbed through the forested slope in the rising sun. Denis could feel the soreness in his thighs from the effort from the day before, but he trudged on following Roger. Their boots crunched on dry twigs and leaves as they moved beneath the trees, but they were less concerned the Germans would be looking for them. The terrain forced them to climb and descend time and again. They had drained the last of their water by midmorning and were desperate for more. Their mouths were dry and parched when, miraculously, they found some in the early afternoon. The small spring was little more than a trickle they spotted in the wet leaves by a limestone outcrop. It took a while to refill the water bottles.

"Water never tasted so good," Roger said, happily taking a swig from his bottle, sensing the mineral-laced moisture replace the dryness of his mouth. "Better than an ice cold beer on a hot day!"

Denis nodded as he sipped and laid back against the stone. "Let's take a break. I'd like to find something to eat, but I need to give my legs a rest." Looking around he thought he could make out a road through the trees. "If that's a road over there, farmhouses could be nearby. We might find something, but I need to get some rest first."

They found a comfortable spot in the leaves and lied down in the dappled shade, drifting off to sleep soon after their heads hit the ground. Sometime later, the rumble of a heavy truck descending the nearby road woke them. Sitting up and peering through the trees, they spotted a green-paneled lorry bearing the German iron cross on the door. A dozen soldiers and a German shepherd dog were sitting in the back. Denis pulled out his map and estimated their position.

"I think they're heading for Pacentro. I hope Harry and his mates aren't there. Anyway, we need to head the other way."

"The road will make it easier," Roger said. "But we should probably stay just inside the trees in case there are more of them coming down the road."

In the late afternoon, moving along in the woods, they came upon a cluster of gray stone houses with tan-tiled roofs. Denis checked his map, but wasn't sure where they were. He knew there were small hamlets the Italians referred to as a *frazione*, and thought this might be one of them—too small to be indicated on his basic map. There wasn't any sign of human activity. They were weary and hungry, having gone two days of heavy trekking without a morsel of food. Decision time. Would they spend another night in the woods or take a chance of reaching out for help?

"I think we're going to have to trust these people," Roger said, looking optimistic. "This is probably the first of many dicey situations were going to face. I can't speak for government leaders or the aristocracy, but the commoners we came across in Sicily seemed like decent people."

Denis mulled it over, wondering about the reception he would get. "Okay. You stay back here in the trees. I'm going to check out that farmhouse over there on the edge of the village," he said, pointing to the small building across the rocky meadow.

Lengthening shadows cast by the late afternoon sun gave Denis some degree of cover as he traversed the meadow in a crouching, serpentine fashion. The small house was constructed of uneven stone and had a rough-hewn, weathered door and two small windows, one on each side facing away. A small barn was situated a few yards from the back door. Denis huddled against the stone wall and made his way to the door. He raised his hand to knock but hesitated. He wondered if these people might be sympathizers, and felt unsure. He edged his way around the corner and peered in. He saw a kitchen with a stone hearth, a round table with two chairs, and a small cabinet. No one was there. An open doorway to a hall revealed doors to other rooms. He inched back to the door and gave a loud rap. He was about to repeat the knocking when the door opened slightly and a young girl gave him a wide-eyed look. She appeared to be a preteen wearing a gray, home-spun dress and apron.

"*Sono un soldato, Inglese. Aiutami per favore,*" he pleaded, identifying himself as an English soldier in need of help.

The girl quickly closed the door. Denis heard her shout in alarm to her father. Denis took deep breaths trying to settle himself to calmness. He hoped Roger could see he had safely made it, but he felt exposed and vulnerable even though he was out of the line of sight from the other houses.

Moments later the door reopened and the girl emerged with a flask of water Standing back in the doorway was her father, a heavy-set, middle-aged man in drab working clothes. He told Denis to follow the girl. She led him to the barn, which was a door-less stable of sorts with slatted walls, a pile of hay at the far end and farm implements stacked against the wall. The girl told Denis to wait here and call his friend; then she returned to the house. Denis signaled Roger to join him. The last rays of the day filtered through the slats as Roger entered the barn. They polished off the water and thirsted for more. While they waited, Denis told Roger what he had learned. The man was a widower. He and his daughter eked out a living farming and tending a few sheep. They seemed to be decent people, just a little scared and uncertain. The man and his daughter reappeared a while later. The daughter led the way with a lantern, a basket of cheese and bread. The father carried two dishes of polenta and the added burden of fear so evident in his eyes. Roger and Denis were halfway through the polenta when the man and his daughter returned with a carafe of water and a goatskin of wine. The flavor of the polenta lingered long after they finished eating and the wine had them feeling mellow Sitting back in the hay, they lit up two of their dwindling supply of prison camp cigarettes, enveloped in the fragrant herbal scent of the ignited tobacco. The lamplight was turned down low barely illuminating their faces and surroundings.

Roger turned to Denis and said, "So far so good. I'm hoping our luck holds out."

"With luck, a prayer, and a man in a red beret, I'm counting on it. When I signed up, I didn't envision this situation."

"Who does?" Roger took a drag on his cigarette and exhaled a stream of smoke with a contented sigh. "Where did you sign up?"

"In my hometown just outside London— Hounslow, a small working-class community."

"What did your folks do?"

"My father was an electrician and my mother stayed home until the war broke out. Then she went to work in a munitions plant."

"You did pretty well speaking with the farmer and his daughter. Where did you learn to speak Italian?"

"Well, my Italian is passable in simple situations like that one. I picked it up at home. My mother immigrated to England from Italy with her parents after the last war.

"Your mother taught you then?"

Denis took a last draw on his cigarette and stubbed it out on the edge of his glass, letting it fall in to the bottom. "Not really. I absorbed it you might say. My mother went through our school system and was as fluent in English as she was in Italian. When she married my father and I was born, I heard both English and Italian in our house, because my grandparents who lived with us spoke mostly Italian. So, to talk to them I had to use Italian, or rather their dialect."

"Well, let's hope it is good enough to get us where we have to go," Roger said and settled back on the hay.

The farmer returned to collect his dishes and glasses and dropped off a blanket. He told them we could spend the night there in the stable, but he asked that they leave at dawn without letting anyone see them. He was clearly worried that if they were discovered he could be reported. He had seen the Germans pass and wasn't sure what was going on with the Italian authority. He begged us not to tell anyone. *"Per favore, dice niente a nessuno."* He was very concerned for his daughter's welfare. Denis filled him in with what he knew about the current situation, thanked him profusely for his help, and reassured him that he would not tell anyone. He offered him some of the lira concealed in the Monopoly play money. At first he refused to accept it, but Denis persisted, and he finally took it gratefully.

It was cold again that night and they were glad to have the shelter. The wool sweaters kept them comfortable, but Roger wrapped himself in the blanket the owner had provided. The hay made comfortable bedding, and they were asleep in minutes.

The sound of a rooster crowing woke them. The early morning light filtered through gaps in the roof and wall boards. Arising, they found another carafe of water, two hard-boiled eggs and two pieces of bread wrapped in a cloth lying on a stone by the barn entrance. They refilled their water bottles and took the bread and eggs. Then quietly they made their way across the meadow to the woods and continued the climb toward Caramanico.

Looking back at the hamlet and its poverty, both Roger and Denis were struck by the abject failure of Mussolini's Fascism, but they were so impressed by the generosity of the good-hearted Italian farmer who shared what he had with them. The sun was rising and it was getting warmer as they moved on. Since they had consumed food and water, the trek was easier on the third day out. The terrain in the woods continued to be difficult. It was tough to get their bearings, but they kept their eye on the road and checked the compass as they trudged along. In time they reached a clearing where they caught a glimpse of two small hamlets in the distance which appeared similar to the *frazione* where they had spent the night. The hamlets were situated on dark-green forested slopes with scattered clusters of hardwood trees in every hue of autumn color. Dried rocky stream beds meandered through a narrow valley below. Passing shadows from moving clouds overhead drifted across the land revealing short tan, ribbon-like stretches of road. In the far distance they spotted what looked to be a larger town, possibly Caramanico. Over the top of that slope there seemed to be blue-green mountains beyond mountains, gradually diminishing in fading rows toward what appeared to be a thin blue strip of sea on the horizon.

"That's got to be the place," Denis said, as he checked the map and compass. "Let's go, old chap," trying to sound optimistic. "We may get there before dark!"

Roger took a swig of water and reshouldered his pack. Taking a deep breath he followed after Denis with his newly found stamina.

They saw no human activity until they approached Caramanico, which they assumed was the right town by its size and position. They stood on a ridge overlooking the earth-colored tiled roofs; the church with its campanile stood out above the other buildings. None of the streets or piazzas were visible from their vantage point. It was late afternoon when they got down to the outskirts. There was too much light and not enough cover, so they decided to hide until it became darker. Then they circled around the edge of town, trying to stay hidden as much as possible as they crossed meadows and small farm plots.

"We have to find a man with a red beret and pipe. The word in camp was that these contacts would be most likely found in the evening around the town's main piazza," Denis said.

They hadn't seen any Germans at that point, and didn't want to chance walking into town and right into German hands. They waited out the rest of the afternoon until dusk. Then when the sun had set, and darkness had fallen, they walked into town on the main road, having no idea of where the piazza was or how to get to it. They were not sure if the townsfolk would help them, although they believed most Italians were probably not fond of the Germans.

The shops had closed. It was the beginning of the dinner hour and few people were out. They shuffled along hunched over trying to appear as naturally Italian as possible. The fragrant aroma of sautéing garlic in olive oil, and the hiss of tomatoes being added to a pan wafted out an open window. Fortunately, no one noticed them. A couple hurried along the other side of the street, but they passed without looking their way. They wished they had broad-brimmed hats to hide their obvious Anglo features—their woolen caps, khaki shirts, and pants were dead giveaways. They put on their sweaters, believing they would draw less attention, but in their soiled and tattered clothing they looked like strangers who had had a rough time in the woods. They just hoped the darkness would hide what would be all too obvious in the light of day. Happily, they surmised correctly that the main road into town would bring them to the primary piazza. It loomed ahead as they walked. No one was about and the shops around it were shuttered.

The street lamps came on and cast a soft glow on the cobblestones and lower aspects of the buildings. There was a bench tucked away in a relatively dark corner of the piazza. They headed to it and sat down. A trash container next to the bench contained a discarded newspaper. Denis retrieved it and gave a section of it to Roger. They used the sheets to hide behind pretending to read. The piazza remained quiet and empty for some time, but eventually people began to appear. Husbands and wives walking arm in arm, young couples, and a group of children came running; they stopped to gather and chat beside the fountain in the center. Denis glanced sideways around the newspaper, looking for someone wearing a red beret and smoking a pipe. No one fit the description, but there were plenty of cigarette smokers.

An engine rumbled down a side street leading into the piazza. The rumble became a roar as a motorcycle driven by a German soldier emerged in the piazza carrying an officer in a side car. The cycle sped on through and exited the far side, the sound of the engine trailing off in the distance. People in the piazza had stopped to stare for a moment; then another motorcycle with sidecar appeared and came to a stop. The officer got out and asked a couple for identification. Satisfied with their cards, he returned them and got back in his vehicle. As the driver sped off, the group picked up where they left off, as if nothing had happened.

Time passed, the evening crowd thinned gradually until only Roger and Denis were left sitting as they were at the beginning of their vigil. They were hungry and had lire to buy food, but decided not to chance buying any from the osteria on the other side of the piazza. It had some activity, but they felt they couldn't chance the exposure. They were about to leave to find some suitable place to spend the night, when a man appeared at the bar's entrance. He stood silhouetted in the doorway and put a pipe to his mouth. His upper lip was crowned with a modest walrus mustache; his face was etched with lines, and he was wearing a red beret.

Roger nudged Denis and whispered, "That guy looks like the Moneybags card. He could be our man."

"You could be right, mate. Sit here and keep reading, I'm going to check him out." Denis got up, folded his sheet of newspaper and slowly walked over to the man. He didn't exactly resemble the Mr. Moneybags caricature on the jail card although he was elderly with gray longish hair and a mustache. The man stepped out of the door way onto the cobblestones, took out a wooden match and struck it to light his pipe. The flame illuminated a serious face. As Denis approached, the man was concentrating on his pipe, puffing the tobacco into greater ignition. *"Sai che ore sono?"*

The man looked at Denis knowingly, removed the pipe from his mouth and said, "English?"

Denis realized his anglicized Italian accent had made his asking for the time obvious he was a foreigner. Crestfallen, he asked sheepishly, "That bad?"

The man merely scoffed. "I've been expecting someone like you to show up since word of the prison escape reached our village. Are you alone?" Denis nodded toward Roger. "Just him."

The man was surprised there weren't more of them, but he indicated it was fine as it would allow him to work out the details of aiding others in the future. He was introduced to Roger and said his name was Fabio. The smoldering tobacco in his pipe had subsided. He replaced it in his mouth and puffed it up, blowing smoke from the corner of his mouth. Then he removed it, pointed the pipe stem at the men and said to them, "Follow me and be very careful from now on. Expose yourselves as little as possible, and to only people you can trust." As he spoke the lines on his face seemed to deepen. "The family I am taking you to is one of the few you can count on in this town. Remember that!"

Chapter 5

Caramanico, Italy. July, 1943

A board game got you here? *Incredibile!*" Francesco exclaimed.

"Well, the game gave us an edge; otherwise we would have been blind. Ask Roger."

Roger wasn't fluent enough yet to respond directly to Francesco, but in English he told Denis to tell Francesco that many of the escapees had the same advice and advantages they did, but they made different decisions—it was a matter of judgment and a bit of luck and the help of his *paisanos*.

Denis translated Roger's opinion. Francesco nodded that he understood. "And who knows you are here besides Pierluigi's family?" Francesco asked. "Very few, only people Pierluigi could trust." Denis brought Francesco up to date with what had transpired in Caramanico before Francesco arrived. On their first night, he and Roger had dinner, bathed finally, and slept soundly. The next morning, while the streets were deserted and before the shops opened, Pierluigi brought them to the local shoemaker where they were surprised to recognize that the shoemaker was Fabio. He measured them for the shoes they needed for the journey as their military boots were badly worn. The next stop was the druggist, another confidant who ushered them into his storeroom where he took their photos for identification cards. Afterward, they returned to the house where they remained for the rest of the day. "I don't think anyone noticed us," he said, seemingly unconcerned.

Francesco was glad to know they had been careful. He thought Pierluigi didn't need any suspicions drawn to him. "What have you been doing to pass the time since then?" he asked.

"Knowing we would have to leave, sooner than later, Annamaria and Angiolina have been drilling us on how to behave and blend in with the Italians. Annamaria has also been helping us with our Italian conversation. She was able to get a book useful for foreigners to learn the Italian language."

"Yes, Pierluigi showed it to me. It looks very good." Francesco wished he had the English equivalent, something to study before he got to America.

"The lessons have been useful. My Italian mostly came from listening as a boy. I took a course in the army, and then talking with the prison camp guards helped. But the review with Annamaria has been good, and Roger is a fast learner. We've had some good laughs through it all."

Francesco got up and pulled the window curtain aside to take a peek at the dimly lit piazza. Frowning he said, "I know staying hidden in his house can be frustrating for you both even though it's the safest thing."

Denis stood up to stretch his legs and yawned. Roger joined him; the three of them stood side by side. Francesco felt a growing attachment to them. Denis and Roger were different personalities, but both were friendly and seemed like good men. He admired how they got each other through the tough days after their escape. They would need that togetherness to continue their quest for freedom. He looked up to them as soldiers and wished he were old enough to be one of them, even fight alongside them. Francesco communicated more easily with Denis who was the more fluent Italian speaker, but in terms of age and disposition he sensed a closer bonding to Roger whose temperament was closer to his. He wondered what their lives were like before the war and told himself he would find out when it seemed right.

"Last evening Pierluigi took us to the thermal baths that were managed by a man he knew he could trust." Denis said. "I think he knew we needed some comfort." The town of Caramanico Terme was well known for the healing power of the warm water and mineral content of its baths. The water attracted visitors from all around the area.

The experience seemed to renew them, Francesco thought. "It's good you got the opportunity," he said. "There may not be another one like that on the road south. Are you ready for the next move in Pierluigi's plan?"

"It's a bit of an unknown," Denis said. "Obviously, we have no experience as shepherds, and we don't know the country, but we can't stay here any longer. We've told Pierluigi that we don't want to put his family in any more danger. We have been ready to set out on our own, but he is trying to convince us that his plan is safer."

"Let's go into the kitchen where I can lay out a map and show you where his brother's farm is located. I don't know the route his friend will take, and I have never been down there, but we can get an idea of the direction and distance from here."

Roger followed Denis and Francesco into the kitchen where he lit up a cigarette. The men dragged chairs to the table as Francesco unfolded the map. He pointed out where they were in Caramanico—situated between Morrone and the other Maiella mountains—and the town of Casoli, which was set on a foothill by a tributary of the Sangro River to the south. Francesco indicated that the Abruzzo region was pretty rugged terrain. He hadn't seen a great deal of it, but he knew its geography from school work. He traced the north-south central spine of mountains with the many east-west ridges and ravines sloping toward the sea. He pointed out the mountainous areas that would likely be challenging, and the easier regions with meadows. Unfortunately most of those meadowlands lay on the lower foothills and plains near the sea.

Denis and Roger leaned over Francesco's shoulder and studied the map talking to one another. They discussed where the British Army might be positioned relative to the German defensive line. Denis knew from talking to the Italian guards in the Sulmona camp that the Eighth army had landed in the area of Brindisi and they were advancing easily along the Adriatic. Roger traced the line with his finger in the southern Abruzzo along the Sangro River to the Adriatic coast and then pointed to an area south, about halfway down the coast. "They might be about there near Bari by now, not that far to go to reach the Sangro," he said. "Sangro," he repeated, "doesn't that mean blood?"

"Yes," Denis said, "River of Blood. I don't know how it got that name originally, but it may earn that moniker again."

Francesco saw them focus on the Sangro. "What do you think?" he asked.

"We're both willing to chance it," Denis said. "Both of us were knocked out of the war early on, and we want to get back into the fight. Now that our army is here in Italy we're anxious to rejoin our outfits. There will a lot of fighting ahead. You pointed out the rugged terrain, which for me translates into bridges to build and obstacles to overcome. That's what I do as a combat engineer. Roger wants to rejoin the infantry just as bad."

Francesco wondered what it would be like to soldier on with them. It was an exciting thought as he looked at Roger. "I know you want to fight again, but do you feel comfortable traveling as a fake shepherd?"

Roger's face indicated he didn't understand the question. He looked to Denis and shook his head with his hands turned out.

"I'll explain in a minute." Turning to Francesco he said, "I think the idea of moving a flock of sheep is a good cover. We both think that traveling the countryside with a couple of Italians to guide us is better than trying to do it by ourselves. At least with you we might be able to negotiate with other Italians and get us through the German line with less risk. The question we have is do you feel up to the task?"

Francesco wrinkled his brow, disappointed Denis might not think him up to the challenge. "Well, I won't be the leader. Pierluigi made that clear," he said. "But I can be helpful to the man he chose to lead. I may be young, but I know I can do it." "If Pierluigi thinks you can do it, then that will be good enough for us. So by all means, let's get on with it, the sooner the better."

"Okay, then," Francesco said brightly. "I would take the risk because waiting around here is more risky. We don't know where your army will be, but as Pierluigi said, moving south toward Casoli as they move north gives us the best chance to meet them."

"That gets us in the game. Once we get close we will have to improvise." Francesco smiled. "I'll tell Pierluigi what we discussed in the morning."

The men both nodded and Denis patted him on the shoulder. "I feel much better about our chances than I did before we sat down to dinner."

Denis and Roger retired to a small bedroom tucked beneath the stairway in the hall beyond the living room.

Francesco felt good about the discussion he had with the men, but realized that he had completely lost track of the time. The house was dark and quiet. He assumed that the family had all gone to bed as he tiptoed up the stairs. No light shown beneath Annamaria's door. Frowning at his missed opportunity, he entered his room and closed the door.

Lying in his bed, Francesco thought about how the war had changed him and his family. The occupation had cast a pall over Roccamorice and everyone in it. The adults seemed quiet, anxious and depressed much of the time. In some ways, his friends and younger children seemed less affected. For them the war and occupation seemed like a curiosity, even an adventure. They were young and could feel that way, he thought. Not that they were happy. In fact, they were miserable with hunger. He recalled seeing some of his younger schoolmates rummaging through trash looking for anything edible. Each day brought new challenges for them, and most of them grudgingly accepted hunger in lieu of starvation. As he drifted toward sleep with half-closed eyes, Francesco thought about how things were before the war when he played football, looked forward to school and writing, and hanging out in the piazza after dinner with his friends. Now he couldn't even get his best friend, Marcello, to kick the ball around. It was the hunger he knew that brought the listlessness, but life under the German occupation had also somehow brought them all more freedom from their parents who had had to loosen their reins on them. They were growing up fast. Adulthood was upon them long before it needed to be, but Francesco was beginning to embrace its responsibilities.

Chapter 6

At dawn, Pierluigi returned from Ennio's cottage and knocked on the bedroom doors where Roger and Denis were sleeping, rousing them from a deep slumber. On the upper floor, Francesco heard the rapping. He rose

and walked to the floor-to-ceiling window, swung the panes open and pushed the wooden shutters aside. He took a deep breath of the fresh morning air gazing at the forested slope of the Maiella rising to its peak, bathed in the rising sun. Getting around that mountain and the rest of the trek was going to be a challenge, he thought.

Downstairs, the morning sun broke through the kitchen window warming the room. Angiolina had prepared breakfast. The roasted aroma of real coffee filled the room. A loaf of bread and plates of cheese, hard-boiled eggs, and sliced pears were on the table. Annamaria sat at one end with the Italian course book opened and reviewed Italian phrases with Roger who was seated beside her.

"*Ripeti dopo di me*," she instructed, giving Roger a phrase to speak.

Roger repeated the phrase. As they practiced, Angiolina and Pierluigi smiled and offered comments. Denis chuckled at Roger's attempts to sound fluent with his Canadian accent. But Roger was serious, enthusiastically attacking each sentence in the lesson; pausing from time to time in midsentence to flip through his dictionary. "The present, past, and future tenses are one thing, not difficult to learn, but this conditional tense is tough," he said. "Why is such a simple phrase—you should have told me that—*avresti duvuto dirmelo*—so difficult to say? It's driving me crazy."

"The Italian language is not easy for us Anglos, mate," Denis said. "I was lucky I had an Italian grandmother and got to converse with the guards in the camp. But you have a good teacher, so hang in there. You'll get it."

Francesco was impressed with Roger, the hardy Canadian soldier who seemed so intent on learning the language. But as he kept one eye on Roger, he focused the other on Annamaria. He felt remorse at missing the opportunity to spend time with her last evening. He knew how he felt about her, a desire that had been initiated too late on his visit to Caramanico a year earlier, but he didn't know how she felt about him. She was sweet, her face gorgeous, he thought, as he focused on her dark eyes and long lashes, but he wondered if there were boys her age in her life.

Annamaria gave Francesco a soft smile as she went about helping her mother at the table.

As they ate, Francesco told Pierluigi what he and the men had talked about the night before. "They want to get going; they don't want to add any more risk to you and your family," he said.

Pierluigi scoffed and brushed Francesco's worry off. *"Non ti preoccupare.* I worked out all the plan details with Ennio last night." He didn't tell Franceso what he discussed with Angiolina—neither of them aired their disagreements in public. He told her about Francesco's encounter with the German officer and soldiers and then he gave her his reasons for sending him on the journey with the escapees. She had challenged him vociferously, but Pierluigi was equally adamant in his response, saying to her that he was more capable than she thought. Angiolina had asked him if he was prepared for the consequences. She watched his face struggle as he nodded. She had sighed heavily, *"fai quello che voi."* The decision was his to make.

Pierluigi set the day aside to gather the necessary supplies. He had to first travel to Sulmona to take care of his business. This morning Francesco thought he looked like the businessman he was, dressed in a suit and sporting a gray fedora. Pierluigi said he planned to contact Fumato to let him know the group was ready to depart so that he could get word to other *partigiani.* He said he also needed to pick up suitable garb for the two men he hoped would pass convincingly as shepherds, and finally collect waterproof *mantellos.* He had given Angiolina and Annamaria their own assignment.

Annamaria finished up her lesson with Roger who closed the book, gathered his papers and walked into the backyard with Denis for a smoke. Annamaria turned to Francesco and indicated it was time to go into town to pick up a few items for the trip.

They walked silently for a few minutes. Annamaria looked beautiful in Francesco's eyes in a bright blue sweater over a dark blue skirt that complemented the curves of her body. The glint of her auburn hair was caught by the morning sun as he turned and reached for her arm. He was pleasantly surprised when she didn't shrug him off.

He told her about his encounters with the Germans at home, which he shared with her father and his decision to let him become a part of his plan. He expressed his strong desire to gain some measure of revenge for what the Germans had done to his family and friends—becoming a part of the resistance, what could be better than that.

"I understand why you want to do it," Annamaria said. "But how old are you now, fifteen?"

"Almost sixteen, that's not much younger than you are." "I like your math," she laughed.

"Let me ask you this, if I'm old enough," he said, a touch of sarcasm in his voice. "How involved are you with what your father is doing?"

"I was surprised when I first found out what was going on. My father seemed like he was quite loyal to the government. I had never heard him speak badly about *Il Duce* until recently."

"When did you find out?"

"I came home from school one day to find these strange men in the house. I thought they might be German until they spoke up in English. My parents sat me down and told me the men's story; how first my father and then my mother had a change of heart. They had decided that Fascism was a wicked thing that should have been evident from the start. Before everything, it stood for war, claiming that war was a good thing. But how can war be a good thing?"

As they entered the core business district, two German soldiers with shouldered rifles came around a corner up ahead. As they drew closer, they focused their eyes on Annamaria and began laughing and speaking loudly in German. Francesco couldn't understand what they were saying, but he caught the innuendo, and he had the distinct impression as they passed that they turned their heads back to look at Annamaria.

"So that's when it started?"

"Yes, I suppose. I don't know exactly, but a week or two later I began forging ID cards."

"What do you plan to do after we leave here tomorrow?" Francesco asked, irritated with the German soldier's behavior which Annamaria seemed to ignore.

"I plan to become more active with the *partigiani* who are planning to help the British once they arrive in the Maiella. My father tells I can be useful besides forging ID cards. I could be a messenger, a courier, lots of things the men can't do, like being their eyes and ears." She smiled and continued, "I could also charm a soldier into divulging information. You just saw how they looked at me." Francesco turned his head to her, wide-eyed.

"Lower your eyebrows, Francesco. The war changes things for women as well as men."

He could tell she wanted to defy—to act right under Nazi noses. "But it is dangerous. You know what they can do. Are you ready for that?"

"I don't think of that since I began to help Denis and Roger. Besides I already made the choice. I have been meeting with a friend of one of my brothers who joined the *partigiani* in the hills. We relay messages, food, and supplies together."

"How did he avoid the army?" Francesco felt a tinge of jealousy that there was a boy in her life, even though it seemed task oriented and platonic.

"He suffered a leg injury as a boy and because of a limp they wouldn't take him. But he is committed to the cause and anxious to help me find my brothers." "Forging documents at home is one thing, but carrying supplies and information is pretty risky. What will you do if you are stopped and questioned?" "I'll tell them I'm bringing food or supplies to the woodcutters or shepherds depending on the situation. Don't worry, I can make something up on the spot." "That may not work after a while. I mean the Germans will become more suspicious of everyone in town the more resistance they encounter. And what about the winter? Who will want to stay out there? Won't they have to come down into the town to survive? You can bet the Germans will be looking."

"You're right," she said gesturing with her hands out wide. "That's when the pressure will be on and we'll have to work harder to shelter them. I have friends— girls like me that the Germans will not suspect. If the men can't come down from their hideouts, my friends and I can bring food, blankets, warm clothes, firewood— whatever else is needed up to those grottos. The men have to stay invisible, at least to the Germans."

"I don't know," Francesco said, the worry etched on his face. "It's risky enough for men and boys, but girls like you..."

"The risk will be worth it if the men get to do their missions and it gets my brothers home. My father is trying hard, and I need to do my part. It's killing my mother too. She is so proud of them, we all are. They are both *bersagliere* you know, our best fighters, so I have to believe they have survived."

"The Germans can be pretty ruthless, this much I know from what I've seen. Can't you be a normal girl?"

"Look at me," Annamaria said, angrily. "Forget the girl-boy stuff. We are both taking risks—me for our men in the *resistenza;* you and my father to save strangers. Let's promise to support each other, so we can both succeed."

Francesco looked at Annamaria. She was lovely, even with her jaw set in determination. Now he found her passion to also be attractive. He had no chance of changing her mind about anything, he realized, except maybe about him.

The street was empty as they approached the shoemaker's shop. Peering in the window Annamaria looked past the shoes lining the display bench but she saw no human activity. She knocked softly on the door window. A gray–haired man with a mustache emerged from the back room and walked to the door. The shoemaker opened the door and bid them *"Buon giorno."* The scent of leather and shoe polish filled the air of the dimly lit shop. Leather -working tools and iron shoe forms rested on the cobbler's bench; scraps of leather lay on every surface and the floor. Shoes and boots of varying sizes and conditions were aligned haphazardly on the shelf behind the counter. The shoemaker peered out the door in both directions before closing it.

"I heard German motorcycles pass a short time ago," he said. "Did you see anyone on your walk here?"

"Just a pair of soldiers on foot. They seemed harmless," Annamaria said

Sighing he said, "Unfortunately the patrols are becoming more frequent."

"Francesco, I want you to meet Fabio," Annamaria said. "This is the man who brought Denis and Roger to our home."

"This is the man in the red beret that I heard so much about?" Francesco's face registered admiration as he shook hands with the man who risked his life for strangers. *"Multo piacere,"* he said enthusiastically.

Annemarie said, "Fabio, my father asked if you could provide Francesco with a pair of boots. He will be going on the trip with Denis and Roger."

"For Pierluigi, it's no problem. Hand me your shoes, Francesco. I salute you, a young man who joins our cause."

Francesco beamed. He relished Fabio's praise.

Fabio took Francesco's shoes and turned to the section of the shelf behind the counter with boots in various stages of construction. He looked for close matches; finally selecting a pair he thought looked appropriate. "I think these will work," he said. "Try them on."

Francesco loosened the boot laces, pulled the tongues forward, placed them on the floor and slipped into them. "They seem comfortable," he said.

"They look good," Annamaria said. "Thank you so much for making them on such short notice."

"It's nothing," responded Fabio. "The other pairs your men need are ready."

"Are the rucksacks ready?"

"Not yet, but I will have them later."

"In that case, let me leave the shoes here until I can return for everything. We have one more stop to make."

"Come back this afternoon."

Francesco bent down to tie the laces of the boots Fabio had given him. "Grazie."

"You can send me *ringraziamente* for the boots after they carry you and the men to freedom."

"Ci vediamo piu tarde," Annamaria said as they left the shop.

As they turned the corner and entered the street where the *farmacia* was located, they passed a pair of German sergeants who had parked their motorcycles up ahead.

"Hey!" one of them yelled back at them in a harsh voice. "Where did you get those boots?" Annamaria and Francesco stopped and turned around.

"At the shoemaker's," Francesco responded matter-of-factly. The two soldiers were young and fit, their athletic bodies molded in their field gray military uniforms, blond hair visible beneath their flanged helmets.

"So those are Italian boots then," the soldier said with a smirk.

"What do you think? They are certainly not German boots," Francesco said, the contempt evident in the tone of his voice.

Annamaria whispered fiercely to Francesco, "Don't annoy them—don't cause trouble."

"Don't worry, these guys aren't the SS."

The smirk on the German soldier's face faded to scorn. He left his fellow soldier where they had stopped and approached Francesco and Annamaria with an arrogant swagger. "So what is wrong with German boots?" he demanded to know.

"Look at your boots. I don't think they have the same quality," Francesco said.

"Maybe you're right, boy. You Italians are a nation of shoemakers so you have had lots of time and experience to master your craft."

Francesco's ears burned. He could not contain himself. "Maybe you should see an Italian tailor while you are here and get properly fitted."

Annamaria flinched. Grabbing his hand, she said "Please, sir, forgive my brother. He means no disrespect. His dog is very sick, and he is very upset. We were just on our way to pick up some medicine."

The officer scowled at Francesco as he considered his options. He turned toward Annamaria, sized her up closely and smiled lasciviously. "Where do you live around here?"

She hesitated a moment. "My house is in the piazza on Via Cavour."

"*Carta di identita!*" he demanded.

She held her breath looking concerned but not frightened. She pulled the card from a waist pocket on her skirt and handed it to the officer.

He looked it over quickly and handed it back to her. Then he pulled a small pad and pen from his jacket pocket and made a note. "I will be back here again, and when I do, I expect you will be much more courteous to me, do you understand?" He turned to Francesco and said, "You better watch your mouth, boy, you're lucky this time; you won't get another chance. There is work in Germany for people like you. Now get out of here while I'm feeling generous."

"C'mon, Francesco, let's be on our way," Annamaria said, breathing normally and looking much relieved. When they were out of earshot of the Germans, she stopped suddenly, turned to Francesco, grabbed his arm and said "Don't you do anything so stupid like that again!"

****

That night at dinner, Denis and Roger joined the family. Annamaria began to recount their morning's activities to her parents, including the encounter with the German soldier. Pierluigi and Angiolina expressed their concerns generally about defying German authority. Denis looked concerned; Roger's face was neutral. Francesco kept his head and eyes down sheepishly. He remained quiet hoping he would not have to defend himself.

Pierluigi changed the subject and told everyone the surprising news that he learned in Sulmona that day on BBC radio. "Mussolini was rescued from prison." Everyone responded with multiple questions at once concerning who, what, where, and when of the incident.

"*Momento*, one at a time," Pierluigi said. "This is what I know. A German commando group pulled off the rescue not far from here in the Gran Sasso, some place called *Campo Imperatore*."

"I never heard of it," said Annamaria.

"Nor did I," Pierluigi responded. "I checked and it's not even on a map."

"The Gran Sasso is just mountain wilderness, no?" asked Francesco.

"Yes, it's the highest peak of our *Appenini*. A ski area on the slopes and a lodge at the base was recently developed up there," Pierluigi said. "The lodge was where he was taken after his arrest."

"How did they get him there?"

"I don't know how, but the BBC said that the rescue was done by a commando group who arrived in a glider."

"They met no resistance?"

"None. Apparently the Italian guards were taken by surprise."

"How did the Germans get him off the mountain?"

"In a small plane. It was able to land in a meadow by the lodge."

"Bloody daring I must say. Where is he now?" asked Denis.

"In Germany with Hitler," Pierluigi said. "The broadcaster did not elaborate."

Denis turned to Roger and asked him if he understood the story. He nodded yes.

"I'm sure they have a strategy for getting Mussolini back in power," Pierluigi frowned, obviously disappointed.

"I wonder what this means for us now. I thought the Fascists were finally on their way out," Angiolina said.

"There is just too much confusion and chaos in Italy now to know what will happen," Pierluigi responded. Anger creeping into his voice, he continued, "What worries me is that the black shirts will rally to him if the Germans bring him back." After dinner, the women cleared the table and left the room. Pierluigi and the men lit up cigarettes canceling the lingering dinner aroma in the room. They began to talk about the trip ahead. The conversation continued through a knock on the door. Annamaria answered to find Ennio standing at the entry. He was a short, robust man with a pleasant face that featured a short beard, dark eyes and curly hair. He was plainly dressed in shepherd's garb and held his wide-brimmed hat in his hand. She welcomed him and led him into the kitchen where Pierluigi was speaking sternly to Francesco. Roger and Denis sat quietly listening.

"*Ascoltami*, Francesco!" I'm counting on you to help Ennio get these men through safely," he said, putting his arm up to acknowledge Ennio's presence. "I know you hate the Germans, but you've got to control your emotions whenever and wherever you meet them. You tell me you want to help; you tell me you want to join the *partigiani*. To do that, you need not only courage but also control and good judgment!"

Wincing, Francesco said, "You're right." The criticism stung him as much as the rebuke Annamaria delivered earlier. "I just didn't think. I'm sorry. I will control my feelings next time." He looked forlorn. "I promise you, it won't happen again." Pierluigi put his arm around Francesco and smiled, rubbed his head. "I know you'll use this *testa dura* next time." Then he introduced Ennio to Francesco and the men. Quietly, they all shook hands with one another. "Sit down, Ennio. Can I get you a glass of wine? I was just telling the men here the latest news of the war." *"Niente, grazie."* Ennio said. He pulled a seat from the table and sat down to listen.

"Pierluigi, besides the Mussolini incident, what's the latest war news from the BBC?" Denis asked, lighting up a cigarette."

"The Allies have advanced to Naples. Apparently the landing at Salerno was difficult and very bloody." He told them that he had heard the Americans were pinned down at the beach and suffered thousands of casualties, the British army as well. But then a lot of firepower from planes and ships forced the Germans to pull back from the beachhead and establish defensive positions until they were forced north to Naples. He had been to Naples on business in years past so he knew how horrible the fighting must have been like in the dense neighborhoods of the inner city, with winding narrow streets that sunlight hardly penetrated. It was the first of October when the Allies finally drove the Germans out and entered the city. By then they had retreated north, but not before destroying anything of use, including the port.

"How much damage?" Denis asked, taking a deep draw on his cigarette. "Quite a bit, but amazingly, they had the port back in working order. The

BBC reporter commented that the effort was remarkable considering how much damage was done."

"Blimy good. That's the work of combat engineers— clearing obstacles, bulldozing rubble, building roads, bridges, port facilities, whatever is needed to support the troops."

"Their work must have been good," Pierluigi said, looking at Denis impressed with his comment. "Liberty ships are arriving in Naples now almost daily, and the people in Naples are getting some relief."

"But what about the rest of the country?" Francesco asked.

"Supplies are also being put on trucks and trains for distribution. It appears from the BBC report that the Americans have taken on the responsibility of supplying food to Italy, not only to the troops but to the civilian population as well."

"Are you getting any of that?" Denis asked.

"It's interesting you ask. I was paid a visit by an OSS agent who had been referred to me by his British counterpart. He told me that the food distribution was becoming a logistical challenge."

"Like what?" Denis asked, exhaling a stream of smoke.

"For one thing, the Allies are a multinational force, not just British and American. The mix of nationalities is causing not only communication issues but also dietary ones too. Some units will not eat pork and demand lamb—they must be Muslims. Others like the French have their own unique demands."

"If I know the French, they probably insist on only French food and wine," Denis responded.

"Then there is the problem of getting food to our civilians. But theft and the black market are becoming a problem. So now, the people in my business are being asked to assist in the food distribution."

"That's good for you, no?" Francesco asked. He thought what was good for Pierluigi's business was good for the people of Caramanico and even his family. "Yes and no. It provides a new source, but actually getting it is one thing, and I still have the dilemma with both the *partigiani* and the German quartermaster."

"Still, not a bad problem to have."

"Not to change the subject," Denis chimed in, "but did the BBC newsreader mention the British Eighth?"

"The update indicated Montgomery's army had advanced up the Adriatic coast as far as Bari. Their next objective would be the airfields at Foggia."

Pierluigi mentioned he had managed to contact Fumato, and relayed the plan of escape. Fumato, he said, couldn't promise anything, but he would try and get word to the partisans in towns along the route.

Denis asked, "What were you able to learn about the British prisoners who didn't escape the area?"

"I'm afraid hundreds were recaptured and brought back to the camp, or shipped to Germany, but many got away," Pierluigi responded. "Fumato said the area is swarming with them. He mentioned the town of Campo di Giove. The whole town seems to have provided clothes and food; even sheltered the men. He said *partigiani* had liberated a prison camp in Avezzano, freeing 2,000 prisoners, mostly British. Similar action took place at the camp near Teramo; he didn't know about the one near Chieti."

"So, at least counting those at the Sulmona and Avezzano camps, about 5,000 men escaped," Denis said. "I suspect, the ones who were not recaptured, like us, are hiding in the surrounding towns and villages. We could run into some of them."

Pierluigi said, "The fate of those men depends on the resources of the local people just like you. Fumato said some of the clergy had even begun to provide shelter and assistance in their rectories. Small bands of *partigiani* are springing up all over. As for our proposed route, Fumato told me he would pass the word to those in the Guardiagrele and Casoli area. How I don't know. I don't think he even knows yet, but he seemed confident."

"Rubbish was my first thought when you mentioned that the church might provide sanctuary," Denis said. "But it's possibly another source to count on."

Pierluigi got up to retrieve his map of Abruzzo from a kitchen drawer. He looked to Ennio who had been sitting quietly through the conversation. He unfolded the map on the table in front of him. "Show us the route you plan to take." The men gathered around, craning their necks to get a good look.

"*Quest e la via,*" Ennio said, drawing his finger across the map from Caramanico over a road, then through forest and meadows up a Maiella slope near Santo Spirito and Passo Lanciano.

"Isn't that going to involve more climbing?" Denis asked.

"Yes, but there is a much less elevation gain than you and Roger had getting here," Pierluigi said. "Go on, Ennio. Where do they go from there?"

Ennio traced the route to Guardiagrele and then on to Pennapiedimonte and Palombaro, making comments on problematic areas where the Germans were planning to build artillery positions.

"You will be close to Casoli at that point," Pierluigi nodded.

Francesco, pointing back at the map, said, "The road through Passo Lanciano is close to the Block Haus artillery site. The Germans will be using the road to bring the supplies up from Roccamorice. Press gangs are bound to be on the road almost every day."

"What do you think, Ennio?" Pierluigi asked.

"It's a problem we have to be prepared for. We will have to face German soldiers sooner or later. When we get near the pass, I plan to stop until nightfall. I don't want to move sheep at night on a poor road."

"I think that's a good idea," Pierluigi said. "Move under the cover of darkness on good terrain; if you're going to risk moving the sheep on a difficult stretch of road, make sure you do it in daylight."

"I agree," said Francesco. "Even the Germans know that no one moves their sheep at night."

"If everything is in order, let's get some sleep. We'll need to be up at daybreak and ready to go," said *Pierluigi,* bidding a *buona notte* to Ennio who left for his home.

Francesco was the last to bed. No light shown beneath the door to Annamaria's bedroom as he walked down the hall to his room.

****

It had begun to rain and Francesco listened to the soft patter of raindrops on the ground outside his window. Then the door of his room opened and Annamaria stood in the doorway wearing a long shirt and holding a candle. Francesco sat up startled. "What's the matter?" he asked.

"I thought you were never going to stop talking down there." She walked closer to his bed.

Her face is so beautiful, he thought in the soft glow of the candlelight. She wore a long-sleeved man's shirt, probably one that had belonged to her brother. She sat on the edge of his bed and the shirt rode up exposing her legs. He had not seen them before. He noticed that the top buttons of the shirt were undone and he could see the upper cleavage of her breasts. His heart was pounding from the erotic arousal, but he looked away.

Annamaria pressed on gently. "Even though you were a bit reckless, I thought you were so brave today trying to defend my honor." Francesco felt himself tremble.

"Look at me, Francesco. Why are you trembling?" she whispered.

"I don't know." he said, barely audible through a tightened throat.

"Don't worry," she said, "its okay," as she slid into bed beside him.

Through her nightshirt, he felt the warmth of her body and breasts against his chest as she caressed him. Then, for the first time, he pressed his lips to hers, and, as they kissed through the embrace, he sensed a warmth spread up to his face and down to his loins, a throbbing he had not felt that intensely before. The wind intensified. Rain lashed against the windowpane, and the shutters began rattling against the stone walls of the house.

****

At daybreak the household arose to the crowing of roosters on the farms at the edge of town. The rain had stopped, the morning was gray and cool. Denis and Roger emerged dressed in their newly acquired shepherd's clothing. As they entered the kitchen, Pierluigi looked up from a book he was reading and exclaimed, "Ah, here are our new shepherds."

Francesco struggled to suppress a grin. Angiolina did a good job, he thought. He saw that Denis's hair was darker, matched his beard and mustache, and was cut to look like a rural Italian. Roger's beard and mustache and his darker features were also passable. The shepherd's clothing had been altered so that the garments seemed to hang naturally on their frames. "I think they just might pass as Italians," he said.

"We just need to fool the Germans. They won't fool Italians," Angiolina said.

"Well, come have some coffee," Pierluigi said to the men who dragged chairs to the table and sat down.

Angiolina placed a fragrant vegetable frittata on the table.

Annamaria walked in with a round rustic loaf of bread her mother had baked in the outdoor wood-burning oven. Smiling warmly at Francesco, she placed the loaf on her hip and made broad sweeps through the crust with a butcher knife that seemed to stir Francesco. She placed the slices in a basket next to a bowl of cherry preserves and a plate of biscotti. The frittata was sliced and passed to each of them. For Francesco, Angiolina had beaten an egg yolk with a teaspoon of sugar in a cup, added milk and then topped it off with coffee.

"*Cosi buono, Angiolina!*" Francesco exclaimed, smacking his lips. "Just the way my mother makes it. Grazie." He savored each sip as he looked at Annamaria, their eyes meeting in a recall of their evening together.

"*Divertiti e mangiate.* Eat and enjoy, all of you. You have a long journey ahead."

"There is an old saying that anyone can make a frittata with eggs; it takes a special effort to make one without them," Pierluigi joked.

Chuckling, Denis said, "Eating eggless frittatas in the days ahead is something I'm not looking forward to."

They ate their breakfast with less banter. Francesco knew it would be his last morning with Annamaria, and he also sensed the impending loss of a comfortable family setting. He wondered why he hadn't felt it when he left his real home. The sudden urgency of escape and the excitement of a new adventure was what he rationalized.

They had all reviewed their plan; now came the time to execute. Angiolina distributed the final food supplies; the men thanked her as they struggled to find room for the additional items in their packs.

"Take this *torrone* with you, Francesco," Annamaria said, pulling the small carton from her apron pocket. *Ricordati di me quando lo assagi.*"

"*Grazie,*" Francesco said, flashing a bright-eyed smile. He loved the Abruzzese nougat candy, but he didn't need to taste it to remember her sweetness. Memories would be reminder enough.

Annamaria turned to Denis and Roger. "Don't forget what I taught you. And try and act Italian!" The remark made them all laugh. Denis and Roger shouldered their packs and grabbed their canteens, and with Pierluigi they left the house through the rear door.

Angiolina followed as far as the backyard with a tear in her eye and waved goodbye.

Francesco lingered with Annamaria at the door. They paused and turned to each other. Francesco had been mulling their relationship over in his mind since he had risen in the morning. "Well, what's it going to be?" Francesco asked.

"About what?" "You and me."

Annamaria frowned. "I don't know if what happened last night was supposed to happen," she said. "I didn't plan it. When I walked in to your room, I was thinking would I see you again, would you come back?"

"But it did happen. You can't expect me to just forget it."

"But you must for the time being," giving him a determined look that said it was settled in her mind. "Focus on what you have to do. I want you back here safely. We can talk seriously about it then."

Francesco sensed she wanted to distract him, to encourage him to leave, and was struggling to find the right words without causing him despair. But despair was just one of the emotions he felt. He was crestfallen and knew he would miss her.

"Be careful!" she said. "You know you will not be as safe as you have been here, and nobody will look out for you like we have. If you're confronted by the Germans again, don't say anything foolish.... "

A shout-out by her mother at the back gate cut her off. "Francesco, hurry, they're leaving without you."

Francesco, realizing there was no time to talk further, sighed in frustration. "Hey, don't worry, I'll be back. You'll be on my mind every day."

"You'll be in my thoughts and prayers too," she said quietly, flashing a warm smile that took the sadness out of Francesco's eyes.

He kissed her softly on the cheek. He wished there was a better way to say goodbye. "*Ciao, ciao,*" he finally said, "And you be careful too. Don't take any risks you don't have to." He picked up his pack and walked out the door. Stopping to give Angiolina a final quick kiss on the cheek, he continued through the gate. In the alley he paused a moment to glance back. The last look he had was of Annamaria standing beside her mother. A sense of foreboding came over him. He had yearned to do what he was about to do, and he didn't know why he felt the sudden change in emotion. He scampered to catch up to the men who were walking to the sheep corral at the edge of town.

Chapter 7

Ennio was waiting by the fold with his long white-haired sheepdogs. The enclosure was packed with sheep; some of the ewes and rams were bleating softly, anxious to move beyond the wall that restrained them.

The ferocious-looking dogs began to bark, causing Denis and Roger to stop in their tracks. Francesco, who was familiar with the breed of sheepdogs, walked toward them without fear. Pierluigi reached into his jacket pocket and pulled out some broken biscotti. He handed one each to Denis and Roger saying, "A dog that eats out of your hand will not bite you."

Ennio held the dogs by their collars and quieted them while Francesco approached and patted them. Cautiously, with Pierluigi's encouragement, the men came forward and held out their hands. The dogs stopped barking, sniffed, then accepted the cookies, looking for more. Francesco knew this fearless breed would become familiar and loyal to their new companions as they traveled together in the days ahead.

The men greeted one another. Pierluigi asked Ennio if he needed anything more.

"I think I have everything I need." A kettle to boil water and a grate for cooking over a fire were hooked to his pack. He handed Francesco, Denis. and Roger each a shepherd's staff. "You will need these," he said. "They serve many purposes."

Indeed, with the staffs, the broad-brimmed hats, scruffy shoes, and peasant garb they looked alike—a group of Italian shepherds if one didn't look too closely.

"Ennio, here are the transit papers," Pierluigi said. "My German quartermaster was able to get them signed by a colonel in Sulmona. They give you permission to move the sheep from Caramanico to Casoli. Show them if you're stopped."

He glanced at the signature and seal before tucking them away in his tunic.

"They may help us with the Germans, but not if our partisans want the sheep." "There is simply no way to cover all situations," Pierluigi said. "Negotiate as best you can. Hopefully, they will be satisfied with whatever you can spare."

"If we need a bribe, we can use the packs of those Seraglio cigarettes you gave us," Denis said.

"As good as cash," Pierluigi said. "Anything else?"

"I can't think of one bloody thing," Denis said. "Let's move out."

"Good luck then," Pierluigi said. "I estimate you will be in Casoli in a week or two. I'll send my man, Roberto, with the produce truck from my shop as soon as I get the word from my brother or the *partigiani.*"

The Eastern sky had turned pale orange and a breeze stirred, bringing the wooly-lanolin scent of the sheep and the odor of their manure. The dogs milled about in front of the gate, anxious to work them.

"If I can get Denis and Roger close to the Sangro, then what?" Francesco asked.

"Your job is just to get them as close to the river as possible, hand them off to the partisans and then get back here. I will have my driver wait for you as long as he can. But remember, he may be the only link between us."

Francesco nodded. He knew they had an understanding of how far he could go and the risks to take. He embraced Pierluigi and quickly backed away toward the sheep.

The rising sun had begun to take the chill from the morning air. The sheep continued to bleat and the dogs moved about the perimeter of the fold. Ennio walked to check the gate and called his dogs next to him.

Denis turned to Pierluigi. "I hope when this war is over we will see each other here in Abruzzo. I understand now why the Abruzzo people are called *'forte e gentile,'* strong and kind. There is much I must thank you for."

Pierluigi reached out his hand to Denis and Roger with a look of sincere appreciation. "I, too look forward to a reunion someday, but in the meantime just focus on getting back to your unit. I think the Allies have underestimated the Germans' determination to hold the line here in Italy."

"I hope that's not the case, but in any event I hope to see a lot more of the Abruzzo in the days ahead," Denis said.

"Well, I expect you and Roger will become familiar with the Maiella," Pierluigi said. This has been an unusually wet autumn, and it may become a bad winter, but you should get to Casoli before then. In the meantime, the rain could make the ravine and river crossings difficult. But you will have to get over the Sangro before it rises to flood stage, the goal of this plan rests on that."

Francesco listened to the exchange quietly, feeling a bit uncertain about the unscripted adventure ahead.

"Well," Pierluig said, choking a bit as he embraced Denis and Roger in turn, "until we see each other again, *buona fortuna.*"

Pausing to clear his throat, Pierluigi turned to Francesco, "Are you ready to go?"

Francesco nodded. "All set," he responded, trying to appear outwardly confident despite some internal apprehension.

Embracing him again, Pierluigi stepped back. "Take care of them, and remember, use good judgment!" he said, trying to smile. Then he turned away, walked over to Ennio and opened the gate of the sheepfold. The dogs entered barking, herding the sheep out. Ennio, Francesco, and the soldiers followed. Pierluigi closed the gate and waved as they started down the road. Then he turned and walked home.

****

Francesco followed Ennio exhorting the flock through the meadowland. The tinkling of bells, soft bleating of the sheep, and the occasional barks of the dogs were the only sounds on this quiet morning. The men chatted, gradually overcoming their communication problems. Francesco and Ennio spoke their lyrical Italian, and Denis and Roger responded with fairly fluent, if less melodic, sentences. They used the basic Italian interrogatives for questions, but sometimes were forced to use largely English sentences interspersed with *"como si dice...?"* Roger searched the Italian-English dictionary he carried, fishing for unfamiliar words to string into sentences that sounded like English rigidly translated into Italian. Francesco knew Denis and Roger were never going to speak colloquially or use idioms, but somehow they began to understand one another quite well.

Francesco thought the gentle terrain starting out offered an opportunity to provide Denis and Roger some basic instruction in shepherding. Ennio agreed and carved out a few sheep from the flock for each of them to manage while he and Francesco walked along coaching. The newly minted shepherds found managing even small flocks not easy. The two groups would intermingle or stray, and they struggled to get control. A sheep would bound off not paying heed to their coaxing causing Roger or Denis to chase after it. Ennio, Francesco, and the dogs came to their rescue time and again, but gradually, they started to get the hang of it. Could they really fool German soldiers, Francesco wondered?

The road through the meadow declined gradually and they entered the forested slopes of *La Maielletta*. The wind overhead rustled yellowed leaves, swirling and flipping those that fell on drafts and rattled along the ground. By afternoon, the flock had been reassembled and the dogs worked the strays and nipped at the flanks of stragglers. Roger and Denis became more comfortable as they walked the edge of the flock. Ennio had marked the trail with rock cairns and pieces of fabric. It skirted rocky outcroppings and ravines before reaching the outskirts of a high mountain meadow in midafternoon. A half-dozen stone piles dotted the grassy expanse.

Roger asked Denis, "What are those? They look like stone igloos." Denis turned to Francesco and pointed. "What do you call those?"

Francesco told him they were *tholos*, constructed by shepherds by layering hundreds of field stones of different size, shape, and shade upon one another, balancing the construction so that the stones supported themselves without mortar. He told them it took patience, but provided protection from the cold and surprisingly admitted little moisture after rain or snow. Denis, Roger, and Francesco walked over to peer inside one of them while Ennio and the dogs rounded up the sheep in the meadow by a natural tank filled with brackish water. The empty hut had an earthen floor. Francesco said, "Not the most comfortable, but with a ground cover and a blanket, good enough. We may want to use them tonight. It looks like rain may be coming. I'll ask Ennio what he thinks."

Ennio indicated the meadow was a good stopping point for the first day out. The men settled between two of the *tholos*, lying back on the grass, using their packs to rest their heads.

After a while, Denis and Roger dozed off. Ennio had rolled over on his side and kept an eye out. Francesco walked about near the sheep that were content to graze, the dogs working back the occasional stray that tried to wander off. He felt good about being in charge of the sheep. When the men awoke, they stretched their legs before settling back down to smoke. Denis drew a cigarette from his pack and lit it.

Francesco thought he knew him well enough to joke around. "Remember to hold that cigarette like an Italian, with your thumb and forefinger, not like an Englishman," he smirked as he walked over and sat on the ground next to Denis.

"Thanks for the reminder," Denis said, smiling.

Francesco asked "What do you plan to do when this is over?" He hoped to learn more about Denis's and Roger's lives before the war, now that the road had given them a growing familiarity.

"I want to get back to England and to work as a civil engineer. There will be a lot of buildings to repair, roads and bridges to rebuild. The Luftwaffe has done considerable damage."

Denis continued the friendly exchange. "What about you?" "Well, if I get back to Caramanico, I'd like to join the resistance."

"Won't you go home to Roccamorice to see your mother and brother?" "Yes, of course, as soon as I can, but I feel the need to do more in this war. "

"Assuming this war will be over one day, what do you want to do afterward?" "That's easy, like I said before, join my father in New York State. That's what we were hoping for when he left. The war changed everything."

Denis took a long drag on his cigarette and exhaled. "That could take a while, Francesco. Pierluigi told me the United States, Canada, and England consider Italy an enemy combatant. They will have to remove that label before you can immigrate."

Francesco frowned. "Well, now that Italy has joined the Allies, won't that happen?"

"Maybe, but not right away."

Roger was following the conversation; his ears perked up at the mention of New York. "Where is your father now, Francesco?"

"He lives in a town in the Niagara region. He got a job in a factory making steel."

Roger's eyes widened. He asked, "Close to the Canadian border? My home in Canada, less than an hour from Niagara Falls."

"Yes. My father sent a postcard telling us it was only a few kilometers from Niagara Falls." Francesco's face brightened. "So where is your town?"

"Aldershot, a village near Hamilton in Ontario. I grew up there on a farm. How is your father doing?"

Francesco's face brightened, pleased to hear the close proximity. "The last letter we received from him was months ago. But he is okay, I think." Francesco thought about how anxious his mother was, how they all were when his father left to look for work in the midst of the Depression. Then the war came and he got the job in the steel mill making armored sheet steel. He remembered how happy they were when he wrote to them about the job. It caused him to work long hours and double shifts. But he was happy making money, and so were they when the American dollars came in the mail.

"So," Roger said. "Immigration was the right thing for your family?"

"Yes, for sure, but I miss him," he said, picturing his father's smiling face on the day he left. He was sorry not to have seen much of his father growing up, always traveling looking for work; but on that day he told him and his brother to help their mother and be strong for each other; to resist any intimidation, and trust yourselves he had said. He would send for us as soon as he could. "The reunion was our hope."

Denis, who had been listening to the exchange said, "Now there you go—a meeting between you two at Niagara Falls after the war and the family reunion."

"That sounds great," Roger said, smiling at Francesco.

"What's Canada like?" Francesco asked. He wasn't that interested in Canada, but thought it would be nice if their relationship could grow into a friendship that continued across an ocean. Across an ocean. It was a pleasant thought.

"Where I come from it looks similar to Western New York. You cross the Niagara River that separates us, but the land looks the same on both sides." He went on to describe the Niagara peninsula of Canada and the borderland with the United States. Like Italy, he said, there were cities and towns of all sizes and lots of farms—it was pastoral like Abruzzo.

"Mountains?"

"Nothing like the Maiella, but there is an elevated ridge that extends inland along Lake Ontario from Canada into New York—we call it the escarpment.

"It sounds different but nice," Francesco said. "I hope the 'enemy' label will be removed when this is over. I really want to get to America, especially knowing you would be so close,"

"I would like that too. The war has robbed us all of the plans we once made. But I hope we get back to them once it's over. I'm sure you do too. I was happy to interrupt my education to serve in the war, but when its over I want to get back to school and get my doctoral degree in history."

"I would like to get back to school too, but after I see my father in America."

Ennio had walked over to check the flock and returned with some firewood he had gathered at the edge of the meadow.

"What about you, Ennio?" Denis asked. "What do you want to do when this war is over?"

"I have sheep in my blood. I love living on the Maiella, moving around these mountains and valleys. I just hope peace and quiet returns," he said, laying down the wood. "I know a man who lives in Vittorito near us," Ennio continued. "He went to New York City where he worked for a time, but he came back before the war. We call him 'Il Americano.' He forgot most of his English except for the swear words he uses to describe the Fascisti. Anyway, he told me that living in New York was not so nice. Terribly crowded streets with no grass or trees. He lived in a two-room apartment on the sixth floor of a building that was packed with families. Six flights of stairs, one bathroom on each floor, and no hot water. Dark and dreary, and the air was bad. They froze in the winter and roasted in the summer. That's not for me."

"Well, that's probably a realistic picture of life in New York City for immigrants, but upstate New York is much different," Roger said. "I've crossed the border and gone as far as Rochester to interview at the university there. People there live in houses with yards and trees. Sometimes those houses get crowded, but they're not the tenements surrounded by concrete that you described."

"Okay," Ennio said, his face registering skepticism, "If you say so."

"You know, Ennio, my father wrote that he missed our village and countryside, too, but he enjoys the freedom to do and say anything he wants over there. The decision to bring us over there instead of returning here was not easy for him." Ennio simply nodded and said nothing.

"Well, so much for that. What are we going to eat?" Francesco asked, feeling a pang of hunger. "I'll start the fire."

"We don't need to cook tonight," Ennio said. "We should eat the *formaggio e salumi* first."

"That sounds good," Denis said, smiling. "I love those cheeses and meats." "Did you taste them at the Sanellis?" Francesco asked.

"When I was a kid in London. There was an Italian grocer in the neighborhood who imported *prosciutto* and *parmigiano* from Parma. Pierluigi's Abruzzo salami and caciocavallo cheese made from his sheep's milk was different, but it was very good too.

Roger added, "The ravioli Angiolina made with that same milk, nuggets of fresh ricotta wrapped in that yellow egg dough, just melted in your mouth."

They sat around eating and reminiscing about food in the amber glow of the fire. The dogs had been fed and settled down with the sheep. The fire crackled as it burned low. Francesco got up and went over to the stack of wood lying on the ground next to Ennio. Adding the branches to the dwindling fire sent sparks in the air that rose and disappeared in the darkening sky. "Did you join the army after you finished school?" he asked Denis.

"I did an apprenticeship for a year with an engineering firm in London, and after that I got into an engineering college. The war broke out when I was about to graduate."

Roger leaned in and said, "I was going to ask before what made you join up." "One night I was listening to a report of the predicament of British forces in Flanders. The broadcast switched to politics and I heard our prime minister give his 'blood, sweat and tears' speech. It was very compelling. The next morning I joined up."

"Just like that, you went to North Africa?" Roger asked. He and Denis hadn't talked much about their early military careers during their prison escape and stay with the Sanellis.

"Not right away. I still had a couple of months before I could graduate. The recruiter told me to come back when I had my engineering degree. So that's what I did, and then I enlisted. I was sent off to training camp and officer's school."

Denis continued by telling them about his North African experience after he was shipped off to Egypt where he joined the Royal Engineers, part of the Western Desert Task Force under Field Marshal Sir Archibald Wavell's command. His job was to direct the building of a railway and a pipeline to deliver supplies and water to the army holding the western edge against the Italian army.

Francesco looked dialed in. Denis mentioned so many places he had never heard of on a continent that was truly dark in Francesco's mind, even though he was familiar with Mussolini's invasion of Ethiopia. The logistics of warfare and the exotic locales had fascinated him. Denis said that by luck and a bluff, Wavell's undermanned forces defeated the larger Italian army that occupied the western desert region. But no sooner had they dispatched the Italians when Rommel's Africa Corps came banging in from the west.

"Did you fight against them too?" Francesco asked wide-eyed, impressed as he was by the German military might.

"Indirectly. We carried more tools than weapons, but I did get up close to the action. Too close. That's how I was captured."

"It's getting late," Ennio said, interrupting the conversation. "We should turn in. We need to get an early start in the morning."

"I want to hear more," Francesco said.

"It can wait," Ennio said. The talk of war was not high on his list of topics. The fire had burned down with the soft-sounding collapse of ashen branches, the scent of smoke drifting in with the night breeze. Ennio extinguished the embers and they all retired to their *tholos*. Francesco had been preoccupied with the daily activity to think of anything except the men and the sheep, but now in the stillness of the night, his thoughts turned to Annamaria. Remembering the torrone in his pack she had given him, he sliced off a piece and savored the sweet nougat. His thoughts became romantic dreams as he drifted off to sleep.

The following morning they emerged from their tholos to clusters of gray clouds silhouetted against a platinum sky. It had rained during the night, but they had slept through it and the *tholos* had kept them dry. But it was a harbinger. They shared bread and a hard-boiled egg with their bitter coffee before starting out on the next leg of the trip.

Just as they had begun the day before, they found the silence of the woods interrupted only by their footfalls crackling on fallen leaves, the soft clang of the bells hanging from the neck of the rams, and the occasional bark of the dogs herding the sheep along. Ennio in the lead swung the group up the Maiella slope following a trail that he had previously marked out to Passo Lanciano.

"Last night you were going to tell me how you were captured," Francesco said to Denis as he and Roger walked along with him at the edge of the flock.

"Let's see, where did I leave off? Let me skip forward to June, 1942, about sixteen months ago. We had established a fortified defensive line from Gazala on the North African coast to Bir Hakem south in the desert. The line was west of Tobruk. I know," he said apologetically, "places you've never heard of."

Francesco nodded. "That's okay, I'm learning now." Denis explained the line was just forward of another town— Knightsbridge which was situated in the approximate center of the line which was fronted by a minefield. Rommel's Africa Korps approached the line from the west. In a bold move, he sent his armor around the left flank while he opened a gap in the minefield allowing his tanks and infantry to thrust forward into the gap. Denis said the British Eighth tried to stem the tide, but were overwhelmed by the Germans and began retreating. That was when he was ordered to gather a group of combat engineers and sappers to salvage pumping equipment and demolish the pipeline before the enemy could get it. He said it was a matter of undoing what they had done earlier—laying five hundred miles of pipe from Alexandria to their forward position in the western desert.

Denis paused to step aside and let some of the sheep herded by one of the dogs pass a narrow defile on the trail. Francesco used his staff to coax one of the strays back to the group.

Roger who was trailing behind, had caught up and heard Denis mention the demolition of the pipeline. "That must have hurt, my friend, undoing all that work."

"It was a real waste," Denis responded with the look of disappointment.

"At least Rommel couldn't make use of our work. Anyway, that was when I was captured.

Francesco was now wide-eyed. "How?" he asked.

Denis went on to say he had his driver swing off to the south into the desert to bypass the traffic on the coast road. What he didn't know was that a German patrol had been shadowing the retreat and saw them turn off the highway. Suddenly an armored car and motorcycle troops emerged from behind a group of high mounds. They pointed their guns and the German officer said in perfect English, 'Hands up. Step out of your vehicle, boys.' After that, Denis said, "We were done!"

Francesco remained wide-eyed listening to the story. *Dio Mio*, he thought, but he didn't want to admit fear. Instead he asked Denis to fill in the details of how he got from the battlefield to Naples, the last part of his journey before Sulmona.

Denis summarized how the Germans bottled them up in one temporary prison after another and eventually turned him and a group of prisoners over to the Italians in Tunis where he was placed aboard a ship for Naples. 'See Naples then die,' the saying went. He wanted to see Naples, but he wasn't keen on dying.

****

Ennio halted the flock in a clearing in the woods and walked back to the men while the dogs kept the sheep together. He told them it was time to rest. They had been traveling all morning and had made good progress. The steel wool sky promised more rain to come. They made a small campfire and pulled food from their rucksacks. Then they settled back, using their canvas mantellos to shield them from the damp ground.

Francesco asked Ennio what he thought about spending the evening at Santo Spirito. He knew it was a diversion, but he wanted to score points with Roger who he knew wanted to be a historian after the war. "At this time of the year, and especially late in the day it should be deserted," he said. He estimated that they could get there by nightfall and just might beat the rain. Francesco felt comfortable making the request because he had scored points with Ennio for the way he handled the sheep.

"My plan was to stop at Passo Lanciano," Ennio said. "But figuring our time, spending the night at the Santo Spirito could work."

"What is Santo Spirito?" asked Roger, overhearing the conversation.

Francesco turned his attention to Roger. "*Un eremo*, a hermitage. I think you would like its history since you want to be a historian. "It was first built centuries ago by the hermit who became Pope Celestine V."

"Sounds interesting. Visiting a site like that always adds to an historical account, especially one I am not familiar with."

Francesco looked to Ennio, and with eyes and gestures between them, the decision was made.

Denis reminded Roger that they had briefly discussed the hermit pope when they broke out of camp. He thought they were safe enough at the moment, so he was willing to go the extra mile if Roger was interested in learning more for his future career.

Francesco smiled and turning to Roger said, "Okay that's settled. I will be happy to tell you the story of our saint and his hermitage, but I would like to trade stories. How did you get to Sulmona? When Denis was a prisoner in Sulmona where were you?" he asked as he added a tree branch to the campfire.

Roger hadn't expected the question, but the fire's crackle and flare cued his memory. He took out a cigarette and lit it. Pausing in thought, he exhaled a puff of smoke and said, "North Africa."

Starting at the beginning, he told Francesco he graduated from McMaster University in Hamilton with his history degree and went to officer's training school. Afterward he shipped out to London. He said the Canadian army had been sent to England in 1940 to bolster Britain's fighting forces. Canadian airmen and sailors saw some action in the early years, but the infantry pretty much remained idle. When he got there in the late spring of '43, they were part of the newly reorganized British Army. "We trained pretty hard and then we shipped out to North Africa," he said. "I was a member of a Canadian Infantry division by then. The crucial battle at El Alamein between Rommel and Montgomery's armies was over when I arrived in May. After that we waited for the allies to execute the next step."

Anxious to hear more, Francesco prompted him, "What did you do in North Africa while you all waited?"

Roger took a drag on his cigarette. "Not much. Life in camp was pretty boring. We did some training exercises to keep in shape, but we didn't know where we would be going to fight. We discussed the scuttlebutt that was going around about Allied strategy."

"What's scuttlebutt?" Francesco asked.

Roger started thumbing through his dictionary.

Denis, who had been chatting quietly with Ennio, saw Roger struggling with his dictionary and interjected, *"la chiacchiera,* I think that's the word."

Francesco laughed and nodded. "You were captured in Sicily, if I remember what Pierluigi said."

Roger said he was in the amphibious landing at Cassibile on the ninth of July. "We were supposed to link up with paratroopers that had landed during the night. A key objective was to capture a bridge over a river just south of the Syracuse-Augusta coastline." Roger saw a stick on the ground and bent down to retrieve it, using it to make an outline of Sicily and indicate all the landing sites with divots. The fire's sudden string of crackles and sparks resembled small arms fire, cueing Roger on. "Things didn't go as planned for a lot of reasons. From the moment the ramps dropped on our landing boats we were in trouble. The machine gun fire was pretty intense, and the water we stepped into was deeper than we expected."

Francesco said, "I talked about the war at home with my friends, but we had no idea of what it was really like. We imagined ourselves fighting on the beaches and towns shooting guns. We'd run around our town, chasing each other ducking in and out of doorways shooting our imaginary guns and throwing grenades of the season—fig fights in summer, snow balls in winter."

"Imagining war—playing make believe with toy guns—and the reality of it are two different things, Francesco," Roger said. "The real battlefield was brutal. After we hit the beaches, there was a lot of confusion. It took a while to get organized." Roger explained what the conditions were like from the landing to the airfield at Pachino that was Army's objective. He said the heat was intolerable. The horror at the beachhead—the dead and dying all around was only the beginning of the misery that lay ahead. Machine gun bullets and artillery shells tore bodies apart. He came across scattered pieces of flesh and the horror of dismembered bodies. He was not used to the intensity of the battle or the tropical Sicilian heat, and the stench of blood and guts was just magnified by the heat. He and his men were constantly thirsty and the fighting was exhausting. "But we pushed on to the Pachino airfield."

Francesco listened to Roger's account with more horror than he had when Denis related his experience. As Roger was talking, Francesco's mind was turning the narration into graphic action, and he realized he and his friends had had childish viewpoints of battle. His stomach felt queasy at the mention of the blood and guts, but he didn't want to admit it.

Roger continued, explaining that the Germans had pulled out north to set up defensive positions in the mountains. They had left the Italians to defend the beaches and towns. He didn't think the Italians were happy about defending the coast, but those who were dug in around the airfield put up a strong resistance. "I started the day with forty men, but by late afternoon I was down to twelve."

Evening brought relief from the heat but not the thirst. By the third day they had pushed the Italians out and captured the airfield. After securing it, Roger said they were ordered to keep going, and sometime in the middle of the night they passed through their first Sicilian town. They stopped at the well in the central piazza to refill canteens and then moved on northward. By morning they halted at a cross roads to rest. They were mostly lounging around smoking and chatting. "Thinking we were safe, I failed to set up a perimeter. Big mistake. Suddenly we were caught out in the open by a Black shirt Militia with machine guns." Roger looked chagrined. "I had no idea those Italian outfits had stuck around. At that point I didn't want to lose more men so we dropped to the ground and I surrendered what was left of my platoon."

The fire flared again, popping and hissing. "Anyway, that's how I got to Sulmona—what we called the 'spaghetti and barb-wire camp.' But after Sicily, it seemed like a rest stop."

Francesco, who had transitioned between fascination and horror, made a mental note not to ask any more war stories.

Denis leaned over and said, "Francesco, I think you're up to speed as we say. And hopefully you're prepared for what might happen if we run into any more Germans. But for now we just have to execute the rest of Pierluigi's plan so we can get back in the game. *Capish?*"

"*Capisco,*" he smiled. "If not for your English accents you could both possibly pass for Italians. Anyway, I think you can fool the Germans."

Ennio had pulled his loaf of bread from his pack and passed it around. Each of them cut off a slice to eat with the Abruzzo salami he also passed. Taking a swig from his wineskin, he reached it over to Denis. They all chatted quietly appearing to relish the mountain stillness around them. "It's time to go," he said finally, getting up and repacking. With his dogs, he and Francesco got the sheep ready to move out. "*Andiamo.*" Denis and Roger resumed their places at the rear, looking around for signs of trouble.

For Francesco, the hours had passed quickly with Denis's and Roger's back stories. He thought he knew both of them better now; he certainly admired them more, and he had gained a greater appreciation of the war from firsthand accounts, not old newspaper stories, propaganda, and rumors. He recalled Annamaria's comment—"How can war be a good thing?" The magical thinking of his childhood where anything was possible was coming to an end.

Chapter 8

Leaving the woods, they crossed up a slope covered with grasses, scattered low shrubs, and rocks. The sheep had been confined by the forest, but now in the open, the flock spread out to graze. Ennio and the dogs kept them moving along in an easterly direction. He and Francesco took the left and right leads with Denis and Roger following along the wings toward the rear and the dogs working back and forth between them. Soon they encountered a narrow dirt road with steep banks that led to the mountain peak where the Germans were building their artillery site. At that point Ennio called a halt as they were nearing the place where it was necessary to confirm the change in plans. He called Francesco over and asked him if he was still intent on the Santo Spirito visit.

Francesco waved for Roger to come forward. "Are you still interested in visiting the hermitage? We need to decide soon as we are close to a crossroad."

"I am if you and Ennio still think it's safe and you know enough of the history."

Francesco was eager to impress Roger. He told him that in school he had studied the basics of Pietro's life, but a few years ago a professor from the University at Chieti came to the village for a sabbatical to do research for a book he intended to title, *The Untold Story of the Pope Who Quit*. "He and my teacher were friends from their days at the university. My teacher asked me to be his guide to Santo Spirito. I spent a few days with him and learned a great detail of Pietro's life from the research he had already done. It was like a special course in history I think you would like to know."

"Sounds like you know enough to make the visit worthwhile. Certainly as a historian I'm very interested, but let me check to see if Denis still wants to chance it." He turned and walked back saying over his shoulder, "I don't want to hold things up unnecessarily."

****

The chug-chugging of a motorcycle coming up the road caught Ennio and Francesco's attention. They both turned and waved their arms to signal Denis and Roger to get low and conceal themselves. But there was nowhere to hide. First one motorcycle, then a second appeared, each ridden by a German soldier with their distinctive helmets and uniforms bearing the insignia of noncommissioned officers. They pulled up and stopped by Ennio and Francesco who had moved to the front of the flock that now filled the roadway. The dogs came running up, barking furiously. Ennio and Francesco each grabbed one and calmed them down.

"Where are you taking these sheep?" the lead officer, a sergeant, demanded.

"To Casoli," Ennio said. "We are moving them to lower pasture before winter." "Who gave you permission to use this road?"

"Do we need permission?" Francesco asked, with a why-are you-bothering-us look. Ever since the incident in Roccamorice and his discussions at the Sanelli home, he had become progressively annoyed with the occupiers; fed up was more like it. He also thought his father would approve how he stood up to authority.

The German officer looked at Francesco. In heavily accented Italian he indicated in no uncertain terms that he would ask the questions, and for the boy to be quiet.

Ennio grabbed Francesco's arm as he pulled the papers from inside his tunic and handed them to the officer. Denis and Roger had pretended to busy themselves with the sheep at the rear, poking about with their shepherd crooks while keeping their faces downcast. They were too far away to hear the conversation.

"These papers are signed by one of your officers," Ennio said.

The officer eyed the papers with suspicion. He didn't recognize the signature, but he thought the seal looked valid. "Where did you get this document?" he asked.

"What does it matter?" Francesco asked, again looking annoyed.

The officer rapidly rolled up the papers and struck Francesco across the face with them. Francesco put his hand to his cheek. He was stunned. The swipe had landed rather softly, but he had not anticipated it.

The officer's jaw set in anger, he said, "Another remark like that and you will be coming with us. Do you understand?"

Francesco clenched his fists at his side, fighting back the temptation to speak out again.

Ennio quickly intervened. "I was given these papers by the owner of the flock who has a business in Sulmona. He works with your quartermaster there."

"Is this your son?" he asked Ennio.

"No, a friend of the owner. He is along to help."

"More like a liability," the officer retorted. He stepped up to Ennio. *"Carta d' identita, subito!"*

Ennio pulled the identification card from his tunic and handed it over. The soldier looked at it and then handed it back. "Who are those men at the rear?"

"Shepherds from our village who have joined their flock with ours for this trip." Francesco hoped that the flock that stood between them and Denis and Roger would shield them from a closer look and the requisition of their ID cards.

"I need to see their identification," the officer said.

Francesco, suddenly fearing what might happen, decided to be more conciliatory. "With your permission, sir, may I retrieve them for you? It will be easier for me to get them. The road is narrow here and the precipice deep. We don't want to cause any of the sheep to stumble off."

The soldier looked about and saw that there wasn't much room to maneuver. "Hurry up then," he said.

Francesco wove his way slowly and carefully through the flock to reach Denis first. Looking back and forth nervously, he said, "Let me have your identification card. I'm hoping this will satisfy the sergeant, but just in case be prepared for an interview. His Italian is not great so just try and use simple sentences like si or no if you can. If that doesn't work, bluff like you don't understand what he's asking. You know, *non capisce.*"

"Here," Denis said, pulling his card from under his tunic and handing it over. "There are only two of them, but they have guns and we don't, so let's not try anything foolish. We won't be able to make a run for it if he pulls his pistol."

Francesco walked over to Roger and repeated his request. "If they let us through, walk on the edge of the road by the embankment, keeping the sheep between you and them and look straight ahead, not at them." Then he worked his way back to the officer and handed him the two cards.

The officer took both cards and looked them over, his eyes traveling back and forth from the images on the card to the men at the rear of the flock. "I need to verify. Wait here," he said to his fellow officer.

Francesco's heart sank as the officer started out through the sheep. He could see Denis and Roger tense as they saw what was happening. Still holding on to one of the dogs, he let go and walked after the officer, making his way through the sheep along the edge of the embankment. He waved to Denis and pointed to himself.

"Get ready to jump this guy," he whispered to Roger.

Roger nodded back. "Why don't you move up and go first. You've got the language down. Maybe you can speak for me."

The German officer reached Denis first and handed his identification card to him. *"Como ti chiamo?"* he asked.

"Mi chiamo Angelo DiCarlo," Denis said, using the alias on his identification.

"Dove habito?"

"Caramanico."

"Dove andare con queste pecore?"

"Casoli."

The officer looked closely at Denis, whose facial features were partly obscured beneath his wide brim hat. He brushed him aside gently, handing him his identification card as he stepped toward Roger. As he had with Denis, his first question was, *"Como ti chiamo?"*

Just as Roger was about to give his name, Francesco nudged one of the sheep over the embankment. It bleated plaintively as it lost its footing, sliding, and then tumbling down the hill. The dogs immediately responded, barking furiously as they bounded thorough the flock to the edge of the embankment, and without hesitation, they leapt after the sheep.

Denis, who had taken back his card, bolted toward the fallen sheep as Roger joined him.

The flock had become agitated and started to panic; Ennio struggled to control them with his staff.

The officer who had been questioning the men started back toward where Francesco was standing.

"Go down after that sheep with the dogs," Francesco said to Roger and Denis who had reached him at the edge of the embankment. "Don't come back up. Pretend that you are taking care of the animal."

Roger and Denis scurried down the bank toward the sheep that had righted itself. It stood frozen and frightened, bleating while the dogs remained barking next to it, not letting it move away.

The officer reached Francesco and looked down at the scene below him. "I just polished these boots today, so I'm not going to go down there," he said. "Ask them if they can get back up."

"Is the sheep okay?" Francesco yelled down to the men in the ravine.

Denis and Roger bent over next to the sheep and dogs waved an okay sign without looking up.

"Good," the officer said, looking at his watch. Then turning toward Ennio he yelled, "Let's go! Move your flock so we can get by."

Francesco breathed a sigh of relief and joined Ennio. Together, they moved the sheep with their staffs, giving the officers room to maneuver their motorcycles. Then the officers remounted and sped up the road toward the Block Haus.

While Ennio stayed with the flock, Francesco scampered down the bank to the men still standing by the dogs and the sheep. "That was close," he said.

"That was quick thinking, Francesco," Denis said.

"Yes, good job," Roger added. "I'm not sure I would have passed the test as Denis did."

Francesco tried hard to suppress a smile. The ewe appeared uninjured. Francesco looked it over, checking each of its legs. "Help him lift it," he said.

Roger carried it up the bank with Denis and Francesco trailing behind, the dogs following after them. They rejoined Ennio who shook his head but seemed much relieved. Out of earshot of Denis and Roger, Ennio said, "You have to grow up or we will be going to prison instead of the Sangro."

Francesco felt the rebuke in the flash of heat in his cheeks. He turned away, his face a blank but sorrow clearly evident in his eyes. He was thankful neither Denis nor Roger brought up the incident with the officer. After they got the animals settled, they resumed their journey with Francesco taking the lead.

****

Continuing down the road, they passed a dirt track that branched off to the east. Ennio pointed it out as the road down the mountain toward Guardiagrele. Seeing it now for the first time, Francesco realized the road would be a real challenge to negotiate in the dark. They pushed on to Passo Lanciano and reached it late in the afternoon.

"This is where we part for the evening," Ennio said. "I think it's better if I overnight the sheep here. I can spend the night in one of the *tholos*. I don't think the Germans will show up here or there. Do you remember where the door key is hidden?"

Francesco assured him he knew how to get into the hermitage.

Leaving Ennio, the sheep, and the dogs behind, Denis and Roger followed Francesco up the road to Santo Spirito. The wind had picked up, it turned cooler, and began to thunder.

Roger turned to Francesco. "You said your town is the gateway to this hermitage, so you must get lots of visitors asking questions."

"People show up in the town piazza asking directions. If they have time we suggest they look at an old inscription chiseled into the wall of one of the houses before leaving. It indicates that the hermit who became pope purchased it—*Casa Celestino,* back when he was building the hermitage."

Francesco told them that his family, often along with others in the town, made pilgrimages to Santo Spirito on some of the feast days, especially. They would start out on foot in the morning, visit the church and chapels, hear Mass, and share meals. Once in a while they would spend the evening, sleeping in the cells of the monastery or on the grounds before heading back the following day. "Pilgrimages here have been going on for generations."

Roger said, "Maybe we can make this a pilgrimage too. I think the hand of God may have helped get us this far; perhaps his holy spirit—Santo Spirito, will get us the rest of the way."

Denis said, "I'm with you, mate. As I remember from what I learned at the camp, there are both secular and spiritual aspects to the story, and a prayer or two up there can't hurt our chances. So tell us what you know, Francesco."

"Well, to begin, the hermit who became a pope, Pietro Morrone, was born here in Abruzzo in the 13th century, sometime around 1215."

"That's a famous date in English history," Denis said, leaning in. "The year the Magna Carta was signed at Runnymede."

"Actually that was an event-filled century in the middle ages," Roger chimed in. Lots of significant religious and secular events."

Francesco thought to himself, these guys know more history than I do, but they don't know the story I'm going to tell—which was largely what he learned shepherding the professor around Roccamorice and Santo Spirito. In his eagerness he hoped he could remember the details.

He told them Pietro was the 11th of 12 children born to a poor couple in a hamlet near here. Not much was known about his childhood although he was thought to be naturally spiritual. Some people said his mother was responsible. But in those days, a young boy choosing the religious life was not that uncommon. When Pietro was old enough, Francesco said he told his parents he wanted to become a monk in the tradition of Benedict who founded the monastic life. "The professor told me he didn't think a life alone was what Pietro intended at first, but while he was at the monastery, he expressed a sincere interest in becoming a hermit, spending his days in prayer with the Lord."

Francesco continued, telling them the abbot insisted that Pietro should first become a priest before joining a hermitage, so he sent him off to Rome. The professor learned that Pietro took his time getting there, stopping for months in monasteries along the way, living and praying with the monks. In Rome he entered a seminary, but as soon as he became a priest he left. He just couldn't adjust to life in the city. He longed for the solitude of the mountains in Abruzzo. He left Rome for Sulmona, and from there he went on to the monastery at Badia. He didn't stay there very long because he wanted more solitude. So he left to live in a nearby cave on Mt. Morrone where he built his first hermitage. "It was there where Pietro lived the simple life spelled out by Benedict; one of mortification, prayer, and penance along with vows of poverty and chastity."

Roger said, "I know the century was filled with religious events—the crusades, religious orders, and secular people like Genghis and Kublai Kahn, the Polos, but I didn't know about this Peter of Morrone. What more can you tell us about him?"

Encouraged by Roger's interest, Francesco told them that Pietro's fame as a holy man spread. The people recognized something new and attractive in his message and they flocked to him. Pietro eventually founded a religious order, similar to the one Francis of Assisi had founded as the Franciscans. The pope at the time made them a branch of the Benedictines, but after Pietro became the pope, they were called the Celestine's after the name he had chosen for his papacy. "Something new I learned was that eventually the Celestine's included a group of Franciscans who were dissatisfied with the changes in the Franciscan order after Francis died. These Fraticelli or Spirituals as they were known became the *Poor Hermits of Pope Celestine.*"

Denis said, "I was told by my prison guard friend, Pepino, that he always wanted to go higher in the mountains physically and spiritually, to get even closer to God."

"He was uncomfortable once his following grew too large. He needed to get away for peace and solitude to pray alone. That was how he came to build Santo Spirito. We're just about there. As you can see, it's still pretty remote. I'll finish the story after we get there. "

Chapter 9

They entered the grounds of the hermitage as it was getting dark, barely able to discern the outline of the monastery and church flanked against the stone wall of the forested mountain slope that towered over the building complex. The men walked past an obelisk with the chiseled Ave Maria, looking up at the layers of jutting limestone, with shrubs and saplings between them, eyeing the top of the mountain ridge to blue sky that was now fading. Continuing toward the door of the church, they passed beside a waist-high trough carved along the stone wall. Slowly moving water gurgled into it from a mountainside spring. Francesco dipped his hand in and brought it to his mouth. The mineral water tasted cool and fresh. Roger and Denis seemed a bit nervous looking around, but then each took a drink.

"Ah, mates, nothing like the taste of a mountain spring, eh?" Denis remarked. Roger took a second, then a third handful, removed his hat and washed the water over his face and head. "Nice," he said. "You wouldn't think there is a war going on."

"Like the eye of a hurricane," Denis said.

Francesco walked over to a ledge, climbed up and retrieved a big brass key from a rocky shelf. The pitter-patter of rain hit the ground as Francesco stepped down and walked over to the door. Above it *Porta Cello* was carved into the lintel. A faded blue and tan coat of arms with a cross was painted on the stone block façade next to it.

"That's the Celestine symbol he said pointing to the wall. This place used to be occupied year round, but now we only see a priest for a few months in the summer," Francesco said. The big metal key clanked as he inserted it in the lock. The heavy door groaned on its hinges as he pushed it open and stepped in. The late afternoon light penetrated only a few feet onto the interior floor. The space beyond was dim and musty; dust motes hung in the air. Francesco flipped the switch by the door, but there was no electricity. He turned and groped for an oil lamp on a ledge beside the door. Lighting it, he beckoned Denis and Roger. They followed Francesco who held up the lamp and moved toward the far wall. It was hard to make out details of the interior in the dim light, but faded frescos could be discerned on the walls below the arched stone ceiling. The main altar held a painting and two smaller altars on the side walls each had a statue. They approached the main altar where Francesco held the lantern up illuminating the painting housed in an elaborate mortared frame. The composition depicted a dozen men clothed in garments of various muted hues all gazing upward to a white dove invested by a glowing light above a woman who sat in a bright blue flowing gown.

"Are they the apostles and Virgin Mary?" Denis asked.

"Yes. It's the Pentecost," Francesco said. He paused for a few moments. Although he had viewed the painting many times, the experience always felt deeply spiritual. Finally, he said, "Come follow me. I will show you where you'll sleep.

The men followed Francesco around the altar and down a mold-scented corridor hewn into the rock. Their footsteps echoed down the corridor as they passed empty devotional niches, carved into the curvilinear wall. He was sad to see that mold had crept in, staining the walls here and there. They made their way to a pair of cubicle rooms next to each other behind the apse of the church. The rooms, like the rest of the building, were stoned-walled with low arched ceilings. A narrow wooden bunk occupied a slightly raised platform at one end. A small curved window with an iron grate looked out to a darkened sky. Each room had a small, soot-stained hearth, and narrow connected gutters ran the length of the floors. Roger swept his hand over the rough, cold stone wall.

"Drop your packs," Francesco said. "Let's go into the kitchen and make something to eat." They followed him into the kitchen adjacent to the cells. It held a hearth, with wood stacked next to it, table and chairs, and a large wooden cabinet. Reaching into a cabinet, Francesco pulled out some kettles and pots. The drawers held plates, glasses, and utensils. I'll get some water," he said to Denis who bent down to make a fire in the hearth.

That evening they prepared a polenta layered over with a lentil stew. The fire in the hearth created a comfortable atmosphere. It was cold and raining outside. Francesco was happy they had made it to the hermitage before the rain, and he was grateful to spend the night sheltered from the elements. He thought Ennio would be okay in the tholos like the many shepherds before him.

As they ate in the flickering lantern light, Roger commented, "This place is impressive considering it was built in the 13th century, especially in such a rugged and remote area."

"It didn't look like this back then," Francesco said. "It was much smaller and more primitive. You're right though. At three hundred meters, this was a difficult place to get to. The professor told me only one of his monks went with him."

"Interesting. I wonder how they got started," Denis said, taking a spoonful of food.

"From what I learned from the professor, the others eventually showed up. They helped Pietro gather stones from the fields and timber from the woods and formed enclosures in the mountain cave that Pietro had found, or as Pietro claimed, God led him to."

"Hopefully his spirit leads us," Roger said. "I can only imagine how uncomfortable it must have been to live and sleep here, but then again, these men had adopted the severe ascetic lifestyle of the period."

Francesco nodded. "The professor's documents indicated that the first buildings were a chapel for prayer, a gathering place of some kind for them all to meet in, and some crude cubicles for sleeping. They probably built fires on the grounds and took their meals outside before they built this kitchen and dining space. You saw how the mountain rock formed an overhang under which they fashioned stone walls to enclose those early spaces. All of this was added over time as the colony grew. The monks also carved stairs to reach a bell tower and a tiny chapel they formed in a natural recess between two rocky overhangs above the main church. They named it, 'La Capellina Magdalene,' for Mary Magdalene."

"That must have taken some time," Roger said, taking a final spoonful of po"lTeinmtae. is what they had plenty of," Franceso said.

"I am impressed with their engineering," Denis said, lighting a cigarette.

"There were periods of abandonment, decay, and vandalism. Much was lost. It looked a lot different then than now, but here and there you can see remnants of the rough stone work from Pietro's period."

"So finish the story about Pietro. How did he become a pope?" Roger asked.

Francesco was happy that he had hooked Roger with his story. He hoped he could hold his interest through the rest of it.

"It's a fascinating story," Denis said. "They chose him because they were looking for a holy man that the church needed at the time."

"So, Denis you heard that story?" Francesco asked.

"At the prison camp in Sulmona, a fellow prisoner showed me an old pamphlet that had been lying around. It was published in the 1930s and titled *Santo Spirito and Saint Pietro, Celestine V.* One of the guards translated it for me. Is it true then that he is the only pope to have resigned of his own free will?"

"Yes," Francesco said. "Most people had not heard of him before or knew that history. That is why the professor wanted to write the book. So here it is, as we Italians say, 'in due parole,' two words." Francesco slid his chair away from the table, leaned forward with his elbows on his knees to expound on the history of it all. Roger swiveled around and listened intently while Denis sat back.

"As the story goes, Pope Nicholas IV was elected in 1288 as the first Franciscan to the papacy. He figured prominently in world politics of the time, but he died four years later. There were twelve cardinals at the time, and they were meeting in Perugia rather than Rome because of an epidemic of malaria. For two years they debated and could not come to agreement, largely because of political factions among the cardinals who favored candidates from one or the other powerful Orsini or Colonna families.

"Eventually, they settled on Pietro as a neutral," Francesco said. "Pietro's reputation as a holy man of God was fairly well known in Italy at the time. So they came for him. That's the story I always knew as a school boy, but there is another that I learned from the professor."

Roger struck a match that flared, momentarily brightening the dimly lit room. The tobacco glowed red as he ignited the tip of his cigarette. He inhaled and exhaled the scented smoke. "What's that story?" he asked intently, as he extinguished the match.

"The other story," Francesco continued, "is that one of the cardinals, Benedetto Caetani, the future Boniface VIII, the most ambitious, influential and persuasive among them, plotted the selection. Caetani really wanted to be the new pope the professor said, but politically he knew that the time was just not right for him, so he purposely influenced Pietro's choice, knowing that Pietro was not up to the challenge. Caetani was wily according to the professor. He was buying time. At any rate, when a delegation was sent to Pietro at his hermitage he was shocked and initially refused the honor. But in short order he realized he could not refuse an offer from the hand of God. He made one demand— that he be consecrated Pope Celestine V at the church that he had founded in L'Aquila when he had made his way back to Sulmona from his seminary in Rome. They agreed. Then after that, and before traveling to Rome for his formal investiture, he went to Naples to visit Charles II. Charles was the head of the kingdom that included Rome and all of Southern Italy. It was there that the poor choice of Pietro became obvious."

"I thought you said he was a very holy man, absolutely immune to corrupting influences," Denis asked.

"He was, but he was an eighty-year-old man who knew nothing of the world. The professor said he completely lacked the skill to be a pope. I was told none of this stuff in school."

"He would need to be politically and diplomatically competent, not to mention have the leadership and administrative skills to manage the office of pope of the Catholic Church," Denis said.

"True," Francesco responded. "He knew no Latin, just the Italian language, and he seemed completely lost with respect to his duties."

"A good right-hand man could have given him administrative help he needed," Denis said.

"To give you an idea of how he chose to live, he had a wooden hut built in the king's castle. Instead of the regal papal wardrobe, he chose to wear the coarse hair shirt that he wore as a hermit."

"To decline the pomp and power of the office to focus on the austerity and holiness of a life devoted to God makes him quite unique among the history of popes," Roger said.

"Yes, a saint really, but the problem was that he started handing out offices and favors to almost anyone who asked. Then he became more reclusive, refusing to see anybody. It became obvious to him in a short time that he was not up to the politics or the requirements of his office, so he made up his mind to resign. Caetani, it was said, at first counseled him against it, but then within a few days he helped him speak the words of abdication at a gathering of church officials in 1294."

Roger shook his head. "Amazing! This humble man's life tracked through most of the 13th century, and yet I don't remember anything about him in any of my history courses. And what about the Celestine's?"

"Well, the Celestine order lasted only a few hundred years. As for Celestine himself, the story that I was told," Francesco said, "is that he resigned because in his prayers he spoke to the Lord who had given him permission to listen to his conscience and to resign of his own free will, if he thought it would benefit the church."

He explained that the professor believed Caetani took advantage of his spiritual devotion and naiveté by speaking to him through a speaking tube in the hut using an angelic voice of God encouraging him to resign for the sake of the church. But he claimed Caetani convinced the other cardinals that the pope's abdication, although unprecedented, was both completely voluntary and legal; after all, he was the pope and there was no higher authority except for God with whom he had a special relationship. After he became Pope Boniface VIII, Caetani appointed an archbishop, Giles of Rome, who subsequently wrote the definitive work on the right of papal abdication. "The professor showed me his copy of Giles's work."

"What happened to Celestine after he abdicated?" Roger asked.

"Maybe we should finish tomorrow," Francesco said. "I think the professor's tale about Caetani speaking for God is a fantasy. I think Pietro prayed but I don't believe it was Caetani's voice he listened to," he said, smiling. "It's getting late and we should get an early start in the morning. I know Ennio wants to travel that road down the mountain while it is still light."

"Good idea," said Denis, yawning.

Picking up the lantern, Francesco said, "Light a candle and follow me.

They left their chairs and followed Francesco down the dark corridor, the darkness receding in the candle glow; their footsteps echoing as they made their way to the rooms. The cells were very cool and damp, but after the day's long trek, dinner and the story telling, Francesco was ready to sleep. In the still of the night, a wolf howled somewhere on the mountain above them; another answered across the valley.

Francesco lay back against his pack and folded his arms behind his head. His mind drifted back to Caramanico and Annamaria. His thoughts began to arouse him, and he struggled to put her out of his mind as he slowly drifted off to sleep.

****

Denis was restless, his thoughts tinged with a melancholic longing for a former life he could scarcely remember before he left England for Egypt and the war. He got up, took his candle, and wandered back through the hallway into the kitchen where the fire in the hearth had become glowing embers. With nothing to do there, he returned to his cell and tried to settle down. Eventually, he fell asleep and dreamt vividly, vaguely aware that his every thought and spoken word was in the fluent Italian dialect he had spoken with his grandmother; not his everyday English. He found himself drawn back to his youth in England with her. He could picture his mother, father, siblings, and grandparents. In his dreams, he spoke to them in Italian and they responded in English. It did not surprise him that they could understand him or that they responded in English, although he couldn't quite capture the sounds of their voices. He spoke similarly to his friends at school and in the pubs, his mind racing from one scene to the next. He pictured the girls he dated and hoped to see again back in England after the war. Abruptly, that scene was juxtaposed to his family gathered around his grandmother's bed in the hospital when she lay dying of cancer. He was just completing officer training and was about to leave for North Africa. He sobbed as he left the bedside realizing he would not see her again. Then he woke up. It was morning and he discovered sadly, his Italian fluency, so perfect in his dreams, had left him.

****

Outdoors in the square, the rising sun gilded the treetops at the edge of the grounds on the far side of the valley, while the square itself, the church, and monastery remained in the mountain's shadow. In the morning light, the men were able to better appreciate how the church fit so well into the mountainside.

Francesco walked out and joined Roger and Denis. He led them up the outside stone staircase so that they could inspect the upper part of the monastery, the tiny chapel dedicated to Mary Magdalene. At the top of the stairs they had a bird's- eye view of the grounds below and the forested valley vista. They entered the tiny chapel that had been formed in a natural recess of the rocky mountainside. Francesco told them how the Magdalena came to be as they stood side by side in close quarters.

"Can you finish that story from last night?" Roger asked."

"We need to get going, but there is not too much more to tell." He leaned against the cool rock wall and picked up where he left off, telling them the professor said after the abdication in Naples, Pietro wanted to return to his hermitage here in Abruzzo, but Caetano, now the newly elected Pope Boniface VIII, persuaded

Pietro to accompany him to Rome for his formal investiture. His real motive was to keep Pietro with him in Rome, because he was unsure of whether he would be considered the legitimate pope by the people. Pietro had a large following and the idea of an abdication was startling. The professor's research found that it had no precedence. Pietro was no threat. He had sworn his allegiance to Boniface as the one true pope, and so even though he didn't want to live in Rome, he traveled with Boniface to the city. "But within a matter of days he realized how unhappy he was in Rome and longed for his Abruzzo hermitage."

"I'm not surprised," Roger chimed in. "In the Middle Ages, the difference between urban and rural living was immense. Look at this place."

"Boniface would not have cared for what Pietro wanted," Francesco said. "He was furious when Pietro slipped away one evening and immediately sent a contingent of soldiers to bring Pietro back to Rome."

Francesco went on to tell how Pietro was aided in his escape by people who loathed Boniface's arrogance and who held him responsible for Pietro's abdication. Included in this group were the Fraticelli, the spiritual branch of the Franciscans. "This is where the legend of the painter of the altarpiece and frescos here at *Santo Spirito* comes in. Some people think this part of the story is pure fantasy. "

"Fact or fantasy, let's have it," Roger said leaning back against the wall. "This is good stuff. Not everything in history we accept as fact actually happened, at least as depicted. Separating fact from fiction, finding the truth can be difficult, but that's what historians try to do, what your professor was trying to do."

Francesco continued the tale reiterating what he had learned from his mentor that as a holy man and hermit, Pietro attracted all sorts of people, including people on the run from crimes they had committed. One such person is said to have been the artist Fabrizio who lived in Bologna. An art historian who the professor interviewed told him that Fabrizio was a talented young artist, but he was not at all known outside of Bologna. He was a kid who liked to fight— to settle disagreements with his fists or a knife.

Denis who had been listening quietly said, "Sounds like what we call a true bovver boy, a real troublemaker."

"Yes, he was often in trouble, but because his family was very influential, he was usually rescued from his troubles. However, one day the professor said he was involved in an argument with the son of another influential family. In the heat of the moment he killed the boy with his sword. For the first time in his life, he found himself in a situation where his family lacked the influence and means to rescue him, so he was forced to flee the city. He ran home and gathered his most important possessions which included his paint brushes, some paints, and whatever money he had. Then he fled south to Marzibotto, an old Etruscan town where he found shelter. He probably didn't stay there long as he always had to be on the move because clan members of the boy he killed were looking for him.

However, in one of the places where he stopped he learned about Pietro, and how he was welcoming pilgrims in all sorts of circumstances. So he traveled to Abruzzo and made his way to Santo Spirito where he sought sanctuary. He never told Pietro his true story. Pietro accepted him and he became one of his followers for a time."

"History doesn't have to be boring," Roger said. "Sometimes you don't have to make this stuff up. What happened to Fabrizio?"

"As *Santo Spirito* was built, Fabrizio came to decorate the walls with frescos and the painting you saw above the altar. It was a new style of painting, the art historian said, one that would be labeled devout realism. It was a style that would be brought to greater fruition by Caravaggio three hundred years later, according to what the professor learned."

"He seems to have mellowed at *Santo Spirito*," Denis said.

"I'm sure that Pietro's piety, gentleness, and peace rubbed off on him as it did for many of the pilgrims who become his followers.

"But after spending some time at Santo Spirito, Fabrizio longed for his old life as an artist in the big city. The life of a hermit wasn't easy. It took good health, stamina, and a strong spiritual commitment. Pietro knew that Fabrizio had the health and stamina but not the commitment, and so with his blessings, Fabrizio left and went to Naples where he was not known. There he resumed his career and as his talent drew attention from wealthy patrons of the arts, he was commissioned to provide paintings at the palace. It was there he reunited with Pietro who was now Pope Celestine. When he discovered Pietro's unhappy circumstances he sympathized with him, but at the time he felt helpless to do anything to ease his misery. However, when he learned of Pietro's escape in Rome, he decided to go to his aid. He rushed to find him in the hills outside the city, and he helped him to find shelter in various monasteries including Benedict's Monte Casino."

"Hard to believe that an old man in his 80s could keep on the run from the troops," Roger said. "I know how hard it was for Denis and me to escape the camp and get to Caramanico."

"Pietro was fortunate in having a strong body that enabled him to sustain the years of tough living. However, you're right; in his eighties it was difficult for him to keep a step ahead of the pope's troops. They remained on his trail for months. Eventually, he realized that he would find no peace in Italy, and he made the decision to leave for Greece where he hoped to live the sort of spiritual life he so much craved."

"Well, we know he never got there," Denis said. "What happened?"

"The professor said while awaiting a ship on the Adriatic, the Pope's men found him and his small entourage. They tried to arrest Pietro, and in the ensuing confrontation between Pietro's men and the pope's soldiers, Fabrizio made a brave attempt to save Pietro from capture. He was as skilled a swordsman as he was a painter. But he and his group were woefully outnumbered and in the melee Fabrizio was stabbed from behind."

"What a terrible ending," Roger said.

"Not entirely," Francesco said. "A priest once pointed out that in laying down his life for Pietro, Fabrizio did redeem himself—you know the scripture 'no greater love… than to lay down your life for a friend.'" And Pietro finally found what he longed for. After the capture, Boniface had Pietro taken to Naples and imprisoned in the castle of Fumone. The professor said the building is still there today in the harbor at Naples. That is where he died there two years later."

Roger said, "Great story, Francesco. And thanks to you, Ennio and the others along the way, we have avoided Pietro's fate so far. I just hope our escape has a better ending."

"It would appear that in the end it worked out well for Pietro," Denis said.

"Yes we think it did," Francesco said. "Although he was unable to return here to his beloved Abruzzo, Celestine was able to find the solitude and serenity he craved in that castle. We always believed that he was able to spend the final months of his life in prayer and contemplation, as he did when he was a hermit here at Santo Spirito."

"It's nice to think that he had a happy ending to his life," Denis said.

"Isn't that what we all pray for?"

"His life would make an interesting book," Roger said. "I can see why that professor wanted to write it." He was about to ask a question when they heard a crunch of tires on the grounds below them.

"Who is that?" Denis asked Francesco.

"I have no idea."

"Wait a minute," Denis said, as he stepped to the small open balcony that allowed a view of the courtyard below. He saw two German officers emerge from a black Mercedes with Nazi fender flags. The officer on the passenger side came around to the driver's side. Both men paused to light a cigarette and leaned against the car in conversation.

"What's happening?" Francesco asked.

"Two SS officers are standing down by their car smoking and talking."

"Did we leave the door locked?" Roger asked.

"No, I left it open. Our packs are still inside," Francesco said. "What are they talking about?" Roger asked.

"I'm trying to make it out, something about a painting," Denis said. "I think I heard 'das Bild, the painting,' but I can't be sure."

"We can't let them steal the altar painting," Francesco said. His words were a plea that matched his anguished look. "That painting has survived so much— the fires, the vandalism, even theft. Miraculously, it was always found, restored, and rehung here. It means too much; we can't let them have it!" He grabbed Denis's arm hoping he could do something to stop the theft from happening. He knew how hard the people in his village would take the loss.

"Are they still out there?" Roger asked.

Denis looked again. The men had thrown their unfinished cigarettes to the ground, stomped them out and gone to the door. One of the two officers reached into his pocket and pulled out a large key. When he placed the key into the lock, he seemed surprised that the door was unlocked. "They just went inside."

****

Roger decided he needed to take action. He was combat-tested where Denis wasn't. He huddled the three together and whispered, "If we want to save that painting, we have to kill them. They have guns and we don't."

Francesco grimaced. He repeated his plea that the painting not be stolen, but fear clearly showing on his face he asked Roger, "Why do it that way? Is there another way, any other way?"

Denis put his hand on Francesco's shoulder to comfort him. "Maybe we just overpower them, tie them up, take the painting and hide it. Then we get back to Ennio and make tracks before they get free."

"You know when they come around they will report to their commander and that will trigger an all-out search for us," Roger responded. "We are carrying a lot of baggage with the sheep. Our disguises may not save us under these new circumstances."

"Still, it's a risky plan. Maybe we just wait it out until they leave," Denis said.

"That's an option, but of course, they steal the painting," Roger said. Roger tried to gauge their thoughts from their facial expressions, hoping they would see his point of view. Dull thuds and shuffling sounds emanated from the church beneath them.

"We need to make up our minds. It sounds like they are taking the painting down."

Finally Denis said, "Okay mate, I don't have a better idea."

Francesco recoiled against the chapel wall, his hands cupping his face.

Denis looked at him sympathetically. "I want you to come down with us, but then cross over the yard and hide in the trees. If this doesn't work, we are captured or don't survive, you have to get back to Ennio, tell him what happened and go back to Caramanico. Pierluigi needs to know."

"C'mon let's go, time's a wasting," Roger said. "Lead the way, Denis. When we get down there, Francesco, I want you to hide like Denis said. Understand?"

They left the chapel and stealthily descended the outside staircase. Roger pointed Francesco to the trees across the courtyard. After Francesco left them, Roger told Denis what he wanted him to do and followed him around to the main entrance. He picked up a baseball-sized rock and handed it to Denis. "Use this," he said.

They positioned themselves on either side of the doorway and waited. It was a clear, cool morning, the sky overcast gray, the ground still wet from the overnight rain. The door was half open. They listened intently to the conversation between the two men inside. Then the talking stopped, replaced by shuffling sounds on the floor just beyond them. Denis looked across to Roger and mouthed, "They're coming, are you ready?"

Roger nodded and gave thumbs up.

The back of an officer appeared in profile as he slowly backed out the door, one arm below and the other clutching the top edge of the large framed painting.

Denis, with his back to the wall, suddenly pivoted and swung his right arm in an arc delivering a heavy blow to the back of the officer's skull. His hat flew with the crack of the rock and the painting fell noisily as the officer crumpled to the ground.

In that instant, as the painting fell from the officer's hand, Roger sprung from his position and was through the door before the surprised second officer realized what was happening. He fell upon him and brought him swiftly to the ground, wrapping his arm in a choke hold around the officer's neck. The officer struggled. He had dropped his end of the painting which had fallen over on the stone floor. He tried desperately to loosen Roger's grip with his arms as his body went rigid against Roger, his legs kicked, and his face became cyanotic. Finally he gave up the struggle and went limp. Roger knelt beside him for a moment and felt his neck for a pulse. There was none. Then he scampered outside to where Denis hovered over the unconscious officer.

Roger looked back and across the yard to where Francesco was hiding. Subtly, shielding himself from Francesco's vantage point, he placed his arm about the officer's neck. "I don't want the kid to see this, Denis, so try and block his view." Then he gave the officer's neck a sudden forceful twist. "That should do it." Roger lowered the officer's head to the ground. He and Denis rose and waved for Francesco to come join them.

****

Francesco saw what happened and horrified, tried to steel himself to calmness. "Are they dead?" he asked, as he approached with an I-know-what-you-did look, turning from one lifeless Nazi to the other. He was deeply pained at the thought they had killed two men for stealing a painting. Deeply conflicted, his mind searched for a rationalization. If I had not brought up *Santo Spirito* this killing would not have happened. But this was not any old painting; it had great meaning for us. The hermitage was not part of Pierluigi's plan, but could it have been in God's plan? he wondered. He wished there had been another way, but he understood that he was with men who had experienced the reality of war. Roger was a combat soldier and killing was what he had to do when it was necessary. He only hoped this incident qualified.

"Yes, I dare say they are," Denis said.

"Let's get on with it," Roger said. "We need to rehang the painting and then get these bodies back in the car. We have to stage a bad accident."

After the painting was deposited by the altar, Roger and Denis picked up the officer by the church door. Francesco held the car door open as they placed him in the passenger seat. Francesco closed the door and waited while Denis and Roger placed the second officer on the front seat behind the wheel and Roger took the keys from his trousers.

Francesco said, "I want to come with whoever is driving to find the best place."

Roger signaled Francesco to get into the back seat. "I need to get something in the kitchen," he said jogging into the church. Returning, he got into the front seat squeezing the soldier toward the middle and started the car as Denis backed away. He circled out of the courtyard and headed down the road.

"Stop here!" Francesco said, pointing to a gap in the trees flanking the roadbed. He got out of the car with Roger.

"Let's make this quick," Roger said. "Find me a stick to let the air out of the tires."

Francesco handed a twig to Roger who used it to emit the air from the right front tire, finally puncturing it with a knife he had retrieved from the church kitchen. Then he opened the driver's side door and maneuvered the officer into a position behind the wheel. While Francesco watched in trepidation, he put the car in gear and sent it over the embankment. It careened noisily down the rocky slope, snapping shrubs and saplings, finally coming to rest against a large tree trunk. He scampered down to check his handiwork. Francesco hoped that if the bodies were found, it would look like a real road accident and not the work of partisans.

When they got back to the church, Francesco saw through the dust-filled light of the open door that Denis had positioned the painting on top of the altar. It looked undamaged, and Francesco felt good about that. While Roger and Denis stood on the altar and lifted it to its former position, Francesco directed them to the heavy hook that had supported it. "Just like nothing happened," he said happily.

"Well, mates, that's jolly good, about as good as we can do," Denis said looking at Francesco. "Hopefully, Pietro, your Celestine will be pleased."

That didn't help Francesco rationalize what had been done. He told himself again that it was war, not murder, but it troubled his conscience, even as he knew the church teaching that killing was not a sin in a just war. "I hope no one else steals it."

"Maybe we can cut the canvas out of the frame, roll it up and hide it somewhere here in the monastery," Roger said.

"It's so old and not in the best of shape. I would be afraid of ruining it," Denis said.

"When I get back to Roccamorice I will warn our priest," Francesco said.

Roger said, "We need to get going. Ennio is going to wonder where we have been."

The road back was littered with wet autumn leaves that had fallen from the bordering hardwood trees. They stopped to survey the wreck in the brush and trees below them. It was quiet except for the trilling of insects and the occasional chirp of a bird. Francesco thought the wreck would not be easily spotted from the road, but he was worried. If the Germans find it, he thought, they might not consider it an accident. But there was nothing more to be done. The side trip to the hermitage had seemed like a good idea to him yesterday, but it hadn't turned out well. He was feeling hollow inside. As he walked down the road with Roger and Denis to rejoin Ennio, he thought about his life in his occupied village. He was often hungry, but not in danger—at least not real danger. There might have been options with the German officer in town if they had taken the time to think. I shouldn't have walked away, he thought.

Chapter 10

Ennio had watched Francesco and the men walk off to Santo Spirito and turned his attention to the sheep. They grazed easily between the rocks of the meadow while the dogs moved about the perimeter forcing the strays back to the main body. Satisfied that the situation was well in hand, he walked to the woods at the edge of the meadow to gather some wood for a fire. He placed the branches close to one of the *tholos* he had chosen to spend the night. He ate sparingly from the *scarmorza* and bread he carried then lit the fire. As night fell, he made one more round of the flock then retired to his layered stone abode.

The loud barking of the dogs roused him in the middle of the night. As he rolled over in the fog of sleep, he realized the cause of the trouble—wolves!

He rose to his knees, grabbed his staff and bolted outside. In weak moonlight, he was barely able to visualize silhouettes of sheep in the landscape. He sensed the flock moving restlessly, and he cued himself to the dogs' ceaseless barking. Running in their direction, he stumbled on one of the rocks and fell spread-eagle on the ground, losing his staff. He quickly righted himself and fumbled for his staff in the dark. Finding it, he resumed his sprint to the dogs that were chasing back and forth at the perimeter of the flock.

He called the dogs; they stopped and turned their attention to him. Clearly agitated and breathing hard, they scampered toward him as he stumbled upon a lamb lying upon the ground. He knelt beside it and put his hands on the body. The dogs stood by sniffing and whimpering, altering their gazes at him with backward glances toward the woods. Shallow periodic breaths signaled that the lamb was in its death throes. He swept his left hand along the body and encountered warm, sticky blood at the neck and throat; his right hand felt bite marks on the lamb's rump.

The work of a wolf pair he thought, likely a breeding pair whose pups were nearby. Wolf predations were a fact of life for the shepherds of Abruzzo, but this did not assuage his anger. His dogs had prevented additional kills and he was grateful for that. He missed his pistols, but realized they would not have helped this time. Before the war, he and fellow shepherds had taken advantage of bounties the Italian government paid for each wolf they killed, but that had come to an end.

He struck the ground in anger. There was nothing more he could do but put the animal out of its misery. Usually, lambs died quickly from blood loss after a bite to the throat, but the dogs must have chased the wolves off before they could sink their teeth more deeply. He took his knife from his waist and finished the animal. Then he dragged it back to his camp site with the dogs trailing after him. He washed the stain and smell of blood from his hands and waited till dawn.

At first light, he and his dogs rounded up the sheep that had strayed. Then he set about to butcher the dead animal, taking enough meat to last for a day or two. He buried the rest and sat down to wait for the return of Francesco and the men.

He hated losing sheep for any reason. The German confiscation was something he could not prevent, and in his mind he had come to terms with it. But these sheep were not his. He knew that if not for Pierluigi, he and his wife would be in serious financial straits, so he felt especially bad. He thought his friend would understand, knowing the risks as a sheep owner. Still it pained him—sheep were the essence of his pastoral life.

****

The rising sun brought with it the clatter of a party traveling up the road. As the group came into view about a hundred or so meters across the meadow, Ennio moved to his knees to get a better view. A column of men carrying crates on their shoulders, some with heavily laden backpacks, were trudging along accompanied by a half-dozen German soldiers carrying rifles. A two-wheeled, wooden cart drawn by a mule brought up the rear. Ennio assumed that it was one of the work parties from Roccamorice delivering supplies to the Block Haus that Francesco had told him about. Suddenly, loud shouts carried across the meadow and the column came to a stop. One of the German guards unshouldered his rifle and scampered up from the rear to a man in the middle of the column who had turned and dropped his pack. An unintelligible exchange between the two men was punctuated by the man's vigorous head shaking, his arms rising and falling with clenched fists, while the guard shouted commands, leveled his rifle and pushed it against the man's chest forcing him to take a step back. The man stood there defiantly for a moment and again shook his head in refusal. Then he abruptly bolted off to the opposite side of the road and disappeared on the down slope, dropping from Ennio's view. The other men in the column who had stopped and lowered their burdens to the ground now clustered together and joined their voices in a chorus of shouts. The German soldier had raised his rifle to his shoulder and took aim down the slope. Two other soldiers rushed up and did the same. Three cracks in rapid succession rang out and reverberated off the surrounding hillsides. Ennio's blood suddenly pulsed faster as he watched two of the three soldiers run off in the direction of the shots and disappear.

Time seemed to stand still as he kept looking in their direction. Then the two soldiers reappeared on the road dragging a limp body which they dropped to the ground. The men tried to gather around their fallen comrade, but they were held off by the soldiers who shouted at them and forced them back into line. Two of the men were ordered to pick up the body and place it on a cart which had been brought up from the rear. Ennio watched anxiously as the driver was made to turn the cart around and head back toward Roccamorice. If only that man could have persevered like the others, he thought. He watched the work party reassemble under the direction of the German guards, and slowly resume their journey up the road toward the Bloc Haus.

****

When Francesco and the men reached Ennio midmorning, they saw that he was troubled. "Bad news," Ennio said. First he told them the story of the wolf attack.

"I heard wolves howl last night, but never gave it another thought. I'm sorry," Francesco said.

"Bloody bad luck, mate," Denis said. "Sorry for your loss."

"Me too, Ennio," Roger added.

"What can you do?" Ennio replied. Then he proceeded to tell them the story of the shooting he had witnessed. Francesco's jaw dropped at the retelling, obviously stunned at the news.

"Who was it?" he asked.

"I don't know, Francesco. I couldn't tell from where I was kneeling. Even if I had been up close I couldn't tell you. I don't know anybody in that town except you."

Francesco looked worried. He was wondering if he should abandon one responsibility—helping Ennio—for another, contacting the family of the slain man. But which family? Several hundred remained in the village following the peak years of immigration when the country seemed to be bleeding out its population. He was still processing the incident at Santo Spirito and the remorse of walking away from home. He would need to be careful if he went back. "Maybe I should go home. We are not that far south. I can get there before dark."

Denis looked concerned. He and Roger gathered around Francesco and Denis put his arms on his shoulders. 'It's a bloody shame, mate," Denis said, "but there is nothing you can do now; the people in your town will deal with it soon enough when that wagon gets back there. Meanwhile, we need you to get us through these mountains."

Francesco realized that Denis was right. It had happened before, the townspeople would deal with it, and they would find and console the man's family. It was an excuse, one he didn't need.

Ennio walked over to the group. "From what you told me, Francesco, we should have enough time to get over to the road to Guardiagrele, downhill and out of sight before the next group departs your village. No sense in risking more contact with the Germans, even with the papers of transit. Let's pack up and get the sheep moving."

By late morning they reached the old road that descended down the mountain to the east. The peaks of the Maiella formed a dramatic backdrop to the coniferous forests and alpine meadows around Passo Lanciano. In the distance the landscape of low hills and meadows sloped gradually to the Adriatic Sea, barely visible at the horizon.

The road quickly narrowed to a track through the forest forcing the sheep into an elongated profile. The dogs worked the outer edges barking at strays wandering off among the trees, herding them back into the pack. The narrow defile and dense woods on either side made for slow going. Gradually, the pines gave way to hardwood as they descended to lower elevation.

It was late afternoon when they emerged from the edge of the woods to a sloping meadow. Before them in the distance was the town of Guardiagrele. The cluster of stone buildings illuminated by the glow of the late afternoon sun appeared to be sitting upon a terrace amid the foothills. The land around the town, was a patchwork of empty grain fields, olive groves and vineyards bordered by banks of trees. Scattered farm houses with terra cotta tiled roofs and faded painted shutters were situated at the edges of the fields.

The road now became wider as it traversed the low alpine meadow, but Ennio halted the flock and told the men that it was too late to travel further. The clear sky at sunset promised a rain-free night, but it would be cold. There was plenty of wood to gather where they stopped and they were able to make a fire they hoped would last the night.

Ennio fashioned skewers from saplings and soaked them in the natural tank by the edge of the road where the animals were drinking. Soon the aroma of roasted lamb wafted in the air. Roger and Denis took potatoes and carrots from their pack, sliced them and boiled them over the fire in the kettle on the grate that Ennio had carried in his pack. There was plenty of meat and vegetables to share; even the dogs enjoyed the change from the dry food that Ennio had been feeding them.

"This is the best meal we've had since we left Caramanico," Denis said. "I was never fond of lamb in England, but this is good. What do you call these?"

"*Li spetucci,*" Ennio responded.

"Lamb shish kebab we call them back home," Roger said. "Our farm workers introduced the style to us. They flavored theirs with olive oil, garlic and wine."

"The only thing better than this is *porchetta,* what we call roast suckling pig, or what some would prefer—*la grabetta,* roast suckling goat," Francesco said.

"Francesco," Denis said with a frown, "I'm picturing a baby goat—I don't think I could eat it, but I hope you will enjoy those classic Abruzzo meats again."

Francesco laughed. "It must be hunger that causes us to think about those special things we miss."

"Actually, here in Abruzzo we don't eat much meat," Ennio said, primarily for the benefit of Denis and Roger. "Maybe up north, but it's not that available for most of us here. We eat a lot of vegetables and pasta."

"And lately not much of that," Francesco said.

Finishing his meal and wiping his hands, Denis asked, "What are the plans for tomorrow?"

"I am hoping we will make contact with the partisans around Guardiagrele," Ennio responded. "Francesco, start out at first light, and find one of those farms we spotted that looks promising. Explain our needing to move the sheep to Casoli. Ask if we can overnight in their field. It will give us more time to find the partisans."

Francesco didn't think he would have trouble finding a place. "What if they say no?"

"Go on to another and do the same. Eventually, someone will be sympathetic. Once you find that place come back and guide us."

The evening had grown very cold. The men built up a base of bedding from the leaf litter on the forest floor and settled down to sleep by the fire with their mantellos wrapped about them. Sometime in the middle of the night they were awoken by the crackling staccato of gunfire in the distance. Rising to look, they saw flashes of light in the distance that seemed to be near the outskirts of Guardiagrele—the town itself was not visible in the moonless night.

"Those look like illumination grenades," said Roger. "It can't be the British, the army could not have gotten this far north. But from the looks of it, it looks like a real skirmish."

The incident lasted only a few minutes; the stillness of the night soon enveloped them again. The fire had died down. Stirring the embers and tossing on some logs, Denis turned to Francesco, and said, "That gunfire is something you need to check on tomorrow."

"I'll see what I can find out," Francesco said, as he laid back down.

The morning broke gray and cold, a harbinger of the days to come. The men awoke to find that the fire had gone out and needed to be rebuilt. After a breakfast of the remaining lamb meat and bread, Francesco repacked, bid farewell, and started down the road toward Guardiagrele.

The gray flat sky extended from horizon to horizon; Francesco had no expectation he would see any sun all day. The road ahead curved down around one of the foothills and disappeared behind it. He walked on briskly, anticipating he would soon encounter one of the farms he had spotted from the alpine vantage point the day before.

As he reached the lower elevations, it began to drizzle. He covered himself with his *mantello* and walked on as the drizzle became soft, continuous rain. He thought back to the discussions at Pierluigi's about the ravines and the worries of rising rivers. He came to a country lane that led through wooded acreage. Glancing up the lane, he spotted a stone structure beyond the trees, a shepherd's cottage he thought. An empty stone shed with a thatched roof and a corral were separated from the cottage by a packed dirt courtyard. The entire complex was invested by a low stone wall. There were no animals around, but the place looked promising. It was isolated and fairly well hidden from the main road. He decided it was safe enough to make an inquiry.

He knocked on the door, and while he waited for a response, he glanced south and saw the very top of a bell tower in the distance; the town of Guardiagrele was only a few kilometers away.

The door opened and he was greeted by a thin, haggard man whose clothing hung loosely on him. His wife stood to the side and a step behind him. She wore a man's much-too-large suit jacket over a black dress. A black scarf covered her hair and black stockings sagged on her legs. Francesco had seen that sad look before—a woman in mourning, now shabbied by the deprivation of war.

Francesco introduced himself and related the journey he was on with his fellow shepherds. He asked if the couple would allow his group with the sheep to spend the evening in their pasture. He realized from their appearance that they had little, and so he assured them that they wanted nothing else from them. They would be no trouble and would leave the following day. The man and his wife seemed surprised that Francesco's group still had their sheep. Theirs had been confiscated by the Germans weeks ago. "We have papers of transit signed by a high-ranking German officer," Francesco said.

The man's wife appeared fearful and tugged at his coat sleeve, beckoning him to step inside.

"Excuse me for a moment. I must speak to my wife," he said, as he stepped inside. Before he closed the door, he asked, "Where do you intend to bring your sheep?"

"To a farm near Casoli," Francesco responded.

Standing next to the door, Francesco could hear raised voices; then silence. He was worried the couple would deny his request. He looked around the rather impoverished property and noticed the lack of a barnyard smell. A moment later the man reopened the door.

"You seem too young to be doing this. Do you know there are lots of German troops in the area?" the man said. "Between here and there you would be lucky to get through unnoticed."

"We have papers if they ask. For tonight we would just be happy to stay out here and be quiet," Francesco said.

"We have no food or anything else to offer you and we don't need any more trouble with the Germans."

"We don't need food, just a place to rest for a short time," Francesco pleaded. "My friends and I could use your shed for shelter and the corral for the sheep."

The man turned to look back at his wife who remained expressionless and said nothing. He was hesitant mulling over the implications and possibilities. "If you have official papers," he said finally. "Bring your sheep and your friends, but you must leave tomorrow." His wife stepped back, leaving him facing Francesco at the door.

Francesco's face brightened. *"Grazie molto,"* he said, happy he would be able to tell Ennio he had been successful. As he turned to leave he asked, "Can you tell me what happened last evening? We heard gunfire."

"Yes. It was close, maybe just a few kilometers away. I got up and went to the door. But it was dark and I saw nothing. It was over quickly. It may have been an attack by the *partigiani* on the German camp near Guardiagrele."

"Good to know. We need to avoid that, but one of us needs to get into Guardiagrele."

"If you follow the road you came in on, you will cross the main north-south road. Just on the other side, on the road into the town you will see the camp. Stay clear of the road to bypass the camp."

"What do you know about *partigiani* in Guardiagrele?"

"Only that they are said to be living somewhere in the hills around the town. What happened last night could have been one of their attacks."

Backing away, he said, *"Grazie."*

As he walked back up the road, it began to rain harder. The ground turned to mud that clinged to his shoes as he trudged on. The autumn weather was not cooperating with the plan; he feared swollen rivers and an early winter. He thought about his brother and hoped he had harvested the grapes with the other men in the village, but he wondered if many families would bother making wine this year with the confiscating Germans in town. Still, making it would be important for morale, and everyone could use the calories.

He heard the dogs first, their barks penetrating the gray mist. Then he came upon them—dogs and men dripping wet, hair plastered to their foreheads.

"I found a place to stay for a day or so," he told them enthusiastically. "A small cottage with a man and his wife, best of all a stone shed where we can get out of the rain."

Francesco told them what he had learned. The man and his wife were rather fearful, the woman especially, but reluctantly he was given permission.

Francesco continued, "We are going to have to be more careful on the road now because there are German military units in the area." He mentioned the German unit that was camped a few kilometers from where they would be staying. "But the good news is that there are *partigiani* in the area too," he said excitedly. "I don't know where they are exactly but I'd like to find out."

Denis said, "One of us has to go look while the rest of us stay here."

"I thought we agreed that I would scout ahead," Francesco said.

"You're right, Francesco. You should be the one to go," Ennio said. Then he called the dogs to begin moving the sheep. Denis and Roger grabbed their packs and followed Francesco who took up shepherding the flock with Ennio.

When they arrived at the farm, they herded some of the sheep into the corral, the remainder they left in the pasture with the dogs to guard them. Denis and Roger settled in the shed looking happy to be out of the rain, while Ennio and Francesco walked across the muddy courtyard and knocked at the cottage door. The owner had seen them coming and opened the door. Beads of rain drops fell from Francesco's hat brim as he greeted him and introduced Ennio who thanked the man for allowing them to use his pasture and shed. "Our two companions are in the shed," Ennio said. "We won't be any trouble. We will be on our way tomorrow. But I wanted to ask if you could give me the name of anyone in Guardiagrele who might put us in contact with the *partigiani* you mentioned to Francesco?"

The man was hesitant, his face reflecting concern. After a few moments of silence he said, "I overheard something in the tobacco shop. Two men were talking about it. I don't know their names."

"Where is the shop?" Francesco asked.

"I don't know if I should say anymore. As I told you yesterday, I don't need any more trouble from the Germans."

"I promise, we will be very cautious," Ennio said.

Silence again. Then he said, "The shop is in the piazza near the cathedral, but why take the risk?"

Francesco interrupted. "We need to know which roads would be safest and where we can find the next shelter south of here."

"Check with the tobacconist. He may know what you are looking for." Francesco and Ennio thanked him and crossed back across the muddy yard to the shed. Roger and Denis had changed their wet clothes. The garments were hanging on a rope they had strung across the back of the shed. The men were sitting on make-shift seats on the straw-strewn floor sharing a tin of sardines.

"I think he knows more than he wants to tell us," Francesco said. "But when he told me he overheard a conversation at a tobacco shop by the cathedral, I thought of something that Pierluigi said. Do you remember he said the priests were joining in the resistance by sheltering people in their rectory?"

"I do remember that," said Denis. "Do you think that's a possibility in Guardiagrele?"

"I don't know, but it's convenient that the tobacco shop is close by the cathedral."

Ennio said to Francesco. "If you nose about the church you might find something, a clue or a lead to someone. If not you can always try the tobacco shop,"

Roger said. "It's risky, but no risk, no reward."

"Well, the priest is the one stranger I would be comfortable asking," Ennio said. "I think he might open up to Francesco. But first you need to dry out and get some sleep."

"If I leave in the early morning while it is still dark, I think I can reach the town after sunrise," he said, pointing to the outline of the elevated town towers in the distance. "That should be enough time to ask around and get back here."

Denis frowned. "I wish there was some bloody way either Roger or I could come with you in case you run into trouble," he said.

"Don't worry, Francesco said. "No one will pay me any attention if I'm alone. If I don't get back by nightfall, you can come looking for me, but be on your best Italian behavior," he said, grinning.

As night fell, they built a fire by the shed's exposed opening, and ate the remainder of the roasted lamb. After dinner the men smoked and chatted while Francesco laid his bed roll on the straw. He thought of Annamaria as he did each time he took a break, but fatigued from the day's trekking, he quickly fell asleep.

****

It was a cold, and starless night when Francesco was nudged awake by Ennio. The rain had stopped.

"It's time for you to leave. Be careful," he whispered. "Don't take any chances and remember—use good judgment!"

It was too dark to see Francesco roll his eyes, but surely the scoff was audible. He retraced his steps along the muddy path that led away from the cottage to the country lane. In the dark, he could barely see his feet in front of him, but his eyes gradually adjusted to the shapes and outline of trees, shrubs, and rocks. The lane was strewn with fallen leaves and puddles of water.

In a short time he reached the main north-south road. He followed it south until he came to the junction with a road that led east. The sign post had arrowed planks pointing in various directions. He got up close and strained his eyes to find the one to Guardiagrele. Satisfied, he started down the road in the dark.

About an hour into the walk he suddenly heard multiple crunching footsteps quickly crossing from the woods up ahead of him. He stopped and crouched in fear, his heart pounding as the vague outline of a half-dozen men crossed the road. From his kneeling position in the dark, Francesco looked left trailing after the men. In the distance he could make out silhouetted tents dimly illuminated by soft light. He presumed it was the German military encampment the shepherd at the cottage had told him about.

He remained fixated on the road, holding his breath, pondering what to do as minutes passed in silence. A sudden explosion rocked the night and lit up the sky above the camp. The burst of light, fire, and smoke was followed by the crack of rifles. Moments later rifle fire was returned from deeper in the camp followed by the stutter of a machine gun. The explosion frightened Francesco who had dropped to his knees, his blood pulsating fast. He rose and bolted off the road and into the edge of the woods to his right where he ducked down behind a tree, his heart still beating rapidly. Then he saw several men running back toward him. He held his breath. The flashes of gunfire from the camp trailed after the men, the bullets whining in the air and thudding the earth around them as they ran toward him.

In the distance, Francesco saw the movement of men silhouetted against the fire in the camp behind them. *Whoomp!* The sound was followed by a hiss and then an explosion on the far side of the road that sent chunks of dirt flying into the air. Someone yelled as a few men crossed the road crouching low and zigzagged into the woods passing him on both sides.

He was scared; not knowing what to do, he lay on the ground behind the tree taking shallow breaths as a second shell exploded on the near side of the road. Clumps of dirt splattered against his tree and the aroma of ignited gun powder filled the air. A third shell shattered the tree behind him sending broken branches flying in all directions. Then silence. He wondered where the men had disappeared to. He listened for footsteps. Nothing. Looking out toward the German camp, no one seemed to be in pursuit.

Rising cautiously, he took a few steps in the dark with outstretched arms feeling his way deeper into the woods. There was no sign of the men and he decided not to follow after them. He wanted to press on to the town, but he knew he would have trouble negotiating the lamp less streets and blacked-out windows. Daylight would come soon enough he thought; then he could go into town to check things out. His heart rate slowed to normal as he sat down and leaned back against a tree to wait for dawn.

As the first traces of gray replaced the black eastern sky, he rose and walked through the woods, paralleling the road until he was well beyond the German camp. Then he crossed over and started up the road. The village of Guardiagrele loomed ahead. The rising sun gilded the cathedral bell tower above the tan stone buildings with shades of tan, gray and terra-cotta-colored tile roofs. He decided the cathedral, not the tobacco shop would be his initial target. He was anxious to see the village. His father was a young man his age when he had gone there to apprentice with a wrought iron craftsman. He remembered how he had praised the town's charm.

The slope leading up to the village was a mixed-patterned landscape of meadows, orchards, and grape trellis. The musty scent of the *vendemia*, the local wine harvest, was in the air and donkeys pulling carts laden with purple and indigo-hued Montepulciano grapes passed Francesco on the road. He stopped by a trellis that still had grapes and plucked a bunch from the vine. He nibbled the purple fruit as he continued up the road toward the town. The grapes were past the peak of flavor, but still had a jammy taste. He finished the last one, tossed the stem aside and passed under the town portal on a cobblestone street bordered by attached stone houses and shops.

The cathedral of Santa Maria Maggiore was an impressive medieval gothic structure that dominated the main piazza. The façade had three levels with a huge stained glass window in the center and a rose window at the top. The main doors at the base of the façade were closed and locked, so Francesco walked into the arched portico at the side. There he found another entrance to the church. The Baroque interior awed him as he stepped inside.

The church interior was cool and had the familiar scent of burning candles and musty hymnals. A few people were seated in the pews before the main altar waiting for Mass to begin. Francesco moved down the side aisle and found the sacristy door at the side of the altar. He knocked softly and then turned the handle to open the door a crack so he could peer in. A priest, a burly middle-aged man with florid cheeks and beard, and a young altar boy were putting on their vestments. "*Mi scusi,*" Francesco said, timidly.

"Yes, can I help you?" the priest responded in a gruff voice.

"I have something I need to ask you."

"Can it wait? It's time for Mass to begin," his tone communicated impatience.

"Yes, of course. I will wait here."

"No. It's better if you come to Mass. We need all the prayers we can get for the war to end."

"Okay, *grazie,* Father." Francesco left the sacristy and found a seat in the church. He felt guilty as he remembered the promise to his mother to pray. He had always taken comfort in his faith, but he was not especially devout; his parish priest might have labeled him *tiepido,* lukewarm. But prayer, for his mother and others in town, had become the one solace from the misery of everyday life during the occupation. He knew many that prayed for help and guidance, so now, he, too quietly whispered a familiar litany.

The early morning weekday Mass was sparsely attended; mostly elderly women were scattered about the pews nearest the altar. In the first row, nuns in their black habits, their faces framed by white wimples, moved their lips in prayer. As the priest and altar boy made their appearance and began the Mass, Francesco's mind drifted to thoughts of how he would discuss his mission with the priest after Mass. How should he pose the delicate issue of partisans? Did he know any in town? Would he introduce him? How much should he reveal about the journey he was on, and should he say the false shepherds were British POWs?

The priest's homily was about Matthew's gospel account of Jesus and his disciples walking along at Caesarea Philippi. "Who do the people say that

I am?" Jesus asks Peter. The acknowledgment that Jesus gave to the answer of that question, the priest said, was crucial to the framing of early Christianity and the Kingdom of God that Jesus preached. Would that kingdom really ever come? Francesco wondered.

When the Mass ended and the people filed out, Francesco returned to the sacristy. Knocking and entering, he saw the priest had removed his vestments and was bidding the altar boy farewell as he left through a side door.

"Please have a seat," the priest said, indicating a set of chairs in the corner of the room. "I don't recognize you. Do you live here?"

"No, Father, I have come from Caramanico."

"I see. Well, I am Father Di Tullio," he said, extending his hand. "What is your name?"

"Francesco."

"You are a long way from home, Francesco. What brings you here?"

"My companions and I are driving our sheep to a farm near Casoli." Francesco felt he could trust the priest. So Francesco told him about leaving Roccamorice for the Sanelli home in Caramanico, finding Denis and Roger there, and how he and Ennio were helping them to escape through the Maiella disguised as shepherds. "We got here after, he said, "but we need some help to go on."

The priest listened, not interrupting Francesco as he finished his story. He said gruffly: "Why have you come to me?"

"We are worried about the Germans between here and Casoli; can you help us?"

"In what way?"

"Last evening I saw a partisan attack on the German camp outside the town. Can you put me in touch with any of them?"

"What makes you think I know any of them?" the priest asked, looking annoyed.

"I don't know you do. I'm just asking because I had heard there were priests in Abruzzo who were helping partisans."

Father DiTullio stood up and walked to the small window that had a view of the courtyard. The daylight highlighted his bearded face in deep thought. After a few moments he turned to Francesco and said, "That attack was the second in as many nights. Some people here feel emboldened to take part in a resistance to the German occupation, as if life here is not dangerous enough. I support my people, but my concern with the resistance is that their actions have consequences. The risks must match the benefits!" Anger had crept into his voice and his clenched fist was emphatic. He moved from the window to his carved wooden desk and sat down. Leaning back in his chair he looked at the ceiling in silence. Francesco slouched and looked up at a series of fine cracks in the ceiling plaster resembling a river delta, wondering what the good Father was thinking. Finally, the priest leaned forward and looked narrowly at Francesco. "I may know someone who might help you on your way."

Francesco's eyes widened. He hadn't expected that response so quickly. He sat up straight and asked excitedly: "Is he here in town?"

"Well, let's just say that he can be found."

"How long will that take?"

"I can't say. You can wait here in the rectory if you like. It could be a few hours or most of the day, I don't know. That's all I can promise now."

"That's fine, Father. It's what I was hoping for," Francesco said. He felt his body relax; he was feeling good about his accomplishment. "I think I'll walk around town for a while and check back later if that is okay with you."

"Suit yourself then."

"Oh, and Father, may I ask one other favor."

"What is it?"

"Can you get word to the parish priest in Roccamorice? Tell him that the Germans tried to steal the altar painting at Santo Spirito. We were able to stop them, but I'm afraid they will try again. It needs to be taken from the monastery and hidden somewhere safe."

"The SS has begun to take some of the best art we have," Father DiTullio said, frowning. "I'm surprised, though, that they reached such a remote place. You are right, we need to hide as much as we can. I will pass the word. You have assumed quite a bit of responsibility for someone so young."

"Thank you, Father," Francesco said, nodding demurely, the pride that swelled his chest remained invisible. He was glad the priest did not ask him how the theft was thwarted.

The priest showed Francesco to the side door that opened onto the street behind the church. "Don't ask too many questions out there, it's dangerous. Be careful and check back in the afternoon."

Francesco ambled along the quiet back street and circled toward the town center. Shopkeepers were opening for business, people were gathering at their doors and people were lining up outside a bakery. He passed an elderly man and his wife at the end of the line. They resembled so many he had seen in his town. She wore a gray shawl over an old housedress with a sagging hem. The man's suit jacket was coming apart at one of the shoulder seams; his pants were worn and faded. Their gaunt ascetic faces and forlorn expressions mirrored those of nearly everyone in line. As he passed, he listened to their complaints of how their ration cards had become nearly worthless.

He spotted a pair of German soldiers leaving a café across the way and decided to go in, remembering he still had the lire Pierluigi had given him. A man sat at the counter with an espresso and a cigarette talking to the proprietor. Francesco ordered a cappuccino and sat at one of the small tables by the bar. He glanced at the pastry case, largely empty except for a tray of biscotti. When the waiter returned with his coffee he asked for biscotti. Just then two German officers walked in with a well-dressed Italian civilian.

"Bring us three espressos!" one of the officers demanded.

The men took a seat at a table close to Francesco, but they ignored him as if he didn't exist; he was thankful they did. The officers removed their hats and the civilian removed his feathered fedora. First one officer and then the other began to question the man about what he knew of people in town who had joined the partisans. The man looked worried as he looked to one and then the other officer with pursed lips and a shrug that implied he knew little.

The proprietor returned carrying a tray with three espressos and a small plate with biscotti. He dropped the plate off to Francesco on his way to the German officers. "Good morning, Mayor," he said, as he placed the coffees down on the table. "Is there anything else I can bring you or your guests?" The mayor nervously indicated they were fine and waved him off. The proprietor returned to his place behind the bar.

Francesco dipped his biscotti in the cappuccino, faced away from the table but listened to the conversation as he nibbled the biscotti and sipped his coffee. The Germans had a passable understanding of the Italian language, but the tone of their heavily accented speech and facial expressions revealed considerable anger. "I am warning you," one of the officers said as he narrowed his eyes at the mayor. "The attacks must stop! If not, we are prepared for reprisal. You are very lucky there were no serious injuries last night; no one died. Let me tell you, for every German that is killed we will take six Italian lives. Is that understood?"

"I can assure you gentlemen," the mayor said nervously, "neither I nor anyone in my office condoned the attack."

"Nevertheless, it happened. Who are they? I want their names."

"As I said on the way here, I know several young men have left the town to avoid the impressments."

"Where are they now?"

"I do not know—in the hills or other towns."

"Prepare a list of the family names of the 'several men' you mentioned. There is one man that we are especially interested in. Supposedly their leader, someone code named Rano, but we believe his real name is Paolo."

"Paolo is a common name here. I do not know the name of anyone who may be in the resistance. Much of what I hear, like you, is rumor."

"I don't have time for debate. I will expect a list this afternoon." Looking at his watch he said, "You've got four hours, don't waste them. One of my men will stop by your office to pick up the list."

Draining the last of their espressos, the officers rose abruptly, replaced their hats, and quickly exited the café leaving the dejected mayor sitting there.

Francesco had listened in anger as the mayor was harangued with the same insolence that the Germans had displayed in Roccamorice over more trivial matters.

The proprietor behind the bar and his customer on the other side of the counter looked toward one another but said nothing. Francesco swallowed the last little bit of milk foam in his cup. He glanced at the small paper bill on the tray, reached into his pocket and placed some money Pierluigi had given him in the tray. Then he got up and left.

Outside he noticed that the line by the bakery had not moved and seemed only to have grown longer. The old people with their sad faces reminded him of his situation at home. He walked on, doubting he would actually make contact or learn any names. For that, he was counting on Father DiTullio assistance. He passed through a small piazza where some small children were playing. Two mothers sat on benches on opposite sides of the piazza staring straight ahead at their chirping children. He walked on aimlessly sightseeing as much to kill time as anything.

Turning a corner, he came upon two German soldiers who had stopped a young man. "Carta d'identita" one of them demanded. Francesco quickly passed them by as the man reached under his sweater for his card. Francesco tensed up. The day had begun well enough, but the German officers in the café and now these two in the street revived his anger. When he was out of sight, he stomped the cobblestone and slammed his fist against the stone wall of a house. The adrenaline surge dissipated and he simmered down as he walked, the sights distracting him. But the town seemed rather lifeless, not what he expected. It was the same everywhere; no small groups had congregated to socialize except in lines at the food shops. He kept walking the cobblestones turning first down one street and then another. At one point he caught a glimpse of a medieval watch tower similar to the one in Roccamorice. He wondered if Guardiagrele's name derived from that period.

It was well into the afternoon when Francesco arrived back at the rectory. As he stepped up to the door he heard shouting beyond it. He paused for a moment and then knocked. The voices silenced and moments later Father DiTullio opened the door. He looked upset.

"Come in," he said in his usual gruff manner. "I have someone here I want you to meet."

The stranger's scrunched face confirmed Francesco's impression the two men had been arguing.

"This is Paolo. Paolo, Francesco."

The young man was seated at a small table on which two espresso cups and a small straw-covered bottle were set. Francesco recognized the bottle of *Centerbe,* the intensely flavored Abruzzese digestive made of a hundred herbs, or so it was said, by the monks. During the occupation it had become a God-send, flavoring the bitter ersatz coffee.

The man rose to greet him. He was a young, dark-eyed man with thick, black hair, a square jaw, and rugged face tanned and creased by sun and wind. He wore an old canvas jacket over a tattered wool sweater and faded canvas trousers. His boots were badly scuffed, a dusty brown fedora rested on the table.

"*Ciao,*" he said as he offered his hand. "I have been on the lookout for your group, but I was not expecting you."

Francesco looked surprised.

"Word of mouth came to us at our camp. The message originated in Sulmona. It said to look out for three men and a boy disguised as shepherds moving a flock of sheep toward Casoli. I expected to see one of the men."

"My job is to scout ahead and report back," Francesco said, matter-of-factly.

"A lot of responsibility for such a young man."

"That's my job." Francesco said forcing a deep androgynous tone and furrowed brow. He didn't see a problem with his role and responsibility. He wanted to convince this stranger by affecting an adult demeanor. "Can you help us then?"

"Maybe. Father filled me in with what you told him. So what is your plan now? Where are you going next?"

"We haven't figured that out yet. We were hoping someone like you would help us find the safest route and places to stop along the way to Casoli."

"Crossing the Maiella is one thing, but the real war is farther south. Getting by the German convoys and installations, crossing the Sangro is going to take a lot of planning and a good deal of luck."

"Do you have any ideas? I'm listening," he said continuing the deep -tone.

Paolo frowned. "Not at the moment. You are the first group we've come upon in this situation. I'll mull it over with my companions and we will come up with a plan. No guarantees. Where are your companions now?"

Francesco described the cottage set back on the country lane and the situation with the farmer and his wife. He also mentioned the attack he had witnessed the previous evening.

Paolo was caught off guard by Francesco's eyewitness account. "We heard about the incident in the café this morning. News travels quickly," he said trying to sound innocent.

"Are you the Rano the German officers mentioned— the partisan leader?"

"Let's talk about this later," Paolo said. He had seen Father DiTullio grimace and shake his head.

"So you will help us then?"

"For now, go back and tell your companions I will find my way there tomorrow morning. There are people I must see and things I must arrange before then." Then turning to Father DiTullio, Paolo asked if the food supplies in the rectory storage room were still adequate.

"*Sufficiente*," the priest nodded as he spoke.

"How are your supplies?" Paolo asked Francesco. "I can spare five hundred grams of spaghetti from our stores. "It's not much, but there is precious little in town."

"*Grazie*," Francesco said. "I didn't come looking for food but I'll gladly take whatever you can spare."

Francesco chatted with Father DiTullio for a few minutes while Paolo went into the store room and returned with some items in a cloth sack. He handed the bundle to Francesco. The pasta, wrapped in paper and tied loosely with twine, protruded out the top. "*Grazie per tutto, Ciao*," he said, as he left the rectory.

Chapter 11

It began raining again as Francesco walked through the town and out the main gate. The sky, as featureless as a sheet of gray paper extending to a low horizon framed his view of the road down the hill toward the misty outline of the woods in the distance. He followed the road until he neared the German camp and then entered the forest, retracing earlier steps. In the gray afternoon light it was much easier returning than it had been coming and he made good time.

It was nearly dark when he walked up the lane to the cottage. The rain had stopped but it was misting and droplets of water fell from the largely bare tree limbs. He skirted puddles of water as he entered the courtyard. The dogs barked and ran up to him. The three men rose and followed. He was greeted in the mud with the scent of wet fur mingling with wet leaves and bark.

"*Grazie Dio, Francesco,*" said Ennio, embracing the sodden figure whose hat still dripped moisture. "I was worried the entire time," he whispered in his ear.

Francesco, wanting to emulate his adult persona responded with: "You needn't have worried. I took care of myself."

"How did you make out?" Roger asked anxiously over Ennio's shoulder.

"I made contact with a partisan," he blurted out, obviously pleased with himself. "He may be able to help us. He gave us some food from the ration stores the priest kept in the rectory. I did my best to keep it dry," he said, as he handed the package under his *mantello* to Ennio.

"Jolly good show, Francesco," Denis said, grinning widely. "How did you do it?"

"It's a long story," Francesco responded. He described the firefight he saw the night before from his close point of view. They were not surprised he had nearly gotten caught up in the shooting; it was what they had feared once they saw where the action was taking place. Then he related his day in the town including his meeting with the priest, the incident in the café, and his introduction to Paolo.

"He should be here sometime tomorrow. I like the man. I think he can help us. He came up with that package. Besides the spaghetti there's a small jar of olive oil, a few cloves of garlic, some dried herbs, maybe oregano, and a dried red pepper."

"Perfect," Ennio said. "Denis take that bucket over there and get some water from the well and grab that old kettle on the wall to boil the water. Roger, use that dry wood in the corner to build a fire by the shed, and rig up that iron stanchion over there so I can hang the pot."

They all pitched in. Francesco changed out of his wet clothes into garments he had left behind. After the pasta had been boiled and drained, Ennio tossed it with sautéed garlic, olive oil, and pepper. Ennio, like most Abruzzese, had a fondness for strong flavoring. *Spaghetti, aglio, olio e peperoncini* sprinkled with *peccorino* cheese he carried satisfied their appetites that evening. The dogs sniffed around for left- overs but there were none. Francesco felt bad they had to be satisfied with the dry food Ennio gave them. After dinner, Ennio checked the sheep and returned to the shed where he, like the others, covered up with his shawl, settled back in the straw to spend another cold, damp night. As the fire died down to embers, sleep came quickly.

In the morning, they rose to dreary light and water dripping off the trees. Puddles had reformed in the courtyard. The pile of dry wood in the shed had dwindled, but there were enough logs for one more good fire. Ennio had found and gathered chicory roots in the forest which he had dried, roasted and then ground up and brewed. Francesco, wrinkling his nose thought it stunk. He remembered the aroma of a real cappuccino the day before and drank water instead. Around midmorning, Ennio, returning to the compound after checking the sheep spotted a man walking up the lane. "Francesco!" he called. "Is that your man coming?"

Francesco emerged from the shed and narrowed his eyes. When he recognized Paolo, he crossed the courtyard to greet him. Paolo wore the same clothes he had on the day before, but he added a *mantello* and carried a large pack and walking stick. "Good to see you," Francesco said, still joyed by the commitment Paolo had made to him. "Come, I want you to meet my friends."

Entering the shed, Paolo unloaded his pack, removed his wet fedora and shook hands with each of the men. Francesco, in introducing him as Paolo, mentioned the fact that his code name had been discovered by the Germans.

Paolo looked around sizing up the men, asked about the residents of the cottage and his flock of sheep. Ennio answered his questions. Then he asked to examine the transit papers and identity card. "Okay," he said, as he handed them back to Ennio, "Good enough. Your boy here told me your general plan, but I need specifics."

They each grabbed whatever was handy to sit upon to talk. Paolo took out a packet of tobacco and cigarette papers and tapped some leaf onto a curl of paper. Licking the edge, he twirled it into a cylinder and put it to his lips. He reached into his jacket for a match, but Denis had already struck and lit his cigarette and reached the still burning flame over to Paolo.

Paolo inhaled and blew out a puff of smoke. "Tell me exactly where you intend to bring these sheep."

"To a farm just south and east of Palumbaro. It's just north of Casoli, I've been there only once before but I can find it again."

"I don't know the place, but I know the general area you are talking about. Here is the situation. There are two main north-south roads that parallel one another in that direction. The western one is less heavily used by the Germans. But every day there are convoys and patrols on both roads."

"Where are they coming from?" Francesco asked.

"The railroad yard in Pescara and the port at Ortona. Mostly men and supplies, boxes of guns and ammunition, on some days, tanks and artillery units. My men and I have been looking for an opportunity to grab arms and ammunition but the convoys are too heavily guarded for an action by a group our size. The word is they are building up the Sangro River front anticipating the British advance."

"What do you suggest?" Ennio asked.

"Get the sheep ready to go. We'll take the road less traveled. The sooner we start the better. I can guide you to Polumbaro. My aunt lives just outside of the town. We can stop there for food and shelter. I sent one of my men ahead to let her know we are coming."

"Then what?" asked Francesco

"Then we figure out the next move. The resistance is just getting started around here. Our networks are incomplete and our communications are less than optimal. We don't have many safe houses now, but we'll get better in time."

Denis had been following the discussion closely. "What's the latest information you have on the war? Do you know where the British Eighth army is?"

"They stopped around Trigno and Campobasso. That's in Molise between Termoli and Vasto on the coast. Once we get to Casoli we can probably learn more."

Denis turned to Roger and said, "Monty seems to still be moving slow."

"But maybe that works in our favor this time. We might still get across the river before they engage the Germans. Ask him about the Allies in the west, does he know where they are?"

Paolo responded to the translated question. "They have had a tough time trying to cross the Volturno River. All the rain has caused flooding and the ground is saturated. Equipment has bogged down. It's been slow going through the mud. I think the British are going to run into the same problem on this side with the Adriatic rivers, but we will see."

"Do you know what has happened with our own soldiers?" Francesco asked.

"My friend in Caramanico is trying to locate his two sons."

"Good luck with that. Everybody is looking for a son, brother, or husband. They could be anywhere if they are alive. If they're not dead, they could be on the run and hiding here in Italy, or stuck in some German prison camp. They might even have been shipped off to Germany." Finding them will be difficult—you need to know the name or number of their outfit, where they were fighting at the time of the surrender on the Eighth of September—things like that. With all the chaos and without a functioning government that sort of information is hard to come by. All I can tell you is that if any of them managed to slip back into Abruzzo we would definitely reunite them with their families."

Francesco looked disappointed. He thought about how hopeful the Sanelli's and especially Annamaria were. He wanted to bring good news on his return. "Maybe we can look out for them as we go."

"Unlikely to be where we are going. Listen to me, first think about keeping yourselves safe, all of you," Paolo said, looking at each of them. "Let's get started. With this weather, there is no time to waste."

The men packed their things, shouldered their packs, and walked out into a drizzling rain to join Ennio and Francesco who had regathered the sheep from the pasture and corral. Ennio left a ram and a ewe in the corral for the shepherd and his wife. He knocked on their door to let them know they were leaving and shouted a thank you through the door. He didn't wait for a response.

When Ennio rejoined the men, Paolo said that they should stay on the road to Polumbaro and to continue to act as naturally as they had to this point, showing their identification and the transit papers if they were stopped. "Remember, the transit papers are real, but the *carta d'identita* the two fake shepherds are carrying are not." To keep things looking less suspicious, Paolo said he would follow them off the road, staying in the woods and meadows, but at a distance keeping an eye out for trouble. The Germans were looking for him anyway, he explained, so he needed to stay out of sight. He expected that his fellow partisan, whom he had sent ahead to Polumbaro, would be heading down the road toward them. In any case he would rejoin them when they paused near the next stopping point, the village of Pennapiedimonte.

They left the country lane and turned the flock south, passing the road to Guardiagrele hoping that Paolo was right about the heavier German traffic on the road farther east. The rain had tapered off, but the morning remained cold and gray. The countryside was sparsely populated with farmhouses surrounded by meadows bordered by hedgerows and clumps of trees. Low stone walls separated the now monochromatic fields from the road. From this vantage point, an artist painting the scene would make up a pallet with shades of grays. Francesco looked for Paolo and thought he might have caught a glimpse of him darting through the trees. It was midafternoon when the church steeple of Pennapiedimonte came into view and they saw Paolo crossing a field waving to them. He carried a small sack in one hand. "Look what I found in the woods," he said. "Hazelnuts! I passed a tree back there that no one had picked."

"That's surprising," Francesco said. "You would think the local people would have picked every nut tree clean by now. Did you happen to spot *funghi di bosco?* I used to hunt for those wild mushrooms back home."

"No, but feel free to take a look for yourself," Paolo said, sweeping his arm to the woods.

"*Grazie.* These nuts roasted will be enough of a treat."

"I think this is as good a place to stop as any," Paolo said. "I don't think we can make Palombaro before nightfall, so we should look for a place to spend the night around here. I really don't know anyone in this town and to be safe, I would rather not inquire. The Germans are looking to set up artillery. I'll go up ahead and see what I can find."

As Paolo walked off, Francesco and the men moved the sheep off the road. They sat in the field and shared some damp cheese and a piece of dry bread that Ennio had wrapped in a cloth.

"You seem a little nervous out here, Denis," Francesco said.

"I am, even disguised as a shepherd. "Does it make sense that a flock of sheep and some shepherds should be out here when no one else with livestock is around?" he asked.

Ennio told him that he believed that they would appear natural enough to an observer who was not from the area, but he was surprised they had seen no other travelers all day.

As they were talking, the rumbling sound of an approaching motorcade drew their attention. A convoy of a half dozen trucks bearing iron crosses carrying German soldiers drove past them toward the town. Some of the soldiers turned and glanced at the sheep and men who were now standing with their staffs looking to tend the animals. They held their breath hoping trucks would not slow down and breathed easily when they didn't.

"I'm glad we looked like we belong here, at least to those Germans," Denis said.

"Let's hope they forget about the sheep they saw," Roger said.

"Amen to that."

They started the sheep back onto the road just as a German staff car drove up to them. The dogs began to bark until Ennio quieted them. The driver remained behind the wheel while an officer in his gray-green uniform got out and motioned to Ennio and Francesco who were closest to him. Denis and Roger slunk at the rear of the flock; they had not yet left the field. They had lowered their heads, and stood still, watching from beneath the wide brims of their hats.

"Where are you going with these sheep?" the officer demanded. "Don't you know that all livestock in this area has been requisitioned?"

"Sir, we have permission to move this flock through this area," Ennio responded.

"And who gave you permission?"

"Your authorities in Sulmona," he said, handing over the transit papers and his identification.

The officer looked over the papers slowly while holding his leather crop under his arm. He seemed perturbed as he looked at the flock, barely glancing at Denis and Roger and paying Francesco no attention.

Francesco recognized the quartermaster emblem on his *Whermacht* uniform. "What's the problem?" Francesco blurted out. "We have authorized papers."

The officer suddenly looked to Francesco and swung his leather crop, catching him squarely across the face. Francesco's face stung, he stumbled back and fell to the ground, as Ennio tried to catch him. "That is for your insolence." Then, turning to Ennio, he said, "You need teach that boy some respect."

Roger had started to bolt forward, but Denis grabbed his sleeve and held him back. "Wait up, mate, let's see what happens," he whispered. "No need to risk it if we don't have to."

Francesco slowly got to his feet and brushed himself off. He tasted blood in his mouth and realized he'd better apologize, and quickly. "I'm sorry sir. I meant no disrespect."

The officer looked at him with disgust, and then he handed the papers back to Ennio. "Be on your way," he said. Then he got back into his car. The driver turned around and sped back up the road.

"Must I remind you again, Francesco, to speak carefully," Ennio said. "You know how sensitive these Germans are about their authority. Don't let your mouth get in the way of a successful trip."

"When he was looking over the papers, I thought he might find an excuse to ignore them," Francesco said. "You could tell he wanted the sheep. I was just trying to make the point that we had the right to move the flock." The tone of his voice betrayed his wounded pride.

"That wasn't the way to do it," Ennio said as he waved to Denis and Roger to move up with the sheep.

When they joined up, Denis asked what the incident was about. When Ennio told him and Roger what had happened, Denis grabbed Francesco's shoulder and said, "Don't be a bloody fool!" We need to make ourselves seem as harmless as ordinary shepherds. That means acting with the kind of humility and subservience these Germans expect. You should know we can't take any unnecessary risks, especially now."

Francesco felt the heat in his cheeks again and nodded, realizing he had used poor judgment. Once again he promised himself to act like a grown-up.

When they reached the outskirts of the town, they saw Paolo walking up to meet them. "Did you see that convoy?" Francesco asked.

"I heard them and was able to duck out of sight. They were heading south, probably to their positions along the Sangro."

Francesco filled him in on the incident with the officer in the staff car, and his concerns about the officer's apparent desire for the sheep.

"For now we can't worry about that. I've found an abandoned farm close by that will keep us out of sight. The house is empty. The door is locked and bolted, but the barn is wide open and there is a well on the property."

He guided them past the outskirts of the town and onto a narrow lane that led through the field to an old stone house. "It will be dark soon," he said. "Let's make a fire. I didn't know if we would reach my aunt's place tonight so I brought a sack of white beans that I have soaking in the barn; also some tubetti pasta, onion, garlic, and a carton of crushed tomato to make a simple minestrone."

They gathered around the fire they had built to eat and discuss the next day's passage. "I expect my associate to join us in the morning once we are on the road. We will likely reach my aunt's house at Palombaro before dark. We can rest there and reassess the situation. I need to learn details of the German movements between there and Casoli before we make ours."

"Maybe you can get an update on the British army position, Roger said, taking a spoonful of soup.

"There might be some information in the village. By the way since you have all been away, have you heard the latest about Mussolini?" Paolo asked, taking a swig of wine.

"The last we heard was that he was rescued by the Germans and taken to Hitler," Denis responded holding his spoon over his bowl.

"Since then the BBC reported that Hitler has reinstalled Mussolini as the head of government here in Italy."

"That's incredible. Mussolini in Rome again?" Ennio shook his head in disbelief.

"No. There is no government in Rome, just the German occupation. You know that Badoglio, the king and the council have all fled to Apulia with their entourage. There is no Italian army anymore and no real leadership from Badoglio. Mussolini and the black shirts have established their government in Gargano."

"Where is that?" Francesco asked. His knowledge of northern Italian geography was limited, but he was anxious to know more about the current events.

"It's in the north just beyond Salo, near Lake Garda. There are plenty of black shirts around there, but it will take the backing of the Germans to keep them in power. The BBC newsreader said Italian resistance fighters were active in the north blowing up bridges and tunnels."

"Hmm, the partisans. So Mussolini is just a puppet then?" Denis asked

"Yes, that's what I think; actually what most people think. Hitler will call the shots, just mark my word," he said, as he passed the flask of wine around.

"It's amazing," Roger said. "Mussolini was once Hitler's model for his vision of Germany. Now, the roles are reversed."

"Sounds to me there could be a civil war within the war," Denis said, taking a swig of wine and passing the flask to Roger.

"It's possible," Paolo said. "I've learned resistance groups are forming all over. Some are Fascist and support the black shirts, some the king, and then there are the socialists, the Catholics, and the communists." About all they or we have in common is the wish to get rid of the Germans—not wait for the Americans and British to do it. But it's not clear who is fighting who."

"A lot of Italians might die," Roger said. "Including us. What about the possibility of getting weapons? I would feel better with a gun in my hand."

"That's the biggest challenge for my group. We have a few obsolete rifles and I carry an old pistol in my pack. We staged a raid on the German camp outside Guardiagrele two nights ago just for that purpose, but we failed."

"That was your group Francesco told us he saw on his way into town that night," Denis said.

"Yes it was. We attempted a diversion with a homemade bomb at one end of the camp while we tried to strike at the other end where we thought the rifles and ammunition were stored. We were badly mistaken. Our plan almost killed us."

Francesco reiterated the conversation that he heard in the café between the German officer and the town mayor. Then he mentioned what he thought was an angry exchange between Paolo and the priest at the rectory. "Is that what you were arguing about?" he asked.

"We were discussing our philosophies and it became heated," Paolo said matter-of-factly. Father DiTullio has been very supportive, but he is worried about reprisals against his parishioners. I told him they were unavoidable, they had already happened. It was the price we had to pay. Our group formed in response to what the Germans were doing; rounding up men for their work details, stealing food, and taking property. The reprisals can't be avoided. The revolt in Lanciano on October fifth is a good example. The people's patience can be tested only so much."

"What happened in Lanciano?" Francesco asked. Although closer to home, he didn't know much about the town.

"The citizens became fed up with the Germans' abuse of power. A group of them were able to get guns from the local police station and attacked the German garrison. The Germans quickly overpowered them and put an end to the revolt. Twenty-two of them were shot and killed."

"I don't blame Father for being upset," Francesco said. "Aren't you?"

"Of course, no one want to lose lives. The good Father countered that nothing like that had happened yet in Guardiagrele. There had been some arrests for various infractions but no shootings."

"What does he expect?" Roger asked.

"His feeling is that the risk had to be justified, and that our raid was not worth it. He wants us to wait until we can act in concert with the British army coming north. I suppose that's where we were when Francesco knocked on the door."

"I think he's right about the timing," Roger said.

"Meanwhile, you can provide intelligence on enemy movement and positions," Denis said. "Maybe harass them with road blocks and sabotage."

Francesco got up and looked for more wood for the fire that had died down, thinking about how he might participate in a harassment.

"Interrupting electricity we've done; roadblocks and even assassinations are possible, but factory sabotage, that's possible only in the larger towns," Paolo responded. "We really don't have those sorts of targets in this part of the country."

"I know Father is concerned about the reprisals," Francesco said, returning with an armful of wood. "I heard the German officer say that he would take at least six Italian lives for every German that was killed. At least what we are doing, helping these two to escape is less risky for the people," he said, as he added the wood to the fire.

"Not really," said Paolo. "You've seen the notices. If we are caught with them it's not just us, it's our families, too, but as I said before, it's the price we have to pay."

"We understand the sacrifice," Denis said.

The men talked on about the potential of the resistance throughout Italy in the weeks and months ahead. It was another cold night. Francesco had roasted the hazelnuts, but his fingers stung as he used his fingernails to pry apart the cracked shells, and his teeth chattered as he tried to eat the nut meat. He thought about Annamaria as he stoked the embers and added branches of wood, hoping the fire would last the night. He wondered if she was thinking of him—the thought brought him comfort, if not warmth as he tucked his *mantello* more tightly.

In the morning under another slate gray sky they were packing their things and getting the sheep ready when the dogs began barking. Looking up, they saw a man and a woman riding up the path toward the house on bicycles. The man wore an old suit with a scarf tied around his neck and a woolen cap on his head. The woman had a heavy wool sweater over a brown dress and a kerchief tied around her head. When they drew near, they dismounted and looked surprised to see the men and sheep. Ennio walked over to greet them.

The man explained that they were the owners of the property. The Germans had confiscated their livestock and most of the valuables in the house. They had left to live with relatives in the town, and had come back to collect a few things they had buried beneath floor planks.

"What do you hear in town?" Ennio asked.

The man told Ennio that the talk in town was about people who were planning to cross over to the southern liberated area of the country controlled by the British army.

"How were they planning to get by the Germans?" Ennio asked.

"Some mentioned trying to find an Austrian regiment because the Austrians would be easier to deal with, at least that's the rumor."

Ennio thanked them for the information. The man and his wife continued up to the house, put their bicycles aside, unlocked the door, and went in.

Francesco had listened in on the conversation and thought it might be a good idea. He walked over to Denis and Roger and asked, "What do you think of finding some Austrians to let us cross? It's possible we could blend in with refugees heading south."

"I would be wary about anyone in a German uniform, Austrian or not," Denis said. "I would want to see refugees passing an Austrian checkpoint first."

Paolo, who had left the group to check for German activity, was back to say that the road was clear. When asked by Francesco, he didn't think the idea of finding an Austrian outfit was a good one. "A Nazi is a Nazi. They wear the same uniform. We don't take chances that one of them is sympathetic. Let's get back on the road. I'll shadow you again like I did yesterday."

Francesco and the men moved the sheep down the lane and onto the main road. As they had since leaving the Guardiagrele area, they traveled through hill country always with the Maiella as a backdrop. Periodically, they passed farms that once had colorful fields of ripening sun flowers, corn, grape arbors, and olive trees; a landscape now monochromatic and barren.

Ennio and Francesco were in the lead and Denis and Roger were trailing the flock when, in the early afternoon, they saw two men in the distance approaching them. As they drew closer, they recognized Paolo who introduced the man he was with as Felice, one of the men in his group. His face was shadowed by the brim of his fedora pulled low on his head, but otherwise in appearance and dress, they pretty much resembled each other.

"We are not far from my aunt's house," Paolo said. "She is not feeling well,

Felice tells me, but if I know her, that will not stop her from preparing something for us to eat this evening."

"Is there any more news about the war?" Francesco asked Felice.

"I went into town to try and find out. One of the shopkeepers told me that a German convoy had stopped briefly but then moved on. They are warning the residents there and in the smaller hamlets to the south of to be prepared to evacuate, so I expect the war is getting close."

They reached the farm late in the afternoon. From the road they looked down on a stone farmhouse and two smaller buildings, a barn and a shed situated at the bottom of the sloping meadow. It was within sight of Palombaro, a hilltop village off to their left. Paolo's aunt Giacomina did not look well when she opened the door to greet them. She was thin, pale, and had a cough, but her face brightened as she embraced her nephew. She wore a black, misbuttoned cardigan over a plain black dress. Her gray-and-black-streaked hair was swept around and tied in a bun in back. Francesco thought she resembled his grandmother and took an immediate liking to her.

While Ennio and Francesco tended to the sheep, the men went in and sat down at the kitchen table. She poured them each a glass of wine.

Paolo briefed them about his aunt's circumstances. Giocomina's husband had passed away several years ago. Two of her sons were away, one in the army and the other, her oldest, had moved to France before the war. She had a married daughter who lived in Palombaro with her husband and children. They came to the farm often to help her manage things, not that there was much to manage anymore. She kept only a small garden and a grape arbor. There was no longer any livestock, but she had a few chickens. She had, in fact, butchered one of them that morning to prepare the soup in the large kettle that was hanging in the hearth. The aroma of chicken broth simmering over the fire was beginning to fill the room. "It's just about ready," she said. "It's not much but it will warm you up."

"You're not feeling well," Paolo said. "You shouldn't have bothered."

She shook off his concerns. "Don't worry about me, I'll be fine." "You should see the doctor in town about your cough," Paolo said. "What can he do? I drink herbal tea with honey and rest, that's all."

She sauntered over to the cabinet and pulled out some bowls and set them around the table. Ennio and Francesco entered and greeted her as she removed a large bowl filled with golden cubes of soft croutons and brought it to the table along with a platter of shredded boiled chicken. "Bring the kettle," she called to Paolo who removed the steaming kettle from the iron hook that held it above the fire. Using both hands, he placed the kettle on an iron trivet in the center of the table. Giacomina lifted and emptied the bowl of Abruzzo-style soup croutons into the kettle of hot clear broth. She had cut the croutons from thin pancakes of flour, eggs, and parsley. Wiping her hands on her apron, she ladled out portions into each bowl.

"Are you not afraid?" Francesco asked, taking a spoonful of soup. Sipping it he said, *"E buona."* Just like home he thought.

"No. I'm an old lady, just a poor wretch now. What can they do to me?"

"The Germans can shoot you, or confiscate your property."

"Let them. I don't care." Coughing, she paused to clear her throat. "I can always go live with my daughter if I have to."

"I think you should leave and go live with her now," Francesco said.

"I'm not ready yet," she said, coughing again. "I like the idea of resisting the barbarians. We all need to help in some way, and that includes helping you and these men rejoin their army. Certainly I want the peace and tranquility we enjoyed before the war, and I want my family around. It's terrible now! But until then, maybe I can find satisfaction in more men like these I can help along the way."

"Well, *Zia*, we can use you and this house in the network, but I'm very concerned for your health," Paolo said. "It's too risky."

"Let's not talk about that now. You're the one who needs to be careful"

After dinner the men discussed the final leg in the journey. Paolo decided to send Felice into Casoli to see if he could make contact with the partisans, while he would start out early in the morning for the farm ahead of the men and the sheep. On a cold November evening, the farmhouse was warm and cozy. They had been on the road for days of unseasonably cold and tirelessly wet weather with the sheep. They had soaked through time and again. Trudging through muddy roads and fields, their clothing and packs had become grimy, and they had taken on a moldy smell. It had been quite a while since they had bathed, and they had acquired that characteristic stale body odor, although an unbiased observer would have simply said they stunk. The hot meal was welcomed, but even more they needed to bathe and put on clean clothes. After bathing, the beds afforded the men the other comfort they needed. No one had trouble nodding off the moment their heads hit the pillows.

Chapter 12

The morning dawned sunny and clear for the first time in days. The men awoke to the aroma of a zucchini-and-onion frittata sizzling on the stove. Giacomina was coughing again as she tilted the skillet and slid the frittata onto a plate. The men had laundered their clothes before retiring—shirts and pants drying on racks by the hearth, assisted by rays of sunlight slanting in from a window.

Felice had left for Casoli. The rest were seated at the table eating and drinking ersatz coffee when a knock on the door got their attention. Giacomina shuffled to the door and opened it to see her husband's old friend from Palombaro, Luigi DiNofrio. His worried face and heavy breathing told Giacomina something not good had happened. *"Buon giorno, che success?"*

Luigi looked past Giacomina to the breakfast table where Paolo was seated with the others. *"I Tedeschi vengano,"* he said waving his hands expressively.

"The Germans are coming? Now?" Paolo asked, startled. Ennio and Francesco, Denis and Roger stopped eating, their forks in midair, their mouths agape.

"Soon I think," Luigi said, looking at Paolo. "The barber told me this morning two German soldiers came to his shop late yesterday afternoon for haircuts. Chatting between themselves, the barber understood they were looking for you. They knew your code name and real name, and that you had an aunt near Palombaro. They intended to pay her a visit."

"Grazie, Luigi. We need to leave," Paolo said, grabbing his pack and signaling the others, *"Subito!"*

Denis and Roger rose quickly. Francesco stuffed another forkful of food in his mouth and got up to join the others. They grabbed their still damp clothes and jammed them in their packs.

Giacomina, coughing, wrapped the loaf of bread she had on her counter and emptied a bowl of hard-boiled eggs by the sink into a sack. She handed the package to Francesco. *"Mangia bene,"* she said.

Paolo came over and hugged her. "Please take care of that cough. I will be back as soon as I can be sure these men are safe, and then we'll go to your daughter's house. You need to see a doctor to get better."

"*Non ti preoccupare,*" she said waving him off. "Do what you have to do. Go and be careful," she said twisting her apron in her hands.

"*Sempre,*" Paolo said, as he kissed her on both cheeks. She blessed him invoking Jesus, Joseph, and Mary. Then he walked out with the men.

"*Grazie per tutto,*" Francesco called back to her. He again thought of his grandmother who loved him unconditionally, lived simply, and gave all she could. "*Arrivederci,*" he said.

"*Adio,*" she responded wistfully from her doorway.

Outside Paolo told the men he needed to stay a step ahead of the Germans. His plan was to cut across the countryside through the woods and a ravine. He knew an approximate location where he expected to intersect them on the road south.

No sooner had the four gotten the sheep moving on the road south, that they were forced to move the flock to the side to let a German convoy carrying military equipment and German soldiers pass them. The dogs barked and nipped at the heels of the stragglers. Denis and Roger kept their heads down as the truck rumbled by, happy to avoid another encounter. They got the sheep moving again. Francesco took the lead with Ennio on the flank and Roger and Denis bringing up the rear. It wasn't long before they reached the junction of the road to Casoli where they turned east.

They had only traveled a short distance when Francesco encountered a group of people off the road to their left sitting on an embankment sharing some food. There were about two dozen men, women, and children with valises and sacks on the ground next to them. The women in peasant dresses were bundled up in sweaters and coats for the cold weather. Most had bandanas wrapped around their heads, their faces drawn and sullen. The men looked hapless in shapeless woolen pants, flannel shirts, and sweaters under old suit coats. Their heads were covered with an assortment of old fedoras and caps. The children, who were dressed for the cold in shabby clothing, sat quietly looking bewildered.

Francesco left the road and walked over to them. Ennio joined him. Most of the men rose to greet them while the women remain seated and stared vacantly.

"*Ciao,*" Francesco said, happy to see a group of people who weren't threatening but sad to see them so forlorn.

"*Buon giorno,*" Ennio said. "*Dove andate?*"

They told him they were headed to Casoli. The Germans forced them to leave their homes in a small hamlet south of the town of Fara San Martino, to the east of where they were now. The Germans claimed they needed their property for a defensive position. But they took more than the homes; they also destroyed their livelihood when they blew up the DeCecco pasta factory where they worked.

Francesco, hearing the story, had a sour look on his face. Just another German abusive overreach he thought, another reason for revenge.

Ennio was stunned. DeCecco was an important Abruzzo pasta business known throughout Italy. The DeCecco's distributed macaroni to the various regions of the country and exported it as well. They were known to use only the finest semolina and the pure cold Maiella water to make their pasta, and they invented a unique way of drying it indoors, something no one else did. "Why did they destroy the factory?"

"The family was proud of its anti-Fascist position," one of the men said. "They helped the new resistance groups in the area but gave the Germans a hard time when they came requisitioning pasta. Of course, the Germans resented that."

"Where are you headed to in Casoli?" asked Francesco.

"A few of us have relatives we hope to stay with; the rest of us are going south across the Sangro toward the British army. We think we can find shelter in Apulia. The old government of Badoglio and the king has reestablished itself there, so that's our plan."

It was apparent to Francesco these refugees had no plan except to rely upon the kindness of others. He and Ennio could offer them little except encouragement and wished them luck on their journey.

Roger and Denis had remained on the road with the flock and dogs. They had witnessed the plight of refugees in North Africa and Sicily, and were sharing their experiences as Ennio and Francesco walked back to the road to rejoin them. "Where are they going?" Roger asked. Francesco told them what he had learned. Turning to Denis he said, "I am almost tempted to join them."

"It's too chancy, Roger," said Denis. "If those refugees get stopped, they're Italians; they can always turn around and go back or try something else. We can't. Let's stick with the plan."

Chapter 13

About two hours later the group rounded a bend in the road, and through a break in the trees the town of Casoli appeared. It was situated on the crest of foothills with the slope of the Maiella rising behind it. The sun illuminated the terra cotta roofs and painted the stone buildings in soft amber light.

Denis had his eyes down thinking about the remaining challenges that lay ahead. When he looked up he said, "I have yet to see an Abruzzi town situated on flat ground. In medieval days they were built on hilltops for defense," Roger said. "But nowadays they probably attract more tourists than marauders."

"And people like us on the run." Too bad, he thought because they look so charming. But he could understand why the German military would want to use some of them for defense.

The men continued their conversation at the rear of the flock as Francesco and Ennio took the lead with the dogs. A short distance down the road they found Paolo smoking a cigarette waiting for them at the junction with a secondary road to the south.

"I see the Germans didn't get you," Denis called out, very much relieved as he and Roger walked around the flock and up to the junction. Denis told him about the truck full of soldiers that had passed them. "I was worried you might have run into them."

"No. Thank God for Luigi's warning. Just another close call." He took a drag on his cigarette and pointed. "The farm is less than a kilometer down that road. I looked it over from the edge of the woods. It fits the description you gave me, Ennio. I saw a small boy and a girl outside playing which also fits with what you told me about the family."

"This is the road I remember," Ennio said. "Any sign of trouble?"

"No," Paolo said relaxed taking another drag on his cigarette. "There was an armored halftrack that came by earlier and headed off on another road through the woods. Everything seemed okay around the house so you should be safe." He dropped his cigarette to the ground and stamped it out with his boot; his expression turned serious. "The most difficult and dangerous part for you lies ahead. The Germans are more concentrated on this slope of the Maiella."

"What's next then?" Denis asked.

"I need to leave you and go into Casoli and find Felice. I was counting on him making contact with someone to get you across the Sangro. I'm worried he has not shown up yet. Anyway, depending on what I learn, one or both of us will rejoin you this evening."

"Wait a minute, Paolo," Denis said. "I'd like to go with you."

"Where did *that* come from?" Roger asked, seemingly annoyed. "Are *you* having second thoughts?"

"I haven't changed my mind about the plan, Denis responded, "but I've thought about what you said earlier and maybe we should keep our options open. As things stand now, finding partisans who can get us across the Sangro is no guarantee. I've been thinking of those folks back on the road—they were hoping to find townspeople who would get them across the river."

"Are you sure you want to do this?" Roger questioned. His frown said he wasn't convinced of Denis's idea.

"Yes, two of us searching will be better than one. But you need to stay safe. If I'm fortunate enough to make a contact, I'll come back with Paolo to get you. Is that all right with you Paolo?"

"Fine, if that's what you want to do, but we will have to split up in town; no connection with me, understand? And you need to fake your best Italian behavior. So, if you agree, let's get going, it's getting late." Then pausing for a moment, "Why not let the boy come too? He could be helpful to you, and I think he can take care of himself."

"What do you think, Ennio? Can you manage?" Denis asked.

"Well, the farm is just down the road so no problem." He gave Francesco a cautious look and asked, "Is this something you want to do?"

"Yes!" Francesco's emphatic response and bright smile, suggested he might have just won a prize. "I can handle this, don't worry."

Denis put his hand on Francesco's back. "We better stop gassing and get going."

Francesco playfully scuffed up the hair of the big, white sheepdogs who had gathered around him. Then he walked off with Denis and Paolo.

Roger stood there for a moment. "Later," he called after them, still looking a little bewildered. Then he joined Ennio who had begun to move the flock south on the narrow road through the woods.

****

The profile of a large stone-mortared farmhouse loomed through the trees now devoid of foliage. As they emerged from the woods with the dogs working the flock, the field in front of them gave way to a meadow on which a two-story house and two barns of substantial size were set back on a rise in the land. An empty sheepfold, a well, a vineyard, scattered hardwood trees, and a grove of olive trees graced the property that was cordoned off by a low stone wall. The lower fields had stubbed rows of corn and sunflowers, long harvested. In the distance, beyond a fruit orchard, the land fell off toward a valley where a line of trees obscured the valley floor.

As they neared the house, the front door opened and a man emerged, paused, and shaded his eyes. Then he walked toward them. A man of medium height and build, he looked comfortably dressed in a country-style cotton shirt, wool sweater, and flannel pants. When he reached the gate, he swung it open and waited. Ennio had quickened his pace recognizing Pierluigi's brother, Dominic. The two men met in an embrace.

"*Grazie Dio*, you finally got here. It's good to see you again," Dominic said. "Pierluigi has been worried. I must tell him you are all safe. Where are the rest?"

"It has taken a little longer to avoid trouble," Ennio said, as the men and sheep passed through the gate. He introduced Roger to Dominic and explained the change of plans regarding Denis and Francesco. Dominic looked concerned, but told the men to herd the sheep into the corral. He thought Casoli might be too risky for Francesco and the other man he didn't know.

When the sheep were settled, Ennio and Roger dropped their packs by the well and washed their hands in a bucket of water. Dominic waited by the door as they walked over to the house, cleaned off their boots, and entered. He led them through the large foyer and down a hallway, past comfortably furnished living and dining rooms into a rustic country kitchen. There he introduced everyone to his wife, Filomena, his young son, Dante, and his daughter, Mia, who were both preteens, several years younger than Francesco.

"Please sit and make yourselves comfortable," Filomena said as she placed a platter of *salumi, provolone,* and slices of rustic bread on the table. Dominic brought a carafe of wine and glasses to the table.

"How do you manage to keep this food from the authorities?" Ennio asked.

"Some luck and my brother's help," Dominic responded. "I discovered a small grotto in the limestone shortly after I bought this property. It had a very small opening when I stumbled upon it. I enlarged it to store my wine. Then when the occupation came it became a good place to hide food as well. I hung my prosciutto there as well as vegetables that Pierluigi sends me when he can. It has a constant cool temperature, so it preserves things well. I could hide Roger and his partner there, if needed, but it would be a little cramped."

Roger and Ennio listened as Dominic continued. "The Germans confiscated a good deal, including a 50-liter barrel of last year's wine. They also took my livestock, and my hunting rifles. But they left the new wine I hadn't yet bottled. Please try a glass," he said, as he poured wine from a carafe for each of the men.

"Thank you," Roger said, as the wine gurgled into his glass. Holding the glass up to the light, he studied the deep red *Mutipulciano* vintage. As he brought the glass to his lips, his nose detected a fresh blackberry sent. *"Salute!"* His face registered contentment as he savored its smooth, dry character.

Dominic looked pleased and poured a glass for himself.

Filomena encouraged the men to eat. Ennio didn't need much encouragement to make a thick panino of *prosciutto* and *provolone*. Roger watched Ennio and then made one of his own. They were both quite hungry. "Help yourselves to more," she urged. "The pasta will be ready soon. I'm just waiting for the water to boil." Ten minutes later Filomena fashioned a pasta of DeCecco spaghetti with a sauce of pecorino cheese, black pepper, and her husband's *prosciutto*.

Between forkfuls of pasta and sips of wine, Dominic responded to questions that Roger asked about where the British army was situated.

"The latest I heard in Casoli is that the army is just beyond the Sangro, somewhere between Atessa and Casalbordino. Let me show you on this map," he said as he turned and reached into a drawer of the cabinet behind him.

"Let them finish eating first," Filomena scolded her husband. "After I clear the table you will have room to spread out that map. It will be easier."

"Is there any more news about the government?" Ennio asked. "The other day we were shocked to learn that Mussolini reformed a government in the north."

"So you have heard of the *Republica Sociale Italiano*, the RSI or the Salo as many refer to it."

"What do you make of it?" Roger asked.

"Mussolini was installed as the head of government only because of Hitler's help and influence. Graziani has been made minister of defense and commander of the army. Several of his other former associates hold various positions."

"Sounds like the same *governo fascisti* with a new name," Ennio said, taking a forkful of pasta.

"Mussolini's military is almost nonexistent and the government is fragile," Dominic responded. "But what worries me are Mussolini's *partigiani*. In the north the black shirts are taking terrible revenge on any Italians who opposed them in the past, especially who they feel betrayed them on the eighth of September. In Casoli the other day I learned that Mussolini's men or his Nazi partners rounded up six of his former Fascist associates, including his daughter, Edda's husband, Ciano. Can you imagine that, his son-in-law?"

Ennio put his fork down and pushed his dish away in a gesture of disgust.

"Where is he getting his support?" Roger asked, pouring himself a glass of wine from the carafe.

"Well, there are partisans of varying persuasions. The people up there who have rallied to him are attacking the anti-Fascists who include the communists, the monarchists, and even those whose sole objective is to rid the country of the Nazis. What surprised me is that many of the leading cultural figures, the 'intellegencia' have rallied around Mussolini. They still believe Fascism is a great revolutionary idea. It's the Allies; in particular, the British who these people think are the real devils. The problem is that Mussolini feels invigorated and he hasn't given up."

"*Orribile,*" Ennio said shaking his head.

Dominic paused to refill the glasses around him. "Mussolini has been whining about what he calls the 'lazy citizens,' Italians who are too lazy to support him. And the black shirts who have joined him in urging the new government to bear down, have Italians on the left killing those on the right and vice versa."

"That's Fascism!" Roger said. They try to divide—to scapegoat those they call lazy and promote as hard-workers, those who support their ideas."

"They have no moral compass. The Salo government has now formally declared the Jews to be enemies, which shows Hitler's influence. They make no excuses for rounding up and killing of any Italians they think are disloyal. Most painful, I was told, are the public displays of the executions."

"It sounds like a civil war within the war; the possibility that Denis mentioned, is actually occurring," Roger said, taking another helping of pasta. "Why aren't you eating, Ennio?"

"All this talk has spoiled my appetite."

"The propaganda and actions seem to be aimed mostly at the people in the north where the Germans have a stronger hold," Roger said "What do you think will happen here?"

"I don't know. The old regime is trying to establish itself politically and socially, but with the war on our doorstep, it's practically dead," Dominic responded, looking disgusted. "The people are too concerned with their own welfare to worry about a government that abandoned them. Besides, they feel that the king and Badoglio are at least partly responsible for the Fascist misadventure."

"We came upon a group of refugees fleeing toward Casoli earlier today," Ennio said, repeating what he had learned from them. "They seem to be just leaving their homes near the front, some on their own and others because the Germans have forced them out, but I don't know if many of them know where they are going, they're just trying to get away."

"My wife and I have been discussing this," he said as he looked at her. "She wants to go to stay with her sister's family in Bari now that it is a liberated city, but we haven't decided. Our options are either to move to Bari or stay here. I think we could be safe here. The British army will probably be moving up the coast to the east of us, focusing on the ports, like Ortona and Pescara. The problem is that we don't know if the Germans will retreat in that direction if they don't hold the Sangro."

The men had finished eating so Filomena called in the children who cleared the table. Filomena brought over another carafe of wine and placed it on the table along with a platter of biscotti.

Dominic unfolded the map next to him, and pushed the plate and carafe aside. The men rose and gathered behind him. Ennio stood to his left and Roger to his right looking over his shoulder. "Look here. All along this area from Sulmona, Scanno, Roccaraso, and the smaller villages, people are on the move. The Germans have built a line of fortifications on the ridges above the Sangro. Now that it has risen to flood stage, many of the bridge crossings are underwater; the German destroyed others, so there are few places left to cross."

"Where do you think is the best?" Roger asked.

"I don't know," Dominic responded. "First you must get over the Aventino River," he said, pointing to a tributary of the Sangro. "It's only a few hundred meters south of the farm. A narrow bridge crosses it but flooding has covered the approaches. After that, you will face the Sangro which has spilled over its banks. The Germans patrol all along it quite often I am told."

"Most refugees, it seems to me, will be trying to cross to the south and west away from the action," Roger said, "But we want to move to the south and east toward our army," he said pointing to Casalbordino. "This is where you said you heard the British army was positioned, correct?"

*****

There were German vehicles and soldiers moving through the streets when Paolo, Denis, and Francesco walked into Casoli. Paolo asked directions to the main piazza from one of the local citizens. Denis kept a low profile as the group walked along the winding cobblestone street lined by stone houses. When they entered the piazza it was relatively quiet. Most shops were closed; few people milled about. Two German soldiers with rifles strapped on their shoulders were smoking and chatting on the far side. Denis thought he overheard words of Anglo-Saxon English being spoken by someone in a group of men sitting outside a small café chatting vigorously, mostly in Italian. One of them threw up his hands in a gesture of futility.

"I'm going to go over and speak to those blokes," he said to Paolo. "By the looks of it, there may be a couple of Brits with those Italians."

Paolo looked at the men dressed like local residents. "Are you sure? You're taking a chance with those Germans over there."

"I overheard spoken English; it wasn't with an Italian accent. They may be POWs who know something. Those soldiers are out of earshot."

"All right, go quietly," he said with a scowl. "I'll wait here with Francesco and watch. If you're okay, we will go look for Felice. Meet me here at sunset no matter what. If I'm not here by dark, don't wait," he said, still scowling. "Try and get back to the farm. You've come this far. Don't jeopardize your chance to escape."

Francesco and Denis looked at one another, then at Paolo and nodded.

Denis walked over to the group of men. The table held a bowl of olives, a loaf of rustic bread and a carafe of wine. He could not tell if the group included foreigners disguised as Italian peasants sitting with Italians, but he decided to give English a try. "Any of you Brits?" he asked.

"Shh, be quiet. There are Jerries all around here."

"Sorry, mate. I don't think those Jerries are within earshot," Denis said, nodding toward the soldiers at the opposite side of the piazza. "Who's with you?"

"My name's Brian," the man said, shaking hands with Denis. He introduced his companion who he said was an escaped POW like him, and their two Italian friends. "Have a seat."

"What camp were you at?" Denis asked.

"No. 78 at Sulmona."

"Me too. Sorry I don't recognize you."

"Well, we were three thousand in that pen after all."

"How did you get here?"

"From the camp to Bagnaturno, then over the Morrone to Salle. How about you?"

"To Caramanico. I'll spare you the story. What are you doing here?"

"We came to collect supplies from people our two friends here know in town. Then we'll go back to our hideout."

"After that?"

"We have been planning to cross the river. We want to get back to the army, but we thought we would wait a bit. It's not very safe just yet."

Denis looked over to where Paolo and Francesco were standing. The piazza was busy again. Shopkeepers had reopened and people were out collecting whatever they could find for their evening meal. He waved to Paolo to indicate he was fine and watched Paolo and Francesco walk off toward one of the side streets. Turning back to the table he asked, "What are you waiting for?"

"For the army to get closer. We figure once the fighting starts, the Germans will be too distracted to notice us trying to cross the river. Another great downpour could help too. Less patrolling."

"Well, both of those scenarios could happen any day now I'm told. You concerned at all about your chances?"

"It'll be a bloody flap, but it's a risk we'll have to take. Meanwhile the cover is great," he said, nodding to the Italians at the table, one of whom, with a cigarette in hand, slid the plate of bread and carafe of wine toward Denis. Brian explained that the people in Salle hid them after their escape. They had nothing to offer beyond the shelter, but they somehow found food to feed them and clothes to give them, and then with the help of local partisans got them to the men who were sitting at the table with them.

Denis shared the many similarities of his and Roger's experience. Between sips of wine, the subject changed to possible escape points along the Sangro. "If we could only predict where the Eighth was planning to cross," Denis said.

As he was speaking, three German soldiers entered the piazza from a side street and walked toward the men seated at the café. One Italian who noticed tapped the other's arm. They both sat up and peered at the soldiers, one of whom carried a tommy gun, the other two had pistols in their holsters. "*Possibile problema*," they whispered to one another. "*Andiamo subito*," one of them said to their British companions.

Brian and his buddy got up quickly to follow the Italians who were rapidly walking toward an alleyway. Brian paused a moment and turned back to Denis with a startled look. "Those Jerries look like they might want identification papers which we don't have. We need to go straight away. Sorry I can't continue this chat, mate. Good luck," he said, as he gave a thumbs up and hurried off to join the others.

"Halt!" one of the German soldiers shouted as he unholstered his pistol. The other soldier followed suit, and the third raised his tommy gun. They surged forward and started firing their weapons at the men running for the alley. Bullets pinged off the pavement and ricocheted off the walls as the last man disappeared around the corner.

Denis leapt to his feet and darted in the opposite direction.

The Germans stopped for a moment, and the officer with the tommy gun motioned to his associates to follow the men in the alley. Then he turned his attention to Denis and shouted for him to halt. Denis ducked into a grocery and past two surprised ladies just inside the entrance who were searching the largely barren shelves. At the back of the store he shouted at the proprietor for the exit. The man nervously pointed to a door behind him. Denis was around the counter into a hallway. A door on the left was labeled *Bagno*; on the right it read *Dispensa*, straight ahead he saw *Uscita*. He ran and pushed through the door, finding himself in a narrow walkway with trash containers next to the rear doors of shops on one side and residences on the other. The position of the afternoon sun had the walkway in shadow. He turned left and walked quickly past the trash containers to the end where the walkway joined a street. To the left he could see where the street entered the piazza. He turned to the right just as the back door of the shop slammed open against the stone wall. The German emerged aiming his tommy gun. A stuttering volley whizzed past Denis who crunched against a wall and darted out of the soldier's line of site. Running down the street, breathing hard, he knew the German would be in pursuit.

He looked back. There he was. More shots ricocheted off the pavement as Denis pressed himself against the wall to catch his breath before starting up the street again past a tobacco store and a tavern. He came to another alley, doors to homes on both sides; at the end another alley ran perpendicular. He stopped again to catch his breath and listen. His pounding heart nearly drowned out the sound of the jackboots on the pavement behind him. He looked back for a moment and then he opted for the alley. At the end he turned to his left. It was a blind end. He turned around and looked to other end. Also blind, but with doors on either side. He made a dash forward toward them just as the German with his tommy gun slid to a stop in front of him. The voice from below the shadowed eyes of a flanged helmet said, "Hands up, English! Come toward me, but slowly."

Memories of North Africa came flooding back as Denis raised his arms. He frowned, his mouth curled down, ashamed and frustrated at being caught again. He wasn't afraid of the German, but the disappointment of losing his freedom for a repeat barbed-wire existence was etched on his face.

As he walked slowly forward, a door behind the German slowly opened and a man emerged in the shadows. A shot rang out. Denis heard a thud as the German exhaled a whoosh of air. A trickle of blood appeared over his lower lip and slid down to his chin as he crumpled to the ground. His head hit the pavement, his helmet snapped off and rolled to a stop by the wall.

The stranger walked toward Denis and the fallen German. The shot had caused a man to peer out his doorway which he quickly closed. It took a moment for Denis, still stunned, to recognize Paolo, now followed by Felice, Francesco and a stranger.

"Are you okay, Denis?" asked a wide-eyed and shaking Francesco, putting his arm around Denis's waist.

Paolo bent down, picked up the tommy gun, removed the clip, and handed it to Felice.

"Yes, I think so," Denis said, glancing down at the German who was lying on his back, a pool of blood beginning to form on the cobblestones near his left shoulder.

"*E morte?*" Francesco asked nervously.

Paolo knelt and placed his hand on the German's neck for a pulse. "*Si, e morte.*" He put his pistol away under his jacket. "Denis, this is Tumulto," Paolo said, nodding toward the stranger, a bearded, muscular man with a serious demeanor. He was wearing a brown beret, a heavy woolen sweater, worn canvas pants and boots. "Felice, Francesco, and I were in the tavern talking to him when Francesco spotted you run past and the German chasing after you.

"Lucky for me you came along, Francesco," Denis said to the boy who still had his arm around his waist. He looked at Paolo and asked, "How did you all meet up?"

"After we left, Francesco and I wandered up and down the side streets around the piazza looking into all the bars and tobacco shops. I spotted Felice going into the tavern and we followed him in. He had made contact with the *partigiani* earlier, and they arranged for Tumulto to meet him there. We were discussing his plan to get us across the Sangro when Francesco saw you run by." "We should leave here quickly," Tumulto said. "The other Germans will be looking for this guy. Leave the tommy gun with my man in the tavern. You can collect it later."

After they left the gun, they hurried out of the alley and turned onto the street, circling away from the piazza on back streets. Ducking for cover in doorways and alleys, they managed to evade patrolling German soldiers. Outside town they stayed off the main road and followed a sheep track that Tumulto knew. On their way, Paolo told Denis what Felice learned in Casoli about a recent massacre from a newly arrived group of refugees. Denis pressed for the details but Felice told him he didn't know; he didn't have time to listen. They reached the road to the farm and arrived at the house as the sun was setting.

******

A knock on the door found Filomena in the living room with the children. She called out to Dominic who went to answer.

Opening the door he was greeted by four strangers and a young man silhouetted by the pale orange sunset behind them. They quickly introduced themselves. Francesco felt comfortable when Dominic embraced him with a smile and told him that he had met him as a child when his family was visiting his brother in Caramanico.

Dominic led the group into the kitchen where Roger and Ennio rose quickly with wide grins and shouted almost in union, "Denis! Francesco!" embracing them in bear hugs.

Roger looked relieved when Denis finished his story. "That was a closer call than you had in North Africa," he said.

"Tell me about it. If it weren't for these men," he said, pointing to Paolo and Tumulto, I might be on my way to hard labor in Germany. Francesco too." He pulled Francesco to his side and hugged him. "This boy has more than redeemed himself, Ennio. He spotted the trouble. You'll have to tell Pierluigi."

Francesco's chest was expansive, smiling as Ennio gave Francesco's hair a friendly tussle. He felt quite proud but said, "It was nothing."

Paolo introduced Tumulto and filled everyone in with what his role would be. The map was lying open on the table. Dominic invited everyone to sit and brought out more wine and glasses. Tumulto, using the map, described his plan for crossing the Sangro. It involved linkage between his group and partisan friends on the south side of the Sangro. It was risky; it would involve stealth and perfect timing, but he thought it could be done. They were discussing the plan and raising questions which Tumulto was attempting to answer when there was a loud knock on the door. A few moments later, Dominic's wife led a man into the room. He was Dominic's friend, Vito from Pescocostanzo, visibly upset. A mutual friend and his family had been murdered.

"Who? Where?" asked Dominic "Guido Donatelli in Pietransieri."

Dominic looked stunned. He, Guido, and Vito were members of an

Abruzzese farming co-op and had become close friends over the years.

Seeing the shocked faces on Francesco and the other strangers in the room, Vito said, "Let me show you where the place is on the map." He pointed to a dot to the east of where they were, near the town of Roccaraso. "It's less than 50 kilometers from here."

"What happened, Vito?" Dominic asked.

"This is how I heard it. A German regiment had been deployed in that area for the past month. They were establishing artillery emplacements. What they didn't want or thought the enemy might make use of, they destroyed. They put up the usual warnings regarding aid to escaped prisoners. Soon after they ordered all the people out of their homes so they could use the town to establish a defensive position, a rocky elevated area just behind the town."

"We met refugees from San Martino who were fleeing toward Casoli under similar circumstances," Ennio said, "No one told us about any atrocity."

"They probably didn't know about it then, in fact; the incident would likely not have come to light if it were not for a man who happened to be hunting in the Limarri forest adjacent to the town. He witnessed the massacre."

"What did he see?" Dominic asked, the lines on his face deepening.

"It seems there was already tension in the village because the Germans suspected several citizens of partisan activity. Most villagers reluctantly responded to the order to evacuate and moved into the Limarri woods, but some refused to leave their home. Then someone attacked or kidnapped a German soldier which drew the ire of the local commander. He called the Gestapo who sent the SS."

"That's always trouble," Dominic said. "What happened to Guido?"

"I can't tell you about Guido himself. But what I know is that in retaliation, when the officer arrived, he ordered the livestock, including sheep and cattle to be strafed and killed. Not content with that, they blew up homes with people in them and chased those that escaped into the woods where they shot every one they could find."

As Vito spoke, Francesco's face was horrified. After listening to Denis's and Roger's war stories and witnessing two killings, he could envision a monochromatic landscape in flat gray light with SS troops chasing men, women and children through the trees amidst the cacophony of screams and the flashes, and staccato of rifle and machine gun fire. He could picture people running, stumbling, falling spread eagle as bullets tore into them; some laying still, others crawling, then rising and running again until bullets found their mark and finished them. Then his mind saw a silent woods littered with bodies like the fallen leaves of autumn.

"*Tutto?*" Dominic asked his mouth agape, his eyes widened.

"There was only one survivor, a six-year-old girl who was hidden beneath her dead mother's body. The witness, who found the girl after the SS left, claimed there were at least a hundred men, women and children lying on the ground. He had hid himself in a thicket and was petrified, afraid to move a muscle to look up. But then he heard soldiers talking about what to do with the bodies. He glanced up and saw through the brambles that one of them was the commanding officer who had a nervous tic and a strange star-shaped scar on his face. He thought he was the one who ordered the massacre."

Tears welled up in Dominic's eyes. His voice quivering, he asked, "What happened to the little girl?"

"The man took her with him into Roccaraso."

"How about all those dead bodies? Was Guido and his family among them?"

"Who knows for sure? They're lying there still," Vito said. "The entire village massacred, so Guido, his wife, and kids were almost certainly among them. A cold front came through there and it snowed a bit before I left, so the bodies are probably okay for now. That's all I know. When I get back I plan to join the burial parties. But I thought you would want to know."

"Yes, of course," Dominic said sadly. "Please look after them. Let me know what I can do."

The story left Francesco with a sour taste in his mouth; tears glazed his eyes. He got up, left the table, and rushed outside. The others watched him go, but Roger got up and followed him out the door.

Outside, Roger looked for Francesco who was bent over the well. Walking up to him, he put his arm on his shoulder and gently pulled him upright. They sat side by side on the stone wall. "It's okay, Francesco; it was a terrible thing, but you have already seen some terrible things in this war."

"Nothing like that," Francesco said, wiping away tears.

"We have to accept what we can't change and hope for justice later. For now have courage, my friend. In time this, too, will pass."

"I don't think it will pass," he said, clearing his throat. He looked forlorn but his tears had dried. "I can't understand how anyone can murder women and children," Francesco said, "I just can't..."

"These are not normal men," Roger responded. "Denis would say they were crackers, crazy. *Pazzo* you would say! These Nazis take an 'eye for an eye' to another level."

"*Bruto*, not *pazzo* is the word I would use."

"Killing people like that is actually beyond brutal; it makes no sense. It just makes the people angrier and only creates martyrs. It's happened time and again in history."

"We need to find out the name of the officer who ordered the killings."

"If there were no survivors except the girl, it will be impossible." "There was a witness."

"But he only overheard soldiers speaking."

"Yes, but he did describe one of them, the officer with a nervous tic and scar."

"But he would be hard to trace."

"But it could be done, right?"

"Well, the military keeps records of officer and enlisted assignments, but getting to those records is another matter. Impossible now. Maybe after the war, when the victors can make formal inquiries into various matters. Come, let's go back in. There is nothing you can do by yourself out here. Better to be with the others."

Francesco shrugged, shook his head, and sighed. He took comfort in Roger's explanation and his realistic expectation. He rose and followed him back to the house, hoping there might be something he could do later.

Denis was speaking when they reentered the room. "We need to haul our arses out of here, Dominic. I told your brother that we didn't want to put his family at risk. Roger and I were planning to escape on our own, but he convinced us his plan was better. He turned out to be right back then, but now it's different. We have put a lot families like yours at risk."

Roger nodded in agreement.

"We just heard how bad the Germans are" Ennio said. "I don't think your brother wants to put you in more danger. So I agree, we need to leave as soon as possible."

Paolo spoke up. "It turns out that the time to leave is at hand. Tumulto and his group claim to have information that the British plan to attack across the Sangro in the next few days, so you must get across the river before then. We talked about the options in Casoli this afternoon where we heard a lot of different stories about escapes. One of the tales was about an escaped prisoner dressed up as a woman, and with two other women, one on either side of him holding his arms, they walked the disguised man out of town right past the German noses."

"*Basta!*" Tumulto said. His face and the tone of his voice showed his impatience. "Enough with the disguises! They got you here but they won't get you across the river. It's time for a bold move. I will get you across a tributary of the Sangro tomorrow and to a safe house in the hamlet of Altino. That's the first step. It's in the Sangro valley. The roads on this side of the river are heavily patrolled by the Germans. They have scattered camps and fortifications on high ground all along that stretch of the river, so you will have to be careful. You won't have the sheep and shepherd guise as cover anymore."

"Is that house safe?" Francesco asked. He had remained quiet during the discussion, the massacre still on his mind.

"Safe enough," Tumulto responded. "There are no sure things, but your two friends are going to have to find the right time to cross the Sangro. One good thing about November weather in this valley is that thick fog fills the river bottom for a few hours in the morning. I am counting on that for cover, but the river has already overflowed its banks so there are few reasonable places to ford. Once you and my man in Altino decide where, a partisan on the other side of the river in the town of Archi will come down to the river. At a prearranged signal, he will row a boat across the river. Looking at Denis and Roger he indicated his friend would pick them up and row back. "When you get to the other side you're on your own finding your way to the British."

If they got to the other side, Francesco thought. Roger and Denis might have been thinking the same thing by the looks on their faces. By now even Francesco knew from the recounting of their military experiences that the best laid plans could go awry.

"If it's okay then, we will go at first light tomorrow," Tumulto said.

"What about me?" Francesco asked. "I can help get them across."

"This has to be the end of the line for you, my boy," Dominic intervened. "You have to stay here with me and Ennio. I will call Pierluigi tomorrow from Casoli, give him the latest update so he can send the truck to pick you up. That's the plan my brother set up, and we have to stick with it."

"The plan was that I was to make sure they got back to their army and then return to Caramanico with Ennio," Francesco said, raising his voice.

"Stay calm, Francesco. You did your job," Roger said. "You were great, but we need to go the rest of the way with the help of Tumulto and his men."

"Yes, but I want to come with you," he pleaded. "I want to know you both made it back. I need to tell Pierluigi that his plan worked out. If I don't come with you, I won't really know. I can do it, you know I can."

"What do you think, Tumulto?" Denis asked. "You've seen how he has handled himself."

Tumulto pursed his lips and frowned. "Why the hell do you want to risk your life? If you were older maybe, but if anything happens to you I could never forgive myself. I have a boy almost your age."

"Look, I have faced German soldiers before. I might be of more help than you think. I could be a messenger in plain sight between you and your men. They wouldn't suspect someone my age of being a partisan."

Tumulto looked down and pondered the idea. "Don't count on it," he said. "The Germans had plenty of 15-year-olds shooting at them in Naples. I'll tell you what, you can come as far as Altino, but then you must return here."

Francesco countered. "Okay, but I want to see them get across the Sangro."

"Altino and no further!" Tumulto responded. "Deal or no deal?"

Francesco's face was scrunched, his lips pursed. He wanted to argue on and convince everyone that he was up to the challenge. The knowledge of what he accomplished getting to the Sangro had changed him. He felt grown-up enough and didn't think it was fair that he was being denied the final opportunity. And he felt an obligation to Pierluigi as well as to Denis and Roger. They had started out as complete strangers, but they had become friends on the trip. He knew what he wanted to do, he didn't want to leave them, but then he didn't want to press his luck either. *"Va bene,"* he said. I'll take it a day at a time, he thought.

"If it's settled then, let's eat and get some rest," Dominic said. "You will want to leave early in the morning."

He thanked Paolo and Felice for guiding the men on the latest leg of the journey, and Vito for coming to tell him about the death of their friend. The room was soon filled with the aroma of a traditional Abruzzo pasta—*maccheroni alla chitarra con salsa di agnello*. After Vito left for home, Dominic showed the men to the rooms where they bedded down for the night.

Roger and Denis looked in on Francesco who sat forlornly on the edge of his bed. Sitting on either side of him, they chatted like any group of friends at the end of a daylong engagement. The banter was driven by Roger and Denis with Francesco mostly silent, listening. But he seemed to perk up when they stressed the essential role he had played these past few weeks on the trek. "Don't lose heart, Francesco," Roger said. "We have the most important challenge ahead of us and you get to come along. It's not over till its over." Francesco was feeling better when they said good night and left the room.

Chapter 14

The following morning the household woke to the sound of thunder. Clouds in hues of gray blanketed the sky forming a low ceiling over Casoli, obscuring the upper reaches of the Maiella and presaging another wet day.

Paolo and Felice had left early at the first rumble to rejoin partisans in the hills of Casoli. The partisans were preparing to guide advanced British units through the forested slopes of the Maiella once they crossed the Sangro. After a breakfast and some last words with Ennio the men left through the farm's south meadow toward the Aventino River beyond the tree line. A slow steady rain began to patter their hats as they neared the river. The approach to a narrow bridge over the tributary was under water on both sides.

Tumulto turned to the men and suggested they wade barefooted. It was cold and wet, but they removed their boots and socks and rolled up their pant legs above their knees. Fastening their boots to their packs by the shoestrings, they entered the cold water cautiously. At first, only ankle deep, the water's depth gradually rose to their knees as they stepped onto the bridge. On the other side, the water's depth receded on higher ground. It continued to rain as they sat and dried their feet and legs, passing a towel around. Replacing their shoes, they rose and moved on turning east through the wet fields. Their shoes sunk into the soft earth as they paralleled the road for a short distance to monitor German patrols.

Satisfied with the absence of military movement along the road, the group quickly sprinted across the muddy path and through a field on the other side into a grove of trees. Ahead of them were low hills and barren fields. They soon came to a secondary road with a road marker with an arrow pointing toward Casoli. Crossing it they continued through the fields to another secondary road with a marker pointing to Altino.

The low rumble of thunder and steady downpour created running rivulets and puddles of water in the road, but without the sheep to slow them, they soon found themselves looking up at the village on the crest of a hill. The slopes below the cluster of stone buildings were covered in spent grapevines and olive groves. Tumulto guided them toward a small stream which they boulder-hopped, and then through a cherry tree orchard barren of both fruit and foliage. A small farmhouse and barn sat at the edge of the orchard. Tumulto led the men into the barn and out of the rain. "Dry off and wait here," he said. "I will let my friend know that we have arrived."

Denis, Roger, and Francesco removed their packs and *mantellos* which were soaked. The interior of the dimly-lit barn contained various implements, ladders, and stacks of empty baskets for the fruit harvests. One of the ladders was propped against a loft where garlands of dry pepper and garlic hung on ceiling hooks. The livestock pen was empty except for a bed of straw. The men looked around and found an oil lamp which they lit causing the darkness to recede to the walls. They turned a couple of empty barrels on their sides, sat down and removed their wet clothes, muddy boots, and socks. They pulled dry clothes from their packs and hung the wet ones to dry.

"So far so good," Roger said.

Francesco said, "The Sangro is next, we are almost there. I can almost smell the water."

"Don't get too excited Francesco, you made a deal, remember?" Denis said. "I can see why Tumulto let you come along; it hasn't been all that risky, but from here on out the German military will be too close for comfort."

"I'm sure Pierluigi would not want you putting your life at further risk," Roger said. "He surely would agree with Tumulto's decision if he knew it."

"I know how you feel," Denis said. "And like I said last night, Roger and I are grateful for everything you have done, but more than anything, we want you to have a life for yourself after this war is over."

Francesco pondered what they were saying. He questioned his willingness to risk his life further; if he was ready to die if the Germans caught him helping the men escape. He questioned what he accomplished in his life. What would his mother do when she learned he risked his life, and what about his father? Would he get to join him in America?

None of the questions had answers he could articulate at the moment so he chose to ignore them and climbed the ladder to the loft.

The barn door swung open and Tumulto entered, accompanied by another man in peasant garb. "This is Serpenta," he said, introducing Denis and Roger. Francesco peered down from the loft. "That's the boy, Francesco," he said to Serpenta, pointing to the loft. "Come down and listen, Francesco."

Francesco climbed down joining with Denis and Roger around Tumulto and Serpenta, a solid, if unimposing, man with dark curly hair protruding beneath a black beret.

"You two will be *i nostri primi*, our first," Serpento said. "We get to test our plan with you, okay."

"Just get us to that river," Roger said. "We'll take our chances from there."
"It's very important that we get you across by tomorrow morning," Serpenta

said. "After that it may be too late. The British army is on the move— they will be trying to cross the river any day now. The Germans are maneuvering on this side. It looks like a chess match to me, but I think the Germans will try to stop them at the river or at least slow them down. They have already blown up most of the bridges."

"Shouldn't they cross tonight then?" Francesco asked.

"It's too risky," Serpenta answered. "The river has overflowed its banks and the current is swift. You could end up way downstream. My compatriot on the other side will need daylight to find you under these conditions."

He went on to tell them the location had been prearranged, taking advantage of cover provided by a grove of trees at flood stage by the river and the morning fog. He explained in detail the signaling system his man and they would use, putting his hand to his mouth and mimicking a squawking raven. He repeated how the calls in sets of three would be the signal for the boatman to depart from his side of the river. "Your response will allow him to maintain the correct bearing and make any necessary adjustment."

"What if there is no fog?" Roger asked.

"Then pray for heavier rain that keeps the Germans at their posts. But the chances are the valley will be filled with fog tomorrow as it has been for the past few days. If we don't have it as cover, we may have to wait for the right conditions again."

"Tomorrow we jog, slog, and pray for fog," Denis said. "Who knows what will happen once the offensive begins."

"Until then we wait," Serpenta said. "Tumulto will reconnoiter the meeting spot on the river. He will let me know if the latest activity forces us to change plans."

The rain finally stopped, and it was getting dark when Serpenta returned. In the dim flickering light of the oil lamp, he told Denis and Roger what lay ahead as Francesco listened attentively.

The sector where they intended to cross the river was heavily patrolled by Germans in both directions. They were moving divisions further east on the coastal plain and several miles deep toward Orsogna and Lanciano to meet the British who they expected would cross the Sangro in that direction. "We have to be careful every move we make from now on. With all the maneuvering it will be hard to predict where the Germans will be at any point."

"Agreed," Denis said, "Stealth is the name of the game."

"Have you eaten yet?" Serpenta asked.

"We were about to break out the food Dominic gave us."

"Well, save that for after you cross the river. You may not know where that next meal is coming from. My wife made a stew with a rabbit that I caught in a trap. It's not much, but it's warm. Let me bring it out."

He left the barn and returned a few minutes later carrying a tray with an iron pot, a carafe of wine, a set of bowls, a partial loaf of bread and glasses. The hearty stew was strongly flavored with garlicky tomato sauce. As the men ate, Serpenta said, "We need to be ready to go at first light tomorrow so we will have the fog for cover. I will call you as soon as I rise. Do any of you have any questions?"

Denis, holding a spoonful of stew in one hand and a hunk of bread in the other asked, "Your man on the other side will be expecting us?"

"Yes. I sent the message to him this afternoon. I expect him to be at the river at dawn. If there is nothing else, let's get some sleep. I will call you at first light in the morning."

"Good night and thank you again for the food and wine," Denis said.

"*Si, grazie molto,*" Roger added.

After Serpenta left the barn, the men climbed into the loft. The scent of combusted tobacco filled the air as the men bedded down for the evening, and Francesco's thoughts turned to his last day with them.

Chapter 15

The next morning they were awakened by Serpenta's urgent call from the barn door. "*Venite subito! Porca misseria,* of all mornings, a bright sun! We have to get to the river before the fog burns off."

The men grabbed their packs and scampered down the ladder. The open barn door revealed a radiant sun causing a mist to rise from the wet ground. Stepping outside, they could see beyond the meadow and trees to the fog-covered river valley, and now to the east for the first time, the full Maiella backdrop beyond the village of Altino. The upper slopes and peak were covered in snow that sparkled in the morning sun. Winter had arrived in Abruzzo, but there was no time to admire the view.

"*Andiamo subito,*" Serpenta urged the men.

Everything was happening too abruptly for Francesco. He needed more time to give Denis and Roger a proper send-off. He knew he couldn't continue the journey. That issue had been settled, and he had agreed. He had given his word, but he was terribly conflicted. He started up the ladder for his pack, then stepped down again and walked rapidly back and forth in the barn rubbing his arms.

Roger read the conflict and disappointment on Francesco's face. "I know we will meet again, Francesco, if not here in Italy, then in America after the war," he said, shouldering his pack. "Take care of yourself and remember me. I know I will not forget you," he said, embracing him. And for the first time, he kissed him on both cheeks.

"That goes for me, too, mate," Denis added, stepping over to put his arms around the boy. "If I survive this war, I will be back in Abruzzo someday and I will find you. You can count on it. *Arrivederci,*" he said, as he turned and hurried away.

Serpenta, who had already started to walk away from the barnyard, turned as he reached the meadow and shouted back to the men to hurry.

Francesco watched them walk off, quickening their pace as they tried to catch up to Serpenta now halfway across the meadow. He wiped a tear and stepped back into the barn starring at his pack. What should he do?

When he stepped to the barn door again, he saw the men had reached the far end of the meadow and were about to enter a stand of trees. He grabbed his pack and walked off in their direction, deciding he would lag far enough behind so they would not see him. But he needed to stay close enough to track them to the river somewhere in the fog, covered valley below.

The rising sun warmed him as he made his way through the tawny meadow and woods, pausing from time to time to duck behind trees and hedgerows to listen. As he descended toward the river he encountered the fog. At first it consisted of only gray misty fingers extending up the slope, but soon he was swallowed up by it, and he found it increasingly difficult to track the men. He sensed a sudden drop in temperature as he continued, and within minutes he moved from the relative warmth of the sun to the chill and dampness of the fog-shrouded slope. He walked and stopped periodically to listen for foot falls. When he heard rustling leaves and snapping twigs he moved on cautiously.

A grinding motor alerted him to a road ahead he could not see. Serpenta had said a road ran along the river. Reaching the edge of the grove of trees, he barely made out the shapes of three men running low up a short incline and disappearing into the mist. Thinking the area before him was clear, Francesco ran across the field to the incline where he stopped to survey the road, visoring his eyes and cupping his ear. He was enveloped in the gray blanket of fog and could only see a short distance everywhere he turned. Quickly he crossed the road and scurried down the embankment into a field on the other side. He wasn't sure how far he was from the river, but he could smell the water's dampness. Cautiously he moved forward, not sure of where the men were. When he heard their voices just ahead of him, he stopped, moved off to his right and waited until the voices faded. Quietly he placed each foot gently on the ground taking care not to make a sound. He was close to the river he knew from the sound of water lapping the shore. He came upon a group of boulders and fallen tree limbs at the river's edge and decided to hide and wait again. He still could not see the men, but he sensed he was close to them.

The scent of the water drifted up to him and he reached down to gather a handful. It tasted cold and fresh. The current moved swiftly along the shore, eddying with bits of debris. As he waited the gray mist began to fill with a pale yellow light, and trees on the far bank became vaguely discernible. This is not good, Francesco thought; the sun is burning through the fog. He looked around. He could now see the three men crouching at the river's edge. Looking backward toward the road, he saw no activity, but trees near the road and beyond were coming into view. Then he heard a harsh squawking sets of raven calls coming from the direction of the crouching men, followed moments later by the same sound from across the river. Hurry, he thought, as he crouched in fear for the men. Soon he heard another set of squawks, and then he saw the silhouette of a man in a rowboat moving in the dissipating fog, the beat of his oars splashing the water as he approached the bank.

Roger and Denis jumped from their crouched position into the boat and took positions in front and behind the rower. The rower reversed his oar strokes and turned the boat, trying to position it optimally in the current for the return trip. As Roger and Denis got into the boat, Serpenta quickly retreated from the river's edge and crossed the road in the disappearing fog bound for home.

As they pulled away into the rippling current, Francesco heard a motor vehicle coming up the road. It sounded like the vehicle he had heard earlier now returning. The vehicle came into view and Francesco saw an armored car. The tan, high-clearance vehicle had an open compartment and two seats, one for the driver and another for a soldier beside him. A semiautomatic rifle with a top-loaded magazine was mounted on the hood. Francesco's head swiveled back and forth between the men in the boat on the river and the armored car on the road. Serpenta had gotten away cleanly, and now Francesco hoped Denis and Roger would too. But his hopes sank when the vehicle ground to a halt. The soldiers had spotted the boat and passengers.

The boat was now clearly visible as the fog lifted; it was moving fast down river propelled by the strong, rapid strokes of the oarsman who struggled in the river's brisk current. The boat was angling toward the far bank when the soldier who was seated next to the driver rose up, sat on the frame of the car behind his seat and drew binoculars to his eyes. He surveyed the river in the direction of the boat and looking down; he said something to the driver that Francesco could not hear. The driver quickly rose and swung the machine gun around toward the boat now on the far side of the river. He shouted "Halt!" several times and then began firing the machine gun. His companion had dropped his binoculars, grabbed his rifle and jumped out of the car. The stuttering machine gun and cracks of rifle fire broke the morning silence as bullets traced across the river sending up spurts of water around the fleeing boat. Close to the shore now, the rower continued his strokes, trying to land the boat against the current pulling the craft downstream. His passengers jumped into the knee-deep river as bullets hit the water around them and the embankment beyond.

Francesco's heart pounded as he watched the scene unfold. Holding his breath he prayed the men would make it. Another volley by the German gunner sent a cluster of bullets across the water that hit the boat and the rower crumpled forward. Denis and Roger struggled onto the shore as the boat drifted away, the rower still slumped over, oars motionless. They sprinted low and serpentine up the embankment. Gunfire continued from the vehicle behind. Francesco could see bullets piercing the ground, sending up clumps of mud around the feet of the men as they neared the top of the bank. His last view was of them zigzagging over the top and disappearing down the other side.

Silence. Francesco began to breathe again. From his concealed position he watched the rifleman climb back into the armored car. The driver secured the automatic weapon, sat down and restarted the engine. Then the vehicle whined and sped off down the road toward Altino. Francesco rose to his knees from his crouched position in the rocks. He remained there still and tense for a few minutes, his deep breaths the only thing audible. *Grazie Gesu!* A sense of relief washed over him. He rose, shouldered his pack, and started back.

Chapter 16

Francesco was energized after the long walk to Dominic's farm. He sat at the kitchen table rapidly forking and spooning a bowl of pasta Filomena had prepared. Speaking to Dominic between forkfuls he recounted the events at Serpenta's cottage and the trek to the river. "Serpenta's arrangement worked," he said, holding a twirl of spaghetti in midair. "It would have been perfect if the fog had not lifted. There were some tense moments with the Germans shooting at them, but they got across."

"They were lucky; they got away and that's what matters. My brother's plan turned out well," Dominic said, watching Francesco gobble down his food. "You did well, Francesco. Pierluigi will be happy to know just how well you and Ennio did."

Francesco beamed inside. Is this what accomplishment felt like? He knew he had only been an observer, but somehow he felt he shared in Denis and Roger's dramatic escape.

Ennio walked into the room with his pack and approached Francesco. "We should be getting back to Caramanico." He had congratulated Francesco earlier on hearing his story when he first returned from the river. "Pierluigi's driver, Roberto, is waiting. His truck is loaded with a bales of hay; the dogs are settled and we have some food and drink for the road, thanks to Filomena."

After they bid their hosts goodbye, Francesco and Ennio began their journey home by traveling southwest from Casoli. The road was largely bereft of traffic. The offensive across the Sangro had developed to the east of Casoli and across the coastal plain. Driving through the towns of Taranta Peligna and Palena, they encountered their first checkpoint, a black-and-white sand-bagged hut flying the Nazi flag. The gate across the road was down and a short line of people waited. A guard with a shouldered rifle stood examining a set of papers. Roberto handed across their official papers which got them through with only perfunctory questioning.

Turning northeast on a secondary road in the late afternoon, they spotted a small group of people: men, women, and children hurriedly crossing the road ahead of them. The refugees disappeared in the thicket when they drove past their crossing point.

At Campo di Giove, Roberto stopped the truck by the fountain in the central piazza so they could eat the food Dominic had prepared for them. Afterward, they got out of the truck to stretch their legs and feed the dogs. Francesco wondered if the town was still the active rendezvous point for refugees Pierluigi had told him about. When he saw a group of boys enter the piazza scampering after a ball, he decided to ask one of them.

"It's true," the boy said. "Many prisoners from the Sulmona camp came through here." He told Francesco that the families in town took care of them. The partisans here were well organized and the whole town cooperated with them. But someone informed the Germans and they staged a raid. Four truckloads of German soldiers suddenly appeared one morning last month, he said. A friend of his was in the watchtower at the time. "He sounded the warning bell. Many got away, but they still captured about two hundred."

"So how are things here now?"

The boy told him the town itself was not safe for any refugees the Germans wanted to arrest. He said German undercover agents come dressed as civilians trying to trick fugitives who are looking for help. Although the town was dangerous, he heard his parents talking about farmers and shepherds to the south of town still helping as much as possible.

"*Grazie. Stai attenti. Arrivederci,*" Francesco said, as he turned away and walked back to the truck.

The boy turned to his friends who kicked the ball to him. He stopped it deftly with his leg and booted it back. "*Ciao, ciao,*" the boy said, waving to Francesco.

*****

It was a dark, cold evening when the truck pattered onto the wet cobblestones of Corso Ovidio, Sulmona's main thoroughfare. Francesco was happy to be back on a familiar street. It was bordered with arcades, but beneath the arches, the storefronts were cast in deep shadow. No one was out walking the dimly lit streets. As they entered Piazza XX Setembre, Francesco glanced at the silhouette of a tall monument gracing the center of the square. Darkness obscured the details of the figure Francesco knew was Ovid, the Roman poet, Sulmona's most famous ancient citizen. The Palazzo was the only building in the square with brightly lit windows. Garish red Nazi streamers hung from the façade. Pierluigi had told him the Germans had seized the building for their headquarters and turned out the municipal office workers when they arrived at the end of summer. Passing the cathedral, they turned down the street toward the city market. It was a city marked by war. Bomb damage was clearly visible as they neared the railroad station. Some buildings were bombed-out shells; others were partially collapsed with rubble piled about the foundations.

Pierluigi's Fiat Cinquecento was parked by his storefront. Roberto slowed his truck and pulled in behind Pierluigi's car. Ennio asked Francesco to get out and check the door. It was locked. Francesco glanced up to the second-floor windows. The blackout curtains emitted no light he could see. He cupped his hands to the sides of his face against the door window and peered inside. The dim illumination from the street lamps revealed a shop with wooden crates stacked along the sides and center before a bare counter. Sacks of what appeared to be grain were lined up against one wall. Francesco returned to the truck and got in. "I don't see anything going on in the shop," he said.

"We'll go around in back," Roberto said. He pulled out and drove into the alley next to the shop. The lot at the rear contained stacks of empty packing crates. He pulled the truck over and the men got out. "I don't see a light in the apartment," he said, "But go up, he must be there. I know he is anxious to see you. I will wait here with the dogs."

Ennio followed Francesco up the stairs that creaked with every footstep. A window with a blackout curtain by the door emitted no light, but a thin stripe of light was visible beneath the door. Francesco knocked.

Pierluigi opened the door. His face brightened in a wide smile as his eyes focused on Francesco. Ennio stood behind him, his hand raised in greeting. "Thank the Lord you are both back," Pierluigi said, as he embraced each in turn, kissing them on their cheeks. "I talked with Dominic on the telephone this morning after you left. He told me all about it. I can't tell you how happy I was to hear the news. Quite an adventure, Francesco. I can't believe the stories. Your mother and father would never have forgiven me had any one of those incidents got you captured by the Germans. "Ennio, thank you for keeping the boy safe" he said.

"We were blessed," Ennio said.

"Well, let's not stand here. Come in. I want to introduce you to some men. We will continue this later. There is so much I want to know." Spotting the idling truck in the courtyard he called down: "Roberto unload, and then you can go, grazie. Ennio take your dogs from the truck and put them in the shop. I will be down to open the front door." Francesco stepped into the apartment and Pierluigi followed, closing the door as Ennio descended the creaking staircase.

Three men were seated at a table in the dimly lit living room. They were young men with dark hair and olive complexions, Italians in their 20s. Pierluigi told Francesco to take a seat, indicating he would be back in a moment after he opened the door downstairs for Ennio. Francesco sat and nodded to the men who had resumed talking. They were in the middle of a conversation about a situation in town. Francesco sensed they were businessmen, shopkeepers. One of them looked particularly worried. He was talking about how the Gestapo had become increasingly present in town. More and more armored vehicles were jamming the streets, and soldiers singing Nazi songs were increasingly seen on the streets and in the piazzas.

Pierluigi reappeared with Ennio, who took a seat on the sofa while he brought another chair to the table. "Let me introduce you, Francesco. This is Fumato," he said, pointing to a young, square-jawed man with a weathered face, good-looking in a rugged sort of way. He has been my contact with the partigiani, the man I told you about when you came to me in Caramanico. You can thank him for helping you to get to Casoli and the Sangro."

Fumato stuck out his hand to Francesco. "So this is the boy who guided the POWs and a flock of sheep to the Sangro," he said. "Amazing!"

Francesco rose and shook hands. *"Grazie molto,"* he said. "I didn't do it by myself. There is the leader," nodding to Ennio on the couch.

But Ennio waved him off insisting that Francesco was the real hero who had saved the day time and again.

"Still, it is a wonder" Fumato said.

"There was a lot of help along the way," Francesco said. "I don't know how you got word to your contact, but once you did, others appeared along the route, guided us, and shared the bread they didn't have."

"I am glad that the system has begun to work. Actually, I wasn't sure we'd have a system to help you, but it's good to know we did. We will make it better. I learned through my allied contact that the partisans in the Piedmonte have put together a military-style organization—young and old, men and boys, and the women have formed support groups. We are forming a similar organization, *la Brigatta Maiella* it's called. In time we will catch up to them."

While they were talking, Pierluigi had gone into the kitchen and returned with a tray containing a pot of espresso, cups, and a small, straw-covered bottle of Centerbe. Pouring the coffee and handing a cup to each of them at the table and Ennio on the sofa, he took his seat and introduced the other two men. "This is Marco Cohen and Cesidio Shapiro," he said, pointing to each of the young men in turn.

These men look Italian, but those names are strange, Francesco thought. He wondered if Shapiro an Italian name.

Pierluigi put a teaspoon of *Centerbe* in his coffee and took a sip as he thought of a way to begin. "These men are Jewish shopkeepers here in Sulmona."

Francesco had heard of Jews, but he had never met one before. None lived in his village of Roccamorice, at least that he knew of.

Pierluigi continued, "You may not know this, Francesco, but since you left, Mussolini has been returned to power by Hitler and has reestablished a government in Northern Italy near Lake Garda."

"Yes, we heard about it on our trip."

"Then do you know that one of the edicts of that government is that the Jews have been declared enemies of the state?"

"We heard that, too, but I don't know what it all means."

"Even though that government has little direct reach here in the south, there are Fascist sympathizers around and, of course, there's the Gestapo. These men and their families have not suffered overt animosity yet, but they sense it's coming. They have felt little pressure in the five years since the racial laws were passed, but now, rather than await the possibility of arrest, they want to leave."

Fumato broke into the conversation. "That is why I brought them here with me tonight. Pierluigi told me he expected you and Ennio back this evening and could tell us about possible routes and safe houses. "

"You want Ennio and me to get them across the Sangro?"

"No, no, Francesco," Pierluigi cut in. "Fumato will engage his partisans for that now that he knows there is a network. Annamaria has provided them with false documents, like the identity cards she made for Roger and Denis."

Francesco was excited to hear her name spoken again; he could feel the pulse of his blood. The challenges of the final trek to the Sangro had kept him focused on the tasks at hand. When was the last time he thought about her? Not since they had made the final push. "How is Annamaria?" he asked, trying not to sound too interested.

"She is fine. You will see her tomorrow when we return to Caramanico. What we need to hear from you and Ennio are your experiences along the route from here to Casoli."

"I don't know if what we know will help much. I am surprised that people in Sulmona want to take the risk."

Cesidio Shapiro turned to Francesco, with anger in his voice and fear written on his face, he said, "Do you know what happened to our people in Germany and how it started here five years ago?"

Marco Cohen gestured to Cesidio to stay calm before Francesco had a chance to answer. He said to Francesco, "Our people believed they were citizens of Germany. Their fathers had served the country in the Great War as our fathers did here in Italy. Like everybody else they believed they were safe and hesitated to leave. Even this past spring when the roundup of Jews began in Warsaw, they hesitated. We do not want to suffer the same fate."

"Francesco doesn't need to know what happened in the past, Gesidio," Pierluigi broke in.

Francesco was, indeed, unfamiliar with the beginnings of Mussolini's increasingly delusional actions. He was only seven when Italian armies invaded Ethiopia without the financial resources to wage war. In doing so Mussolini became increasingly dependent on Hitler, who by 1938 had become the dominant partner in the relationship. Arriving in Rome that year to a hero's welcome, Hitler upped the pressure on Mussolini to follow his lead in making Jews second-class citizens. The racial laws were passed in 1938, but Mussolini resisted full enforcement until he fell from power the past summer.

Turning to Francesco, Pierluigi said "It's not important you know their history now, but what's happening in Sulmona is important. Know that these men fear for their families' survival. The Nazis and their collaborators don't care where these people were born or what they did for this country."

"We've learned that the Gestapo raided the Jewish ghetto in Rome and rounded up over a thousand people," Cesidio said more evenly. "We just received word that most of them are being deported to God knows where. We also learned from friends here in Sulmona that the Gestapo is gathering names of Jews who live here. There is no time to waste, so we need to get our families into the liberated areas as soon as possible."

Ennio had listened quietly, but now left the sofa and came to the table. "Let's look at a map," he said. "There is a way south to freedom if you are willing to try it."

Pierluigi retrieved a map of Abruzzo from a drawer and spread it out on the table as the men and Francesco gathered around. "Show us, Ennio."

Fumato leaned over, pointed to the map, and said, "The latest information I have on the war is that the heavy fighting is around Orsogna. Casoli may be liberated and safe by now."

Tracing the map with his fingers, Ennio looked at Fumato and said, "One way is through Anversa and Scanno, but I think it would be best to follow the route we took to get back here from Casoli. So, I would suggest your people travel to Campo di Giove, then Palena, Taranta Peligna, Lama, and finally Casoli— that's the safest route in my opinion."

"Wait," Francesco said, raising his hand. "I learned in Campo di Giove refugees need to avoid the town itself. The Germans patrol it now. It was a rendezvous point for escaped POWs and they raided it last month."

Fumato said, "It may be best to head straight south toward Campobasso. If the fighting is around Orsogna, the British army will be focused on crossing the Moro River, so the Campobasso area is likely to be safer."

"If you are going to go that way, I was told by a boy in Campo di Giove today that the people in the countryside are still helping people," Francesco said,

"The crossing can be difficult over the mountain passes on the route you suggest, especially if the weather is bad," Marco Cohen said. "I don't know if my wife and children will be up to it."

"We have seen families on the run," Francesco said. "You just have to be prepared and dressed for the weather. You can do it. Use the roads as guideposts to avoid the tough terrain at the passes. Stay near but clear of the roads. That's what my friends did when they escaped the Sulmona prison camp. There are Germans in the towns disguised as civilians claiming to be POWs or fugitives. Don't be fooled."

"We were always fortunate in finding people who gave us food and shelter. They asked nothing in return, they just wanted to help," Ennio said. "Will they help Jews?" Cesidio asked.

"I don't know," Francesco said. "That didn't come up, but there is another Italy, a generous one we found on our trip. *Speriamo.*"

"We have given up hope, even though friends here told us they would hide us if need be." Cesidio said.

Marco said, "We appreciate their offer, but we don't want to put them in danger, and I don't know how safe it would be. I don't know who we can really trust anymore. Some people have grown desperate—they could turn us over to the Gestapo for a reward. Everyone is needy."

"Who is going to guide?" Francesco asked. "I would love to do it." "Don't you even think about it," Pierluigi said sternly.

"With what you've told us, Francesco, my men can take over from here," Fumato said.

"But I would really like to help, "Francesco said. I've been there and seen how tough it is to cross the river with the Germans patrolling and…"

Pierluigi cut him off. "There is no way I am letting you go so just get it out of your head. I should have had my head examined for letting you go in the first place. You'll be coming back to Caramanico with me. We have work to do there."

Francesco was disappointed. He knew better than to argue with Pierluigi, but he sensed a new calling to rescue people, and in his heart he believed he could guide these men and their families to freedom. He shrugged his shoulders and sat down.

Turning to Fumato, Pierluigi said, "I can give you some of the provisions I have in the crates downstairs—U.S. Army rations in 18 kilo packages. The German quartermaster knows about them, but he has not asked for them yet."

"We would be grateful for that." Fumato said. "Thank you. I'll talk to my men and get back to you." They were about to shake hands when the stairs began to creak.

Suddenly startled, Pierluigi said, "Quick Fumato, take Marco and Cesidio into my bedroom and be very quiet. Take the cups with you. I don't know who this could be so late."

The three men quickly picked up their cups and went into the adjoining room. Moments later there was a loud knock on the door. Pierluigi motioned for Francesco and Ennio to stay calm and remain sitting as he went to the door. When he opened it he found the German quartermaster standing there. "Good evening, Captain," he said, his mouth agape. "What brings you here so late?"

"I saw your car parked out front and assumed you were here. I came to inquire about the field rations."

"Come in. Let me introduce you to my guests."

The German officer, a tall austere man, stepped inside and looked at Francesco and Ennio seated at the table. Two espresso cups and the bottle of *Centerbe* rested on the table along with an ash tray full of cigarette butts. His eyes fell on the ash tray. "I didn't know you smoked Sanelli."

"Actually, those were left by my other guests earlier this evening." Changing the subject quickly, he said, "Let me introduce you to my Caramanico neighbor, Ennio and my young friend, Francesco." Ennio and Francesco rose from their seats.

Francesco had recoiled the moment the officer walked in. All of the incidents he had witnessed or heard about involving German officers reeled through his mind. His heart was racing as he tried to suppress his sense of fear.

Fortunately, the officer missed the look on Francesco's face as his gaze was diverted by Ennio who offered his hand.

The officer simply stood back and raised his arm in the Nazi salute. "Be seated. I will be brief," he said turning to Pierluigi. "I will send my men to pick up the crates with the food rations tomorrow morning. Here is a list of what to include," he said, handing the sheet of paper to Pierluigi."

"Certainly, Captain. I will have them ready for you, but I have need of a few for my family and friends in Caramanico."

"Fine, you know our arrangement. As long as you cooperate with us there will always be something for you. We know the difference between pigs and hogs, don't we?"

"Yes, of course sir."

"Well then, till tomorrow," the officer said as he turned, walked to the door and opened it without looking back. He departed quickly closing the door behind him.

When the creaking on the stairs ceased, Pierluigi turned to Ennio and Francesco with a look of relief. "That was close. I wouldn't have wanted to explain who my other guests were."

Francesco had visibly relaxed once the sound of the officer's footsteps had receded off the steps. He thought about the German officers at Santo Spirito. How easy would it have been to dispatch this one too.

Pierluigi walked over to the bedroom and opened the door. "Fumato, come out. You will have to collect the crates tomorrow morning before sunrise. I will be waiting. Try not to be seen"

Fumato thanked Pierluigi, walked to the kitchen door, opened it cautiously, and looked down into the empty courtyard. Then he motioned to Marco and Gesidio who, shaking hands with Pierluigi, followed him out and down the steps.

Pierluigi brought a cot and blankets for Ennio to sleep on, and he made up the sofa for Francesco. Then he retired to his bedroom where he slept restlessly, waking periodically and then falling back into the edges of sleep.

****

It was still dark when Pierluigi arose and roused Ennio from a sound sleep, telling him he needed to come down to the shop to keep the dogs quiet. In the shop Pierluigi lit an oil lamp, pulled the shades over the windows and waited.

At dawn's first light, Fumato and one of his men drove up and parked. Pierluigi opened the door and helped the men load four of the cases of field rations and a sack of wheat into the back seat.

At sun rise he and Ennio returned to the apartment. Francesco was still sleeping. Pierluigi made some coffee and handed a cup to Ennio who had begun folding his blanket. Pierluigi whispered to him; "I will be leaving soon with Francesco. Roberto will come for you and the dogs in a little while. My manager will be here to open the shop before then."

"What do you want me to tell him?" Ennio asked softly.

"There is little for him to do except wait for Roberto to arrive. You can help him load the truck, and then he can wait for the Germans. I left a note on the counter that specifies what to provide to whom."

"I will see you then in Caramanico. It's been a long journey. I will be happy to get home. I hope you don't ask me to do that again," he said, as he took a sip of coffee.

Pierluigi raised his arm, his hand palm up and shook his head. "Don't worry, I wouldn't think of it. I fretted the entire time you were gone. Every day I regretted asking you and Francesco to take the risk. There was no way I was going to let that boy guide the Jews, let alone allow you, even though I want to help them get away from here. "

"You had a good plan, but we were lucky. I thank the Lord for that good fortune. And I will tell you this, I could not have done it without Francesco."

"My brother said he seemed older than he was."

The sound of their voices, though softly spoken, reached Francesco in his slumber. He turned over with his eyes closed, vaguely aware he was being praised. After a few moments, he fell back to sleep.

Ennio swallowed the last of his coffee. "That's true, but more than that, he showed courage and fortitude. He never complained once, and he always wanted to do more than we expected of him. It was tough to convince him otherwise."

"I expected that he would be helpful, but I didn't think he would be quite as resourceful as he turned out to be. He seems much more grown up now to me as well, even though it's only been weeks."

"He went with Denis and Roger on the last part of the trip to the Sangro while I waited at the farm. At Altino near the river he was told to stay behind, but he went anyway."

"Yes, my brother told me. He said Francesco just had to see for himself that the men got safely across the river."

"They became close, we all did on the road. It was hard for him to leave them.

I know that he misses them."

"I told him to use good judgment."

"I reminded him from time to time, and for the most part he did. I know he wanted to personally assure you that your plan worked. That seemed important to him."

"Well, there will be much to talk about. I better wake him so that we can get started to Caramanico." The rising sun had gradually brightened the room. Pierluigi walked over to the sofa and nudged Francesco awake. "Time to get up, sleepyhead."

****

Francesco rolled over and rubbed his eyes. "What time is it?" "It's about seven. Time we left for Caramanico."

Francesco cast the blanket aside, sat up, and put on his shoes and shirt. He was anxious to get going. By morning he had replaced the disappointment of not guiding the Jews out of Sulmona with the anticipation of seeing Annamaria again. Pierluigi went into the kitchen to make another pot of espresso, and returned with three cardboard boxes labeled K Rations and handed one to each of them. Then he went back for the coffee. Francesco eyed the boxes curiously.

"It's what the soldiers call their breakfast pack," Pierluigi said. "The small packets are a coffee powder that you pour hot water over. It's pretty weak, not like our espresso, but better than the bitter substitutes we have had this past year. The biscuits are nourishing so I would recommend those. Forget the coffee."

Francesco, the coffee critic who had sampled both the good and bad, nodded his head. "I'll take your word for it."

After they finished their breakfast, Pierluigi and Francesco bid Ennio goodbye. Francesco grabbed his pack and followed Pierluigi to the shop downstairs. He paused to play with the dogs for a few moments, and then left through the front door where Pierluigi was waiting to lock it. Francesco got into Pierluigi's car parked at the curb and stowed his pack behind his seat. Pierluigi got into the car and pulled away. It was a cool, crisp morning. Sulmona was just beginning to stir with the first pedestrians and vehicles on the street.

"Francesco!" she exclaimed with a bright smile and a little short of breath. "I'm so happy to see you. I passed my father near the *municipio*. I couldn't get here fast enough," she said as she pulled off her coat and tossed it on a chair. Francesco rose to greet her matching her smile and joy.

His heart picked up a beat and he reached out his hands to hers kissing on her cheeks as she kissed his.

He tried to contain his excitement with her mother in the room. "Annamaria, I missed you."

"I missed you too; I'm so happy you're back safe. Let me look at you. *Dio mio*, you've lost weight!"

"Not you too!" He knew he had lost weight; he was forever cinching up his belt. "That's what a long walk in the woods will do."

"Really? Some walk! You're older too. Didn't you have your birthday while you were away? How did you celebrate?"

"Alone with *torrone* and thoughts of you." "How sweet."

"I'm catching up to you."

"Not really. I'll be eighteen soon." "Perfect, you'll be legal."

"But you still won't be," she laughed.

Francesco put up his hands gesturing she had gotten the best of him. "So what have you been doing while I was away?"

"Oh, I don't want to talk about me," she said, pulling out a chair and taking a seat at the table. Francesco sat down next to her. "Is it true what we heard from Uncle Dominic?"

"What did you hear?"

"Don't be so humble, Francesco," Angiolina chimed in. "You did a man's job."

"Well, what we did was have some close calls with the Germans, but everything worked out. What's important is that your father's plan worked. Denis and Roger got away. They should be back with their army by now, I hope."

"My friends all want to meet you," Annamaria said. "We want to throw you a party!"

"He deserves a *panarda*—a banquet for the special man he is!" Angiolina said.

"I didn't do this by myself. Ennio was the leader, and everyone looked out for me."

"It's nice to be modest, Francesco, but you should be proud," Angiolina said, as she rose and walked to the pantry. A beaded curtain covered the entrance. The strands clicked apart as she stepped through. Looking back she said, "I'm thinking of doing a *gallina arrosto* tonight. How does that sound, Francesco?"

His mind conjured up the sight and aroma of roasted chicken surrounded by crisp garlicky potatoes and caramelized onions. "Sounds good to me," he said, with his thumb up. Of course he knew that would be the second course, the *secondo;* the *primo* would be a pasta, probably a *maccheroni alla chitarra* or *a brodo.* One can't have too many courses in Abruzzo. The *panarda,* a multicourse banquet for special occasions and reunions, is served in such a way that when one thinks the last course is served, another begins. In this manner thirty or more courses would not be unusual.

Pleased with Francesco's response, Angiolina turned into the recess to gather her supplies.

Francesco reached for Annamaria's hands and drew her close to him. "I've missed you so much," he said as he attempted a kiss on her lips.

Annamaria pushed him back gently sweeping her eyes to the pantry and back to indicate her mother's near presence. Turning and walking into the hallway, she motioned Francesco to follow her. She turned to him and he reached for her.

With his arms about her waist, he drew her to him again. She put her arms around his neck and kissed him passionately on the mouth. They separated for a moment to look intently at each other before bringing their mouths together more passionately. Francesco moved his hands up and pressed her more tightly to him, just as Angiolina called from the pantry.

"Annamaria, I can't find the herb basket. Do you know where it is?"

"I may have moved it to the kitchen cupboard," Annamaria called from the hall. "I'll take a look." She lowered her hands to Francesco's arms and gently pushed them down.

Francesco's heart was still beating rapidly, but he sighed and stepped back, releasing her. "Tonight?" he asked.

"Yes," she said softly. Her cheeks were blushed as she reentered the kitchen with Francesco trailing behind. In the kitchen she looked at Francesco and put her forefinger to her lips as she nodded toward the pantry. "Tell me about what you saw on the way to Casoli," Annamaria asked, turning and bending over to look into the lower shelf of the cupboard.

He found it difficult to shift his thoughts back to her question. "Where do you want me to start?

"I found the herbs, Mama," she said, as she rose with the basket. She turned and looked at Francesco. "I want to know everything you saw and did."

"And I want to know everything you did since I left."

"I still do the identification cards and some other things for the partisans. You remember the friend of my brother who has been involved with them?"

"Yes, I remember you told me. It goes well?"

"He gives me the names and photos. I make the cards at home, and then I give them to him when we meet."

"You see a lot of him then. Is that all you do together?"

"Yes, Francesco, it's all we do, no more, no less. We're quite serious about our work; his job and mine are interconnected don't you see." She pouted her lips and waved her forefinger at him. "You shouldn't be jealous."

"Hey, just asking. What does he do with the cards?"

"He hides them in slots he made in the seats of bicycles and they get peddled to wherever they have to go."

"Very clever."

"The bicycles are used to smuggle other things too. We roll up documents like forged birth certificates, important maps, plans for sabotage, that sort of thing and they get inserted into the steel tubing of the bicycle frames. The Germans search people and vehicles, but so far they have not thought to look into bicycle frames."

"Maybe I can help with those bicycles, maybe do some of the riding. I want to stay involved."

The beaded curtain clicked and Angiolina emerged from the pantry as Francesco was uttering his last remarks. "Francesco, you need to make a trip home to see your mother before you do anything else."

"My mother is right," Annamaria said. "Your mother asked about how you were getting along in a note that was delivered by a friend of your brother's. We had to send back a note that you were doing well, that you were working at my father's shop in Sulmona for a few days. We felt bad enough with that lie. Maybe you should go home and talk to her."

"You can say you have been working with my husband's food distribution project. That's less of a lie," Angiolina said.

Francesco looked annoyed, thinking of an excuse. "If I do tell her what I have really been doing these past few weeks, she will be very upset, so will my brother. The Sulmona story might be better. Anyway with all the snow now, I can't go back the way I came."

"I am sure my husband will take you in his car. It's something you are going to have to do sooner or later."

"Later will be better. Until then I can help Annamaria and her friends."

Angiolina looked exasperated. "Look, Francesco, we're thinking about what's best for you. Let's talk about this later, when my husband comes home. He needs to hear what you have to say, what we all have to say. I'm sure he will have a strong opinion about what you should do next."

"Fine, whatever you decide. I owe you that much."

"Annamaria, can you help me prepare lunch?"

"Certainly mama, what are you making?

"*Le sagnette.* How does that sound, Francesco?"

Francesco never much cared for the pasta his mother made with flour, water and salt; no eggs. *Cucina povera*—poor people's food he knew it was called, but he felt he couldn't say that to Angiolina. *"Va bene,"* he said.

"Well, then, why don't you unpack your bag and make yourself comfortable? Maybe you would like to go to the thermal baths."

Francesco sighed, realizing Annamaria would be busy helping her mother; so he said, *"Buona idea."*

Pierluigi returned from the municipal building in the early afternoon with the news that Roberto had arrived and dropped off the food crates after taking Ennio home. But he seemed more haggard than usual with tired-looking eyes. Playing his many roles was taking a toll.

Francesco had enjoyed his time at the thermal baths. His dark wavy hair was still damp and combed back from the temples. He looked refreshed and handsome. Angiolina and Annamaria were scurrying about the kitchen preparing the pasta when Francesco walked in. He sat down to chat with Pierluigi while the women worked around them.

In late afternoon after the meal, they were all still seated having coffee, chatting merrily, relaxed and smiling. The aroma of Angiolina's cooking lingered in the air. Angiolina had surprised Francesco by dressing the pasta in a lamb ragu. Pierluigi was telling them about Roberto's description of Ennio's homecoming and how happy his wife was to see him again. Angiolina was about to bring up Francesco's future when the rumble of vehicles pulling up in the front of the house brought the conversation to an abrupt halt.

****

Pierluigi frowned and turned toward the hallway. "Hmm," he murmured. "Who can that be?" He rose from the table and walked down the hall to the front door. As he peered out the narrow window by the door he caught a glimpse of military vehicles. He couldn't imagine why they were there, but he sensed that many of his neighbors' eyes were peering through the slats of the window shutters of their homes flanking the piazza. He opened the door to get a better look at the unfolding scene, and then he closed it quickly. Hurrying back into the dining room, he exclaimed, "It's the SS!"

He had seen an officer step out of a black Mercedes bearing the Nazi fender flag. The dreaded black uniform was tailor-fit to a robust body. His officer's hat with the spread eagle and gray cord was smartly set on his forehead framing a stern face with a strong jaw line— the determined look of someone who got things done. A squad of riflemen stood in the back of a green lorry that had pulled up behind the car. They were dressed in their army field tunics. One of them bore the insignia of a sergeant.

"Do you recognize them, Gigi?" Angiolina asked.

"I've never seen any of them before," Pierluigi said.

"What could they want?" she asked

"I don't know." He was worried. He felt comfortable dealing with the

German military in Sulmona, but they were the Wehrmacht, not the SS or Gestapo. And here in his home, not his shop, he felt particularly vulnerable.

Heavy pounding on the door was accompanied by a muffled, German-accented voice. *"Sanelli, apri la porta, subito, snell!"*

Pierluigi walked quickly to the door and opened it slowly. The black-uniformed officer with SS insignia on the raised collar of his uniform faced him. Steely eyes peered beneath his officer's hat visor. He held a black leather crop in his hand. His sergeant stood behind him. The black Mercedes was parked a few yards away. Several soldiers descended from the lorry and gathered in front of their vehicle, their rifles off their shoulders at the ready. Behind them townspeople appeared from the doorways of their homes and stood along the far side of the piazza.

"Yes, sir, may I help you?" Pierluigi asked, looking at the officer's insignia. "I am Standartenfuhrer Hoffmann. Where are the British POWs?"

"There are no POWs here, Colonel." He knew it would be foolish to deny an encounter with the escaped prisoners, too many people in town knew prisoners from the Sulmona camp had escaped to Caramanico. It took nothing to be labeled a collaborator, a whispered accusation would be enough, but he hoped he could deflect the accusation. He said, "It is true that prisoners from the camp at Sulmona came seeking shelter, but I refused them, and they left."

"Listen, Sanelli, the trouble with you Italians is that you lie to us. Do not lie to me," he said again, giving Sanelli a dark look. "My informant told me that they have been here for several days." Annoyed, he slapped his leather crop against his leg and asked, "Where is your family?"

"In the dining room."

"Take me! Lead the way!"

****

Pierluigi turned and the colonel and his men followed him into the dining room. As they entered, Francesco looked up stunned—his eyes drawn to the stellate scar on the officer's cheek. Could it be, he thought— the butcher of Pietransieri— the SS officer who had ordered the mass killing he learned about at Dominic's farm.

"This is Colonel Hoffmann." Pierluigi said. His voice was subdued and hesitant; his face taunt. He rubbed his hands.

"I take it, Sanelli, this is your wife?" Hoffman stepped around the room with an arrogant swagger.

Angiolina rose, faced and bowed toward the officer, but she remained quiet and grim-faced, nervously tucking at her apron.

"And is this is your daughter?" he asked, nodding toward Annamaria.

One of the soldiers who stood next to the officer said, "Colonel, she and the boy there were the ones who were so insolent to us a few weeks back."

Francesco now recognized the soldier as one of the two that had stopped to question him and Annamaria after they had left the shoemaker shop. He looked at her, a tinge of remorse quickly crossed his face and he averted his eyes.

Annamaria sighed deeply, her eyes downcast.

Francesco refocused on the officer whose eyes he now saw as pure evil. The officer's right eye blinked rapidly. It was that tic and the scar that now convinced Francesco he must have been the officer in charge at Pietransieri.

"Yes, this is my daughter," Pierluigi stuttered, "but the boy…"

Pierluigi was suddenly cut off by the colonel who raised his hand demanding silence. "Be seated all of you." Then he turned to his sergeant and said "Call two others and have the rest remain at their post. I want a complete search of the house."

The soldiers pushed past the group in the dining room and began rummaging through the house as Pierluigi, Angiolina, Annamaria, and Francesco sat anxiously at the table. Francesco saw anguish etched on Angiolina's face and her struggle to fight back the urge to cry. Pierluigi nervously ran his hands through his hair as he noisily fidgeted with the dinnerware. What are they doing Francesco wondered, and why are they here? Could it be that the dead officers were discovered at Santo Spirito and the trail led the SS to this house he shuddered to think?

Several minutes passed with the muffled sounds of the men moving through the various rooms of the house rattling doors and drawers. The ceiling creaked as Hoffman reached into his jacket for a pack of cigarettes. Pulling and lighting one, he took a drag and tossed the still burning wooden match on an empty dinner plate.

"No one else is here, Colonel," his sergeant said, returning from his search. A few moments later the others appeared, one of them held the identification card instrument in his hands. "I found this in the girl's bedroom," he said.

Annamaria slumped in her chair crestfallen. She looked at her father and saw the defeat in his face.

"Well, Sanelli, care to tell me how you acquired a British document machine? You know, of course, such contraband is illegal and severely punished."

****

Francesco shifted uneasily in his chair with a sense of foreboding. He hoped Pierluigi had a convincing alibi, something that would save Annamaria and the family.

"I have had it for some time, even before the war," he said. "When the British embassy in Sulmona acquired a new model, I found this one among its discarded items at a warehouse."

"A likely story," Hoffmann, smirked bitterly. And the two other British objects I'm looking for—the POWs, Sanelli, what is your story for them?"

Pierluigi continued to deny any knowledge beyond the brief encounter he had with them when they first appeared unannounced at his door.

Hoffman was clearly irritated, the frequency of his ocular tic increased. Slapping his crop on the table, he took a final drag from his cigarette, exhaled and ground it out on the plate with the burnt-out match. He rose from the table smiling coldly. He walked around to Annamaria and grabbed her arm, pulling her forward. He said, *"Signorina,* you've made your last card!" His jaw set in anger, a cold fury in his eyes, he squeezed hard with his thumb and forefinger, pressing the soft tissue above her wrist against bone.

Annamaria grimaced, let out a cry of pain and fell back in her seat.

Francesco's instinct was to reach out to her. Anticipating his reaction, Pierluigi held Francesco's wrist to the chair.

"Follow me— outside now! All of you," Hoffman barked.

Francesco's foreboding became sheer fright. He froze and looked to Pierluigi for what to do.

Alarmed, Pierluigi said "My family was not involved with the prisoners. I alone spoke with them. I gave them directions to reach the far side of the Maiella, that's all."

"Why do you insist on continuing this charade, Sanelli? My informant is unimpeachable. I know two men were here. Now bring your family outside! Don't make me repeat myself!"

Pierluigi stood dejectedly. He walked into the hallway, motioning his family and Francesco to follow him.

They followed behind apprehensively, the sounds of jackboots trailing after them. When they stepped out the front door, Hoffmann directed them to stand against the wall of their home on the cold, snow-dusted cobblestones. Annamaria was trembling as she gave Francesco a pleading look and clutched her mother around her waist. Francesco read the fear on Annamaria's face and wanted desperately to reach out and comfort her, but he could not find the words. Grimly, he stood next to Pierluigi, his mind in turmoil.

"Please Colonel, this is a mistake," Pierluigi pleaded. "Please spare my family.

They are innocent, I swear to God."

"Your God can't help you, Sanelli. He is powerless, if he, indeed, exists, which I doubt."

Francesco bristled, his fear modified by indignation. These godless Nazis had shown disrespect for his faith, his church, and his people; now this man who lacked a soul or even a trace of moral fiber flaunted his imagined moral superiority. He would slay this Goliath then and there. But he was empty-handed.

"Sanelli, you know the penalty for assisting escaped prisoners, warnings have been widely posted and clear to everyone." He gestured his men into firing squad alignment. The crowd that had gathered remained silent as they looked on solemnly.

"Please, sir, whatever I can do, I will, anything you ask, just let my family go," Pierluigi pleaded again.

"There can be no compensation except by lives for lives, Sanelli, you know that by now." He motioned his men to lift their rifles.

The women suddenly clutched one another, their eyes glazed with tears. "*O Dio mio, O Dio mio,*" Angiolina murmured, holding her hand over her rapidly beating heart. Annamaria, the girl who had become a *partigiana* without a second thought, clung to her mother as her knees nearly buckled under her. She looked to her father.

Pierluigi was crestfallen. With hanging head and slumped shoulders he clasped her hand as he put his other arm around Angiolina's shoulder.

Francesco stood next to them with his heart pounding. His hands began shaking, but he stood straight with shoulders back. He tried to steel himself to calmness and hold back his tears. He glanced sideways past Pierluigi to Annamaria who had turned her head to him. And in that visual connection, all their pain, sorrow, and anguish flowed between them — just the two of them; all other existence faded to another place, as they nodded to one another.

In the crowd, men and women folded their arms or wrapped them tightly, some women held their hands up to their opened mouths; others made the Sign of the Cross. Hoffmann glanced about the scene before him and the crowd behind him, and slowly raised his arm.

As the rifle squad raised and cocked the bolt action of their rifles, the metallic sliding and clicking caused Francesco's chest to tighten and startled everyone in the crowd. Cold, expressionless faces beneath gray flanged helmets stared down their rifle barrels at Francesco. In their eyes, he saw the futility of his situation. His body relaxed as a wave of resignation swept over him. The chill of the late afternoon was augmented by a sudden breeze that flapped the Nazi fender flags on the Mercedes. Then it became eerily quiet.

The colonel stood expressionless to the side, midway between the Sanellis and his men. He looked at the family huddled against their house, and prepared to drop his arm as a signal for his men to shoot.

"*No, aspeto, aspeto!*" shouted someone beyond the crowd. It was the Mayor running up and holding onto his fedora as he jostled through the crowd. "Please stop, don't shoot, Colonel!"

The captain slowly relaxed his arm as he turned to the mayor, the look of annoyance on his face. "What is it?" he asked.

"That boy," he said pointing to Francesco, "is not part of the Sanelli family. He is from a nearby village. He is just here to help with household chores and care for sheep."

The captain eyed Francesco suspiciously. "Step forward, boy. Is that true?

What is your name?"

Francesco turned toward Hoffman and stared at the peculiar scar on the officer's cheek. He found the nervous tic of the officer's right eye and cheek unnerving and looked away.

"Look at me, boy, when I ask you a question," Hoffmann ordered. "Your name?"

"Francesco," he said softly, turning his head back to the black uniform but avoiding his face.

"Look at me, I said. Speak up! What is your name?"

Francesco slowly raised his head and looked at the cold, slate gray eyes. "Francesco," he mumbled.

"This is not your town?"

"No, sir, I am from Roccamorice." "Sanelli, this is not your son?

"No, Colonel, the mayor is correct."

"Why didn't you tell me this earlier?" "I tried to."

"Are these Sanellis your relatives, your *congiuniti*, Francesco?"

"No, sir, but they are my friends."

The colonel paused to consider his options. The mayor approached and took him aside to intervene for the whole family. But the colonel dismissed him and motioned Francesco to stand at his side.

Glancing at Francesco he said, "You might want to remember who you make your friends." He turned his gaze back toward his rifle squad and nodded. They lifted their rifles into firing position.

Standing next to Hoffman, Francesco reached out to the family, but Hoffman pushed Francesco's arms down with his left arm as he raised and quickly dropped his right arm.

A barrage of rifle fire rang out, the sound reverberated off the walls around the piazza and drowned out Francesco's shout. It lasted only a second, but in a blink, Francesco's horrified eyes saw the bodies of Pierluigi, his wife, and daughter crumple to the pavement.

Time seemed to stand still as the reverberations ceased and the crowd gasped. The smell of gunpowder filled the air. The bullet-ridden family laid on the cobble- stones beneath the pocked wall, their arms flung out, their legs askew as blood began to stain the snow-covered pavement around them. Francesco's mouth opened in a soundless scream; he dropped to his knees and froze.

The colonel turned to face the mayor and in a voice loud enough for everyone in the in the piazza to hear he said "Let this be a lesson! If I have to return because of the assistance given to any other escaped prisoner, I will shoot every man, woman, and child in this village."

He then stepped into his staff car. His driver circled the piazza and drove off. The rifle squad boarded the truck and followed.

The crowd that had gathered began to disperse in silence, as a woman emerged carrying a purple shroud and covered the bodies. The color seemed unusually vivid in the drab afternoon light.

Apart from the soft swish of leather on the snowy pavement, the only other sound was Francesco's slumped figure on the cobblestones sobbing, his face contorted in agony. Clutching his sides, nausea swept over him; he stifled the urge to vomit. The mayor reached down to touch his shoulder. "Francesco . . ." His words faltered.

Francesco raised his arm and pushed the mayor's hand away. "No, leave me alone!" he screamed as he glanced at the shroud-covered bodies.

He rose and began walking away toward the piazza's exit, slowly at first then more quickly until he broke into a run. He did not stop running until he passed through the village entrance to the road down the mountain.

He paused at the side of the road. He looked back and then he turned to peer toward the adjacent slope of the Maiella, from where he had come weeks ago. The staccato of rifle fire still echoed in his head, and a wave of nausea washed over him again. He clutched his belly, and fell to his knees. Tears welled up and coursed down his cheeks. His mind was in turmoil, one incoherent thought following another, none of them in focus. He had heard stories, and he had witnessed death, but nothing like that—an execution. He had run from hunger but the path he chose brought him to this moment. A black Fiat Cinquecento emerged through the village entrance and came to a stop next to him. The mayor got out of the vehicle and came around to Francesco and lifted him to his feet. He embraced the boy but said nothing at first. Several moments passed, with only Francesco's soft sobs interrupting the stillness. Finally, the mayor spoke softly, "Cosa sara, Francesco, cosa sara."

But Francesco knew the mayor was wrong—everything was not going to be okay. Everything had suddenly changed and nothing would be the same again.

The mayor kept his arm around Francesco's shoulder and walked him over to his car. "Let me drive you home."

"How can I go back?" sobbed Francesco.

"That's where your family is, and you need to be with them, especially now."

"I was so hungry in Roccamorice, that I left my family because I thought that I would be so much better off here with the Sanellis," Francesco said. "And now look, they are all dead. I don't know what to do."

"It wasn't anything that you did or did not do that cost the Sanellis their lives. They knew the risks. They believed in what they were doing; you must remember that," said the mayor.

As Francesco got into the car next to the mayor, guilt, anger, and remorse merged into one emotion wrapped in an overriding sense of helplessness. Turning toward the mayor he asked, "What can I do? I don't know what to do," he said, choking back sobs.

"Listen, Francesco, the Sanelli's knew the dangers of maintaining a safe house; still they risked it as did so many others. This changes nothing for those who will continue to resist. You must pray for them all and remember their courage."

"That's not enough, it's just not enough."

The mayor paused, thinking. "Maybe after you have had some time to reflect, you can write about them. I was told you enjoyed writing."

"What will that do?" "It will bring solace."

"To whom? Not to the Sanellis."

"To you. You may come to understand what they sacrificed, not only what happened and why, but also you may see that God made you a witness to the love that one man has for another."

But Francesco didn't respond. He slumped forward in the seat and held his hands over his face and sighed deep breaths between sobs of pain.

The mayor circled back to the Sanelli house so that Francesco could retrieve his belongings. The bodies had been removed from the street and the blood-stained snow had been swept away when they arrived in front of the house. Francesco cringed at the bullet marks on the outside wall as he ran in the front door to the bedroom to grab his pack. He quickly returned to the car. As they drove down the mountain toward Roccamorice, Francesco, thinking about what the mayor had said, recalled the passage from John's gospel: *There is no greater love than to lay down one's life for one's friends.* But the scripture didn't bring him much comfort. He knew he had paid a dear price for his failure to deal with the German occupation and assuage his hunger. And now he had no sense of how to cope with what he was feeling, the horror, the loss of love, and the consuming guilt. The idea for a story was quickly blotted out by anger and shame.

Part II
A Time to Mourn

Chapter 18

Roccamorice, Italy. Late December, 1943

It's late, Antonio. How long has he been sleeping?" Luisa was seated at the kitchen table mending a pair of woolen socks. Antonio was seated next to her holding a cup of coffee and smoking a cigarette. It had turned colder. The fire in the hearth had burned down but glowing embers warmed the room.

"I don't know, it's hard to say. I heard him up last night sobbing. Sometimes he moans, sometimes whimpers; last night he cried."

Luisa knew that Francesco was suffering from nightmares from what Antonio had told her—the shooting played over and over in his brother's mind— "Nooo, nooo, don't!" he would scream, thrash about in his bed, hitting the wall. He woke Antonio many nights. The knowledge of her son's night terrors grieved her. She prayed for it all to end.

"Once he wakes, I know it is difficult for him to get back to sleep," Antonio continued. "I try to console him, but last night I was too tired. I just turned over and went back to sleep."

"What are we going to do? It's been weeks now and he's not getting better."

"I don't know. I think he's losing his mind."

"Please don't say that! He's your brother. Don't you think you would be in shock if you saw what he saw?"

"I suppose so, but I don't know how to pull him out of it."

"He is living through a nightmare. We have to pray for him. Show him that we understand his sorrow."

"Mayor Santini told me how broken he was after the shooting. He wept all the way back here. When he did speak it was about the guilt he felt. I've tried to talk to him, to make him feel better about himself, but it just hasn't worked. I thought that maybe his friends might get him out of his depression, but you see how he reacted to Marcello, his best friend."

"I know. I was surprised he wasn't very happy to see him," Luisa said.

"He was very rude, I thought. Definitely not like him at all."

"I feel so bad about letting him go to Caramanico in the first place. We should have thought about ways to hide him here, maybe with some of your friends. I should never have given in. None of this would have happened."

"Who knew he would have gotten involved with escaped prisoners? Of all things I could imagine that was not one of them. He was just supposed to help out Pierluigi. I didn't know that Pierluigi had had a change of heart regarding the government and the war, did you?"

"No, but why on earth did he share that with Francesco and why did he put that boy in such a terrible situation, all that risk? Why didn't he ask me what I thought? It may have been difficult to reach us, but I will never understand why he didn't try."

"I think Francesco had a lot to do with that," Antonio said, exhaling the last draw from his cigarette and stubbing it out in the ashtray. "From what little I have been able to get out of him, I think he begged to get involved. He didn't want either you or me to know. You know how he is. What were the words his teachers used to describe him: bold; independent? Those were traits our father encouraged, even on the day he left."

"But not foolish. He was never foolish."

"No more foolish than you and your friends who hide food under your skirts and pass it out to messengers."

"That's different. We take the chance here because the Germans pretty much ignore us. Anyway, it's too much to expect of someone so young," she said, clearing the coffee pot and empty cup from the table. She placed the pot on the wood-burning stove. The iron rack overhead held a black skillet, a garland of garlic, and a string of dried red pepper. She reached for the skillet and placed it on the stove. "I think a lot of his grief is loneliness, especially the loss of Annamaria," Antonio said. "Whatever, it's holding him like a hawk's talons and won't let go."

Returning to the table and sitting down, Luisa said, "That was a surprise to me. I didn't think he was interested in that girl. When did he express feelings for her?"

"I began to notice little things on our last visit, the looks they gave one another and the giggles. I think an attraction developed between them then. I think it drove him to Caramanico, maybe more than the hunger or the Germans did."

"She was older, I wouldn't have thought," Luisa said, as she cupped her hands over her face and slowly rocked her head. Her emotions had ranged from one extreme to another over the days since her son had returned. She had prayed and spoken to the parish priest, but the advice he had given did not console her. Her neighbor friends offered encouragement, but the sympathy was always short lived. "I'm so angry at the Sanellis," she screamed.

"Mama, please, there is no sense being angry. It was bad luck that someone informed on them, and so tragic, considering what they did for the town."

"I know, I know," she said, wringing her hands. "I grieve for them and I pray for their souls, but I still feel angry, I can't help it."

The sound of footsteps on the stairs caused them to lower their voices. Francesco appeared at the head of the stairs looking disheveled in a badly wrinkled shirt and trousers. His hair, tussled and uncombed, was badly in need of a haircut. "Come over here and sit down," his mother said, with a smile turning to a scowl.

"And put on these socks." She pushed a pair of heavy wool socks she had knitted across the table. "The floor is cold."

Francesco said nothing but ambled over to the table and took a seat. His brother passed him the socks and he slowly slipped one on and then the other. "What time is it?" he asked.

"It's just about noon. You've slept a long time." his mother said.

"I feel like I just fell asleep an hour ago."

"How about I make you something to eat? I saved an egg just for you."

"I don't feel like it."

"You need to eat something."

"I told you, I'm not hungry!" he snapped.

"Stay calm, Francesco," his brother said. "She is just thinking about your health."

A knocking at the door startled Francesco and he started to rise and leave the table.

"Sit a minute, Francesco," his mother said, as she walked over to open the door. "It's just Concetta from next door. She told me she was coming over to bring a few biscotti for you." She opened the door and her neighbor walked in carrying a plate covered with a cloth.

Francesco's eyes, however, were drawn not to the plate but to the purple shawl that covered the woman's head and shoulders. He opened his mouth wanting to scream, but uttered nothing; instead he rose and quickly ran to the stairway leading to his room.

"What did I do to frighten him like that?" Concetta said, seeing the fear on Francesco's face.

"Oh, Concetta, it's nothing you did. He's just has not been himself. It's hard to know what makes him react the way he does. Sometimes it's something that is said; other times it's something that we do. I'm at my wits end."

"I'm so sorry, Luisa, I wish I could do something. I know it must be difficult for him. It would be tough for anyone of us to witness a killing, but for someone his age I just can't imagine."

"Yes, I know. Please come in and stay awhile. I can use your company."

Antonio, who was startled at Francesco's sudden departure, got up and said to Concetta: "Yes, please sit. I am going to check on Francesco.

"How do you plan to celebrate *la Vigila* this year?" Concetta asked Luisa after Antonio departed the room.

"I don't know. With the occupation I'm not sure. I hope the Germans will give us Christmas Eve to celebrate the birth of our Lord."

"I heard the mayor asked the German commandant to relax the rules and curfews for the holidays and supposedly he agreed."

"That's good. I hadn't heard that."

"Just this morning my husband told me he heard it at the bar."

"Well, that might cheer up Francesco a bit. Of course the Vigil will not be like the past. Without the fishmonger from Pescara selling his eel and salt cod I won't be able to prepare the meal the family usually enjoys."

"Me too. My brother was going to come up with his family to celebrate with us. I was expecting him to bring the fish, but with the war so close now they are staying home. Otherwise, I would have shared with you, Luisa."

"Thank you for the thought, Concetta. I will be happy if the Germans let us have more pasta. I saved a tin of anchovies, so pasta with anchovies will have to be our 'Feast of Seven Fishes.'"

****

On the lower level, Antonio found Francesco face down on his bed sobbing softly. He sat next to him and put a hand on his back. "Hey, it's okay, what's wrong? Why did you run off like that?"

His arms remained cradled about his head. "That purple shawl! Some woman, a neighbor of the Sanellis, covered the bodies of the family with a purple shroud after the shooting. I never want to see that color again."

"That's okay," Antonio said, putting his hand on Francesco's back trying to sooth him. "Listen, how about we go for a walk and get out of this house for a while?"

"I don't want to run into anybody. You know how they are. They want to know how I'm doing, am I feeling any better about what happened? I just don't want to talk about it."

"You mean the Sanellis."

"Yes, all of them. It's true when I saw Annamaria again in Caramanico after my trip I knew I loved her. I think she felt the same way, but I'll never know." His abdomen tightened in sadness and regret as he spoke those words to his brother. "I can't believe she's gone, that they are all gone."

"We are so sorry, Antonio, for her, her parents, and for you," Antonio said, continuing to rub Francesco's back. "Everyone shares that grief."

"I know people mean well, but I just don't want to talk about it."

"Okay. C'mon, get up; you'll feel better walking in the fresh air."

Francesco turned over in his bed and crossed his arms across his chest. He didn't want to be bothered. "I just feel numb, and I can't explain it. It's like one moment nothing is real, it's just a dream, and then I realize it wasn't a dream at all."

"You won't believe it now, Francesco, but those dreams will fade and only the good memories will remain, trust me. Get your coat. I'll meet you upstairs."

Reluctantly, Francesco sat up and swung his feet over the edge of his bed. Then he rose slowly and took out a sweater from his chest of drawers and grabbed his coat from his closet.

****

Upstairs, Antonio whispered to Concetta to hide her shawl that she had placed on a chair beside her.

"What's the matter?" his mother asked.

"I don't want Francesco to see it. I will explain later. We're going out for a walk now."

Concetta handed the shawl to Luisa who quickly placed it into the sideboard cupboard. She had just closed the door and returned to the table when Francesco entered the room. He saw the plate of biscotti on the table.

"Thank you for those biscotti, Senora, I know getting the flour and sugar to make them is difficult now, so I appreciate you're sharing with us," he said with little emotion.

"I hope you like them, Francesco, I didn't have the nuts this year, and very little anise so they may taste a little plain."

"I'm sure they're good," he said quietly.

****

The boys departed and walked down the Corso Umberto toward the center of the village. It was cold. Several inches of fresh fallen snow covered the cobblestone. Francesco shuffled along, kicking up snow with Antonio at his side. "I don't want to run into those Germans who made me leave town," he said.

"Don't worry. Like I told you when you came home, their platoon was transferred to another unit somewhere else in the region."

"How about that officer that day at *Zio* Donato's?"

"He was transferred too. No one came looking for you after you left. And now that it's cold, most of the military pretty much stay inside. Supplying the Block Haus has slowed down. The work details now mostly shovel snow."

"They haven't called you since I've been home, how come?"

"I've done my share of work for them. But I'm sure they'll come for me again, probably after Christmas when the work picks up."

"I'm sorry about Pietro."

Pietro was Antonio's friend who had been shot at Passo Lanciano. The two of them often worked together hauling supplies to the Bloc Haus. They encouraged one another when the going got tough, when they were tired and needed to stop and rest. On the morning of the incident, as the work party was being assembled,

Antonio had responded to a request from a German officer to work on a project at headquarters, leaving Pietro to go on the Block Haus work detail without him. "I still can't forgive myself," Antonio said. "I feel like I abandoned him."

"It's not your fault," Francesco said.

"It's not your fault either about the Sanellis. There was nothing you could have done. Try telling that to yourself."

"It doesn't work," he said gloomily.

"Hey," Antonio said, suddenly stopping. "Wait a minute. Here's Taglio's shop. Let's go in. Your hair is a disaster. You can use a haircut for Christmas." Francesco, who had walked on a few steps, stopped and turned back, frowning. "I don't know. You know how much he likes to talk, and I'm not in the mood."

"Don't worry; I will do the talking."

"Look and see if there is anybody in there with him. I don't want to go in if he has customers."

"I looked in the window when we passed. He was sitting in his chair alone reading something."

"Okay, but let's make it quick."

"*Buon giorno,* Rosario," Antonio said, as he entered the shop with Francesco trailing behind. My brother needs a haircut."

"I can see that. Sit down here Francesco," the barber said as he got out of his barber chair and gave the seat a quick sweep with his towel. Francesco paused to think if he wanted his hair cut. He sighed and removed his jacket and hat, handed them to his brother and sat in the chair. "It's nice to see you again," Rosario said. "I heard you were back in town. I'm so sorry to hear what happened in Caramanico." Antonio gave Rosario a stern look and a head shake to let him know not to continue that line of conversation. "What have you heard about the war?" he asked, changing the subject.

Francesco felt relieved his brother had interceded. He just wanted to sit and not talk.

"One of the German officers was in here yesterday for a haircut. They usually tell me to mind my business and just do my job when I ask a question about the war. But this one was in a talkative mood, so I just asked how things were going."

"And what did he say?"

"He said that there has been a big battle going on in Ortona for the past several days."

"Did he say how it was going?"

"He was boasting. He said they had one of their best fighting units in the battle—the German 1st Parachute Division. They were very experienced troops he said, so he predicted a victory against a Canadian division that had much less experience."

Francesco's ears perked up at the mention of the Canadian unit. He immediately thought about Roger and Denis. Roger was the one person he especially yearned to see again. He felt the need to share what happened to the Sanellis. "What did he say about the Canadians?" Francesco asked

Working with his scissors and comb, Rosario clipped away strands of Francesco's shaggy, long, dark hair; it fell about the apron covering Francesco's shoulders and chest. "He didn't elaborate, and I didn't ask. I learned when not to probe too much. But I know this much from the general chatter among the soldiers talking around town. Ortona is important. The British need the port for its supply line and the Germans want to stop them from using it. They have been ordered by the top command to defend Ortona at any cost."

"Antonio," Francesco said. "The two soldiers I helped escape may be in that fight."

"Getting there will be damn near impossible with the fighting, Francesco. Maybe afterward if the Canadians win."

"I don't think the Canadians are going to win," Rosario said. "That German officer sounded pretty confident about his army's chances."

"But what if the Canadians do win?" Francesco said. "I need to see Roger again. I need to share what happened to the Sanellis, and with Denis, too, if I can find him. It's important to me." His mood had changed; the tone of his voice indicating he was less despondent.

Antonio saw how Francesco's eyes brightened and he perked up at the news about Ortona. It was the first sign of Francesco's old persona since coming home.

"Well," he said. "I have friend in Chieti. That can get us close, but getting there in this weather will be difficult."

"Getting to Chieti and from there to Ortona will be a problem. There is a German garrison in Chieti. Even if you deal with that, you've got the curfew and the war itself."

Antonio stopped to think.

"I wouldn't make any plans yet," Rosario said, as he put down the scissors and started smoothly shearing Francesco's hair with sweeps of his straight razor.

"Maybe they will call for a cease fire over Christmas?" Francesco said, his tone and face much brighter. "We could go then."

"I doubt it. The Germans have shown no sentiments for the holidays," Rosario said.

"Even if a truce was called, there would only be a narrow window of opportunity," Antonio said. "Rosario is right. We just have to wait and see what happens. But I do think that it might be good for you to see your soldier friends again. I'll find a way."

"Here's a way. What do you think of contacting Pierluigi's driver in Caramanico?" Francesco asked. "We could meet him down the road in San Valentino and he could drive us to Chieti."

"It sounds a bit complicated, Francesco. I don't want to discourage you."

"Let's try," Francesco said, pleading. There was nothing to lose by making a plan. He thought of all the planning that Pierluigi did. His plan to get the POWs to freedom worked, even though the family had paid a high price afterward.

Rosario finished trimming Francesco's neck, brushed the loose hair from his shoulder, and removed the apron. Then he swiveled him around in the chair so that he could face the wall mirror, while he passed a hand mirror behind Francesco's head. "Well, Francesco, how do like it?"

"It looks okay, I guess." "That's all you can say?"

"It looks very good, Rosario, thank you." his brother said.

"At least you will be presentable at Christmas Mass, Francesco," Rosario said.

"If I go."

"You need to go and make your mother happy," Antonio said. "You can pray for the Canadians at Ortona. You want to see your friends again, right?"

"I haven't been able to pray; I don't know if I want to pray anymore."

"It's not something you forget; you just need a reason and now you have one. Besides, you don't want to disappoint your mother on Christmas of all days."

Francesco shrugged. "Let's go over to the municipal building and see if we can make that phone call."

While Francesco waited by the door, Antonio thanked and paid Rosario for the haircut, and the brothers left the shop. Outside the wind had picked up. It had grown colder with the wind chill. The brothers raised and drew their jacket collars more closely around their necks. Francesco wondered if another storm was coming, just in time for Christmas. It was late afternoon and already getting dark as they entered the main piazza and walked to the municipal building. Inside, the halls were empty. Lights were burning in some of the offices on the main floor. They climbed the stairs to the mayor's office on the second floor. A clerk Antonio knew was working on a ledger in the outer office. They knocked and walked in.

"Is Mayor Rotondo in his office?" Antonio asked.

"Hello, Antonio. Yes, have a seat and I will ask if he can see you."

Antonio and Francesco took a seat as the clerk knocked on the mayor's door and entered. Francesco noticed the phone on the clerk's desk. "Let's hope it's working," he said as Antonio nodded.

The clerk emerged from the mayor's office; holding the door open, he said, "The mayor will see you, please go in."

"You go, Antonio," Francesco said. "I'll wait here."

When Antonio entered the mayor's office, Francesco picked up an old Fascist magazine and flipped through the pages idly as the clerk went back to his ledger. How could the people believe all this Fascist propaganda: *"Mussolini ha sempre ragione"*—Mussolini is always right. His thoughts were interrupted by the unmistakable sound of jackboots in the corridor. His body suddenly stiffened.

He looked for a place to hide, but there was no place to go. The clerk kept at his work unaware of Francesco's reaction. The sound of the boots clicking kept on past the door, and the faded down the hall. As it did, Francesco relaxed and his heart stopped pounding. A few moments later, the mayor emerged with Antonio, and Francesco rose to greet him.

"Francesco, I was wondering when you were going to show your face around town. *Come va?*"

"*Sto bene,*" he lied. "Not much to do in this weather."

"We heard about what happened in Caramanico. You were very lucky that Mayor Santini vouched for you. What happened there is not something we want to see happen here. Do you know what I'm saying?"

"Yes sir, I understand," Francesco said. He was angry but didn't want to let the mayor know it. This fascist doesn't want any partisan action from me or anyone else, he thought.

"He didn't know what he was getting into when the Sanellis took him in," Antonio spoke up. "None of us knew, or we would not have allowed him to go."

"Well, I am glad you're back. I understand that you want to speak to a shop manager in Sulmona, is that right? Your brother told me that you left some personal articles there you would like to get back."

"Yes, that's right. I would appreciate it if I can use the telephone. I have no other way to get in touch with him."

"Well, it's rather late now and the shop is sure to be closed. Tomorrow is the Vigil so I doubt that he would be there even then, so why don't you come back after Christmas."

Francesco frowned, but realized the futility of persisting. "We can come back after Christmas. Thank you."

Outside on the walk back to the house, Francesco turned to Antonio, "Did you catch the threat from the mayor?"

"I took it as a warning, Francesco. It was just his way of telling us not to get involved with partisans around here, but I pay him no attention."

"The mayors of Roccamorice and Caramanico could not be more different in terms of how they see the German occupation."

"It's easier for Santini. The Germans are not underfoot there every day like they are here."

"Maybe so, but they're different politically. Rotondo still wears his fascist lapel pin. He still believes in Mussolini and the Salo group."

"As long as he lets us use the phone, I'm not going to complain."

"Maybe we should rethink the phone. Who knows who might be listening?"

"Well, there may be another way. Let me do some checking."

When they got home it was dark. Luisa was bent over the hearth, about to hang a pot on the hook above the fire. "Just some soup tonight and a little bread is all we have. Tomorrow night will be better," she said. As she was speaking, the pot handle slipped from the edge of the hook and the kettle crashed to the floor below spilling the broth and scattering burning embers.

The cast iron hitting the tile startled Francesco and he backed away holding his hands over his ears. "No, no," he shouted and scampered down to his room.

"It's okay, Francesco," his mother called after him. "Just a little spill. It will be fine."

Antonio quickly walked over to the hearth and rehung the kettle, swept back the embers into the hearth, and readjusted the burning wood. "He is still very sensitive to noises," he said.

"He startles so easily. How long can this go on?"

"He was actually much better today." Antonio told her about the time they spent in the barber shop; how his spirits were lifted by the news that the Canadian army was fighting in Ortona, and the possibility of seeing those soldiers again. "For the first time since he has been home, his mood has improved. I think he has found something to hope for."

"There's a war! Luisa's brow was furrowed and there was no mistaking the anger in her voice. "How does he think he can see those men again?"

"Well, that's the problem. Right now we can't do anything until we find out how things turn out in Ortona. If we're lucky, it will go our way."

"We can't let him just go off again," she said sternly.

"No, I wouldn't let him go alone. First we would need to get to Chieti. I'm sure my friend Claudio would let us stay with him while we figure things out."

"How are you going to get to Chieti in this weather?" Her voice and manner had softened but the scowl remained.

"That's something we are working on now." Antonio explained the visit to the mayor's office and the hope that they could make contact in Sulmona for a ride to Chieti. "Our idea is that if the driver in Sulmona is willing, Francesco and I can walk down to San Valentino where he can pick us up. Anyway, it's not anything we can do until after Christmas."

"It's not something I want to see either of you do, even if you go together. Do you really think it will help Francesco to heal?"

"I don't know, but it's worth a try. Nothing else has worked."

"Well, let me think about it. Go call your brother; the soup will be ready soon." The morning on the vigil of Christmas was again cold and gray with flurries slanting through the air suggesting a storm was coming. Francesco had spent another night of delirium tossing and turning, experiencing nightmarish replays of the shooting. He dreamed that Pierluigi got up from the pavement and walked off. The next moment Pierluigi was lying in bed with him. That woke him with a fright. Antonio heard him scream, "Nooo!" and get out of bed, but he let him be.

It was still dark when Antonio awoke troubled. He got up, tiptoed past Francesco's room and climbed the stairs to the kitchen. He knew he would need help for the trip into the war zone, a friend who had friends or contacts along the way. His best options to get things rolling was a friend hiding out with partisans in the nearby hamlet of Abbateggio. As the first pale streaks of dawn appeared, he trudged over the snow-covered road to the hamlet and reached the outskirts in the early morning. He went directly to the barn where he knew his friend was hiding and called his name up to the hay loft.

"Ah, Antonio, what brings you here this morning?" his friend Tulio said with drooping eyes, still half asleep. He was on hands and knees, looking down from the loft wrapped in a gray wool blanket.

"I need your help," Antonio said. "Do you know anyone who can get me to Chieti?" He went on to explain the situation with the battle in Ortona, his brother's condition, and his hopes of reuniting his brother with the British and Canadian soldiers.

Tulio climbed down the ladder from the loft, the heavy blanket draped around his disheveled clothes. He was unshaven and his hair was a mess. He looked and smelled as though he hadn't had a bath in a long time. "I know a guy in Scafa who had a car he used to get supplies for his bakery business. He is one of us, but I'm not sure if he still has the car, or whether he would risk taking you all the way to Chieti."

"Can you find out for me?

"Let me see what I can do; if it's even possible. You sure you want to take the chance? You know what the Germans would do if they catch you out there without proper papers."

"I have to try for my brother's sake, for his peace of mind."

Tulio placed his hand on Antonio's shoulder. "I will meet you at San Donato after Christmas Mass. The church is the one place I won't have to worry about the Germans. And by then we may know more about the situation in Ortona."

They chatted a while longer, catching up. Antonio expressed his gratitude for any effort he could make. He wished he could have been one of them. He reiterated how much getting to Ortona would mean for his brother's mental state. When he returned home, he found his mother making pasta for the evening's dinner. Most of the town had been living in a state of semi starvation, but for the Vigil of Christmas the townspeople had come together to pool resources and share with one another. The Germans had relaxed restrictions for the holiday, and they provided the town more flour from their grain stockpile. Fruit, especially citrus from Sicily, cabbage, and other vegetables would be unavailable, but there would be enough pasta and wine.

"Where have you been this morning?" she asked.

"To see Tulio in Abbateggio." He went on to fill her in on the conversation he had with Tulio about the possibility of a car and driver in Scafa.

"How would you get to Scafa in this weather?"

"I think we can get part way there with a work crew. With the snow coming, the Germans will want to clear the road down the mountain at least to San Valentino. We could slip away from there."

"If you get caught leaving then what? Don't forget about Pietro."

He was sorry she brought up his friend. "If we do the work, we'll be okay. I'll know when the time is right so it doesn't look like abandonment. Where is Francesco?"

"He went out for a walk by himself. His friend Marcello came by to invite him to a party the young people were planning for this evening after dinner, and then they were going to the Midnight Mass together."

"He agreed to that? I'm surprised, but then I thought his mood was better today."

"No, he didn't. He told Marcello he wasn't on good terms with God and had no interest in parties. When Marcello kept trying to encourage him to go he got real irritable. He told him again that he was not in the mood for a party. I listened and wanted to say something, but I know how he reacts to my suggestions. Finally, when Marcello tried to cheer him up and said the party would be good for him, he got angry and started shouting at him. Poor Marcello didn't know what to do or say at that point. He looked shocked. Francesco just grabbed his coat and left. I tried to console Marcello. But, of course, he doesn't really understand what Francesco went through."

"I will look for him. Maybe the information I got in Abbateggio will put him in a better mood. Do you need anything before I go?"

"Go to Concetta's and borrow the *chitarra* for the pasta? Too many wires on ours are broken."

"I can fix that by the time you have the dough ready. I'll be back soon."

Antonio left and walked down to the piazza. Even though it was a dreary cold day with continuing snow flurries, more of the citizens were out and about getting ready for the Vigil. Everyone who passed nodded and greeted each other with *Buon Natale*. Antonio was feeling upbeat, hoping that Francesco would also sense the spirit of the holiday.

He looked for Francesco in the bar and cantina but he was not in either establishment. Some young people were walking across the piazza but Francesco was not among them. He crossed over to the municipal building and went up to the mayor's office. The clerk told him that Francesco had been there earlier and had tried to make a phone call to Sulmona, but there was no response and he left. Where could he be? He doubted that he would walk to his Uncle Donato's farm on the outskirts of town, but he went anyway. He wasn't there but he paused for a glass of wine with his uncle, whom the Germans had detained for only a few days. His aunt and uncle were concerned for Francesco ever since he had returned to town acting so depressed. They had tried to cheer him with invitations to the house, but he avoided social activities, be it friend or family. Before Antonio left, his aunt gave him a piece of salted cod that she had wrapped in heavy paper and tied. She had washed it thoroughly for hours to remove the salt.

"Give this to your mother so she can make the *bacala* tonight. I just received it from a friend in San Valentino; she got it from someone in Pescara."

On his way back into the village Antonio stopped off at several family friends, but no one had seen him. Frustrated, he circled back through the side streets. On one of them he passed the parish priest who was bundled up with a scarf around the collar of his long, black coat. He had one hand on the top of his round black clerical hat. Off-handedly, he asked the priest about Francesco, not expecting to learn anything about him.

"Why yes, as matter of fact, he was sitting in one of the pews." He told Antonio that Francesco had lit a devotional candle and seemed to be quietly praying. He didn't want to interrupt him. "You must tell him again for me how grateful we all are for getting word to us about the altar painting at Santo Spirito."

This was the first Antonio had learned of Francesco's role in saving the painting from theft. He knew that the priest in Guardiagrele had alerted the town about the Germans' attempt to steal the altarpiece, but none of the details. At any rate, the priest sent some men from Roccamorice to bring it back to the village, where they hid it in the grotto of the old abandoned church. He shook his head at the thought that Francesco had played a significant part in still another incident.

"*Buon Natale*, Father," he said, as he walked past the priest toward the church. In the darkened interior, Antonio found Francesco in the first row by the altar. Several small devotional candles were burning on a rack; and behind it, on an elevated platform, a wooden manger scene of the first C Christmas was arranged with the ceramic nativity figures.

"Francesco, I've been looking all over for you."

Francesco snuffled and wiped away tears from his eyes. "I don't know why I came here," he said. "I guess I was cold walking around. I knew I didn't want to talk to anybody. I thought no one would bother me here."

"It's Christmas Eve, so it's a good place to be."

"When I saw the candles burning, I thought I would light one for the Sanellis. I tried to pray, but I can't concentrate. My mind just wanders. Annamaria, her parents, that miserable Gestapo officer crowding their images. It just will not go away, day or night; whether I'm asleep or awake."

Antonio took a seat next to Francesco and put his hand on his back. He had offered words of consolation so many times since Francesco returned home. In this setting, he simply chose to be quiet and let the silence speak for him. After a while, he said, "I may have found a way for us to get to Chieti."

Dry-eyed now, Francesco asked "How?

"One of my friends in Abbateggio knows someone in Scafa with a car." He told Francesco the situation. "We can't worry about it now anyway; everything will depend what happens in Ortona. Let's go. Mother can use our help with dinner tonight."

"What's that I smell?" Francesco asked, now noticing for the first time the package next to Antonio.

"*Bacala* from *Zia* Francesca. There will be at least two of the seven fishes on our table tonight. What's the Vigil without bacala?"

They rose from the pew and genuflected in the aisle. Francesco turned and walked toward the rear of the church. Antonio instead went up to the candle rack, picked up a taper, and lit a candle. He put a coin in the slot, made the sign of the cross, and paused briefly; then he turned and joined Francesco for the walk home in the cold.

****

Luisa had kneaded the yellow pasta dough ball to a smooth elastic consistency. It rested on a floured surface of the wooden table. She was about to begin rolling it out when Antonio and Francesco walked in the door. "Antonio, fix the *chitarra* so I can make the pasta before it gets too late," she said.

"In a minute. Here is a little something from Aunt Francesca," He said as he handed her the package of salt cod. "*Bacala in umido*, just like always."

"What a nice surprise!" she said with a wide-eyed smile. "I was so sad this morning thinking we would not have *bacala* for the first time ever."

Antonio retrieved the wooden-framed pasta cutter from the cabinet and restrung the broken wires. His mother grabbed her heavy iron pan from the rack and began sautéing garlic in olive oil. She followed with diced onions and when they had caramelized, a jar of her squeezed tomatoes. The hiss of tomatoes in the hot pan added to an aroma that spread through the room lifting everyone's spirit.

Francesco, who hadn't said much, looked around and seeing the dough on the table, he divided it into four sections as he had seen his mother do. Then he began rolling each of them out thinly with the rolling pin. Luisa looked surprised at his initiative, and praised his efforts. Working together, she gathered up each of the pasta sheets he made and placed them on the strings of the *chitarra* frame, pressing them with the rolling pin against the wires to form the long square-cut strands of *maccheroni alla chitarra*. She laid them out on a cloth on the table while Antonio began boiling water in the large pot hanging in the hearth. With the *bacala* simmering in the light tomato sauce and the pasta water boiling on the hearth, they set the table.

When everything was prepared, they sat down together to commemorate *la Vigilia di Natale*. Antonio offered the prayers of grace before the meal, remembering his father and others who could not be there to share with them. Francesco looked down but did not bow his head. He remained silent.

"It's been so long since we have heard from your father," Luisa said. "I miss him, especially today."

Antonio added his thoughts that his father would be spending the feast day with paisanos in America, probably enjoying all seven fish courses. "What else should we pray for?"

Francesco felt he should say something. "Victory at Ortona." When Antonio concluded with a prayer for the souls of the Sanellis, Francesco, thinking of Annamaria, finally bowed his head.

****

Later that evening as the bells of San Donato pealed their invitation to the Midnight Mass, Francesco lay on his cot unable to sleep, still unable to suppress the nightmare of Caramanico. He tried unsuccessfully to substitute better images and thoughts, but in the end he resigned himself to a sleepless night. Tossing and restless, he anticipated the dawn and the hope that the road to Ortona would be open to him, and the two people who would understand his sorrow, and who could share his mourning.

Chapter 19

The bells began pealing at eleven for the Christmas Day Mass at noon. Reluctantly, Francesco put on his jacket and walked to San Donato with his mother and brother. The snow had stopped overnight, but the sky was leaden and the early chill remained at that late morning hour.

They joined a stream of parishioners approaching the church from every direction, nodding and wishing each other *Buon Natale.* Surprisingly, the German military had continued to keep the same low profile they had on Christmas Eve. The pews were nearly full with families, unlike Sundays when most of the parishioners were women and children. Francesco tried hard to concentrate on the liturgical service. Praying had become difficult for him. He would listen to the beginning of the various rites, but his mind wandered, and he remained mostly silent during the priest's invitation to prayers. He listened to the beginning of Luke's Gospel but his mind drifted during the reading, and he paid almost no attention to the homily that followed. His thoughts were on Antonio's friend and what news he might have for them.

After mass, the people filed out, pausing in the courtyard in front of the church to exchange well wishes with one another. Luisa and Francesco stopped to talk to her brother and sister-in-law. Antonio sought out his friend Tulio who kept a low profile at the edge of the crowd. He appeared much different than the man Antonio had encountered in the barn, having cleaned up and disguised himself with a heavy woolen shawl and broad-brimmed hat.

"Good news and bad news," Tulio said. "The car in Scafa is available, but unfortunately there is no petrol. The supplies all around are practically gone, and the Germans are hoarding as much as they can. But my friend Ottavio has offered to help you get to Chieti. You just need to find a way to his house," he said. He handed Antonio a slip of paper with his friend's address.

On the way home, Antonio told Francesco the situation regarding the transportation problem and the contact in Scafa.

"I don't care how we get there, as long as we do." Francesco said.

Two days later, on the morning of the twenty-seventh, Antonio was sitting in the bar having coffee where he learned that most of the people in Ortona had fled the town when the battle commenced a week earlier. Some went up the coast or to the smaller villages in the hills, but a few had made it as far as Chieti. The fighting had been intense; the Germans were setting booby traps all over Ortona and deliberately blowing up buildings to block the roads. The fighting and artillery shelling continued through Christmas. The person relaying the information had spent a fretful time in Chieti. It was not a Christmas he wanted to remember. His family had gotten back only because his cousin was a railroad worker and was able to get them seats on the train.

Antonio was intrigued with the idea of the train, something he hadn't seriously considered because he thought the railways had been damaged by allied bombing. But the man said repairs to the line between Chieti and Scafa had been made although the trains were unpredictable.

When Antonio got home he was excited to tell his mother and brother what he learned about the fighting in Ortona and his thoughts on using the trains. "I don't know how the battle will turn out, but it might be better to wait down in the valley for a train that may or not come than to wait here."

"My pack is ready to go. I just need to fill it." Francesco said. His face had perked up, registering the excitement in his voice which matched his brother's. "We'll need to dress for the weather and get food from somewhere," Antonio said.

By now Antonio had convinced his mother the trip to Ortona was important for Francesco. He told her that Francesco's brooding had turned into active mourning, something he could share with the one person who would understand. "It would help him to heal," he said. She hoped he was right—that the road to Ortona would be the road to Francesco's recovery, and she resigned herself that they were going regardless of her concerns. So she helped them gather supplies including the heavy woolen shirts, sweaters, and the socks she had made them earlier. But the problem was food. She had nothing to spare.

"I'm going out to see what I can find," Luisa said. "Someone may be able to help."

"*Mama non ti preoccupare,*" Francesco said. "We always found something to eat on the way to Casoli. And there were four of us with the dogs and sheep. People are quite generous. We'll be fine."

Antonio went out in the afternoon to see what more he could find and rushed home with fresh news. There was a lot of activity in the piazza when he went to the bar. German soldiers seemed unusually animated as they stood next to their trucks when the local commandant's black staff car pulled up in front of the municipal

216

building and he went in for a meeting. Antonio waited a few minutes and then went into the bar to wait. Later, after the German left his office, the mayor walked over to the bar to chat with his cronies. Antonio listened, barely able to contain his excitement as the mayor told them the Canadians had managed to break through at Ortona. During the night, the last German regiment in Ortona, believing they were going to be outflanked by the Canadians, pulled out of town.

While the mayor's friends expressed serious concern with the unexpected turn of events, there were some like Antonio who seemed cautiously optimistic. Someone asked the mayor where the Germans retreated, but he wasn't sure. The commandant told him only that they headed up the coastal road toward Pescara. Francesco's face lit up at the news. "If the Canadians won, our luck is changing. Anyway, it's time to get going!"

"Okay then, let's go," Antonio responded, equally energized. "We don't know how long the Canadians will stay in Ortona. Will they rest a while or chase the Germans?"

"We won't know waiting here," Francesco said.

They decided to walk down to San Valentino and then on to Scafa in the valley. On the road out of town, a German soldier in an armored car pulled up next to them. Francesco froze, but Antonio, who recognized the soldier from one of his work details, calmed him with a pat on his arm.

In late August, the German soldier had been supervising a work detail walking backward watching the progress when he stumbled and took a nasty fall breaking his arm. Antonio rushed to his side, gave him aid, supporting his arm with a stick and cloth wrappings from the sleeve he tore away from his shirt. He hadn't seen him since the incident.

"Where are you going?" the German asked.

"Hello. I did not recognize you at first," Antonio said. "How's your arm?"

"It has healed nicely, thank you. Where are you going?" he repeated.

"To visit friends in San Valentino."

"I am going there to pick up an officer. Get in and I will give you a ride."

Antonio looked at Francesco and smiled. He hadn't planned on good luck so soon. Antonio got in first at Francesco's urging. He didn't want to sit next to the driver. They squeezed together tossing their packs in the cramped space behind the seats.

****

Francesco slumped down against the door and remained silent during the short trip. He was uncomfortable remembering the day on the Sangro when the armored car had pulled up and the German soldier began shooting. The terror of that moment gripped him again as his mind replayed the bullets tracing across the water, striking the boatman, Roger and Denis jumping out and scampering away. He winced at the thought.

Antonio chatted amiably with the German, hoping to learn anything more about the battle in Ortona, but the soldier was unable to add to what they already knew.

When they reached San Valentino, the officer dropped them off in front of the church on the main piazza.

"It's early," Antonio said. "If we keep walking we can be in Scafa before dark and leave for Chieti in the morning. What do you say?"

"Let's just keep going, the closer I get, the better I'll feel."

They continued down the Corso Umberto to the road out of town into the Pescara River valley. The dull morning sky had faded to a gray overcast afternoon and snow began falling as they trudged on. Francesco was happy they had the road to themselves. Snow-covered meadows, forests of bare trees, and a few scattered farmhouses were all the brothers saw that wintry afternoon. The wind picked up along with heavier snow when they reached the edge of Scafa. They crossed a set of railroad tracks and the main east-west highway that bordered it. Antonio checked the address of the contact Tulio had given him. The snow was coming on when they found the house on a side street two blocks from the train station.

Ottavio was a plump young man with thinning hair, strong arms and hands, in Francesco's mind, what a baker should look like. Ottavio was not surprised to see them. "Listen, my friends," he said as he invited them in, "I told Tulio that I thought I could get you to Chieti, but the weather is getting bad and the only option I can think of is the train."

Antonio told him how they had come to that same conclusion before they left Roccamorice. "Problem is I heard the passenger trains were unpredictable."

"Yes, that's true," Ottavio said, "But there is a freight train that comes through here most nights around eight o'clock. It's a local that stops at Chieti before going on to Pescara."

"You think we can sneak on?"

"Only way to find out is to go and see. But we have a couple of hours before then so sit and rest. I'm afraid I don't have much to offer except a glass of wine."

Antonio and Francesco sat in Ottavio's one room living space while he crossed over to the kitchen area to pour glasses of wine. The wind picked up and softly whistled through the cracks around the window of the cottage. Peering out, Antonio frowned watching the snow piling up. Ottavio handed him a glass of wine, and a glass of water to Francesco.

"That weather is better for you and your brother. There will be fewer agents or soldiers checking the trains on a night like this."

Periodically glancing at the clock as they talked, the three men left the house around 7:30, bundled against the cold. Lamplights cast lucent circles on the glinting snow as they walked to the station. At the terminal, a misty yellow corona invested the platform light and revealed an empty walkway below. The men huddled and waited in a railroad shack a few hundred meters away from the freight terminal.

The train's whistle announced its impending arrival. Right on time. Mussolini would have been pleased, Francesco thought. The approaching steam locomotive drew a series of hoppers and flat cars, some of which carried military vehicles; a string of boxcars brought up the rear. As the engine chugged to a stop issuing a hiss of steam, the car couplings clanged together. The three men left the shack and made their way through the falling snow to the last boxcar. Its door was locked but the door to the one forward was slightly ajar.

Up ahead, an agent opened the terminal door and walked onto the platform. He called something up to the locomotive engineer, then he turned and walked back inside.

"Hurry," Ottavio said. "This train may not be here very long."

Ottavio and Antonio rolled the door open enough for Francesco to hop inside. It was completely dark and his eyes were not able to make out any interior details. He felt around with outstretched hands moving along the side walls forward and aft encountering nothing. Reappearing at the door he said, "Empty."

"Okay," Ottavio said, "Jump in, Antonio. I'm going to slide the door back and leave just a crack so that you can get out in Chieti." Bending down he swept away the snow and picked up a stone pebble which he placed in the door track.

"Ottavio, thanks again for your help," Antonio said. "I'll be sure to let Tulio know when I get back home."

"*Buona fortuna*," Ottavio said. He headed back across the tracks toward home.

Through the slit in the doorway Francesco watched him cross the tracks until he disappeared in the darkness and falling snow. He and his brother huddled together silently on the wood plank floor, their backs braced against their packs placed against the metal wall of the boxcar. Footsteps crunched the snow outside. A brief shaft of light came through the crack in the door. Someone carrying a lantern was checking the cars.

"Be ready to jump and make a run for it if he opens the door," Antonio whispered to Francesco. They go up quietly and stood on each side of the opening, backs braced the wall, their packs at their feet.

Neither Francesco nor Antonio were able to see who it was that had stopped at their car, a soldier or railroad worker. Whoever it was attempted to close the sliding door all the way but he met resistance at the pebble obstructing the track. The man put his lantern down and tried harder with two hands. Rolling and slamming the door as hard as he could, he still met resistance short of the mark. He reached into the track and felt the problem, and then he picked up his lantern and let the light fall on the pebble. He could not dislodge it with his finger. Once again he slid the door back in an attempt to gain momentum. Rolled with more force the door slammed loudly but failed to close. Francesco and Antonio pressed themselves harder against the wall of the car and held their breath. The man picked up his lantern and illuminated the car's interior, but the two brothers' profiles remained in the shadows.

The man gave the door another try, but only managed to embed the stone more firmly. Mumbling something, he left the door ajar, picked up his lantern and moved on to the last car. When he passed back, the lantern's light flashed through the cracked-open door as he crunched through the snow. Calling out and waving his lantern, he signaled the engineer to start the train moving.

Antonio and Francesco felt the jolt as the couplings clanged and cars began to move. Slowly, and then with increasing speed, the train left the station behind. From inside the car, Antonio and Francesco were able to push the door open a smidge, and with shoulders and arms slide the door part-way open. The rush of cold air through the open door and the rumble of the locomotive engine blended with the rhythmic clicks and clacks of the train's wheels on the steel rails. The brothers sat silently in the dark as the train rushed past periodic flashes of light illuminating signs for villages along the route. The train never lost speed until they passed a sign that indicated Chieti ahead; then it slowed as it entered the town.

When the train pulled into the railroad yard and came to a stop, Antonio and Francesco grabbed their packs and peered into the darkness along the row of train cars. They were in the freight yard well away from the station house. No one was in sight. They jumped down and scurried across the tracks and headed toward the few dim street lamps of the town they could see. The accumulated inches of snow covering the ground and tracks made crossing the yard tricky. They both stumbled a few times before they reached the edge of the commercial district.

Antonio was familiar with the city having visited several times, so he was able to negotiate the streets cautiously knowing the city was under German occupation with a probable evening curfew. They ducked into doorways and alley ways at the sound of passing vehicles and worked their way around the central piazza with the dominating bell tower of San Giustino.

"We're almost there," Antonio said, his voice misting the air as he pointed to one of the side streets exiting the piazza.

Francesco trailed behind Antonio, his head angled downward shivering. "Good," was all he could utter. It was too cold for anything more.

At the door of his friend's home, Antonio knocked softly hoping to raise someone without waking the neighbors; but it took some pounding before he heard someone shuffling to the door.

"Who is there?"

"Claudio, it's me, Antonio."

"Antonio? From Roccamorice? What are you doing here?"

"Open up and let me and my brother in so I can explain."

Claudio opened the door. He was a slender man with dark, wavy hair, wire-rimmed glasses and a three day beard. Dim back light from the hallway fell on the two snow-covered brothers. "My God, in this weather at this hour with the curfew? Are you crazy? Come in, you must be freezing."

"I am sorry I couldn't let you know earlier," Antonio said, as he and Francesco kicked the snow off their boots and stepped inside. "This was a last-minute decision, and you know how hard it is to get word by telephone."

"But why are you here? What happened?" He motioned for them to follow him down the hall to the kitchen. "Sit down and tell me what's going on," he said as he reached for a pot on the stove to make ersatz coffee.

"It's a long story," Antonio said. "We need to get to Ortona."

"Why? What's so important? You realize there is a war going on, don't you?" He opened a cupboard and retrieved three cups placing them on the table.

Antonio slowly told his friend the story of Francesco's trek to Caramanico where he encountered the escaped British and Canadian POWs at the home of a family friend. As he explained his brother's involvement in helping them get back to their units in the British Army and the tragic aftermath that happened to the Sanelli family, Claudio listened intently, his face lined with concern as he looked back and forth from Antonio to Francesco.

Francesco, who wished he didn't have to relive the experience, listened with downcast eyes as Antonio explained what had happened to him and why the reunion was important.

"Anyway, he's hoping to find the two soldiers in Ortona, now that the British army has reached there," Antonio concluded.

Claudio got up and walked around the kitchen table to the stove to serve the coffee. He lifted and swirled the pot to mix the content. Turning to Francesco, he filled his cup and said, "You have lived with this tragedy for quite a while, Francesco. I sympathize; I want to help you, but you see the weather, the beginning of another bad storm. I don't think anyone will be moving out there to or from Ortona, not even the military."

"It's important, Claudio," Antonio said. "Maybe you know people who can help us."

"Maybe, but its late and you need the sleep. Drink this," he said, as he poured Antonio a cup from the pot. "I'll think on it. We should talk in the morning."

"Thanks for letting us spend the night. I don't want to upset Maria. We can just rest right here."

"Don't worry. She and the kids are staying over another night at her parents' home. It's no trouble. You've used the room in the back before." When they had finished their coffee he said, "Bring your things and follow me."

In the morning they awoke to the smell of chicory. Dressing quickly they emerged from their bedroom to find Claudio at the table.

"Have you checked the weather, Antonio?" Claudio asked.

"No, not yet." he said. He reached for a biscotti and glanced toward the window coated with ice.

"Go take a look. The snow stopped, but everything is coated in ice."

Antonio walked over to the kitchen window. The thin layer of ice on the inside of the glass obscured his view. He scraped some away with his fingernail and glanced into the narrow alley at the side of the house. "I don't see much," he said.

"Are you sure you want to leave for Ortona today?

"How far are we from Ortona?" Antonio asked. "Can we make it there today?"

"About thirty-five kilometers," Claudio said. "On a good day, driving there would only take a half hour, but today who knows. I have an uncle who lives on a farm. He has a sled and horses. It may be possible to get there that way."

"How far is the farm from here?" Francesco asked.

"Not far from the edge of town on the way to Ortona."

"Do you think he'll take us?"

"Only way is to go ask him. Are you up for it?"

Francesco got up. "We can't wait here, we need to keep going. We take our chances at your uncle's. If he says no we try to make it on foot. I have walked to the Sangro. I should be able to make it to Ortona from here." He looked to his brother whose facial expression offered no opinion one way or the other.

"Not in weather like this, especially not knowing the way," Claudio said.

When they left the house, they had layered up for the cold and found themselves in foot-deep snow. The low gray sky added gloom to Chieti's medieval streetscape. Even though they were bundled in woolen caps, trousers, and sweaters beneath heavy jackets, the cold penetrated and the crunch of their boots confirmed the icy conditions. Turning onto the main thoroughfare, the going was easier as military halftracks and other vehicles had tamped down the snow. On the walk, Claudio motioned them into a snow-filled courtyard where a few pedestrians had cut a path to an old wooden door.

"Let's stop at this cantina," he said. "We can warm up. My friend Stefano may have some useful information. It's a popular spot for the Germans."

They opened the door and descended a few steps into a basement level cantina. The light was dim and the aroma of wine was in the air. One side of the space was lined by large oaken barrels; the other side had a bar with stools. Two small tables were set in the middle of the room. A fire in a large hearth at the back warmed the stone-walled space. There were no customers. The proprietor, a stout unshaven man wearing a half apron and a black beret, a towel over his shoulder, stood by the hearth adding wood to the fire.

"*Ciao, Claudio,*" he said turning to the men. "What brings you out on such a terrible morning?"

222

"*Ciao*, Stefano. We just stopped to warm up a bit. Actually, we were wondering if you had any information about what it's like now in Ortona. I know you get German soldiers stopping in."

"Why? I hope you aren't thinking of going there."

"I'm not, but I am trying to help these friends get there." He explained Antonio and Francesco's situation as they took a seat at one of the tables.

Stefano brought a carafe of wine and glasses to the table. They politely refused a pour, telling him it was too early and too cold. "The wine will warm you up. How about some brandy then?"

"*Grazie*, but nothing, Stefano, we're fine," Claudio said. "I was just wondering if you heard anything."

"Four German noncommissioned officers came in just after I opened. I don't know exactly where the German army is now. They left Ortona and moved up the coast but I don't know how far. That's what they were talking about this morning. The British army is still in Ortona, they said. I don't know what it's like there now. This storm has pretty much brought everything to a halt. I'm sorry, Claudio, that's all I know."

"At least we know the battle in the city is over and the Germans have left. My friends here will just have to find out what the conditions are for themselves."

Francesco got up and walked over to the hearth. He stood there warming himself by the fire.

"What do you plan to do in all this snow and ice?" Stefano asked Claudio. "It would be a tough trek under the usual peace time conditions. But now…."

"I just hope to get them as close to Ortona as possible then they're on their own. My uncle has a team of horses and a sled that could make things easier. He's just outside town on Via Adriatico. Thanks again for the chance to warm up, but we had better get going."

"*Buona fortuna*. Just don't freeze yourselves out there."

The men gathered their packs and walked back up the stairs onto the snow covered street. On the town's outskirts the ground was blanketed in deep snow obscuring the boundary between road and meadow. The tree limbs and electric wires were coated with ice. The men trudged along, huddled against the cold that penetrated their layers and boots.

Chapter 20

Claudio's uncle and aunt were surprised to see their nephew and his companions on such an inclement day. After the introductions, explanations, and request, Claudio's uncle said he was willing to take his friends part of the way—San Tomasso maybe, or Miglianico It was too risky to go farther. The ice storm has taken down a lot of tree limbs. He didn't know what the road ahead would be like. After a lunch of hot broth and bread, the men gathered their packs and stepped outside where two hardy chestnut horses were harnessed to a four-person sled. The horses tossed their heads and snorted, manes sweeping away the misted air. Francesco and Antonio stepped into the back seat while Claudio's uncle took the reins and Claudio got in next to him. The misted words of goodbye identified each of the travelers who spoke to the woman who had stepped out to wave them off.

The sled moved along quickly, the runners gliding easily over the packed snow. The ceiling had lifted and the sun came out, glinting off the ice-covered branches of the bare hardwood trees flanking both sides of the road. The weight of the ice had caused the branches to lean inward so that they formed a glistening canopy above the horse-drawn sled. The wind swayed the branches and the ice-covered tendrils crackled as they rubbed against one. The bitter cold canceled any joy the sun might have spread over the crystal cathedral, but thoughts of Annamaria came to Francesco's mind, thoughts that weighed heavily on his heart.

No one spoke; it was just too cold to talk, but a poem began to form in Francesco's mind. It had been a while since Francesco had composed a poem.

> beech trees in winter
> covered in ice prisms on branches
> cast rainbows of light.

breezes sway boughs
clicks fill the air
the collision of branches
cause cracks to appear.

fairies emerge,
they dance all around,
tilting toward sunlight
and then falling down.

fairylands vanish
in the afternoon sun.
sweet birds of youth

Francesco repeated the last stanza of poem over in his mind trying different phrases for the last line, but nothing worked. He knew it was a pretty rough piece but it made him feel good trying to reach out in remembrance. He hoped he could recall the stanzas later, write them down, and polish the piece.

Just before they turned off for Miglianico, a German truck convoy passed them heading toward Chieti. The convoy reminded Claudio of the incident at their nearby prisoner-of-war camp that turned out so differently from the situation at Sulmona. He recited the failure of the prisoners to run for their lives from the camp outside Chieti when the armistice was declared. The POW leader told them to wait for the British Army to rescue them. Instead, the Germans showed up and sent them packing to camps in Germany. Antonio shook his head; Francesco stared ahead and said nothing. But his jaw tightened as he pictured the scene and thought about the futility of it all.

On the secondary road the sled runners sank lower in the snow, but the horses were powerful animals and didn't falter; the sled swished on through the heavier accumulation. After a while Claudio's uncle stopped to rest them. Resuming the journey, the snow-covered rooftops of the village of Miglianico appeared on a hillside to their left. They turned onto the road that led gradually uphill into the village.

They were surprised to see a British jeep parked in front of the municipal building as they entered the piazza. Claudio's uncle brought the horses to a stop as Antonio jumped out and went inside hoping to find the British soldiers. Two noncommissioned officers were in the main foyer talking to a clerk at his desk. One was speaking to the clerk in Italian. Antonio approached the soldiers and introduced himself, explaining why he was there and who he was trying to find. The British officer queried Antonio about the reason for the search of the war-torn town so he summarized Francesco's story. The officer didn't know any of the

Canadian soldiers by name, but he knew that the Canadians were bivouacked in Ortona and offered to bring him and his brother back to the town, or "what was left of it," he said. Antonio hurried outside excitedly and gave Francesco the news.

Francesco quickly climbed out of the sled with his and Antonio's packs as the British soldiers emerged from the municipal building. Antonio made the introductions and after shaking hands with everyone, Antonio and Francesco were invited to throw their gear in the jeep and hop aboard.

"Good luck," Claudio called out to them, his words enveloped in mist as they got into the jeep. "I hope you find who you are looking for, Francesco."

Francesco nodded his head, raised and cocked his arm and fist in victory. "Stop in Chieti on your way back," Claudio said.

"We will, God willing. *Grazie*," Antonio said, turning and waving.

The officer inserted his key in the ignition and turned over the engine startling the horses. Claudio's uncle quickly brought them under control as the jeep pulled out and left the piazza.

Heading down the snow, covered road out of town the jeep's canvas canopy blocked out the wind but not the cold. Their breaths continued to be visible as they spoke. Antonio asked the officer if he could comment on his earlier statement regarding what was left of the town.

The officer explained that the battle for Ortona had been the toughest and bloodiest battle the Eighth had fought to date in Italy. "Sicily was tough, but nothing like it had been this past week," he said. "We have to give the Canadians credit for this one. It was their fight and they pulled it off, although I wasn't sure how it was going to turn out when it started."

He explained that after crossing the Moro River, the Canadians got themselves bogged down in a ravine south of Ortona called *Torrente Saraceno*, about three miles long and a few hundred yards wide that the locals used for farming. The Germans planted it with mines and booby traps. Then they dug themselves in and tried to bottle the Canadians up to keep them out of Ortona itself. The Canadians called the salient "the gully" at first, and later after the casualties mounted, "dead man's gulch." Finally, after nine days of fierce fighting they took it with a flanking maneuver.

Francesco was listening to the officer's account. "Why did they go into that gully in the first place?" he asked.

"Good question. I don't have a good answer. Anyway, by the time they entered Ortona, the Germans were well entrenched. They had demolished the town, beginning with the watch tower. Then they blew up buildings and filled the side streets with rubble so nothing could pass, not even tanks. This forced the infantry down the main road through town. The Germans had placed snipers, planted booby traps and mines everywhere."

"It must have taken courage to go down that road," Antonio said.

"No one had experienced fighting like that; they're still counting and burying bodies. All I know is that since crossing the Sangro we have had thousands of casualties. I don't know many have died."

Mention of the Sangro caused Francesco to lean forward in the jeep and raise his voice over the noisy rumble: "What about the townspeople?"

"Most of them left before the fighting began. Where they went I don't know, but I know that the Germans stopped some of the younger men and forced them into work parties."

"But the Canadians won. We got word of that a couple of days after Christmas. How did they manage it?" Antonio asked. "It sounded like the Germans had the upper hand."

"The Canadians fought harder. They were more determined. As I said earlier, it was a fight unlike any we had since landing in Sicily. It went street by street, house by house, even room by room. It was tough and bloody, but there was no other way, the Germans had seen to that."

"I can't even imagine," Antonio said.

"They improvised. They climbed to the upper floors, blasted holes in the outer walls, threw in grenades, and used their guns to clear the room. Then they had to break through adjacent walls, clear out those spaces. When they secured one level, they dropped through ceilings into rooms below; worked their way down stairwells floor by floor cleaning out the rooms on each floor. They repeated that process from house to house, moving down entire blocks without ever going outside."

"I still can't grasp it," Antonio said.

"Mouse-holing' was what they called it," the officer said. "The Germans put up one hell of a fight. They had brought in one of their best fighting units to hold the town."

"Why did they want to hold Ortona so badly?" Antonio asked.

"It's a deep water port. The German high command didn't want it to fall into Allied hands, so they ordered their men to hold it at all cost."

Still leaning forward with his hand on the back of the driver's seat, Francesco yelled, "How did it end?"

"For such an intense struggle, it ended pretty quietly. I guess the Germans realized that it was going to be a losing battle, so they decided to cut their losses and leave. During the night, someone gave the order to pull out and they just melted away."

The snow-covered ruins of Ortona came into view as the officer finished his story. Antonio and Francesco fell silent in wide-eyed wonder at the bombed and hollowed buildings at the edge of town. Rubble was everywhere. Groups of British soldiers were camped along the road; tents laid out in clusters in snow clearings. The jeep crunched to a stop at a makeshift field hospital marked Battalion Aid Station.

"We'll stop here. I'll ask about your Major Jones, and Lieutenant Ellis," the officer said, hopping out of the jeep.

The British flag was flying from a pole adjacent to the large tent marked with a red cross. Antonio and Francesco got out of the jeep and followed the officer inside. Beyond the front flap, soldiers were moving about with paper records; some were rummaging through file boxes at improvised desks. Rows of cots with wounded men occupied most of the interior space. Medics were attending to men with heads and splinted extremities wrapped in blood-stained bandages. The smell of blood and antiseptic filled the air replacing the acrid odor of the spent battlefield outside. A makeshift operating room was situated at the far end. Bottles of plasma hung on poles next to tables where battlefield surgeons huddled over men with chest and abdominal wounds. The officer stopped at a desk marked Registration.

"I'm looking for a Lieutenant Roger Ellis, and a Major Denis Jones," he said. "Ellis was with the Canadians and Jones was with us the last time anyone knew. Do you know if either has been treated here or where I can find them?"

The clerk looked through his admission log. "I don't have anyone by those names here," he said looking up. "But that doesn't mean they weren't casualties; just that those men were not brought in here. You might find out more at HQ."

Francesco's chest tightened when he entered the tent, but he breathed easier when he left with the officer and Antonio.

The clerk shouted after them: "If you don't get any information at HQ, try the Canadian divisional HQ. They've taken over a house in town on the main drag near the piazza. Look for the red Canadian flag."

They hopped back in the jeep and headed down the road to the battalion headquarters.

Inside the BQ, staff officers were conferring in makeshift office spaces. Some were standing before maps with pointers indicating movements and features. The sergeant walked to a bench marked Personnel. File boxes were stacked along the sides, top, and rear. A noncommissioned officer was seated flipping through a box of records.

"Corporal," the sergeant said. "We are looking for two officers." He again provided their names, rank, and services.

The corporal checked his log book and then went to one of his files. He pulled out a record, flipped it open and scanned it. "It looks like Major Denis Jones, an engineer with the 78th has been sent down to Vasto with Montgomery's contingent. I heard they were shipping out for England."

"They're not moving up to Pescara?"

"I don't know what's going on for sure. I heard General Oliver Leese is coming in to take over from Monty. I guess there's been a change of plans."

"What about Lieutenant Ellis?"

"I don't have anything here. You say he's a Canadian? They may have a record of him at their divisional unit in town."

Francesco had breathed a sighed a relief when he heard Denis was still alive. He smiled at Antonio as they left the headquarters tent with the sergeant.

The drive into the heart of Ortona was eerie. Bulldozers had begun to clear a path through the snow and rubble on the main thoroughfare. They were forced to drive slowly, navigating through piles of stones, bricks, and beams that lined both sides of their path. Some of the heavily damaged buildings had completely collapsed; the facades of others had fallen away, downward tilted roofs and floors exposing the inner rooms. Some of the homes were still standing, largely intact, but the walls were gouged with bullet and shrapnel strikes. They passed military personnel along the street climbing over debris going in and out of buildings. A few citizens were out surveying the damage and chatting. A lady had strung a clothesline and was hanging freshly laundered sheets and clothing while another was bent over picking through the rubble. A man struggled to push a ramshackle cart along. They came upon a group of boys kicking a soccer ball in the street where debris had been bulldozed away. Laughing and shouting, they seemed inured to what had happened. The entire street scene seemed surreal to Francesco. The Canadian flag hung from a pole on a house next to the piazza, the one building that appeared to have suffered only minor damage. At the front entry soldiers were entering and leaving; inside a corporal was seated at a desk that had been fashioned from a door resting on two chairs. A field phone and stacks of papers were lying upon it and the corporal was making entries in a log book. The British sergeant introduced himself and exchanged a salute.

"We are looking for a Lieutenant Roger Ellis," he said.

"It's Captain Ellis now. That's his office there," he said, pointing across the hall.

Francesco and Antonio suddenly wide-eyed and smiling yelled in unison, "*Grazie Dio*," and slapped their hands together. Francesco had maintained a private optimism that Roger was still alive, but now he let loose his inner joy.

"He's out making rounds but he should be back shortly," the sergeant said. "Have a seat there if you like," pointing to a row of mismatched wooden chairs against the wall.

Francesco turned to the sergeant, his face overjoyed and thanked him for getting him and his brother to Ortona.

The sergeant shook Francesco and then Antonio's hands. "I was happy to help. After what you did to help our men escape, Francesco, I was glad I could return the favor." Putting on his helmet he said, "I need to get back to headquarters. If you need me, look for me there. Good luck!" Then he turned, walked out the door, and hopped into his jeep.

Chapter 21

An officer wearing a captain's double bars on a heavy jacket walked in carrying a tommy gun. A sidearm was strapped to his waist. His facial features were darkened by a helmet set low on his brow and the stubble of a beard on his jaw and chin. Francesco noticed the man enter, but he didn't give him a second look.

"Captain," the corporal turned and said. "These men have been waiting for you."

Roger Ellis turned toward the men seated against the wall. He narrowed his eyes and asked uncertainly, "Francesco, is that you?"

Francesco looked back again. Realizing it was Roger who spoke, he jumped up and threw his arms around him in a crushing hug. Roger swung out his left arm with the tommy gun while he embraced Francesco with his right.

Antonio rose and introduced himself as Francesco's brother.

Nodding to Antonio, he pulled back a bit from Francesco for a better look. His face had that stunned expression of suddenly recognizing someone they once knew, but now out of context. "Hey, my friend, so good to see you again. I can't believe you're here."

Francesco's eyes teared up but he held them back and remained silent holding onto Roger.

Antonio said, "When we heard the Eighth army had reached Ortona, Francesco said he needed to find you. I didn't think it would be possible at first, but we found a way."

Roger nodded again to Antonio and looked down to Francesco. "Okay, my friend. C'mon, let's go into my office."

Antonio followed Roger, still holding on to Francesco, into his office, a converted bedroom off the main hallway. A wooden table served as his desk. Wooden chairs were positioned in front and behind the table. A map of Italy and another of the Abruzzo region with colored pins were tacked side by side on the wall. "Ever since that day at the Sangro, Francesco, I hoped I would see you again, but I expected it would be across the ocean, not here. Tell me how you got here; better yet, why are you here?"

"They are all dead," he said. The tears that had formed earlier, that he held back, began to trickle down his cheeks.

"Who are all dead?"

"The Sanellis."

Roger's eyes widened. He turned to Antonio. He closed his mouth then asked, "What happened?"

Antonio pulled up a seat in front of Roger's desk and had Francesco sit; he took one next to him. Roger sat behind his desk and listened as Francesco began his story.

He started with the unexpected arrival of the Gestapo officer at the Sanelli home. "We were sitting at the table one afternoon when this SS officer and his men showed up. They questioned us, Pierluigi, me...I... I saw his face, I can't forget." The pain of remembering was too much. He stopped speaking and scrunched down sobbing. It was left to Antonio to pick up the story and finish it.

"My brother has not been the same since he came home," he said when he had finished telling the story.

Roger had listened silently to Antonio's recitation of the events. Then he got out of his chair, turned and suddenly slammed his fist against the map on the wall, startling Antonio and Francesco. He paused a moment to take a deep breath and recompose himself; then he came over and put his arm around Francesco. "They were a wonderful family. They paid the ultimate sacrifice for us, Francesco. I feel your pain, but I don't want to see you torture yourself. We all have regrets. Denis and I wanted to go off on our own. We were afraid something like that would happen."

"I know," Francesco said, sniffling. The sobbing had stopped. "Pierluigi was so sure you would be safer doing it his way."

"We were. Who knows what might have happened if we just left on our own that night."

"The plan worked, you escaped, and you're here. It's just a terrible shame they were found out," Antonio said.

"I've seen a lot of death this month, not just soldiers, but civilians caught in the crossfire," Roger said. "Collateral damage, we called it. Unfortunate, but the deliberate execution of civilians is another matter—that's a crime that turns my stomach."

"Francesco, your brother says you remembered the Gestapo officer who called himself Hoffmann. He had the same scar and nervous tic as the officer who ordered the massacre at Pietransieri, is that right?"

Francesco, who was still looking down at the floor, nodded.

Roger paused a moment thinking. "I am going to write up the incident in a formal report and pass it on up the line to Eighth Army Command. I don't know how or when this war will end, but we will win it I'm sure; and when we do, a report like this will be useful for war crimes investigations."

"I want him killed!" Francesco said in anger. "I can't get his face out of my mind."

Antonio reached over and put his hand on Francesco's arm. Then he looked up at Roger and began to relate the symptoms Francesco had manifested in the days and weeks since the incident—the nightmares, anxiety, and irritability; his arousal at seemingly unrelated events that triggered bad reactions; the social withdrawal and sobbing at unexpected moments.

Roger told them the symptoms were similar to what many of his men were experiencing in the recent weeks of fighting on the Adriatic front. Some of the medics were calling it "shell shock" or "nervous shock." A medical corps psychiatrist had visited the camp and discussed the state of his men with him. He especially noted the combination of hysteria and paralysis—some were simply paralyzed with fear. "War neurosis," he labeled it. He wasn't sure it was a real medical diagnosis.

Turning to Francesco he said, "Francesco, that doctor is returning to our camp today for a follow up," Roger returned to his seat behind his desk and leaned toward Francesco. "I would like you to talk to him about what you are feeling. I think it might help you deal with what you are going through."

Francesco sat up and thought about what Roger was asking. "I don't think talking to a stranger will help."

"The thing is, Francesco, this doctor is a specialist who helps young soldiers deal with the things that are bothering them. You might not have been in a battle like them, but you experienced the same sort of trauma. I don't have this resource after today. There might not be another opportunity. What do you say?"

Antonio turned to Francesco. "I think it would be a pity not to take advantage of talking to this doctor."

Francesco had crossed his arms and was looking down at the floor again.

Roger and Antonio stared at Francesco. Moments passed in silence. Francesco looked up. "It's not what I want to do, but if you think it will help..."

Roger said, "I think we should give it a try. Give me a minute to make the arrangements." He stepped out of his office and yelled to his corporal to contact the company medic. "Tell him to find the doctor, Captain Wallace." When he came back in his office Roger said, "You'll see the doctor, and then tonight we will celebrate. Do you know what night this is?"

"Not really," Francesco responded. "I've lost track of the days."

"How about you, Antonio?"

Antonio scratched his head. "To tell you the truth, since Christmas it's been a blur. We must be close to the New Year?"

"It's New Year's Eve! The Brits are throwing a party in the church. It should be, as they say, 'a jolly good time.' We can catch up some more."

"Don't we have to leave today?" Francesco asked his brother.

Roger interjected before Antonio could reply. "Well, certainly not tonight. There is another storm coming and there's the party. See how things look tomorrow."

"What about you, Roger? What's next?" Antonio asked.

"My time here is about over," Roger said. "Command is giving up the Adriatic campaign. We just don't have enough firepower to continue. Part of the army will stay here and pin down the Germans. What is left of my unit is being transferred to the west of the country. We're joining up with the United States Fifth Army."

"Sir," the corporal called from the outer hallway. "I have Captain Wallace on the phone for you."

"Be back in a minute."

Roger walked out to talk with Wallace on the field phone. He arranged for Francesco's consultation that very afternoon and came back to give them the details. "Let me get you both settled," he said. "There are cots and blankets upstairs where you can sleep tonight after the party. I will have one of my men show you the way. When the doctor gets here, I will call you down, Francesco. Antonio, he may want your input as well. Until then, rest up. I have to write up and file my reports for the day."

****

The psychiatrist arrived a short time later. He was a young, serious-looking man with dark hair and black-framed glasses. Captain bars and the medical corps emblem were pinned to his uniform. He removed his officer's hat and introduced himself to Roger who told him to use his office for the interview. The corporal brought Francesco down from his room and introduced him to the doctor.

"Nice to meet you young man," Dr. Wallace said, with a soft smile. "Please take a seat. May I call you Francesco?"

"Okay," Francesco answered shyly, sliding into the chair he had occupied earlier.

After some small talk in an attempt to get Francesco to relax, Dr. Wallace began with: "Tell me how you first met Captain Ellis."

Responding to prompts from Dr. Wallace, Francesco recalled his trip to Caramanico, the circumstances at Pierluigi's house and family; where he met Roger and Denis, and how he helped them escape across the Sangro. All the while, he shifted uncomfortably in his chair, his voice sometimes fading out. Wallace found himself frequently asking Francesco to repeat his answer. "Please speak up," he said, looking up from his notes from time to time. Francesco struggled but handled the session fairly well, that is until he came to the incident with the Gestapo at Pierluigi's home. Then intense visceral feelings came flooding back and he burst into tears. The doctor kept reassuring him as the session continued, stressing he was doing well. His soft voice and easy-going style were able to restore Francesco's sense of well-being and bring the interview to a conclusion. An hour after he began, he ushered Francesco out and brought Antonio in for an interview. Antonio related how one moment his brother was sad, and later seemed fine, as he related the past several weeks of Francesco's behavior following his return to Roccamorice.

"He's a young boy, Antonio. They have those sort of mood swings." Wallace said.

"He blames himself for the Sanellis' deaths."

"It's natural for a youngster to feel that way, although there is no age limit for guilt."

When the interview with Antonio was over, Wallace said to him: "What you have been describing, Antonio, and what your brother has related is similar to what I have seen with many of the troops here in Ortona especially. The battle left them with a terrible sense of foreboding or doom, and a kind of emotional numbness that goes along with it. Like Francesco, some are having trouble sleeping and nightmares. Many of them feel depressed, but no one here is suicidal, at least not yet. Let me bring in Francesco and talk to you and him together about my diagnosis and treatment plan."

After Francesco took his seat, Wallace addressed him and his brother with an upbeat tone of voice: "The good news in your case, Francesco, is that you are young," the doctor said. "You are a strong young man and have the support of family and friends. I think sharing your grief with Captain Ellis was a good thing to do. It helps to have someone who understands, someone you can commiserate with."

"I don't know if it's going to matter," Francesco said, looking skeptical.

"I think it will. The sadness you feel will not linger. That's easy for me to say, but you have to take my word for it that such cases with young people do not last. In fact, from what your brother has told me, your mood has begun to improve on this trip. Do you feel that it has?"

"I suppose so. Maybe a little; I don't know."

"There has been a lot to distract him," Antonio said.

"But in any case, with your permission, I would like to write up a report you can take with you. If you need to see a doctor in the future, the report will contain my assessment and recommendations for counseling if you need it. How does that sound?"

"Okay, I guess," Francesco said quietly.

"One other thing. I'm told by your brother and Captain Ellis you enjoy writing. It's good to focus on the things you enjoyed doing before the war began. So I am going to recommend when you are ready, you might want to write about your trip to the Sangro and back. It could help you wipe away the darkness you feel."

"Someone else suggested that, but I'm not in the mood. It just doesn't appeal to me right now," Francesco said.

"I'm not totally certain that the horror stories in the mind can be released between the pages of a book, but it's worth a try. Time itself has healing properties. You will know if and when you're ready to write."

Dr. Wallace ushered Francesco and Antonio out to the corporal who indicated they should go up to their room and rest before the party. With the session concluded, Wallace found Ellis, and they spent a few minutes together discussing Francesco's case. "I'm optimistic that boy will be okay, eventually," Wallace said. "I will dictate my report for one of your clerks to write up."

"Hey, thanks much Doc. I appreciate you seeing him. Can you hang around for the party tonight?"

"Wish I could, but I have to report down the line. This campaign is keeping me busy. Enjoy the evening, it should be good for Francesco," he said, as he saluted and left.

Chapter 22

After sunset, Roger brought Francesco and Antonio down to his office to chat before walking to the church for the party. Roger poured Antonio and himself a glass of Canadian whiskey. Francesco was satisfied with water.

"I hope the session with Dr. Wallace helped you, Francesco," Roger said.

Francesco nodded, tight-lipped. From his point of view, talking it out seemed to have helped him feel better, but he wasn't sure and he was not ready to admit anything.

"I think the doctor's recommendations will help," Antonio added.

"He was quite positive about the session," Roger said. "I feel optimistic for you, Francesco. I wish I could say that for all my men."

Francesco fidgeted with his glass of water and shifted in his chair. He got up and put the glass on the desk and stepped over to the map wall. He studied it for a moment thinking and turned to Roger. "The British sergeant who drove us here told us about the fighting around Ortona. You told me about your men, but are you okay?"

"Everyone handles the war differently. Some are affected more than others. The war opens up cracks in some that don't exist in others. But, yes, I'm doing okay."

"Francesco told me that you were a lieutenant," Antonio said. "I see that you were promoted since you got back with your unit."

"We lost several officers after our landing in Sicily. I was one of the lucky ones to survive. I was made captain just a couple of weeks ago as we fought our way north."

"How bad has it been?" Antonio asked, taking a sip of his whiskey. "I mean how many casualties have you had?"

"I don't have a count yet, but I know we have a lot of bodies to bury from the fighting this month, maybe a thousand or more."

"Tell me about Denis," Francesco said, reaching for his glass of water. "Before we found you, we learned at British headquarters that he made it here alive. But his unit is going back to England with Field Marshal Montgomery, is that right?"

Roger's face registered surprise. "We were in completely different units, so I did not know that. But I'm happy for him. I know he was looking forward to going home, rebuilding England. But he'll likely rest up there with his unit before they deploy again.

"What happened to him after the Sangro?" Francesco asked, putting down his glass.

"After we crossed the river and got back to our Army, Denis was sent to join the engineers in the British 78th Division, and I was assigned to the Canadian 1st Infantry. With all the rain, Denis's group had a tough time of it building roads through all the mud around the flooded rivers and then bridging over them. The rains never stopped and more than once those bridges were washed out and had to be rebuilt."

"So you never got to see Denis again?"

"Only once, briefly. His outfit was always working up ahead of us. Right before the Moro River crossing our division was swapped with the British 78th. They needed the rest. They were pretty much exhausted from the fighting and working in all that rain, snow, and mud. It was during the transfer that I saw him again. They were lined up on both sides of the road as we passed through. He recognized me and called out."

"How did he look?"

"Tired and grimy, they all did. We made small talk. We were just happy to see each other again."

"I wish I could have seen him. I would have wanted to tell him about the Sanellis."

Roger picked up his drink. "I will write him a letter. I need to get some closure, just like you. I told him we would try to stay in touch. The letter might not get to him for a while, but at least he will know. If you would like to add a note, I can include it."

"I don't write English. You will know what to write for me."

"I am sure I can find the words. I know he will be very grateful for the news, sad as it is. And I know he will appreciate the great effort you made to come all the way here under these conditions to let us know about the Sanellis." He took the final sip of his whiskey and put down the glass. He smiled, and in a brighter voice he asked, "So are you two ready to go to a party?"

"I'm not feeling so happy right now," Francesco said.

"Happiness is relative," Roger responded. "We can't be happy all the time, but we can be happy we are alive at this moment. We need to stop and celebrate these moments when we can. It has been one tough year."

"I agree," said Antonio, putting his glass down on Roger's desk and turning to his brother. "Let's enjoy the evening. Who knows what will happen tomorrow." "Speaking of tomorrow, I want to make sure you both can get back to your home. The Germans still control much of the area you came through, so I can't have you escorted back."

"It's true," Antonio said. "We were expecting to run into them before we found you, so we were surprised when we met the British sergeant in Miglianico."

"I talked to one of my men and asked him to see if there is a civilian vehicle somewhere we can get our hands on. We have the mechanics who can fix anything they find."

"What about petrol?" Francesco asked.

"We have enough of that to spare, at least to get you where you need to go." Roger said. "So if you are ready, let's go over to the church. To accommodate everyone, headquarters set up a system of shifts." Glancing at his watch he said, "Our unit is due there next."

The men rose from their chairs and walked into the hallway and put on their jackets. Roger stopped to give some orders to his clerk who jotted some notes on a pad while Antonio and Francesco waited by the door. Joining them, Roger wrapped a scarf around his neck and zipped up his jacket. Putting on his hat, he said to Francesco, "I'm sure you will enjoy what they have to eat. I've heard the British are roasting a suckling pig. Didn't you tell me once how much you liked porchetta?"

"Oh my," Antonio said. "How long has it been, Francesco?"

"A couple of years at least. I don't remember having any since the war began." Roger opened the door and they all stepped into a gusting wind. It was dark and the snow was coming at them sideways, stinging their faces. They walked quickly up the rubble-strewn street to the heavily damaged church of San Rocco a block away. Huddled up soldiers were streaming in from all directions joining them as they approached the entrance. Singing, punctuated by the soft roar of laughter greeted them as they opened the door.

The atmosphere was festive with enlisted men, commissioned and non-commissioned officers milling about, singing and drinking, toasting one another. British and Canadian flags were suspended from cross-beams below the vaulted ceiling. The altar had been blocked off to separate the sacred from the profane. Doors pulled from the town rubble became tables set upon on tops of the pews. Scattered lanterns provided halos of light.

Bottles of beer, pale and brown ales, and Guinness rested on some, while others held bottles of whiskey, gin, and brandy. Champagne for the midnight toast rested in barrels of icicles gathered from roof eves. For the nondrinkers, like Francesco, there were bottles of ginger beer. Part of the right side wall of the church had been shattered open by an artillery shell. In the space a large hearth had been fashioned where enlisted men were taking turns rotating a young pig on a spit over a wood fire. To accompany the roast, cooks had scrubbed and roasted potatoes and made Yorkshire pudding. Dessert tables were stacked with pound and sponge cakes, fruit jams, and chocolate sauce made from Cadbury chocolate bars that lay in stacks on a table.

Francesco and Antonio were stunned. The sheer volume and variety of food and drink overwhelmed their sensibilities.

"What's the matter, Francesco?" Roger asked seeing the expression on Francesco's face. "You seem troubled."

He frowned. "Look at all there is to eat and drink in here while so many are hungry. You know it was hunger, *la fame,* that's why I went to Pierluigi's in the first place."

"I remember," he said. "That and those German soldiers who forced your hand." He paused to consider Francesco's dilemma. "I can understand why this party might upset you. But if we can sympathize and mourn, Francesco, can we not also console one another with food and drink?"

Francesco had nothing to counter. He was feeling guilty. What did he have to celebrate? It didn't seem right somehow, although being with Roger felt right. "Consider what these men have been through," Roger continued. "They fought hard liberating this part of Italy. Do you think they should be denied the opportunity to fill their bellies and celebrate victory and the New Year? If it makes you feel better, the townspeople who remain here have been invited to attend."

"Maybe we're being too critical," Antonio said. "That's a nice gesture, Captain. "Let's get something to eat, Francesco, I'm hungry."

They made their way through the crowded aisles to the hearth where the pig had been removed to a set of wooden planks. Several enlisted men greeted Roger as he passed them, the grim look of war now replaced by smiling faces. Soldiers were lined up with plates in their hands, and as they filed past the cook standing over the pig.

The *porchetta,* in the Abruzzo tradition, was a savory pork roast. Francesco thought the military chef must have enlisted the help of one of the local residents to prepare it. He knew the young pig had to be deboned and stuffed with liver, garlic, fennel, and other herbs, then heavily salted and roasted for hours with the fat and skin turning to a crispy texture. For each man the cook cut a slab of the fatty aromatic pork and placed it on their plate. Francesco looked down at his plate. As the aroma wafted up to him, he remembered the many festive occasions in Roccamorice that now seemed so long ago.

After they filled their plates with the other offerings, Francesco and Antonio followed Roger to the other side of the church where amid lively chatter and laughter they found a spot on a table in the pews. Fellow officers stopped by to greet Roger. He introduced each of them to Francesco and Antonio. The brothers responded with a brief *"Piacere,"* holding their forks of porcetta over their plate with one hand, the other raised in greeting, more intent on the food than the introductions. While they were eating, Roger's staff sergeant stopped by to tell him that they had located a civilian automobile in a collapsed garage. They were able to extricate the vehicle and got it running after they added fuel and made a few repairs. The vehicle belonged to a town official who was not anxious to part with it.

Thanking and dismissing his sergeant he said, "Tell the man I will talk to him tomorrow morning and make him an offer." Then he turned to Antonio and asked him how far he thought he could safely drive toward home.

"I think Chieti," Antonio said. "I have a friend there where we can leave the car. Do you think the owner would be happy with that?"

"That sounds workable. I'll make that arrangement with the owner tomorrow. We'll compensate him fairly and he'll have a salvaged auto repaired and refueled. Why wouldn't he be happy?" Roger looked at his watch. "We have a couple of hours until midnight, but we need to give up these seats for the next group due in. We can go back and put our feet up, and then come back to toast the New Year if you are up to it."

"It's been a long day," Antonio said. He glanced at Francesco who managed a tired smile and nodded. Looking across the table to Roger he said "I would never have dreamt that we would have found you; that we would be sitting here talking at a party when we left Chieti this morning."

Roger winked and smiled. "Hope you both have some pleasant memories to replace the unpleasant ones. Tonight is what I want you to remember."

"And a better story to tell," Antonio added.

"That reminds me, Francesco," Roger said, finishing the last dregs of his beer and putting the bottle down on the table. "I'm going to give you my home address in Canada. I want you to send me your story if you write it, the memoir Dr. Wallace encouraged you to write."

"I can't promise to write, Roger. I just don't know."

"Whether or not you write it or fulfill the plan of going to America after the war, you must let me know how things turn out for you. Keep me informed. I am going to write up my report too. Maybe we can find some justice for the Sanellis."

An enlisted man wearing an apron came by to clear the empty plates and pick up the empty bottles. Roger rose from his seat to leave. Francesco sighed deeply as he rose to follow Roger. Antonio joined them and they wove their way through the noisy crowd to the vestibule at the front door of the church. Soldiers were coming and going through the entryway. Francesco stepped aside, slumped against the wall and frowned. The party was over he realized. Roger, noticing Francesco's sadness, took him aside.

"Look at me Francesco, look at me," he repeated, embracing him. "This war will end, but think about this not just as the end, but as the beginning of something, a friendship, a reunion and who knows." He repeated his encouragement and his earlier offers. "Maybe we get some justice."

Roger's words made him feel better, lighter, and more hopeful; a smile brightened his face. "That would be something wouldn't it?"

The three men made their way to the door where they bundled up before they stepped outside. The wind howled and rushed after them as they walked back to the headquarters building pelted by the wind-driven snow.

The party would last into the early morning hours. Midnight would be marked with a champagne toast and the singing of *Auld Lang Syne*, but Francesco and Antonio would not be there. Neither they nor anyone at the party would be sad to see the year pass into history. What would the coming year bring, Francesco wondered as he lay in bed and closed his eyes on the final minutes of 1943.

Part III
A Time to Heal

Chapter 23

Hamilton, Ontario. March, 1953

Professor Ellis, do you have a minute?"

Roger Ellis was deep in thought. His left arm was propped on his desk, his hand on his forehead. He was making notes in the margin of a manuscript he was working on—a book tentatively titled, *Nazi War Crimes in Italy, 1943-1945*. He lost his train of thought at the interruption. He flashed a frown of annoyance at his graduate assistant, Dan Travis, standing in the doorway. "What's up, Dan?"

"There is something interesting in this story that you gave me a while back with the file on the Italian campaign."

"What story was that?"

"The one written by that Italian kid, Francesco, the one who helped you and your buddy escape."

"Ah, yes, Francesco, my lifesaver. Come in and have a seat."

Roger's office was piled with books, journals, and manila file folders stuffed with articles on his desk, counter top, and file cabinets. A sepia print of *Santo Spirito alla Maiella* hung on one wall; a battle map of the Italian campaign on another, and personal photos and documents on a third. A stack of books rested on the chair at the side his desk. He picked them up and looked around trying to decide where to put them before bending down and shoving them under the chair. "Sit here."

Dan sat with the open manuscript as Roger returned to his swivel chair and placed the manuscript on top of the Royal typewriter resting on the table behind his desk. His office window was cranked open. The fresh scent of spring wafted in, easing the musty smell of old books and papers out the office door. From his second floor office, Roger looked down on the quadrangle of Hamilton, Ontario's, McMaster University campus. The greening grass and the newly leafed maple trees framed the crisscrossing walkways and benches where a group of students sat chatting.

Turning back to his graduate assistant he asked, "So, Dan, what did you find in that manuscript?"

"Do you remember the SS officer Francesco described—the one with the stellate scar and the nervous tic?"

"I do. Francesco's description was quite vivid as I recall. What about it?" "I think I may have seen a man fitting the description."

Roger's eyes opened wide. "Are you kidding me?"

"Well, I could be wrong, but the description was so compelling that I immediately thought of it when I saw this guy the other day."

"Where?"

"Downtown in the Ukrainian section."

"What were you doing down there of all places?"

"Shopping with my wife in an antique store. She was looking for a copper amphora she needed for a floral arrangement."

"An antique store?"

"Sort of a thrift store that had some old stuff."

"And you bumped into him there, in the shop? He was a customer?"

"No, I think he was the proprietor or manager."

Roger picked up a pencil and began tapping it on his desk. "You saw that scar and tic that Francesco described?"

"It was uncanny, really. Here, take a look at the description again." Dan handed the manuscript to Roger.

The pages were folded back to the Caramanico incident immediately preceding the shooting. Roger read Francesco's description again furrowing his brow. Rubbing his chin, he handed the manuscript back to Roger. "I have to admit, that scar and tic make a pretty unique combination."

"That's what I thought too. The story was one of the sources I was checking for your book."

"Did you speak to him?"

"I was actually afraid to."

"Did you hear him speak?"

"He was talking to a customer in English about a vase she was interested in. He had an accent, but I couldn't place it. It sounded Eastern European, but it could have been Ukrainian."

"Could it have been German?"

"I don't know. I'm not very good in distinguishing those European accents." Dan got out of his chair and walked over to glance out Roger's window. Students were crossing the diagonals on their way to classes.

"What else did he look like, besides that scar?" Roger swiveled around in his chair.

"Medium height, round face with dark-rimmed glasses, graying hair. Kind of portly. I wouldn't have given him a second look until he turned his face and I saw the scar and the twitch around his eye."

"So where is this neighborhood again?"

Dan sat back down. "Downtown. The steel mill and railroad tracks border it on the north lakeshore. It's between Sherman and Gage, north of Cannon. The actual shop is on Barton Street."

"Did you get his name?"

"No, I didn't ask. Foolish I know. We left the shop quickly after spending just a few minutes because my wife didn't find what she was looking for."

"Well, he probably wouldn't have used his real name—Hoffmann, anyway, if he was hiding out."

"Do you want to go down there and have a look?" Dan asked.

"I am intrigued. I wouldn't be able to identify him any more than you could. I wasn't in Caramanico when the incident happened."

"What about bringing Francesco up? He's in the States now, isn't he?"

"Yes, in Lockborough, not far away. But before I do that, I would need to have more suspicion about this guy."

"Well, then it wouldn't hurt to take a ride and have a look, would it? Maybe getting into a conversation with him might help," Dan said.

"Wait a minute; I should have a file around here on Hoffmann. When Francesco came to Ortona, I filed a report and sent it up to headquarters. Eventually it made its way to London and British Intelligence offices. We should have a copy of the reply."

"Yes, those declassified intelligence files on Nazi war crimes from the National archives," Dan said. "I looked into them for that project you had me working on about the early Resistance movement in Italy. They should be back in your files."

Roger got up and walked over to one of his file cabinets stacked with books and file folders. "Check those files on my desk," Roger said to Dan, as he pulled open a file drawer.

Dan moved over to Roger's desk. Books, manuscripts, notebooks of various types and sizes, and manila files crowded the work surface leaving only a small space to write. A neat stack of letters, a cupful of pens and pencils, a stapler, and Scotch tape dispenser provided the only semblance of order around his desk lamp. Roger flipped through the headers on the manila files in the first file drawer. Finding nothing, he opened the next one below and repeated the process. "Well, here's something," he exclaimed, pulling out a file labeled *Limarri Massacre.*" In it was the official British intelligence report on the atrocity at Pietransieri that he, Francesco, and the others learned about at Dominick's farm near Casoli. He skimmed the sheets and records, his eyes falling on Colonel Hoffman, the SS Commander of the outfit responsible for the incident. He put the file back and flipped through the rest in the drawer, chiding himself for his poor filing system, which he had left to his graduate assistants. There was no rhythm or rhyme to the arrangements; no dates or locations, nothing. But the Caramanico file had to be there. "Any luck, Dan?" he asked.

"I'm not finding anything in this stack. Just some incidents that were reported in Northern Italy, but I did find that misplaced file you were looking for to write the Pope Celestine book."

"Okay, but first things first," Roger said, as he closed the drawer and opened a third drawer to continue his search. "Here it is, finally." He pulled out a thick file labeled *Roccamorice Memoir*. In it was a copy of Francesco's story in the original Italian, dated September 27, 1945. Roger recalled the short story Francesco had sent him as a courtesy, or more of an obligation he thought. It had never been published. The file also held a copy of Roger's written report at Ortona dated December 31,1943, and a copy of the British Intelligence report from August, 1947, which listed Hoffmann as the commander of the unit that had carried out the Sanelli execution in Caramanico. It also linked him to Pietransieri, and several other Italian village killings. Specific dates and places were listed, and there was a Nazi payroll sheet signed by an SS officer confirming that Hoffmann collected his salary as a member of the SS in the Italian campaign. There was also a photograph of Hoffmann, a frontal view, without evidence of a scar. He was dressed in his *Schutzstaffel* officer uniform with the skull-and-crossbones cap. He appeared young and stern faced. The photo was likely taken just after he received his commission. "Those Nazis never cease to amaze me. I'm grateful as a historian that they recorded everything—they actually thought the Third Reich would last a thousand years."

He walked the file back to his desk and sat down. Dan retook his seat next to him. Roger took out the photo and handed it to Dan. "Is this the man you saw in that shop?"

Dan stared intently at the photo of the man in his SS uniform not wearing glasses. "I'm trying hard to compress ten years in my mind, but I just don't know."

"Well, before we can do anything, get the authorities involved, we need to at least have a much stronger suspicion; some presumptive evidence."

"Isn't there enough in your files?"

"There could be with an actual eyewitness. Someone that is credible."

"Francesco could fit that bill?"

"Yes, I think he could with everything else we have, especially if we can find witnesses in the towns where he committed the atrocities."

"There is nothing in the files that says Hoffmann did any of the killings," Dan said.

"If he was a commander of a unit that perpetrated the atrocity, as the files indicate, then he's responsible even if he didn't pull the trigger. He gave the order, and that's all that matters."

"What do you want to do next?"

Roger closed the file and thought a moment. "I'm going to be busy the rest of the day. I have a class at eight o'clock tomorrow morning, and then a meeting with the department staff after that. Why don't you come by here, let's say around eleven? I should be free then. We can grab a bite on campus and then head downtown to that shop. I need to take a look at this guy before I do anything more."

"That works for me. I have an early class myself, and then a tutorial with a group of undergrads, but I can meet you in your office at eleven."

"Okay, I'll see you tomorrow, and by the way, Dan, good work! If this pans out, this is going to be a big story, front page news. But I'm getting ahead of myself."

"Thank you, sir. See you tomorrow."

Roger swiveled in his chair, stood up and gazed out his window. The butterflies were in his stomach, not flitting about the flowers. The idea of justice and redemption for the family that had sheltered and saved him, and the opportunity, finally, to erase the guilt he carried with him for a decade was exciting to contemplate.

His mind drifted back to his escape to Caramanico from the POW camp in Sulmona, and the time he spent with the Sanelli family. He saw them all so clearly now, confident and courageous. Friends among the foe. Pierluigi, confident, self-assured and committed. Angiolina, dutiful, industrious, and loyal. And then there was the lovely and innocent-looking Annamaria, who had been so patient with him, coaching and teaching him the basics of the Italian language. He had lost much of what he once knew—disuse atrophy he called it, but he retained enough to identify important documents that needed translation for his research projects. He remembered all the many gestures of kindness in that war-torn country as they made their way south and across the Sangro to freedom.

The next morning, Dan arrived at Roger's office promptly at eleven. They decided it was too early for lunch on campus. They could get a bite later downtown. "Do you want me to drive?" Dan asked. "My car is parked downstairs in the ten-minute visitors' space."

"Yes, that's fine," Roger said. "It will save me a walk over to the parking garage."

They left the campus and drove down the escarpment to the lower city. It was a beautiful spring morning. With the windows rolled down and the fresh air rushing in, Roger breathed in deeply the scents of spring. As they descended they passed stately homes with manicured yards he glanced at the flower beds containing brightly colored tulips in shades of red, pink and yellow, and various species of spring flowers he couldn't identify.

"Where is this place again?" Roger asked.

"On Barton Street around the corner from Gage Avenue."

As they entered the working class community on the lower level of town, the streets they now traveled were lined by closely set brick houses of similar style. They soon became aware of the industrial sector to the north as the scent of coal and smoke reached them from the massive steel mill on the lakeshore. Roger rolled up his window.

Dan turned onto Barton Street and pulled over to a parking space in front of the Ukrainian Orthodox Church. "That's the shop across the street," Dan said. It was in the middle of an older, somewhat dingy commercial block.

On the way, they had decided that Dan would conduct an interview with the man using the ruse of doing research on immigration, while Roger would observe and listen.

They got out of the car. Roger came around from the passenger side, and after letting cars pass, he hobbled across the street with Dan at his side. A number of older men and women were walking along the street, checking items in shop windows, carrying parcels, and chatting with one another. They heard a smattering of English, but most of the conversations were in what they assumed was the Ukrainian language.

They passed a grocery next to the antique shop. A wooden stand out front was loaded with fruits and vegetables. They paused to let a customer pass who had just emerged from an open door carrying a bag of groceries. The unique foreign scents of the store's interior followed the shopper onto the street.

Dan opened the door to the antique shop next door. It was a small, stale-smelling shop, one that could be entirely encompassed visually from front to back in a fairly quick glance. The interior was crowded with all types of implements and tools. Glass cases held various types of dishware and pottery, jewelry, orthodox religious items, and icons. Racks of clothing were situated along one wall and old paintings, mirrors, and religious calendars adorned the walls. Two women in different aisles were examining items. Dan and Roger walked to the back toward the counter with a cash register.

"I don't see our man," Dan said.

"Maybe he is not working today," Roger offered, "but someone must be running the shop."

Hearing their voices, a man emerged from a curtained space behind the counter. "May I help you?" he asked.

Roger was not immediately struck by his appearance—a middle-aged man with a portly face and thinning dark hair flecked with gray. He wore black-framed glasses with unusually thick lenses. He certainly didn't resemble the file photo. But then the man turned slightly revealing the scar, and at the same time began to manifest the distinctive facial tic Francesco had so vividly described. Roger drew in a sudden sharp breath and wondered. "I'm Professor Roger Ellis from McMaster University, and this is my graduate assistant, Dan Travis," he said. He removed his wallet from his pocket to display his faculty identification card.

"Sorry, my eyesight not too good," the proprietor said, leaning close to Roger's outstretched hand.

"We have been interviewing citizens in the neighborhood for a research project on the *History of the Ukrainian Community of Hamilton, Ontario.* And we were wondering if you would be so kind as to spare a few minutes for an interview."

"The Ukrainians of Hamilton. Who would be interested?" the shopkeeper's tone was rather sarcastic.

"Oh, on the contrary," Dan said. "Lots of people are interested in ethnic history. It's an active area of investigation for graduate students working on their master's and doctoral dissertations, especially here in Canada with the recent wave of immigrants."

The man seemed ill at ease as he fidgeted with a keychain lying on the counter. "Well, this not convenient," the man replied with a voice that implied annoyance. "I'm very busy, you see, don't have time to answer questions."

"I'm sorry I did not call ahead or send a letter, but this will be quick," Dan said, removing a questionnaire from the briefcase he was carrying. "The other shopkeepers were quite satisfied with our questions. There are only a few questions, and they are really quite basic. I won't take up much of your time."

"Okay, okay," the man responded grudgingly, "Just be quick."

"First, let's start with your name. You are—"

"Pavlov Karpenko."

"You are the listed as the proprietor of this shop. When was it established?" Dan asked, as he began filling out the questionnaire.

"Well, I don't own it, I am the manager. Why you need to know this?"

Roger, who had been flipping through a stack of old postcards on the counter while Dan asked the questions, interrupted to explain the purpose of the interview. "There have been three distinct waves of immigration from Ukraine," he said. "The first began in the late 1800s and lasted until about 1920. The second wave occurred between the wars, and the third is what we are now working on, the period of 1945 to the present. Dan would like your help with this period, because these years are the focus of our project. So we just need to place your information in the proper context."

"I see. You want to know after the war," Karpenko said with narrowed eye, shifting uneasily. "I think this shop was started before the war."

"Thank you," Dan said, folding over the questionnaire sheet. "May I continue?" "I'll try to tell you what I can, but I can't promise much," Karpenko responded.

"My memory not that good," he said.

"So where were you born in the Ukraine?"

"Rovina."

"That's in the western part of the country. You were raised there, I take it. What sort of work did you do there before you immigrated?"

"I was an iron worker with my father. We made wrought iron things like tools."

"When the war broke out you were old enough to serve. Did you join the army?"

"No. I could not pass the physical; my eyesight was too bad, but we made tools that the Russian army could use in the war."

"What sort of tools?"

"Folding shovels for the soldiers to carry were one thing."

"So you were a Ukrainian citizen at that time; not a Russian, is that right?"

"Correct."

As Karpenko answered the questions, Roger tried to seem disinterested, continuing to glance at the cards. But he wondered if the black-framed glasses with thick lenses Karpenko wore were part of a disguise to give some credence to the poor vision story. He recalled the man in the file photo did not wear glasses, but he thought Karpov's accent was German, not Ukrainian; certainly not the same as Ukrainians he had heard before, and not like those people who were speaking on the street.

"Why did you decide to immigrate?" Dan resumed.

"I did not want to live under Communist rule."

"Was it difficult? You know, getting the approvals. How were you able to do it?"

"There was an agency helping us. I had to travel to Kiev to work with people there. Finally, after about four years, in 1949 I was granted permission and the necessary papers to leave the country."

"You had a sponsor here then I take it."

"Yes, like everybody who came, I had to show I could have a job, you know, go to work, and they were hiring at the steel mill."

"So you started at the steel mill. When did you get this job?"

"About a year later," Karpenko responded, his face contorted. He took an exasperated breath, a sign of his growing impatience. He turned to the table behind the counter and rifled through a stack of receipts. With his back to Dan he said, "The Ukrainian owner was looking for someone to take over the business. I could run the place and pay for it little by little. It was easier than being a steelworker."

Roger frowned and gave Dan the high sign.

"Thank you, Mr. Karpenko. We promised you a short interview. You have been very helpful. I need to ask a few more questions but I can come back again. May I call to set up a good time?"

"Yes, of course," he said, looking relieved. "But I don't know much more than what I told you."

Roger and Dan walked back through the store and out the door. On the sidewalk Dan asked Roger, "What do you think?"

"Well, first of all, he doesn't resemble the man in the military photo, but more important I think he is lying. I don't think he's Ukrainian; I think he is a German trying to affect a Ukrainian accent."

"Is that it—the way he looks and speaks?"

"Like I said, he doesn't look like Hoffmann, but he could fit his description ten years later. The glasses bother me. The thick lenses could be plain glass. It's the scar and the tic that convince me the most. Francesco was pretty clear about those features when he relived the horror he described to me in Ortona. I think they were permanently etched in his mind, and he faithfully reproduced them in his memoir."

"What do you want to do now?" Dan asked. "I could talk to some of the other shopkeepers; maybe talk to neighbors where he lives."

"That's a good thought, but I think we can hold off for a bit. What I could use is a current photo of this guy."

"What for?"

"I'd like to show it to the authorities, maybe Francesco too. Get his reaction."

"I don't have a very good camera."

"You can use my 35mm. It has a telephoto lens. Take as many photos of him as you can coming and going from his shop. Track him around town if you have to. Don't be afraid to get as many shots as you can."

Pulling his car keys out of his pocket, Dan said, "No problem. I can get that done in the next few days. Is there anything else?"

"No, not right now, but I'm suspicious enough about him to go to the Canadian Immigration Office in Toronto. I need to make a case with the evidence I have, but I'll need those updated photos."

"What about Francesco? You suggested showing the photo to him. Shouldn't we bring him up here for a real look, just to confirm your suspicion?"

"Not yet. I want to try and build the case first at ground level. Francesco's testimony is going to be crucial, no question about it, but I don't want to disappoint him with a false alarm. I want the Canadian authorities on board before I contact Francesco. It will help me to convince him to come up."

"How are you going to convince Canadian Immigration you have a case?"

"I need to show he is not who he says he is. His immigration records are probably located in Halifax. That's where most immigrants entered the country."

"How are you going to get access? That's a pretty private government office. They like to keep their records confidential."

"I have a very good friend in the Justice Department in Ottawa. I think he can get me what I need. I'll call him from the office when we get back."

"Sounds good. Listen, can you spare me a moment? I want to pick up a loaf of a special Easter cake—*Paska* the Ukrainians make at this time of the year. They'll have it in the grocery next door."

"No, go ahead," Roger said, pulling a small notebook and pen from his jacket pocket. "I'll be on that bench over there. I want to make some notes before I forget."

Dan was back in a few minutes carrying a brown bag. "I asked the lady at the baking counter if she knew our friend Karpenko. She told me that he pretty much keeps to himself, and he doesn't say much to anyone."

"That would fit with someone who wanted to conceal his real identity," Roger said, as he got up and folded his notebook.

They crossed the street, got into the car. Roger took one last look at the antique shop. He thought he caught a glimpse of Karpenko's silhouette looking at them from behind the window of the shop as they pulled away.

On way back to the university, Dan asked Roger about his contacts with Francesco since he last saw him on New Year's Eve in 1943.

"After the war when he mailed me his memoir. It contained information about the end of the German occupation of Roccamorice, and how he spent the last two years of the war. I wrote back to thank him."

"I was going to ask you about that. When I read it, there was this vignette about the German officer ordering the citizens to evacuate the town, because they were going to fortify it in anticipation of an advance by the British army."

"Yes, that part about the citizens pleading with the Germans to allow them to stay in their homes was kind of dramatic—the part where the women of the town, a few of the men and children got down on their knees and processed to the old chapel on the edge of town where they prayed for the Germans to relent. Francesco wrote that he didn't participate, but he watched the procession as the soldiers stood along the route with pointed rifles."

"Amazingly it worked." Dan said. "I read when the officer reported back what had happened, the unit commander relented and canceled the evacuation order." "Well," Roger said, "I don't think he so much had a change of heart, as a change of orders from up the chain of command. The battle for that part of Italy was essentially over after Ortona. There would be no push to Pescara, and the pivot to Rome for the British army was canceled."

"What did Francesco do during that time?

"The new strategy for the German army was to establish another defensive perimeter further north. The war had another year and a half to go after that. After he immigrated I met him briefly at Niagara Falls. I had to get to Buffalo to fly to New York for an overseas meeting the next day, so we didn't have a lot of time to catch up. It's been a while since we talked. I should have stayed in touch, but I got busy and, well, you know how that goes."

"Well, you have a perfect opportunity to reconnect now."

Chapter 24

Easter week bracketing the Catholic and Orthodox celebrations had come and gone. Dan and Roger had been busy with their teaching and research projects. In the interval, Dan had taken several surveillance photos of Karpenko and gave the prints to Roger. Roger had spoken to his friend in the Justice Department, laying out a convincing case to get him Karpenko's file.

Roger felt the thrill of discovery reading through Karpenko's immigration file. He called Dan to his office in the afternoon on May 11th to share what he had found. Dan sat while Roger narrated a summation: "After the war, Karpenko was in a camp for displaced people in Ukraine, according to documents from the International Tracking Service." Roger went on to say that the record was moot on how he got there, but his other documentation showed he was transferred to the Eastern front from Italy.

Dan said, "I know Ukraine has a long history of annexation and partition by neighboring countries, and in 1941 it was invaded and annexed by Nazi Germany." "Yes," Roger answered. "Many Ukrainians in the western part of the country hated the Russians and actually worked with the Nazis to defeat them. Karpenko, rather Hoffman, probably shed his German uniform and identity, and blended into that Ukrainian population. To get into Canada, however, he had to find an agent who could locate a Canadian sponsor."

"He must have reinvented himself in Ukraine to find an agent for sponsorship," Dan said. "Wasn't that the common route for immigration in those days?"

"Yes, having a legitimate sponsor allowed immigrants to leave the country of origin. There were agents who served both the needs of the farmers who wanted help, and the Canadian Immigration Service who could provide the immigrant manpower. The documents showed that he arrived in Halifax on September 30, 1949."

Roger paused to shuffle through the file to check the date on the immigration form. Then he continued in his matter-of-fact tone. "The usual way for immigrants to reach various Canadian cities was to take the train from Halifax. The records showed that Karpenko traveled to Toronto on September 30th and then to Aldershot. He signed a contract to work one year on a farm as a requirement to enter the country." Looking up at Dan, he said, "This guy settled in my hometown while I was here in graduate school, and I never ran into him. So close and yet so far until you spotted him."

Shaking his head he continued. "Then in the fall of 1950, he moved into the city and got a job at the Dofasco Steel Company. He worked there a year and then left to work in the shop on Barton Street. Here, look over this other file while I get us a couple of cups of coffee."

"What file is this?" he asked as Roger handed it to him.

"It's the SS dossier."

"Where did that come from?"

"The U.S. Intelligence Department. Please don't ask me how."

"Friends in high places I assume."

"Right. I'll be back in a minute. While you're at it, compare the Karpenko and Hoffmann signatures."

Roger returned with two cups of coffee and handed one to Dan who was studying the dossier. Roger took a sip and asked, "What do you think, Dan?"

"Well, this is interesting stuff," he said, looking up. "It shows all of Hoffmann's postings in Italy. It puts him at all of those towns where the atrocities occurred, and it shows his transfer in 1944 to the Eastern front. Somehow he evaded the Soviets sweeping the Germans out of Ukraine that spring. But with everything else you have, this is a slam dunk! And you're right; Karpenko and Hoffmann's handwriting look identical."

"I agree. We can track him all the way from Germany to Italy, the Ukraine, Canada, and that shop on Barton Street."

"He must have become the manager of the shop sometime after he worked at the steel mill," Dan said. "He was at least truthful with that part of his story." "He bought into it a year ago; about the same time he was taking classes for citizenship."

"Everything checks out with what he told us in the interview we had with him last month. So how are we going to accuse him of being someone else?"

"I think we can get him in a lie—namely that he is a German and not a Ukrainian. It's time we get Francesco involved. We have lots of written documentation. What we need now is the key eyewitness. I have gone over all of this with the Immigration Service. They are willing to consider Francesco's testimony as part of their own investigation."

"Are you going to call him?" Dan said, passing back the file to Roger and taking a sip of coffee.

"Yes, I am going to set up a meeting, probably in the States first. I need a face- to-face. I can't go through all this over the phone."

"How do you think he'll react?"

"I don't know, but it could definitely stress him again. I need to be with him when I tell him. Back in Ortona my battalion surgeon said, his youth would likely protect his mental health, but he is older now. When I first saw him at Niagara after he immigrated with his mother and brother I thought he was doing as well as could be expected. He had become a steelworker, not the writer he had hoped to be as a boy. But it was a good job with wages that allowed him to live comfortably. I didn't detect any sign of the depressed teenager I said goodbye to on that New Year's Eve in Italy."

On Saturday morning Roger drove to his office to catch up on some academic work. The building was quiet; few students moved about the quad below his office window. He was enjoying a cup of coffee at his desk when the thought came to him to put in a call to Francesco who was probably not working on a Saturday.

He checked his personal directory and dialed the number. He got an answer on the third ring. "Hello, Francesco, It's me, Roger in Hamilton."

"Roger!" Surprised to hear his voice, he said, "How are you?"

"I'm fine, Francesco. I have been thinking of you and thought it was time to call and catch up again. Too much time has passed since that brief meeting at Niagara Falls." After they exchanged some pleasantries, Roger got to the point. "Look, the reason I'm calling is that I thought I would drive in to see you if that's all right."

"I'd love that! Come to the house. We would love to have you for dinner. When was the last time you had a good dish of pasta?"

"Well, the pasta is tempting, Francesco, but would it be okay if just the two of us met privately somewhere? I need to talk to you about something in confidence."

"What needs to be so private?"

"It's not something that I can discuss over the phone. It's important, though, and it's something I need your help with."

"Hey, you know I'm not going to say no to you. When do you want to come to town?"

"I have been invited to give a lecture at Niagara University in Lewiston on Monday afternoon. How about if we meet for dinner that night? I can make the short drive to Lockborough."

"I get out of work at the mill at 3:00 pm. I could get home, clean up, and meet you between five and six. Is that okay?"

"That will work. Where should we meet?"

"The Rex Grill. Drive in on Route 31. It becomes West Avenue as it passes through our west-end neighborhood. The restaurant is there on the right, you can't miss it. Are you sure you can't tell me what this is all about?"

"I'll tell you Monday night—the whole story." So far so good, Roger thought. Francesco's voice was bright and he seemed upbeat. It was a positive sign he hoped would hold through the news he planned to deliver.

****

Francesco was at the bar having a beer when Roger limped in. He saw him enter and quickly left the stool to embrace his old friend. "*Ciao*, Roger, so good to see you," he said, greeting him with a kiss on both cheeks. He was struck by Roger's professorial look—the tweed sport coat and striped regimental tie. Francesco, in his casual after-work street clothes, still had the bright dark eyes and full head of wavy hair, but had added the broad shoulders and large forearms that came from work in a steel mill. As they gripped each other's hands, Francesco's fingers and palms with the scratches and calluses of manual labor sensed the softer texture of Roger's palm. "Let's sit down by the window."

Late afternoon sun cast lengthening shadows along the tree-lined street in the working-class neighborhood. The scent of beer mingled with the aroma of slow roasting beef as they took their seats.

The restaurant had several customers. Some patrons were sitting at the bar drinking, and a few couples were dining in the booths. The bartender was talking to one of the men at the bar, laughing at the response to one of his questions. Two men played shuffleboard, the soft metallic clicks of the pieces striking one another formed a background to Dean Martin's rendition of *"That's Amore"* emanating from the Wurlitzer.

A waitress came to take their order, pulling a pencil from her hair.

"What do you want to eat here, Francesco?" Roger asked.

"They make a good 'beef on wick.'"

"What's that?"

"A roast beef sandwich on a special bun they call kimmelwick. It has a crust of coarse salt and caraway seeds."

Wrinkling his nose, Roger said "I think I'll have the steak."

"I will too. I'm hungry tonight. They have good butcher steaks here. Nice and tender; cheap, too, so they won't set you back on your professor salary. "

Roger laughed. "Two of those steaks he's talking about, medium rare," he said to the waitress. "And a bottle of Chianti."

She took the order and returned with the wine and two glasses. She poured the wine and left.

"Salute!" They smiled at one another as they clicked their glasses.

"So tell me, Roger, how are those legs of yours doing?" Francesco asked. "We had that short time at Niagara, but we didn't get around to talk about what happened after you left Ortona. I thought you brushed me off. Seemed like you didn't want to talk about that part of your war experience."

258

"Some things you try to forget."

"Well, I don't want to bring up bad memories. God knows we've had our share."

"Since there is something I need from you, I'll trade stories again like we did on the road back in Abruzzo."

"It's a deal."

"Okay, I'll make this quick—as you say in due parole."

Francesco smiled at Roger's recall of idiomatic Italian he had struggled to learn.

"So, after Ortona, my unit was transferred to the Casino front where the Allies were having a tough time. My Canadian outfit broke through into the Liri Valley with the Brits. During our assault on an enemy position I was hit in both legs by low-grazing machine-gun fire."

Francesco winced.

"My comrades put pressure on the wounds until the medics arrived. Then they got me to an aid station where they were able to patch me up before they shipped me to a beachside hospital at Anzio. From there I got shipped to a big medical unit in North Africa. A surgeon did a good job fixing the fractures. After I recovered, I got shipped home. The rest you know. After rehab, I went to graduate school and got my PhD."

"I'm glad you were able to heal. Best of all, you got to do what you talked about. The war—it threw a monkey wrench into my dreams, but it didn't stop yours."

"You're right, Francesco. I got to do what I wanted to do thanks to you. Becoming a historian and writing about the war helped me get rid of my demons."

Francesco thought back to the Sangro escape with pride in what he had done for Roger and Denis. He also remembered what Roger had done for him in Ortona. "You saved me too."

"I was happy to see you had bounced back. What happened after I saw you? You brushed me off, too, at the Falls."

Francesco paused a moment and looked out the window unsure of whether he wanted to share his experience. Then he turned back to Roger with a downcast expression. "I didn't appreciate how bad that civil war would become when we first heard about it on our way to Casoli. Nearly two years passed before things got back to what seemed like order, but even those years after the war were not very good."

Roger saw Francesco's sad expression and tried to be empathetic. "I know it was a horrible time in Italy, even those years after the war. I can understand why you didn't want to talk about it. I hoped writing about the trek and what happened afterward would help you to come to terms and heal like the doctor suggested."

"I did write, but it took a while. I had had long talks with my brother. He was a good listener and encouraged me—things would work out he said, but I struggled. My parish priest suggested I go up to Santo Spirito to reflect and pray. When I did, I got into a discussion about the war with a visitor. He asked me what I remembered most. 'La fame,' I said to avoid the real remembrance. Until then I hadn't been able to write, but alone that night with my thoughts, words I could not find before came to me."

"I'm glad you found those words and sent me that story."

"Roger, I never told anyone this, but what happened that night was a repeat of what happened to me for a moment when I faced that firing squad in Caramanico."

"In what way was that?" Roger asked uncertainly. "You never mentioned it to me in Ortona."

"It was something that I remembered much later. I was scared to death looking at those rifles pointed at me. I was sure I was about to die. Then suddenly a strange release, an acceptance, a peace I can't describe washed over me. Just then the mayor yelled out and that moment passed. I don't know where that feeling came from that day or at *Santo Spirito.*"

"Perhaps it was God breaking through to you—a sacred experience at a horrible moment, and later—maybe that same spirit prompted you to write."

"I don't know," Francesco said, shaking his head. He knew his faith had wavered over the years, and that he had been changed by what had happened. "I can't describe it. I just know that writing it down brought me some peace."

"Some things are what are called ineffable." "What's that mean?"

"Indescribable, like what Dante experienced returning from heaven in the *Divine Comedy.* Did you write anything else after that?

"I wanted to. My old teacher set me up with a friend at the university in Chieti after the war. I tried, but I just couldn't focus. The classroom didn't work for me. My mind wandered too much, and when I wrote nothing felt right."

The waitress returned with two plates, each wafting the fresh-grilled aroma of a juicy steak and French fries. She put the plates down, and asked if they needed anything else.

"No, we're fine, thanks," Roger said. After the waitress left he said, "So then, go on; what happened after your time in Chieti?"

Francesco cut into his steak wondering if he should continue to open up. "I met this girl in Chieti and got married, but it didn't work out. I knew I had made a mistake. I just couldn't get over the loss you know. Anyway, the marriage got annulled." He looked down to avoid eye contact. "Not long after that, my father brought us here."

Roger reached over and patted Francesco's arm. "I'm sorry, Francesco, but I know you will find someone, and maybe even write again. The universities and colleges nearby offer programs in creative writing. You could apply; I could help you. "

"Maybe. I'll never get those years back. I know I miss what I can't replace, and the stories I thought about I may never write. I'm okay with that now. I'm just glad to be here."

"I'm glad you are here too," Roger responded, finishing off a piece of steak with a sip of wine. "So, how is the life of a steelworker? I know you didn't imagine that in Italy."

"Funny how things work out. The job is good." Francesco's voice and face were much brighter now. "The mill is booming all day and night. Salary and benefits are great. The older workers like my father are buying houses and new cars. Not me yet, but in time."

"Sounds like what they call the American dream. Do you miss the old country?"

"I miss the Abruzzo, the mountains and countryside. I would like to visit Roccamorice when I can afford it. But I am thankful I am here now. My life is here."

"What about the people you left behind?"

"Most of the ones that matter are here now. Guys from Roccamorice and other parts of Abruzzo and southern Italy work at the mill with me." He thought to himself that he didn't leave a lot behind except memories, not all of them good, and he certainly didn't want to go back and live out his life there.

"You're keeping busy?"

"I'm enjoying myself. After work, I usually stop for a beer and play cards with my bar mill crew. Not every night, sometimes we go to the track. And I bowl a couple of times a week on a team."

"You don't miss the food?"

"Believe it or not, some things are much better here. The sugo my mother makes on Sunday with pork and beef is so delicious, much better than the marinara she made there. You should have accepted my invitation to dinner."

"I won't say no next time." Roger smiled softly. "I'm glad you're enjoying yourself, Francesco. You seem much happier now."

"So tell me, Roger, what is the big mystery that you couldn't tell me about on the phone?"

Roger put his knife and fork aside his plate and paused to wipe his lips with his napkin. Assuming a more serious demeanor he said, "The write-up of our escape you sent me. I was reviewing the English translation with one of my graduate students. I need you to clarify something about that SS officer for me."

"Like you, Roger, not everyone likes to talk about the war." Francesco frowned as he put his fork into the piece of steak. He shifted in his seat and turned his face to the window. A few moments ago he felt contented; now he wondered. Turning back to Roger, his voice heavy with emotion he said, "I wrote the story, but I've tried to put that stuff out of my mind. Nobody in this town knows what happened to me except my parents and brother. We don't talk about those times.

There are mornings I wake up soaking wet and don't know why. I don't remember my dreams, but I think maybe that Nazi was in them. Your army doctor said I just needed to get through the grieving process and I would be fine. I am...most of the time."

"Are you seeing anybody about it?"

"No. I can handle it."

"I'm sorry about that Francesco, and I'm so sorry to bring it up, but it's why I'm here. You remember the report that I filed in Ortona from your account of the Sanelli tragedy? It was sent up the chain to British Intelligence. They put together a file on Hoffmann."

The mention of the Nazi officer's name conjured an image that knotted Francesco's gut. He put down his knife and fork and pushed his plate aside. Anger crept into his voice at the thought of the man. "For years I've tried to push that bastard's name and memories out of my mind. I thought coming to America would make me forget; I thought I did, that I got over that tragedy, but now you won't let me forget!"

"Look, Francesco, what happened to you was traumatic, but nothing says you have to let this bother you for the rest of your life. Be open to the possibilities life brings you. You've kept those bad memories at bay, but obviously they break through in your dreams; maybe in more ways that you know. I can give you the opportunity of saying goodbye to them forever."

"Easy for you to say, you didn't lose someone you loved."

"No, you're right. My relationship with the Sanelli family may not have been as close as yours, but I still owe them my life, and I want justice for them, same as you. Trust me, you are going to want to hear the rest of what I have to say. I know how you can write the fitting ending to the story you sent me. I think we found Hoffmann."

Francesco's jaw dropped. His voice wavered. "Are you serious? How is that even possible?"

"He's in Hamilton, living under an assumed identity."

Roger went on to tell Francesco about the investigation that was launched by his graduate student's discovery based on the description of Hoffmann that Francesco had written in his memoir. "He's calling himself Pavlo Karpenko. He is hiding out with that alias as a postwar immigrant from the Ukraine."

Francesco scowled. "I swore I would kill that bastard if I ever got my hands on him."

"Me too. But then I thought, maybe I could get justice and satisfaction by having the Italians do it. You want justice, Francesco, same as me. I think we can get him arrested and extradited to Italy where they can put him on trial and hopefully execute him for all the atrocities. That's what we said we wanted for the Sanellis, remember?"

"I suppose I said that back then." Francesco's eyes squinted. It was painful to remember. He turned his head nervously from side to side, sweeping his hand up and down from his cheek to his jaw. His throat tightened, his voice struggled for release. "Now I'd rather do it myself, slashing his throat or better yet, twisting a knife slowly in his belly, looking into those twitching eyes and telling him, 'This is for Pierluigi and Angiolina and Annamaria,' giving him one thrust for each of them," he said, wiping away tears that had welled up.

"Listen, my friend," Roger said, taking a sip of wine and reaching his hand out to Francesco's. "I discussed this with the Canadian Immigration officials in Toronto and they have spoken to the Italian counsel. They have reviewed all of the documentation. We have a strong case against him for what he did in Caramanico, Pietransieri, and some of the other towns we didn't even know about. If we can get him extradited, the Italian counsel thinks there could be several eyewitnesses for the trial, like the mayor of Caramanico."

"Can't he be arrested, tried, and executed right here?" Francesco asked.

"Canada hasn't established the necessary jurisdiction to prosecute Nazi war criminals—someday maybe, but not now. But if the authorities can show the suspect lied to immigration officials, they can do a denaturalization and removal action."

"What does that mean?"

"It means he can be extradited to stand trial. Ten years, Francesco, but finally, justice is possible with your help." Roger beamed optimism. He gave Francesco's hand a tug.

Francesco wiped his eye again. "I heard some of those Nazis were let go at those trials in Germany, the ones they had at that town in Nuremberg."

"Listen, Francesco," Roger said, as he looked at him in earnest, "most of the those who committed or directed the murders were sentenced to death, and Hoffmann was among the worst of the worst. Believe me, there is no way he will escape justice."

Francesco looked skeptical, but he trusted Roger's judgment. "What do you want me to do?"

"Come up to Hamilton and make a positive identification. You are an eye witness, up close and personal as they say. With all the other documentation, your testimony will be enough for an arrest. It's the last piece we need." Roger reached into the breast pocket of his jacket and pulled out two photographs. "Here is the German file photo of Hoffmann and the most recent one that my assistant took of him in Hamilton." He handed them to Francesco. "Do you think you can make the ID?"

Francesco rubbed his jaw as he looked them over, comparing the two photos taken at least a decade or more apart. Dan's profile photo clearly showed the distinctive scar. "That's him. The bastard looks like a tired bum now—a bad dream

I thought I would never see him again."

"Finish your steak, it's getting cold."

"What's that saying you told me once, 'Revenge is a dish best served cold?'" Francesco picked up his fork and knife and cut a piece of steak. Holding it on his fork he asked, "Do you think we can really do this thing?"

"Now that you're on board, I know we can."

They picked up their glasses and clicked them together. "Just one more thing," Roger continued, "This encounter can also be an emotional boomerang. It can come back to bite you if you're not prepared. So prepare yourself."

Chapter 25

Francesco woke just before dawn, aware he had spent a restless night. Rubbing his tired eyes he walked into the bathroom and retrieved his shaving mug and straight razor from the cabinet over the sink. He rhythmically honed his razor on the leather strap and then lathered up his facial stubble. He looked at himself in the mirror as he slowly swept the sharp blade over his face, deep in thought. He had led men to freedom during the war despite some lapses in judgment, and they had survived. He had adjusted to the unexpected loss of the love of his young life, while nearly losing his own, and he had crossed an ocean to begin a new chapter. These experiences had changed him, made him stronger and more resilient. But there was this unfinished business—justice, something he had not realistically considered until his dinner with Roger.

When he finished shaving, he folded the razor back in its case and replaced the shaving mug in the cabinet. He hesitated with the razor before putting it away.

Crossing over the Rainbow Bridge at Niagara Falls, he was barely aware of the billowing mist from the nearby cascade. He stopped to identify himself to the border agent, show his papers and answer the perfunctory questions about his destination and purpose of his visit. Hamilton, to kill someone, he thought. "To visit friends," he said.

It was a dull, gray morning when he arrived in Hamilton, the kind that augured the possibility of rain. The summer wind came drifting in from the industrial lakeshore bringing with it the acrid smells from the foundries and mills. On the drive downtown from McMaster, Francesco sat silently in the back seat, head turned to the window while Roger and Dan in front focused on the road ahead, keeping their thoughts to themselves. Ever since the dinner meeting with Roger, Francesco had replayed again and again the fateful day in Caramanico. Ten years later, he thought he had finally adjusted, but thanks to Roger, the specter of the Nazi killer had intervened to upset his life again. He was feeling particularly glum this day. Maybe it was the weather he was looking at out the window. Maybe not a great day to do this he thought; on the other hand he had come to the conclusion on his drive to Canada that this was something that had to be done.

Dan drove up and parked across the street from the antique shop. He waited while Francesco and Roger got out of the vehicle and crossed the street to the shop. An Ontario Government sedan bearing the logo of the Border Service pulled up and parked just beyond the shop. Francesco glanced at the vehicle and the two officers seated in the front seat as he paused by the shop's door.

"Are you ready, Francesco?" Roger asked.

Francesco gave an uncertain nod. "As ready as I can be I guess." He crushed out the cigarette on the sidewalk that he had lit upon exiting the car. "I never thought I'd see this butcher again." With a hard edge in his voice, he said, "Let's go!"

Roger opened the door to the shop and followed Francesco in. As Francesco walked he took in and exhaled deep breaths through pursed lips, clenching and unclenching his left hand while patting his pants pocket with his right hand. It was early, the shop had opened but no customers were inside. "That's him behind the counter," he whispered to Francesco, as they made their way to the back of the store.

Could it be him? Francesco wondered, trying to match a resemblance to a conjured up memory of a man he had once stood face to face with. Is it possible?

Hoffmann had just finished adjusting the hands of an antique clock. He reached for a large glass platter from the shelf behind the counter and began wiping it with a cloth. He turned at the sound of the approaching footsteps. "Good morning," he said frowning, as he recognized Roger. "Not more questions, I hope?"

"None for me, but perhaps you can answer some for my friend here," Roger said, nodding to Francesco.

Francesco could feel the thumping in his chest, almost hear his heart sounds. He moved up to the counter, jaw firmly set, his eyes narrowed. He stood no more than three feet from his nemesis, staring.

Hoffmann gave Francesco a look of annoyance, showing no sign of recognition. Turning to Roger he said, "I don't want to be bothered with any more questions from your students, professor. I said what I had to say."

"I'm not his student," Francesco said, still steely-eyed. "My name is Francesco.

Do you remember me? You must remember me!"

Hoffmann gave Francesco a quizzical look. He registered the Italian accent but he shook his head, again showing no sign of recognition. "I don't know you. Who are you? Have we met?"

"Maybe this will remind you—Caramanico, or how about Pietransieri?"

The plate Hoffmann was holding slipped from his hand, hitting the edge of the counter and fell to the floor, shattering into myriad pieces. The crash traveled through the store, catching the attention of a woman passing by the storefront. Karpenko's jaw dropped and the blood drained from his face. He bent awkwardly behind the counter. His face manifested the shock of discovery. He remained there for a few moments picking up glass shards, anything to delay having to confront his questioner.

When he finally rose, he said, "I don't know any Caramanico. I have never heard of it or the other place you mentioned. Where are they?"

"You know very well, in the Abruzzo of Italy, Mr. Karpenko, or should I call you Standartenfuhrer Hoffmann," Francesco said, his voice rising in anger.

Hoffmann glared. His voice rose to match Francesco's anger. He shouted "My name is Karpenko! You have mistaken me for someone else."

The blow came suddenly without warning. Francesco exploded, lunging upward and at the same time swinging his steelworker's fist, delivering a haymaker to the side of Hoffmann's face. The force of the impact sent Hoffmann staggering back. He fell against the counter, rattling the shelves, toppling bowls and vases, sending them crashing to the floor. He tried to steady himself against the edge of a shelf, but failed to get a grip and slumped to the floor. A trickle of blood appeared on the corner of his mouth.

Francesco leaned over the counter and looked down at the dazed figure sitting in glass and ceramic debris. "No, Colonel," Francesco said defiantly. "I could never mistake that face, the scar, and those twitching eyes when you made me stand next to you on that cold afternoon ten years ago in Caramanico. You called me over, don't you remember? I was standing with Pierluigi Sanelli and his wife Angiolina and his daughter Annamaria. We stood in front of your firing squad. I was with them waiting to die until the mayor told you I didn't belong to the family."

Roger had rushed to the counter when Francesco struck Hoffmann. He pulled Francesco upright and leaned toward Hoffmann who was struggling to sit up. His face contorted in anger as he said, "You and your men had come looking for me. I had escaped the Sulmona POW camp. Someone in Caramanico had informed on the Sanellis, but I had left long before then. You murdered that fine family for what?"

Hoffmann returned Roger's angry look as he tried to right himself. He wiped the blood that had dribbled onto his chin. His voice again rising, he said, "I don't know those people, and I don't know this crazy Francesco. I am a Canadian citizen. In 1943, I was in Ukraine, not Italy!"

"Let me refresh your memory, Colonel," Roger said, pulling a photo from the breast pocket of his jacket. "This is you, Colonel Hoffmann, an SS officer of the Nazi party," he said, as he handed the photo to Hoffman who had struggled to his feet.

"No, that is not me!" he shouted, as he pushed the photo back into Roger's hand. "Now, get out of my shop, both of you, before I call the authorities." He reached for the telephone on the counter.

"That won't be necessary," Roger said. "I think we have what we came for, don't you agree, Francesco? Let's let the rest of this play out."

Francesco was still livid; the cold hard glint in his eyes flashed as he raised his hand in a fist and slammed it on the counter. "You said that Pierluigi's God would be of no use to him, but you were wrong. You'll get what you deserve, you can be sure of that!" His voice sputtered and cracked; he was barely able to get the words out of a throat choked with emotion. He suddenly pulled the straight razor from his pants pocket and flicked his wrist, brandishing the steel blade as Hoffmann recoiled.

Roger grabbed Francesco's arm. "No, Francesco! We came here for justice. Tell me you want that too!" Forcing Francesco to look him in the eye he said, "You have a new life, why ruin it by killing him?"

Francesco was conflicted between the advice Roger was urging and his own sense of justice. His face still creased in anger, he decided to fold the razor as he glared at the frightened face of Hoffmann.

Roger put his arm around Francesco and whispered, moving him to the front of the shop, "We need to let our desire for justice be stronger than our hate." As they exited, two uniformed Canadian Border Service men brushed by them and entered the shop.

Francesco turned his head back to Hoffman. "If they don't kill you, I'll cross the ocean myself and do it!"

Outside a soft rain fell from the leaden sky. Francesco paused at the curb as Roger crossed the street to Dan Travis waiting in his parked car. He walked around to the passenger side and opened the door.

Looking over at Roger as he got into the vehicle, Dan said, "Well, that should make the rest of your day better."

Roger smiled wistfully. He looked toward the sidewalk where Francesco was staring through the shop window. The government agents emerged with a struggling, handcuffed Hoffmann between them. They muscled him into their vehicle and pulled away from the curb.

Francesco lingered for a moment and gave a shrug. Then he crossed over in the rain and got into the rear seat of Dan's car. Roger and Dan were silhouetted against the windshield in front. Roger turned to Francesco. "It's over, my friend. You can let it go and get on with your life."

Francesco looked past him at the government vehicle receding down the street. He closed his eyes and saw the boy in Italy who played football and wrote essays and poems, until the war came to his village and changed the course of his life. His journey to the man he was now was something he could not have imagined then.

He tightened his closed eyes. The faces of the men he rescued and the family he failed to save—a wonderful man and the girl he loved were before him, filling the spaces between the objects on the street. He sighed and placed his hand on his chest. He was heartsick remembering, but at the same time he found peace knowing he had brought the Sanellis justice. His new life was better, he thought. That poem? Those stories? He would enroll in a creative writing program and write them after all.

The moment passed and he opened his eyes. The vehicle in the distance was just a speck, vanishing with the last bit of the darkness that haunted him.

Author's Note

Although based on a true life event, this is a work of fiction. The characters, apart from Francesco, are truly fictional and do not resemble anyone living or dead. However, I must add that Francesco's dialogue, and many of his situations are the product of the author's imagination.

The village of Roccamorice was under German occupation in 1943. A boy named Francesco, out of sheer hunger, did leave the town and walked to Caramanico where he was taken in by a family. There were no prisoners of war living in the family's home at the time Francesco arrived; they had left days before. The family was accused of harboring escaped prisoners and was executed by a firing squad. Francesco's life was spared at the last minute when the mayor testified that Francesco was not a member of the family. Following the atrocity, he returned to Roccamorice with signs and symptoms of what today would be labeled posttraumatic shock syndrome. He eventually recovered and emigrated to the United States, became a steelworker, married, and raised a family.

Several books were helpful in developing the historical background. The war in Italy is drawn from *Day of Battle, The War in Sicily and Italy 1943-1945* by Rick Atkinson and *Mussolini's Italy* by R.J.B. Bosworth. Two novels by Ignazio Silone, one depicting the life of Pietro Morrone—*The Story of a Humble Christian*, and the other, Fontamara, about life in Abruzzo in the Mussolini era, provided additional cultural context. Jon Sweeny's nonfiction account of Pietro Morrone, *The Pope Who Quit*, informed Francesco's story at Santo Spirito; but the character, Fabrizio is fictional, based on *Caravaggio, A Life Sacred and Profane*, by Andrew Dixon. The Hermitages of Roccamorice by Errico Centofanti and Alberto DiGiovanni allowed me to fill in the physical details. Roger's character and history was shaped in part on Farley Mowat's account of his WW II experience in *The Regiment*, and that of Denis by Major Peter Ranier's chronicle of the British Army in North Africa, *Pipeline to Battle*. Their escape was shaped in part by Uys Krige's *The Way Out*–a soldier's escape from an Italian prisoner of war camp.

The escape from Prisoner of War Camp 78 is considered one of the most successful of World War II. Much of the camp remains intact near Sulmona today. The escape trail depicted in the novel is highly imagined; however, there is a historic trail which traces one of several routes prisoners used to flee the camp in September 1943. At least one group, disguised as shepherds, made it across the Sangro with the aid of Abruzzi villagers and partisans. An annual commemorative trek along this Freedom Trail from Sulmona to Casoli is held each year.

Acknowledgments

I would like to thank a few people who were with me in spirit as I wrote this book—my parents and relatives who told me about their history and culture in the Abruzzo and shared their family stories with me. I apologize for any liberties I may have taken.

And then there were those who encouraged me to develop the story from its rudimentary beginnings. First, Mark Young at Scottsdale Community College found my nonfiction short account "interesting" and my protagonist, Francesco, "likeable," and worthy of further development. I am also much indebted to Katy Grant whose, introductory course on writing the novel at Mesa Community College, encouraged me to transform the nonfiction account into the historical novel it became. After I had set the manuscript aside to pursue other projects, she gladly reviewed later drafts, and made valuable suggestions. I know she is relieved this egg is finally hatching.

I must thank the staff and faculty at the Piper Writer's Center at Arizona State University for the many workshops that helped me fine tune the prose. I am also indebted to Carol Test for aspects of developmental editing that brought the novel closer to publication.

I can count the people who read the near-final drafts on the fingers of one hand. In addition to the aforementioned, my wife, Rosalie, and my friend Nancy Wallace were my beta readers par excellence. They allowed me to test ideas, and responded with patience, kindness and support.

Finally, my book designer, Joe DiPastena, *705market.com*, made valuable suggestions, hung in with me as I made the final touches on revisions, and guided the files to the bookmaker, and beyond to a website he created for me—*larosatiauthor.com*.

About the Author

Louis A. Rosati, born and raised in Western New York, became a physician specializing in pathology and laboratory medicine. Now retired, he resides in Mesa, Arizona, with his wife, Rosalie. He has published two nonfiction books— *My Winning Season* and *Men of Steel*. The Boy in Abruzzo is his first novel.

www.ingramcontent.com/pod-product-compliance
Lightning Source LLC
Chambersburg PA
CBHW030614120726
47904CB00006B/1891